Anno-Dracula

Also by Kim Newman

The Night Mayor
Bad Dreams
Jago

Anno-Dracula

Kim Newman

Carroll & Graf Publishers, Inc.
New York

First published in Great Britain by Simon & Schuster in 1992.

This edition published by arrangement with the author.

First Carroll & Graf edition 1993

Carroll & Graf Publishers, Inc.
260 Fifth Avenue
New York, NY 10001

Library of Congress Cataloging-in-Publication Data

Newman, Kim.
   Anno-Dracula / Kim Newman.
      p.   cm.
   ISBN 0-88184-967-7 : $21.00
   1. Dracula, Count (Fictitious character)—Fiction. 2. London
(England)—Fiction. 3. Vampires—Fiction. I. Title.
PS3564.E91626A56   1993
813'.54—dc20   93-21934
                                       CIP

Manufactured in the United States of America

For Steve Jones, the Mammoth Bookkeeper of Vampires

'We Szekeleys have a right to be proud, for in our veins flows the blood of many brave races who fought as the lion fights, for lordship. Here, in the whirlpool of European races, the Ugric tribe bore down from Iceland and the fighting spirit which Thor and Wodin gave them, which their Berserkers displayed to such fell intent on the seaboards of Europe, ay, and of Asia and Africa too, till the peoples thought that the were-wolves themselves had come. Here, too, when they came, they fought the Huns, whose warlike fury had swept the earth like a living flame, till the dying peoples held that in their veins ran the blood of those old witches, who, expelled from Scythia, had mated with the devils in the desert. Fools, fools! What devil or what witch was ever so great as Attila, whose blood is in these veins? Is it a wonder that we were a conquering race; that we were proud; that when the Magyar, the Lombard, the Avar, the Bulgar, or the Turk poured his thousands on our frontiers, we drove them back? Is it strange that when Arpad and his legions swept through the Hungarian fatherland, he found us here when he reached the frontier? And when the Hungarian flood swept eastward, the Szekeleys were claimed as kindred by the victorious Magyars, and to us for centuries was trusted the guarding of the frontier of Turkey-land; ay and more than that, endless duty of the frontier guard, for, as the Turks say, "water sleeps, and enemy is sleepless". Who more gladly than we throughout the Four Nations received the "bloody sword", or at its warlike call flocked quicker to the standard of the King? When was redeemed that great shame of my nation, the shame of Cassova, when the flags of the Wallach and the Magyar went down beneath the Crescent, who was it but one of my own race who as Voivode crossed the Danube and beat the Turk on his own ground? This was a Dracula indeed! Woe was it that his own unworthy brother, when he had fallen, sold his people to the Turk and brought the shame of slavery upon them! . . . Again, when, after the battle of Mohacs, we threw off the Hungarian yoke, we of the Dracula blood were amongst their leaders, for our spirit would not brook that we were not free. Ah, young sir, the Szekeleys – and the Dracula as their heart's blood, their brains, and their swords – can boast a record that mushroom growths like the Habsburgs and the Romanoffs can never reach. The warlike days are over. Blood is too precious a thing in these days of dishonourable peace; and the glories of the great races are as a tale that is told.'

Count Dracula

'I have studied, over and over again since they came into my hands, all the papers relating to this monster; and the more I have studied, the greater seems the necessity to utterly stamp him out. All through there are signs of his advance; not only of his power, but of his knowledge of it. As I learned, from the researches of my friend Arminius of Buda-Pesth, he was in life a most wonderful man. Soldier, statesman, and alchemist – which latter was the highest development of the science-knowledge of his time. He had a mighty brain, a learning beyond compare, and a heart that knew no fear and no remorse. He dared even to attend the Scholomance, and there was no branch of knowledge of his time that he did not essay. Well, in him the brain powers survived the physical death; though it would seem that memory was not all complete. In some faculties of mind he has been, and is, only a child; but he is growing, and some things that were childish at the first are now of man's stature. He is experimenting, and doing it well; and if it had not been that we have crossed his path he would be yet – *he may yet be if we fail* – the father or furtherer of a new order of beings, whose road must lead through Death, not Life.'

Dr Abraham Van Helsing

I

In the Fog

Dr Seward's Diary (kept in phonograph)

17 SEPTEMBER

Last night's delivery was easier than the others. Much easier than last week's. Perhaps, with practice and patience, everything becomes easier. If never easy. Never . . . easy.

I am sorry: it is difficult to maintain an orderly mind and this marvellous apparatus is unforgiving. I cannot ink over hasty words or tear loose a spoiled page. The cylinder revolves, the needle etches, and my ramblings are graven for all time in merciless wax. Marvellous apparatuses, like miracle cures, are beset with unpredictable side-effects. In the twentieth century, new means of setting down the human thought mind may precipitate an avalanche of worthless digression. *Brevis esse laboro*, as Horace would have it. I know how to present a case history. This will be of interest to posterity. For now, I work *in camera* and secrete the cylinders with what remain of my earlier accounts. As the situation stands, my life and liberty would be endangered were these journals exposed to the public ear. One day, I should wish my motives and methods made known and clear.

Very well.

The subject: female, apparently in her twenties. Recently dead, I should say. Profession: obvious. Location: Chicksand Street. The Brick Lane end, opposite Flower & Dean Street. Time: shortly after five *ante meridiem*.

I had been wandering for upwards of an hour in fog as thick as spoiled milk. Fog is best for my night-work. The less one can see of what the city has become in this year, the better. Like many, I've taken to sleeping by day, working by night. Mostly, I doze; it seems years since the bliss of actual sleep. Hours of darkness are the hours of activity now. Of course, here in Whitechapel things were never much different.

There's one of those cursed blue plaques in Chicksand Street; at 197, one of the Count's bolt-holes. Here lay six of the earth-boxes to which he and Van Helsing attached such superstitious and, as it eventuated, entirely unwarranted importance. Lord Godalming was supposed to destroy them; but, as in so much else, my noble friend proved not equal to the task. I was under the plaque, unable to discern its wording, pondering our failures, when the dead girl solicited my attention.

'Mister . . .' she called. '*Missssster . . .*'

As I turned, she settled feathers away from her throat. Her neck and bosom showed mist-white. A living woman would have shook with the cold. She stood under a staircase leading to a first-floor doorway above which burned a red-shaded lantern. Behind her, bar-shadowed by the stairs, was another doorway, half-sunken below the level of the pavement. None of the windows in the building, nor in any close enough to see clearly, showed a light. We inhabited an island of visibility in a sea of murk.

I traversed the street, boots making yellow eddies in the low-lying fog. There was no one nearby. I heard people passing, but we were curtained. Soon, the first spikes of dawn would drive the last new-borns from the streets. The dead girl was up late by the standards of her kind. Dangerously late. Her need for money, for drink, must have been acute.

'Such a handsome gentleman,' she cooed, waving a hand in front of her, sharp nails shredding traces of fog.

I endeavoured to make out her face and was rewarded with an impression of thin prettiness. She angled her head slightly to regard me, a wing of jet-black hair falling away from a white cheek. There was interest in her black-red eyes, and hunger. Also, a species of half-aware amusement that borders contempt. The look is common among women, on the streets or off. When Lucy – Miss Westenra of sainted memory – refused my proposal, the spark of a similar expression inhabited her eyes.

'. . . and so close to morning.'

She was not English. From her accent, I'd judge her German or Austrian by birth. The hint of a 'ch' in 'chentleman', a 'close' that verged upon 'cloze'. The Prince Consort's London, from

Buckingham Palace to Buck's Row, is the sinkhole of Europe, clogged with the *ejecta* of a double-dozen principalities.

'Come on and kiss me, sir.'

I stood for a moment, simply looking. She was indeed a pretty thing, distinctive. Her shiny hair was cut short and lacquered in an almost Chinese style, a fringe like the cheek-guards of a Roman helmet. In the fog, her red lips appeared quite black. Like all of *them*, she smiled too easily, disclosing sharp pearl-chip teeth. A cloud of cheap scent hung around, sickly-sweet to cover the reek.

The streets are filthy, open sewers of vice. The dead are everywhere.

The girl laughed musically, the sound like something wrung from a mechanism, and beckoned me near, loosening further the ragged feathers about her shoulders. Her laugh reminded me again of Lucy. Lucy when she was alive, not the leech-thing we finished in Kingstead Cemetery. Three years ago, when only Van Helsing believed . . .

'Won't you give me a little kiss,' she sang. 'Just a little kiss.'

Her lips made a heart-shape. Her nails touched my cheek, then her fingertips. We were both cold; my face a mask of ice, her fingers needles pricking through frozen skin.

'What brought you to this?' I asked.

'Good fortune and kind gentlemen.'

'Am I a kind gentleman?' I asked, gripping the scalpel in my trousers pocket.

'Oh yes, one of the kindest. I can tell.'

I pressed the flat of the instrument against my thigh, feeling the chill of silver through good cloth.

'I have some mistletoe,' the dead girl said, detaching a sprig from her bodice. She held it above her. 'A kiss?' she asked. 'Just a penny for a kiss.'

'It is early for Christmas.'

'There's always time for a kiss.'

She shook her sprig, berries jiggling like silent bells. I placed a cold kiss on her red-black lips and took out my knife, holding it under my coat. I felt the blade's keenness through my glove. Her cheek was cool against my face.

I learned from last week's, in Hanbury Street – Chapman, the newspapers say her name was, Annie or Anne – to do the business

swiftly and precisely. Throat. Heart. Tripes. Then get the head off.
That finishes the things. Clean silver and a clean conscience. Van
Helsing, blinkered by folklore and symbolism, spoke always of the
heart, but any of the major organs will do. The kidneys are easiest
to reach.

I had made preparation carefully before venturing out. For half an
hour I sat, allowing myself to become aware of the pain. Renfield is
dead – truly dead – but the madman left his jaw-marks in my right
hand. The semicircle of deep indentations has scabbed over many
times but never been right again. With Chapman, I was dull from
the laudanum I take and not as precise as I should have been. Learning
to cut left-handed has not helped. I missed the major artery and the
thing had time to screech. I am afraid I lost control and became a
butcher, when I should be a surgeon.

Last night's went better. The girl clung as tenaciously to life, but
there was an acceptance of my gift. She was relieved, at the last, to
have her soul cleansed. Silver is hard to come by now. The coinage
is gold or copper. I hoarded threepenny bits while the money was
changing and sacrificed my mother's dinner service. I've had the
instruments since my Purfleet days. Now the blades are plated, a
core of steel strength inside killing silver. This time I selected the
post-mortem scalpel. It is fitting, I think, to employ a tool intended
for rooting around in corpses.

The dead girl invited me into her doorway and wriggled skirts
up over slim white legs. I took the time to open her blouse. My
fingers, hot with pain, fumbled.

'Your hand?'

I held up the lumpily gloved club and tried a smile. She kissed
my locked knuckles and I slipped my other hand out from my coat,
holding firmly the scalpel.

'An old wound,' I said, 'It's nothing.'

She smiled and I quickly drew my silver edge across her neck,
pressing firmly with my thumb, cutting deep into pristine dead-
flesh. Her eyes widened with shock – silver *hurts* – and she released
a long sigh. Lines of thin blood trickled like rain on a window-pane,
staining the skin over her collar-bones. A single tear of blood issued
from the corner of her mouth.

'Lucy,' I said, remembering . . .

I held up the girl, my body shielding her from passers-by, and slid the scalpel through her stays and into her heart. I felt her shudder and fall lifeless. But I know the dead can be resilient and took care to finish the job. I laid her in the well of the sunken doorway and completed the delivery. There was little blood in her; she must not have fed tonight. After cutting away her corset, easily ripping the cheap material, I exposed the punctured heart, detached the intestines from the mesentery, unravelled a yard of the colon, and removed the kidneys and part of the uterus. Then I enlarged the first incision. Having exposed the vertebrae, I worried the loose head back and forth until the neckbones parted.

2

Geneviève

NOISE REACHED INTO her darkness. Hammering. Insistent, repeated blows. Meat and bone against wood.

In her dreams, Geneviève had returned to the days of her girlhood in the France of the Spider King, *la Pucelle* and the monster Gilles. When warm, she had been the physician's daughter not Chandagnac's get. Before she turned, before the Dark Kiss . . .

Her tongue felt sleep-filmed teeth. The aftertang of her own blood was in her mouth, disgusting and mildly exciting.

In her dreams, the pounding was a mallet striking the end of a snapped-in-half quarterstaff. The English captain finished her father-in-darkness like a butterfly, pinning Chandagnac to the bloodied earth. One of the less memorable skirmishes of the Hundred Years War. Barbarous times she had hoped deservedly dead.

The hammering continued. She opened her eyes and tried to focus on the grubby glass of the skylight. The sun was not yet quite down. Dreams washed away in an instant and she was awake, as if a gallon of icy water were dashed into her face.

The hammering paused. 'Mademoiselle Dieudonné,' someone shouted. It was not the director – usually responsible for urgent calls that dragged her from sleep – but she recognized the voice. 'Open up. Scotland Yard.'

She sat, sheet falling away. She slept on the floor in her under-clothes, on a blanket laid over the rough planks.

'There's been another Silver Knife murder.'

She had been resting in her tiny office at Toynbee Hall. It was as safe a place as any to pass the few days each month when lassitude overcame her and she shared the sleep of the dead. Up high in the building, the room had only a tiny skylight and the door could be secured from the inside. It served, as coffins and crypts served for those of the Prince Consort's bloodline.

She gave a placatory grunt and the hammering was not resumed. She cleared her throat. Her body, unused for days, creaked as she stretched. A cloud obscured the sun and the pain momentarily eased. She stood up in the dark and ran her hands over her hair. The cloud passed and her strength ebbed.

'Mademoiselle?'

The hammering started again. The young were always impatient. She had once been the same.

She took a Chinese silk robe from a hook and drew it about herself. Not the dress etiquette recommended to entertain a gentleman caller, but it would have to do. Etiquette, so important a few short years ago, meant less and less. They were sleeping in earth-lined coffins in Mayfair, and hunting in packs in Pall Mall. This season, the correct form of address for an archbishop was hardly of major concern to anyone.

As she slid back the bolt, traces of her sleep-fog persisted. Outside, the afternoon was dying; she would not be at her best until night was about her again. She pulled open her door. A stocky new-born stood in the corridor, long coat around him like a cloak, bowler hat shifting from hand to hand.

'Surely, Lestrade, you are not of the kind that needs to be invited into any new dwelling?' Geneviève enquired. 'That would be very inconvenient for a man in your profession. Well, come in, come in . . .'

She admitted the Scotland Yard man. Jagged teeth stuck from his mouth, unconcealed by a half-grown moustache. When warm, he had been rat-faced; the sparse whiskers completed the resemblance. His ears were shifting, becoming high and pointed. Like most new-borns of the bloodline of the Prince Consort, he had not yet found his final form. He wore smoked glasses but crimson points behind the lenses suggested active eyes.

He set his hat down upon her desk.

'Last night,' he began, hurriedly, 'in Chicksand Street. It was butchery.'

'Last night?'

'I'm sorry.' He drew breath, making an allowance for her spell of rest. 'It's the seventeenth now. Of September.'

'I've been asleep three days.'

Geneviève opened her wardrobe and considered the few clothes hanging inside. She hardly had costume for every occasion. It was unlikely, all considered, that she would in the near future be invited to a reception at the Palace. Her only remaining jewellery was her father's tiny crucifix, and she rarely wore that for fear of upsetting some sensitive new-born with silly ideas.

'I deemed it best to rouse you. Everyone is jittery. Feelings are running high.'

'You were quite right,' she said. She rubbed sleep-gum from her eyes. Even the last shards of sunlight, filtered through a grimy square of glass, were icicles jammed into her forehead.

'When the sun is down,' Lestrade was saying, 'there'll be pandemonium. It could be another Bloody Sunday. Some say Van Helsing has returned.'

'The Prince Consort would love that.'

Lestrade shook his head. 'It's merely a rumour. Van Helsing is dead. His head remains on its spike.'

'You've checked?'

'The Palace is always under guard. The Prince Consort has his Carpathians about him. Our kind cannot be too careful. We have many enemies.'

'Our kind?'

'The un-dead.'

Geneviève almost laughed. 'I am not your kind, Inspector. You are of the bloodline of Vlad Tepes, I am of the bloodline of Chandagnac. We are, at best, cousins.'

The detective shrugged and snorted at the same time. Bloodline meant little to the vampires of London, Geneviève knew. Even at a third, a tenth or a twentieth remove, they all had Vlad Tepes as father-in-darkness.

'Who?' she asked.

'A new-born named Schön. Lulu, Common prostitute, like the others.'

'This is . . . what, the fourth?'

'No one is sure. The sensation press have exhumed every unsolved East End killing of the past thirty years to lay at the door of the Whitechapel Murderer.'

'How many are the police certain of?'

Lestrade snorted. 'We'll not even be certain of Schön until the inquest, although I'll stake my pension on her. I've come direct from

the mortuary. The trade marks are unmistakable. Otherwise, Annie
Chapman last week and Polly Nichols the week before. Opinions
differ on a couple of others. Emma Smith, Martha Tabram.'

'What do you think?'

Lestrade nibbled his lip. 'Just the three. At least, the three we
know of. Smith was set upon, robbed and impaled by roughs from
the Jago. Violated, too. Typical rip-mob assault, nothing like our
man's work. And Tabram was warm. Silver Knife is only interested
in us. In vampires.'

Geneviève understood.

'This man *hates*,' Lestrade continued, 'hates with a passion. The
murders must be committed in a frenzy, yet there's a coolness to
them. He kills out on the street in broad darkness. He doesn't just
butcher, he *dissects*. And vampires aren't easy to kill. Our man is not
a simple lunatic. He has a *reason*.'

Lestrade took the crimes personally. The Whitechapel Murderer
cut deep. New-borns were jerked this way and that by misunder-
standing, cringing from the crucifix because of a folk tale they
half-knew.

'Has the news travelled?'

'Fast,' the detective told her. 'The evening editions carry the story.
It'll be all over London by now. There are those among the warm
who do not love us, Mademoiselle. They're rejoicing. When the
new-borns come out, there could be a panic. I've suggested troops,
but Warren is leery. After that business last year . . .'

She remembered. Alarmed in the aftermath of the Royal Wedding
by increased public disorder, Sir Charles Warren, Commissioner
of the Metropolitan Police, had issued an edict against political
meetings in Trafalgar Square. In defiance, warm insurrectionists,
preaching against the Crown and the new government, gathered
one November afternoon. William Morris and H. M. Hyndman
of the Socialist Democratic Federation, with the support of Robert
Cunningham-Grahame, the radical Member of Parliament, and
Annie Besant, of the National Secular Society, argued for the
declaration of a Republic. There was fierce, indeed violent, debate.
Geneviève observed from the steps of the National Gallery. She
was not the only vampire to consider aligning with the putative
Republic. You did not have to be warm to take Vlad Tepes for
a monster. Eleanor Marx, herself a new-born, and authoress with

Dr Edward Aveling of *The Vampire Question*, made an impassioned speech calling for the abdication of Queen Victoria and the expulsion of the Prince Consort.

'. . . I can't say I blame him. Still, H Division isn't equipped for riot. The Yard has sent me over to goose the local blokes, but we've got enough to do catching the murderer without having to fend off some scythe-and-stake mob.'

Geneviève wondered which way Sir Charles would jump. In November, the Commissioner, a soldier before he was a policeman and now a vampire before he was a soldier, had sent in the army. Even before a flustered magistrate could finish reading the Riot Act, a dragoon officer ordered his men, a mixture of vampires and the warm, to clear the Square. After that charge, the Prince Consort's Own Carpathian Guards set about the crowd, doing more harm with teeth and claws than the dragoons had with fixed bayonets. There were a few fatalities and many injuries; subsequently, there were a few trials and many 'disappearances'. November 13th, 1887 was remembered as 'Bloody Sunday'. Geneviève spent a week in Guy's Hospital, helping with the less seriously wounded. Many spat on her or refused to be ministered to by one of her kind. Were it not for the intervention of the Queen herself, still a calming influence on her adoring subjects, the Empire could have exploded like a barrel of gunpowder.

'And what, pray, can I do,' Geneviève asked, 'to serve the purpose of the Prince Consort?'

Lestrade chewed his moustache, teeth glistening, flecks of froth on his lips.

'You may be needed, Mademoiselle. The Hall will be overrun. Some don't want to be out on the streets with the murderer about. Others are spreading panic and sedition, firing up vigilante mobs.'

'I'm not Florence Nightingale.'

'You have influence . . .'

'I do, don't I?'

'I wish . . . I would humbly request . . . you would use your influence to calm the situation. Before disaster occurs. Before more are unnecessarily killed.'

Geneviève was not above enjoying a taste of power. She slipped off her robe, shocking the detective. Death and rebirth had not shaken out of him the prejudices of his time. Lestrade shrank behind his smoked glasses, as she swiftly dressed, fastening the seeming hundreds of small catches and buttons on her bottle-green skirt and jacket with neat movements of sharp-tipped fingers. It was as if the costume of her warm days, as intricate and cumbersome as a full suit of armour, had returned to plague her. As a new-born, she had, with relief, worn the simple tunics and trews made acceptable if not fashionable by the Maid of Orleans, vowing never again to be sewed into breath-stopping formal dress.

The Inspector was too pale to blush properly, but penny-sized patches appeared on his cheeks and he huffed involuntarily. Lestrade, like many new-borns, treated her as if she were the age of her face. She had been sixteen when Chandagnac gave her the Dark Kiss. She was older, by a decade or more, than Vlad Tepes. While he was a warm Christian Prince, nailing Turks' turbans to their skulls and lowering his countrymen on to sharpened posts, she had been a new-born, learning the skills that now made her the longest-lived of her bloodline. With four and a half centuries behind her, it was hard not to be irritated when the fresh-risen dead, still barely cooled, patronized her.

'Silver Knife must be found and stopped,' Lestrade said. 'Before he kills again.'

'Indubitably,' Geneviève agreed. 'It sounds like an affair for your old associate, the consulting detective.'

She sensed, with the sharpened perceptions that told her night was falling, the chilling of the Inspector's heart.

'Mr Holmes is not at liberty to investigate, Mademoiselle. He has his differences with the current government.'

'You mean he has been removed, like so many of our finest minds, to those pens on the Sussex Downs. What does the *Pall Mall Gazette* call them, concentration camps?'

'I regret his lack of vision . . .'

'Where is he? Devil's Dyke?'

Lestrade nodded, almost ashamed. There was much of the man left inside. New-borns clung to their warm lives as if nothing had changed. How long would it be before they grew like the bitch vampires the Prince Consort had brought from the land beyond the mountains, an appetite on legs, mindlessly preying?

Geneviève finished her cuffs and turned to Lestrade, arms slightly out. It was a habit born of lifetimes without mirrors, always seeking an opinion on her appearance. The detective gave grudging approval. Settling a hooded cloak about her shoulders, she left her room, Lestrade following.

In the corridor outside, gaslights were already lit. Beyond a row of windows, hanging fog purged itself of the last of the dying sun. One window was open, letting in cool air. Geneviève could taste life in it. She must feed soon, within two or three days. It was always that way after her rest.

'The Schön inquest commences tomorrow night,' Lestrade said, 'at the Working Lads' Institute. It might be best if you attended.'

'Very well, but I must first talk with the director. Someone will have to take care of my duties for the duration.'

They were on the stairs. The building was coming to life. No matter how the Prince Consort changed London, Toynbee Hall – founded by the Reverend Samuel Barnett in the name of the late philanthropist Arnold Toynbee – was still required. The poor needed shelter, sustenance, medical attention, education. The new-borns, potentially immortal destitutes, were hardly better off than their warm brothers and sisters. For many, the East End settlements were the last recourse. Geneviève felt like Sisyphus, forever rolling a rock uphill, losing a yard for every foot gained.

On the first-floor landing sat a dark-haired little girl, a rag-doll in her lap. One of her arms was withered, leathery membranes bunched in folds beneath it, the drab dress cut away to allow freedom of movement. Lily smiled, teeth sharp but uneven.

'Gené,' Lily said, 'look . . .' Smiling, she extended the spindly arm. It grew longer, more sinewy; the hairy grey-brown flap stretched. 'I've been working on my wings. I'll fly to the moon and back.'

Geneviève looked away and saw Lestrade similarly examining the ceiling. She turned back to Lily and knelt, stroking her arm. The thick skin felt wrong, as if the muscles beneath were pulling against each other. Neither the elbow nor the wrist locked properly. Vlad Tepes could shape-shift without effort, but new-borns of his bloodline could not carry off the trick. Which didn't prevent them from trying.

'I'll bring you some cheese,' Lily said, 'as a present.'

Geneviève stroked Lily's hair and stood. The director's door was open. She entered, rapping a knuckle on the wood as she passed. The director was at his desk, going over a lecture timetable with Morrison, his secretary. The director was youngish and still warm, but his face was lined, his hair streaked grey. Many who'd lived through the changes were like him, older than their years. Lestrade followed her into the office. The director acknowledged the detective. Morrison, a quiet young man with an interest in literature and Japanese prints, stood back in the shadows.

'Jack,' she said, 'Inspector Lestrade wishes me to attend an inquest tomorrow.'

'There's been another murder,' the director said, making a statement not asking a question.

'A new-born,' said Lestrade. 'In Chicksand Street.'

'Lulu Schön,' Geneviève put in.

'Did we know her?'

'Probably, but under some other name.'

'Arthur can go through the files,' the director said, looking at Lestrade but indicating Morrison. 'You'll want the details.'

'Was she another street girl?' Morrison asked.

'Yes, of course,' said Geneviève.

The young man looked down. 'I think we've had her here,' he said. 'One of Booth's cast-offs.' His face screwed up as he mentioned the General's name. The Salvation Army deemed the un-dead beyond redemption, worse than other drunkards. Although warm, Morrison did not share the prejudice.

The director's fingers drummed his desk. He looked, as usual, as if the weight of the world had just unexpectedly settled on his shoulders.

'Can you spare me? Geneviève asked.

'Druitt can take your rounds if he's back from his cricketing jaunt. And Arthur can fill in once we've got the lecture schedules arranged. We weren't, ah, expecting you for a night or two yet anyway.'

'Thank you.'

'That's quite all right. Keep me informed. This is a dreadful business.'

Geneviève agreed. 'I'll see what I can do to pacify the natives. Lestrade is expecting an uprising.'

The policeman looked shifty and embarrassed. For a moment, Geneviève felt small, teasing the new-born. She was being unfair.

'There may be something I can actually do. Talk to some of

the new-born girls. Get them to take care, see if anyone knows anything.'

'Very well, Geneviève. Good luck. Lestrade, good evening.'

'Dr Seward,' said the detective, putting on his hat, 'good night.'

3

The After-Dark

FLORENCE STOKER DAINTILY tinkled her little bell, not to summon the maid but to call her parlour to attention. The ornament was aluminium, *not* silver. The clatter of tea-taking and conversation died. The company turned to play audience to their hostess.

'An announcement is imminent,' Florence declared, so delighted that the lilt of Clontarf, usually rigorously suppressed, insinuated itself into her tone.

Beauregard was suddenly a prisoner in himself. With Penelope on his arm he could hardly refuse the fence, but the situation was instantly different. For some months, he had teetered on the brink of a chasm. Now, screaming inside, he plunged towards the doubtless jagged rocks.

'Penelope, Miss Churchward,' Beauregard began, pausing then to clear his throat, 'has done me the honour . . .'

Everyone in the parlour understood at once, but he still had to get the words out. He wished for another gulp of the pale tea Florence served in exquisite bowls, in the Chinese fashion.

Penelope, impatient, finished for him. 'We're to be married. In the Spring, next year.'

She slipped her slim hand about his own, gripping tight. When a child, her favourite expression had been 'but *I* want it *now*'. His face must be flushed scarlet. This was absurd. He hardly qualified as a swooning youth. He had been married before . . . Before Penelope, Pamela. The other Miss Churchward, the elder. That must cause remark.

'Charles,' said Arthur Holmwood, Lord Godalming, 'congratulations'.

The vampire, smiling sharply, pumped Beauregard's free hand. Beauregard assumed Godalming knew how bone-crushing was his un-dead grip.

His fiancée was detached from him and surrounded by ladies. Kate Reed, by virtue of her spectacles and unruly hair the perfect Penelope's favourite confidante, helped her sit and fanned her with admiration. She chided her friend for keeping the secret from her. Penelope, honey over salt, told Kate not to be such a drip. Kate, one of those new women, wrote articles about bicycling for *Titbits* being currently much excited by something called a 'pneumatic tyre'.

Penelope was fussed over as if she had announced an illness, or an expected baby. Pamela, never far from mind when Penelope was present, had died in childbirth, her huge eyes screwed tight with pain. In Jagadhri, seven years ago. The child, a boy, had not survived his mother by a week. Beauregard did not care to remember that he had to be dissuaded from shooting dead the fool of a station doctor.

Florence was conferring with Bessie, her one remaining maid. Mrs Stoker dispatched the dark-eyed girl on a private mission.

Whistler, the grinning American painter, elbowed aside Godalming, and playfully thumped Beauregard's arm.

'There's no hope for you, Charlie,' he said, stabbing the air in front of Beauregard's face with a fat cigar. 'Another good man fallen to the enemy.'

Beauregard successfully sustained a smile. He had not intended to announce his engagement to Mrs Stoker's after-dark gathering. Since his return to London, he had been less frequently a guest at the get-togethers. Florence's position as a hostess to the fashionable and noted remained secure, though the question of her vanished husband hovered about always. No one had the courage or the cruelty to enquire after Bram, who was rumoured to have been removed to Devil's Dyke after an altercation with the Lord Chamberlain on a point of official censorship. Only the distinguished intervention of Henry Irving, Stoker's employer, prevented Bram's head from joining that of his friend Van Helsing outside the Palace. Lured by Penelope to this much-reduced gathering, Beauregard noted other absences. No vampires were present, apart from Godalming. Many of Florence's former guests – notably Irving and his leading lady, the incomparable Ellen Terry – had turned. Presumably others did not wish to associate even with the rumour of Republican sentiments, though the hostess, who encouraged debate at her after-darks, often made mention of her disinterest in politics. Florence – whose tireless struggle to surround herself with men far more brilliant and women marginally less pretty than herself Beauregard had to admit he found faintly irritating – entertained no question about the right of the Queen to rule, no more than she would query the right of the earth to resolve around the sun.

Bessie returned with a dusty bottle of champagne. Everyone discreetly set down their tea-bowls and saucers. Florence gave the maid a tiny key and the girl opened a cabinet, disclosing a small forest of glasses.

'There must be a toast,' Florence insisted, 'to Charles and Penelope.'

Penelope was by his side again, holding fast his hand, showing him off.

The bottle was passed to Florence. She regarded it as if uncertain which end could be opened. She would normally have a butler to perform uncorking duties. Momentarily, she was lost. Godalming stepped in, moving with a quicksilver grace combining speed with apparent languor, and took the bottle. He was not the first vampire Beauregard had seen, but he was the most perceptibly changed since his turn. Most new-borns fumbled with their limitations and capabilities, but His Lordship, with the poise of generations of breeding, had adapted perfectly.

'Allow me,' he said, draping a napkin over his arm like a waiter.

'Thank you, Art,' Florence babbled. 'I'm so feeble . . .'

He flashed a one-sided smile, baring a long eye-tooth, and dug a fingernail into the cork, then flipped it out of the bottleneck as if tossing a coin. Champagne gushed and Godalming filled the glasses Florence held beneath the bottle. His Lordship accepted mild applause with a handsome grin. For a dead man, Godalming practically burst with life. Every woman in the room was fixated upon the vampire. Not entirely excluding Penelope, Beauregard could not help but notice.

His fiancée did not much resemble her cousin. Except sometimes, when, catching him unaware, she would produce some phrase of Pamela's or make a trivial gesture that exactly duplicated a mannerism of his late wife's. Of course, there were also the Churchward mouth and those eyes. When he first married, eleven years previously, Penelope had been nine. He recollected a somewhat nasty child in a pinafore and sailor hat, deftly manipulating her family so the household revolved around her axis. He remembered sitting on the terrace with Pamela, and watching little Penny taunt the gardener's boy to tears. His bride-to-be still had a sharp tongue sheathed in her velvet mouth.

Glasses were distributed. Penelope managed to accept hers without for a moment leaving go of his hand. She had her prize and would not let it escape.

The toast fell, of course, to Godalming. He raised his glass, bubbles catching the light, and said, 'For me this is a sad moment, as I experience a loss. I've lost again to my good friend Charles Beauregard. I shall never recover, but I acknowledge Charles as the better man. I trust he will serve my dearest Penny as a good husband should.'

Beauregard, cynosure of all eyes, experienced discomfort. He did not like to be looked at. In his profession, it was unwise to attract notice of any kind.

'To the beautiful Penelope,' Godalming toasted, 'and the admirable Charles . . .'

'Penelope and Charles,' came the echo.

Penelope giggled like a cat as the bubbles tickled her nose, and Beauregard took an unexpectedly healthy swig. Everyone drank except Godalming, who set his glass down untouched on the tray.

'I am so sorry,' Florence said, 'I was forgetting myself.'

The hostess summoned Bessie again.

'Lord Godalming does not drink champagne,' she explained to the girl. Bessie understood and unbuttoned her blouse at the wrist.

'Thank you, Bessie,' Godalming said. He took her hand as if to kiss it, then turned it over as if to read her palm.

Beauregard could not help but feel slightly sickened, but no one else even made mention of the matter. He wondered how many were assuming a pose of indifference, and how many were genuinely accustomed to the habits of the thing Arthur Holmwood had become.

'Penelope, Charles,' Godalming said, 'I drink to you . . .'

Opening his mouth wide on jaw-hinges like a cobra's, Godalming fastened on to Bessie's wrist, lightly puncturing the skin with his pointed incisors, Godalming licked away a trickle of blood. The company were fascinated, Penelope shrank closer to Beauregard's side. She pressed her cheek to his shoulder but did not look away from Godalming and the maid. Either she was affecting cool or the vampire's feeding did not bother her. As Godalming lapped, Bessie swayed unsteadily on her ankles. Her eyes fluttered with something between pain and pleasure. Finally, the maid quietly fainted and Godalming, letting her wrist go, caught her deftly like a devoted Don Juan, holding her upright.

'I have this effect on women,' he said, teeth blood-rimmed; 'it is most inconvenient.'

He found a divan and deposited the unconscious Bessie on it. The girl's wound did not bleed. Godalming did not appear to have taken much from her. Beauregard thought she must have been bled before to take it so calmly. Florence, who had so easily offered Godalming the hospitality of her maid, sat beside Bessie and bound a handkerchief around her wrist. She performed the operation as if tying a ribbon to a horse, with kindness but no especial concern.

For a moment, Beauregard was dizzy.

'What is it, dear-heart?' Penelope asked, sliding an arm around him.

'The champagne,' he lied.

'Will we always have champagne?'

'As long as it is what you wish to drink.'

'You're so good to me, Charles.'

'Perhaps.'

Florence, her nursing done, was swarming around them again.

'Now, now,' she said, 'there'll be plenty of time for that after the wedding. In the mean time, you must be unselfish and share yourselves with the rest of us.'

'Indeed,' said Godalming. 'For a start, I must claim my right as the vanquished sir knight.'

Beauregard was puzzled. Godalming had blotted the blood from his lips with a handkerchief, but his mouth still shone, and there was a pinkish tinge to his upper teeth.

'A kiss!' Godalming exclaimed, taking Penelope's hands in his own. 'I claim a kiss from the bride.'

Beauregard's hand, fortunately out of Godalming's view, made a fist, as if grasping the handle of his sword-stick. He sensed danger, as surely as in the Natal when a black mamba, the deadliest reptile on earth, was close by his unprotected leg. A discreet cut with a

blade had separated the snake's venomous head from the remainder
of its length before harm could come to him. Then, he had good
cause to be thankful for his nerves; now, he told himself, he was
overreacting.

Godalming drew Penelope close and she turned her cheek to his
mouth. For a long second, he pressed his lips to her face. Then, he
released her.

The others, men and women, gathered round, offering more
kisses. Penelope was almost swamped with adoration. She wore
it well. He had never seen her prettier, or more like Pamela.

'Charles,' said Kate Reed, approaching him, 'you know . . . um,
congratulations . . . that sort of thing. Excellent news.'

The poor girl was blushing scarlet, forehead completely damp.

'Katie, thank you.'

He kissed her cheek, and she said 'gosh'.

Half-grinning, she indicated Penelope. 'Must go, Charles. Penny
wants . . .'

She was summoned to examine the marvellous ring upon
Penelope's dainty finger.

Beauregard and Godalming were by the window, apart from the
group. Outside, the moon was up, a faint glow above the fog.
Beauregard could see the railings of the Stoker house, but little
else. His own home was further down Cheyne Walk; a swirling
yellow wall obscured it as if it no longer existed.

'Sincerely, Charles,' Godalming said, 'my congratulations. You
and Penny must be happy. It is an order.'

'Art, thank you.'

'We need more like you,' the vampire said. 'You must turn soon.
Things are just getting exciting.'

This had been raised before. Beauregard held back.

'And Penny too,' Godalming insisted. 'She is lovely. Love-
liness should not be permitted to fade. That would be
criminal.'

'We shall think about it.'

'Do not think too long. The years fly.'

Beauregard wished he had a drink stronger than champagne.
Close to Godalming, he could almost taste the new-born's breath.
It was untrue that vampires exhaled a stinking cloud. But there was
something in the air, at once sweet and sharp. And in the centres

of Godalming's eyes, red points sometimes appeared like tiny drops of blood.

'Penelope would like a family.' Vampires, Beauregard knew, could not give birth in the conventional manner.

'Children?' Godalming said, fixing his gaze on Beauregard. 'If you can live for ever, surely children are superfluous to requirements.'

Beauregard was uncomfortable now. In truth, he was unsure about a family. His profession was uncertain, and after what had happened with Pamela . . .

He was tired in his head, as if Godalming were leeching his vitality. Some vampires could take sustenance without drinking blood, absorbing the energies of others through psychical osmosis.

'We need men of your sort, Charles. We have an opportunity to make the country strong. Your skills will be needed.'

If Lord Godalming had an idea of the skills he had developed in the service of the Crown, Beauregard supposed the vampire would be surprised. Since India, he had been in Shanghai, at the International Settlement, and in Egypt, working under Lord Cromer. The new-born laid hand upon his arm, and gripped almost fiercely. He could hardly feel his own fingers.

'There will never be slaves in Britain,' Godalming continued, 'but those who stay warm will naturally serve us, as the excellent Bessie has just served me. Have a care, lest you wind up the equivalent of some damned regimental water-bearer.'

'In India, I knew a water-bearer who was a better man than most.'

Florence came to his rescue, and guided them back into the mainstream. Whistler was recounting the latest instalment of his continuing feud with John Ruskin, savagely lampooning the critic. Grateful to be eclipsed, Beauregard stood near a wall and watched the painter perform. Whistler, accustomed to being the 'star' of Florence's after-darks, was obviously happy the distraction of Beauregard's announcement had passed. Penelope was lost somewhere in the crowd.

He had cause to wonder again whether he had selected a proper path, or even if the decision had been his own to take. He was the victim of a conspiracy to entrap him in the webs of femininity, orchestrated between China tea and lace doilies. The London to which he had returned in May differed vastly from that which he had left three years ago. A patriotic painting hung above the mantel; Victoria, plump and young again, and her fiercely mustachioed, red-eyed consort. The unknown artist posed no threat to Whistler's pre-eminence. Charles Beauregard served his Queen; he supposed he must also serve her husband.

The doorbell rang just as Whistler made an amusing speculation, perhaps unsuited to predominantly feminine company, regarding to the long-ago annulment of his hated enemy's marriage. Irritated at the interruption, the painter resumed his flow as Florence, herself irritated because Bessie was unavailable for the menial task, hurried off to answer her door.

Beauregard noticed Penelope sitting near the front, laughing prettily as she pretended to understand Whistler's insinuations. Godalming stood behind her chair, wrists crossed under his evening coat in the small of his back, the sharp points of his fingers dimpling out the cloth. Arthur Holmwood was no longer the man Beauregard had known when he left England. There had been a scandal, shortly before his turning. Like Bram Stoker, Godalming had sided with the wrong lot when the Prince Consort first came to London. Now he had to prove his loyalty to the new regime.

'Charles,' Florence said, quietly enough not to interrupt Whistler further. 'There is a man for you. From your club.'

She gave him a calling card. It bore the name of no individual, just the simple words: THE DIOGENES CLUB.

'This is in the nature of a summons,' he explained. 'Make my apologies to Penelope.'

'Charles . . .?'

He was in the hallway, Florence following close behind. He took his own cloak, hat and cane. Bessie would not be up to her duties for a while yet. He hoped, for the sake of Florence's dignity, the maid would be available to see to the guests when the time came for their departure.

'I'm sure Art will see Penelope home,' he said, instantly regretting the suggestion. 'Or Miss Reed.'

'Is this serious? I'm sure you don't have to leave so soon . . .'

The messenger, a close-mouthed fellow, waited out in the street, a carriage at the kerb beside him.

'My time is not always my own, Florence.' He kissed her hand. 'I thank you for your courtesy and kindness.'

He left the Stoker house, stepped across the pavement, and climbed up into the carriage. The messenger, who had been holding the nearside door open, joined him. The driver knew their intended destination, and immediately set off. Beauregard saw Florence closing her door against the cold. The fog thickened and he looked away from the house, settling in to the steady motion of the carriage. The messenger said nothing. Although a summons from the Diogenes Club could mean no good news, Beauregard was relieved to be out of Florence's parlour and away from the company.

4

Commercial Street Blues

A T COMMERCIAL STREET Police Station, Lestrade introduced her to Frederick Abberline. At the sufferance of Assistant Commissioner Dr Robert Anderson and Chief Inspector Donald Swanson, Inspector Abberline had charge of the continuing investigation. Having pursued the Polly Nichols and Annie Chapman cases with his customary tenacity but without notable results, the warm detective was now saddled with Lulu Schön, and any yet to come.

'If I can help in any way . . .' Geneviève offered.

'Listen to her, Fred,' Lestrade said; 'she's wise to the ways.'

Abberline, obviously unimpressed, knew it was politic to be polite. Like Geneviève, he could not see why Lestrade wanted her dogging the case.

'Think of her as an expert,' Lestrade said. 'She knows vampires. And this case comes down to vampires.'

The inspector waved the offer aside, but one of the several sergeants in the room – William Thick, whom they called 'Johnny Upright' – nodded agreement. He had interviewed Geneviève after the first murder, and seemed as fair and smart as his reputation would have him, even if his taste in suits did run to lamentable checks.

'Silver Knife is definitely a vampire-slayer,' Thick put in. 'Not some rip-merchant killing to cover theft.'

'We don't know that,' Abberline snapped, 'and I don't want to read it in the *Police Gazette*.'

Thick kept quiet, satisfied that he was right. In their interview, the sergeant admitted his personal belief was that Silver Knife imagined he had been wronged – or, more likely, actually had been wronged – by Vlad Tepes's get. Geneviève, expert enough to know the capabilities of her kind, agreed, but knew the description fitted so many in London that it would be fruitless to extrapolate a list of suspects from the theory.

'I believe Sergeant Thick is right,' she told the policemen.

Lestrade assented, but Abberline turned away to give an order to his own pet sergeant, George Godley. Geneviève smiled at Thick and saw him shiver. Like most of the warm, he knew even less about bloodline, about the infinite varieties and gradations of vampire, than the Prince Consort's glut of new-borns. Thick looked at her and saw a vampire . . . just like the bloodsucker who had turned his daughter, violated his wife, taken his promotion, killed his friend. She didn't know his history but supposed his theory was formed by personal experience, that he guessed the murderer's motive because he could understand it.

Abberline had spent the day first interrogating the constables who were first at the scene of the murder, then going over the ground himself. He had not immediately discovered anything of any relevance and was even holding off from committing to a statement that Schön was indeed another victim of the so-called Whitechapel Murderer. On the short walk from Toynbee Hall, they had heard newsboys shouting about Silver Knife; but the official flannel was that only Chapman and Nichols were demonstrably dead by the same hand. Various other unsolved cases – Schön now joining Tabram, Smith and sundry others – linked in the press could conceivably be entirely separate crimes. Silver Knife hardly held the patent on homicide, even in the immediate locality.

Lestrade and Abberline went off to have a huddle. Abberline, possibly unconsciously, made elaborate movements with his hands whenever the likelihood of pressing flesh with a vampire arose. He lit a pipe and listened as Lestrade ticked off points on his fingers. A jurisdictional dispute was in the offing between Abberline, head of H Division CID, and Lestrade. The Scotland Yard interloper was assumed to be one of Dr Anderson's spies, dispatched by Swanson to check up on the detectives in the field, ready to swoop in whenever glory was to be claimed but anonymous if results were lacking. Anderson, Swanson and Lestrade were the Irishman, the Scotsman and the Englishman of the music hall stories, and had been pictured as such by Weedon Grossmith in *Punch*, traipsing over a murder site and obliterating clues, to the annoyance of a local copper who somewhat resembled Fred Abberline. Geneviève wondered if she, hardly the epitome of the French girl from the same stories, fitted into the scheme. Did Lestrade intend her for a lever?

She looked about the already busy reception room. The doors pushed open constantly, admitting foggy draughts, and banged shut. Outside were several groups of interested parties. A Salvation Army band, flying the Cross of St George, supported a Christian Crusade preacher who called down God's Justice on vampirekind, upholding Silver Knife as a true instrument of the Will of Christ. The Speakers' Corner Torquemada was heckled by a few professional insurrectionists, ragged-trousered longhairs of various socialist or Republican stripes, and ridiculed by a knot of painted vampire women, who offered expensive kisses and a quick turning. Many new-borns paid to become some street tart's get, purchasing immortality for as little as a shilling.

'Who's the reverend gentleman?' Geneviève asked Thick.

The sergeant glanced out at the mob and groaned. 'A bloody nuisance, Miss. Name of John Jago, so he says.'

The Jago was a notorious slum at the upper end of Brick Lane, a criminal jungle of tiny courts and overpopulated rooms. It was undoubtedly the worst rookery in the East End.

'Any rate, that's where he comes from. He talks up an inferno, makes them all feel righteous and proper about shoving a stake through some trollop. He's been in and out of here all year for fire-breathing. And drunk and disorderly, with the odd common assault tossed in.'

Jago was a wild-eyed fanatic but some of the crowd listened to him. A few years ago, he would have been preaching against the Jews, or Fenians, or the Heathen Chinee. Now, it was vampires.

'Fire and the stake,' Jago cried. 'The unclean leeches, the cast-outs of Hell, the blood-bloated filth. All must perish by fire and the stake. All must be purified.'

The preacher had a few men soliciting donations in caps. They were rough-looking enough to blur the line between extortion and collection.

'He's not short of a few pennies,' Thick commented.

'Enough to get his bread-knife silver-plated?'

Thick had already thought of that. 'Five Christian Crusaders claim he was preaching his little heart out to them just when Polly Nichols was being gutted. Same for Annie Chapman. And last night's too, I'll lay odds.'

'Strange hours for a sermon?'

'Between two and three in the morning, and five and six for the second job,' Thick agreed. 'Does seem a trifle too done up in pink string and sealing wax, doesn't it? Still, we all have to be night-birds now.'

'You probably stay up all night regularly. Would you want to listen to God and Glory at five o'clock?'

'It's darkest just before dawn, they say.' Thick snorted, and added, 'Besides, I wouldn't listen to John Jago at any hour of the day or night. *Especially* on a Sunday.'

Thick stepped out and mingled with the crowd, getting the feel of the situation. Geneviève, at a loose end, wondered whether she should be getting back to the Hall. The desk sergeant checked his watch and gave the order to turn out the station's regulars. A group of shabby men and women were let out of the cells, marginally more sober than they had been when they were pulled in. They lined up to be officially set free. Geneviève recognized most of them: there were plenty – warm and vampire – who spent their nights shuffling between the holding cells, the Workhouse Infirmary and Toynbee Hall, in the constant search for a bed and a free feed.

'Miss Dee,' said a woman, 'Miss Dee . . .'

A lot of people had trouble pronouncing 'Dieudonné', so she often used her initial. Like many in Whitechapel, she had more names than the usual.

'Cathy,' she said, acknowledging the new-born, 'are you being well treated?'

'Loverly, miss, loverly,' she said, simpering at the desk sergeant; 'it's an 'ome from 'ome.'

Cathy Eddowes looked hardly better as a vampire than she'd done when warm. Gin and nights outdoors had raddled her; the red shine in her eyes and on her hair didn't outweigh the mottled skin under her heavy powder. Like many on the streets, Cathy still exchanged her body for drink. Her customers' blood was probably as alcohol-heavy as the gin which had been her warm ruin. The new-born primped her hair, arranging a red ribbon that kept her tight curls away from her wide face. There was a running sore on the back of her hand.

'Let me look at that, Cathy.'

Geneviève had seen marks like these. New-borns had to be careful. They were stronger than the warm, but too much of their diet was tainted. Disease was still a danger; the Prince Consort's Dark Kiss, at whatever remove, did something strange to diseases a person happened to carry over from warm life to their un-dead state.

'Do you have many of these sores?'

Cathy shook her head but Geneviève knew she meant yes. A clear fluid was weeping from the red patch on the back of her hand. Damp marks on her tight bodice suggested more. She wore her scarf in an unnatural fashion, covering her neck and the upper part of her breasts. Geneviève peeled the wool away from several glistening sores and smelled the pungent discharge. Something was wrong, but Cathy Eddowes was superstitiously afraid of finding out what it was.

'You must call in at the Hall tonight. See Dr Seward. He's a better man than you'd get at the Infirmary. Something can be done for your condition. I promise you.'

'I'll be all right, love.'

'Not unless you get treatment, Cathy.'

Cathy tried to laugh and tottered out on to the streets. One of her boot-heels was gone, so she had a comical limp. She held up her head, wrapping the scarf around her like a duchess's fur stole, and wiggled provocatively past Jago's Christian Crusade, slipping into the fog.

'Dead in a year,' remarked the desk sergeant, a new-born with a snout-like protrusion in the centre of his face.

Geneviève said, 'Not if I can help it.'

5

The Diogenes Club

BEAUREGARD WAS ADMITTED into the unexceptional foyer off Pall Mall. Through the doors of this institution passed the city's most unsociable and unclubbable men. The greatest collection of eccentrics, misanthropes, grotesques and unconfined lunatics outside the House of Lords was to be found on its membership lists. He handed over gloves, hat and cane to the silent valet, who arranged them on a rack in an alcove. While deferentially slipping off Beauregard's cloak, the valet subtly established that he was carrying no concealed revolver or dagger.

Ostensibly for the convenience of that species of individual who yearns to live in monied isolation from his fellows, this unassuming establishment on the fringes of Whitehall was actually much more. Absolute quiet was the rule; violators who so much as muttered under their breath while solving a crossword puzzle were mercilessly expelled without refund of their annual dues. A single squeak of marginally inferior boot-leather was enough to put a clubman on probation for five years. Members who had known each other by sight for sixty years were entirely unaware of one another's identity. It was, of course, absurd and impractical. Beauregard imagined the situation which would eventuate were a fire to break out in the reading room: members stubbornly sitting in the smoke, none daring to call out an alert as the flames rose around them.

Conversation was permitted in only two areas, the Strangers' Room, where clubmen occasionally entertained indispensable guests, and, far less famously, in the sound-proofed suite on the top floor. This was set aside for the use of the club's ruling cabal, a group of persons connected, mostly in minor official capacities, with Her Majesty's Government. The ruling cabal consisted of five worthies, each serving in rotation as chairman. In the fourteen years Beauregard had been at the disposal of the Diogenes Club, nine men had served on the cabal. When a member passed on and was discreetly replaced, it was always overnight.

As he was kept waiting, Beauregard was carefully watched by unseen eyes. During the Fenian Dynamite Campaign, Ivan Dragomiloff had penetrated the Club, intent on executing a commission to exterminate the entire ruling cabal. Detained in the foyer by a porter, the *soi-disant* ethical assassin had been noiselessly garrotted so as not to offend the sensibilities or excite the interest of the ordinary members. After a minute or two – no ticking clocks disturbed the peace – the valet, as if acting on telepathic command, lifted the purple rope that barred the unremarkable staircase leading directly to the top floor, and gave Beauregard the nod.

On the stairs, he remembered the several times he had been summoned before the ruling cabal. Such a call inevitably resulted in a voyage to some far corner of the world, and involved confidential matters affecting the interests of Great Britain. Beauregard supposed he was something between a diplomat and a courier, although he had at times been required to be an explorer, a burglar, an impostor, or a civil servant. Sometimes the business of the Diogenes Club was known in the outside world as the Great Game. The invisible business of government – conducted not in parliaments or palaces but in Bombay alleys and Riviera gambling hells – had afforded him a varied and intriguing career, even if it was of such a nature that he could hardly profit in his retirement by writing his memoirs.

While he had been away pursuing this Great Game, Vlad Dracula had taken London. Prince of Wallachia and King of Vampires, he had wooed and won Victoria, persuading her to abandon her widow's black. Then he had reshaped the greatest Empire on the globe to suit his tastes. Beauregard had vowed death would not interfere with his loyalty to the Queen's person, but he had thought he meant his own death.

The carpeted stairs did not creak. The thick walls admitted no noise from the bustling city without. Venturing into the Diogenes Club was like sampling stone-deafness.

The Prince Consort, who had taken for himself the additional title of Lord Protector, ruled Great Britain now, his get executing his wishes and whims. An elite Carpathian Guard patrolled the grounds of Buckingham Palace and caroused throughout the West End like sacred terrors. The army, the navy, the diplomatic corps, the police and the church were all in Dracula's thrall, new-borns promoted over the warm at every opportunity. While much continued as always, there were changes: people vanished from public and private life, camps such as Devil's Dyke springing up in remote areas of the country, and the apparatus of a government – secret police, sudden arrests, casual executions – he associated not with the Queen but with Tsars and Shahs. There were Republican bands playing Robin Hood in the wilds of Scotland and Ireland, and cross-waving curates were always trying to brand new-born provincial mayors with the mark of Cain.

On the top landing was a man with a military moustache and a neck the thickness of his head, even in civvies the absolute image of a sergeant-major. Beauregard passed inspection and the guard opened the familiar green door, stepping aside to allow the clubman to enter. He was inside the suite sometimes referred to as 'the Star Chamber' before a realization sank in: Sergeant Dravot, the man on guard, was a vampire, the first he had seen within the walls of the Diogenes Club. For a horrid, sinking moment, he assumed his eyes would get used to the gloom within the Star Chamber and alight upon five bloated leeches, sharp-fanged horrors ruddy with stolen blood. If the ruling cabal of the Diogenes Club had fallen, the long reign of the living would genuinely be at an end.

'Beauregard,' came a voice, normally pitched but sounding, even after only a minute in the silence of the Club, like a thunderclap from God. His moment of fear passed, replaced by a mild puzzlement. There were no vampires in the room, but things were changed.

'Mr Chairman,' he acknowledged.

It was convention not to address any of the cabal by name or title in their suite, but Beauregard knew he faced Sir Mandeville Messervy, a supposedly retired admiral who had made his name in the suppression, twenty years earlier, of the Slave Trade in the Indian Ocean. Also present were Mycroft, an enormously corpulent gentleman who had been chairman on Beauregard's last visit, and Waverly, an avuncular figure Beauregard understood to be personally responsible for the downfall of Colonel Ahmad Arabi and the occupation of Cairo in 1882. There were two empty seats at the round table.

'Alas, you find us depleted. There have, as you know, been changes. The Diogenes Club is not what it was.'

'A cigarette?' offered Waverly, producing a silverwork case and offering it.

Beauregard declined but Waverly tossed him the case anyway. He was fast enough to catch it and return it. Waverly smiled as he slipped the case into his breast pocket.

'Cold silver,' he explained.

'There was no need for that,' said Messervy. 'I apologize. Still, it was an effective demonstration.'

'I am not a vampire,' Beauregard said, showing his unburned fingers. 'That much should be obvious.'

'They're tricky, Beauregard,' said Waverly.

'You have one outside, you know.'

'Dravot is a special case.'

Formerly, Beauregard had considered the ruling cabal of the Diogenes Club impregnable, the ever-beating lion-heart of Britannia. Now, not for the first time since his return from abroad, he was forced to realize how radically the country was altered.

'That was a fine piece of work in Shanghai, Beauregard,' the chairman commented. 'Very deft. As we have come to expect of you.'

'Thank you, Mr Chairman.'

'It will be some years, I believe, before we hear again of those yellow devils in the Si-Fan.'

'I wish I shared your confidence.'

Messervy nodded sagely. The criminal *tong* was as impossible to root out and destroy as any other common weed.

Waverly had a small pile of folders in front of him. 'You're a well-travelled man,' he said. 'Afghanistan, Mexico, the Transvaal.'

Beauregard agreed, wondering where he was being led.

'You've been of great service to the Crown in many situations. But now we need you closer to home. Very close.'

Mycroft, who might have been sleeping with his eyes open for all the attention he seemed to pay, now leaned forwards. The current chairman was obviously so used to deferring to his colleague that he sat back and allowed him to take over.

'Beauregard,' said Mycroft, 'have you heard of the murders in Whitechapel? The so-called Silver Knife killings?'

6

Pandora's Box

'WHAT'S TO BE done?' shouted a new-born in a peaked cap. 'What's to stop this fiend slaughtering more of our women?'

Coroner Wynne Baxter angrily tried to keep control of the inquest. A pompous, middle-aged politician, Geneviève understood him to be unpopular. Unlike a High Court judge, he had no gavel and so was obliged to slap his wooden desk with an open hand.

'Any further interruptions of this nature,' Baxter said, glaring, 'and I shall be forced to clear the public from the room.'

The surly rough, who must have looked hungry even when warm, slouched back to his bench. He was surrounded by a similar crew. She knew the type: long scarves, ragged coats, pockets distended by books, heavy boots and thin beards. Whitechapel had all manner of Republican, anarchist, socialist and insurrectionist factions.

'Thank you,' said the coroner ironically, rearranging his notes. The troublemaker bared his fangs and muttered. New-borns disliked situations where someone warm had the authority. But a lifetime of cringing when officials frowned left habits.

This was the second day of the inquest. Yesterday, Geneviève had sat at the back of the Hall while sundry witnesses gave testimony relating to Lulu Schön's origins and movements. She had been out of the ordinary among East End streetwalkers. Countess Geschwitz, a mannish vampire who claimed to have come from Germany with the girl, blurted out something of Lulu's history: a procession of acquired names, dubious associations and dead husbands. If she had been given a name at birth, no one knew it. According to a telegraph from Berlin, the German police still wanted to talk to her in connection with the shooting of one of her more recent husbands. All the witnesses – including Geschwitz, who had turned her – were transparently in love with Lulu, or at least desired her beyond all reason. Evidently the new-born could have been one of *les Grandes Horizontales* of Europe, but foolishness and ill fortune had reduced her to fourpenny knee-tremblers in London's meaner streets and finally delivered her to the sharp mercies of Silver Knife.

Throughout the testimony, Lestrade muttered about opening up Pandora's Box. It was almost certain the only connection between the Whitechapel Murderer and his victims came at the point of their deaths, but the police investigation could not afford to overlook the possibility that these were pre-meditated killings of specific women. Back in Commercial Street. Abberline, Thick and the others were assembling and cross-referencing biographies, more exhaustively detailed than any life of a great statesman, of Nichols, Chapman and Schön. If any connection could be established between the women, beyond the fact that they were all vampire prostitutes, then that might lead to their killer.

As the inquest, commenced in the early afternoon, proceeded into the evening, Baxter had turned his attention to Schön's doings on the night of her death. Geschwitz, face red from a recent feeding, said Lulu had left their attic some time between three and four in the morning. The body had been discovered by Constable George Neve, walking his beat shortly after six. After finishing Lulu, presumably in plain sight on Chicksand Street, the murderer had dumped her on the doorstep of a basement flat. A family of Polish Jews, of whom only the littlest child could speak anything approaching English, had been inside. They all stated, as translated by the tiny girl after a Yiddish babel of argument, that they had not heard anything until Constable Neve roused them by practically battering down their door. Rebecca Kosminski, the self-assured spokeswoman, was the only vampire in the family. Geneviève had seen her kind before; Melissa d'Acques, who had turned Chandagnac, was one. Rebecca might live to become the all-powerful matriarch of her extended clan, but she would never grow up.

Lestrade fidgeted throughout, describing it cruelly as 'comedy relief'. He would rather have been out combing the crime scene than sitting on a hardwood bench made for the tough bottoms and short legs of twelve-year-olds, but he could not get in Fred Abberline's way too often. He gloomily told Geneviève that Baxter was known for the length of his inquests. The coroner's approach was characterized by an obsessive, not to say tedious, insistence on dragging out irrelevant details and the flamboyant off-handedness of his summings-up. In his closing remarks on Anne Chapman, Baxter had invented the theory, on the basis of gossip overheard at the Middlesex Hospital, that an American doctor was either the murderer or the employer of the murderer. The unknown doctor, researching the physiognomy of the un-dead, was rumoured to have offered twenty guineas for a fresh vampire heart. There had been a brief flurry of activity as Abberline tried to locate the foreigner, but it turned out vampire hearts, mainly somewhat damaged, could be unethically purchased from mortuaries for as little as sixpence.

Baxter had adjourned before midnight, and reconvened the inquest this morning. Now evidence from the post-mortem was available, and today's business mainly concerned a succession of medical men, all of whom had crammed themselves into Whitechapel Workhouse Infirmary Mortuary to examine the mortal remains of Lulu Schön.

First came Dr George Bagster Phillips, the H Division Police Surgeon – well known at Toynbee Hall – who had done the preliminary examination of the body in Chicksand Street and performed the more detailed post-mortem. It boiled down to the simple facts that Lulu Schön had been heart-stabbed, disembowelled and decapitated. It took much desk-banging to quieten the outrage that followed these not unexpected revelations.

By law, inquests had to be held in public places and be open to the press. From the several appearances Geneviève had made as a witness in connection with the deaths of paupers in Toynbee Hall beds, she knew the audience was usually confined to a bored stringer from the Central News Agency, with the occasional friend or relation of the deceased. But the lecture hall was even more thickly populated today than it had been yesterday, the benches as heavily burdened as if Con Donovan were on the stage, rematching with Monk for the Featherweight Title. As well as the reporters hogging the front row, Geneviève noticed a gaggle of haggard mainly un-dead women in colourful dresses, a scattering of well-dressed men, some of Lestrade's uniformed juniors, and a sprinkling of sensation-seekers, clergymen and social reformers.

In the centre of the room, spaces all around unoccupied despite the surplus of attenders, sat a long-haired vampire warrior. Not a new-born, he wore the uniform, including a steel breastplate, of the Prince Consort's Own Carpathian Guard, augmented by a tasseled fez. His face was withered white parchment but his eyes, blood-red marbles set in the dead waste of skin, constantly twitched.

'Do you know who that is?' Lestrade asked.

Geneviève did. 'Kostaki, one of Vlad Tepes's hangers-on.'

'That sort gives me the creeps,' commented the new-born detective. 'The elders.'

Geneviève almost laughed. Kostaki was younger than she. His presence was almost certainly not due to mere curiosity. The Palace was taking an interest in Silver Knife.

'People die every night in Whitechapel, in ways Vlad Tepes couldn't devise, or live lives worse than any death,' Geneviève said, 'yet from one year's end to the next, London pretends we're as remote as Borneo. But give them a handful of gory murders and you can't move for sightseers and prurient philanthropists.'

'Maybe some good will come of it,' Lestrade commented.

Dr Bagster Phillips was thanked and dismissed, and Baxter called for Henry Jekyll, MD, DCL, LLD, FRS, etc. A dignified, smooth-faced man of fifty, obviously once handsome, approached the lectern and took the oath.

'Whenever a vampire's killed,' Lestrade explained, 'Jekyll comes creeping round. Something rum about him, if you get my drift . . .'

The scientific researcher, who first gave a detailed and anatomically precise description of the atrocities, was warm only in the sense that he was not a vampire. Dr Jekyll was self-controlled to a point that suggested a disturbing lack of empathy with the human subject of the inquest, but she listened with interest – certainly more than that expressed by the yawning reporters in the front row – to the comments Baxter solicited from him.

'We have not learned enough about the precise changes in the human metabolism that accompany the so-called "turn" from normal life to the un-dead state. Exact information is hard to come by, and superstition hangs like a London fog over the subject. My studies have been checked by official indifference, even hostility. We could all benefit from research. Perhaps the divisions which lead to tragic incidents like the death of this girl could then be erased from our society.'

The anarchists were grumbling again. Without divisions, their cause would have no purpose.

'Too much of what we believe about vampirism is sheer folklore,' Dr Jekyll continued. 'The stake through the heart, the silver scythe. The vampire corpus is remarkably resilient, but any major breach of the vital organs seems to produce true death, as here.'

Baxter hummed and questioned the doctor. 'So the murderer has not, in your opinion, followed what we might deem the standard superstitious practice of the vampire killer?'

'Indeed. I should like to put certain facts into the record, if only to provide a definitive contradiction of irresponsible journalism.'

Some of the reporters hooted quietly. A lightning sketch artist sitting directly in front of Geneviève was deftly portraying Dr Jekyll for reproduction in the illustrated press. He pencilled in some dark shadows under the witness's eyes to make him look more untrustworthy.

'As with Nichols and Chapman, Schön was not penetrated with a wooden stake or paling. Her mouth was not stuffed with cloves of garlic, or fragments of communion wafer, or pages torn from a sacred text. No crucifix or cruciform object was found on or near the body. The dampness of her skirts and the residue of water on her face was almost certainly condensation from the fog. It is highly unlikely that the body was sprinkled with holy water.'

The artist, probably the man from the *Police Gazette*, drew in heavy eyebrows and tried to make Dr Jekyll's thick but immaculately combed hair look shaggy. He went too far in distorting his subject and, tutting at his overenthusiasm, tore the sheet off his pad, crumpled it into his pocket, and began afresh.

Baxter jotted down some notes, and resumed his questioning. 'Would you venture that the murderer was familiar with the workings of the human body, whether of a vampire or not?'

'Yes, coroner. The extent of the injuries betokens a certain frenzy of enthusiasm, but the actual wounds – one might almost say incisions – have been wrought with some skill.'

'Silver Knife's a bleedin' doctor,' shouted the chief anarchist.

The court again exploded into uproar. The anarchists, about half-and-half warm and new-borns, stamped their feet and yelled, while others talked loudly among themselves. Kostaki looked around and silenced a pair of clergymen with a cold glare. Baxter hurt his hand hitting his desk.

Geneviève noticed a man standing at the back of the courtroom observing the clamour with cool interest. Well dressed, with a cloak and top hat, he might have been a sensation-seeker but for a certain air of purpose. He was not a vampire, but – unlike the coroner, or even Dr Henry Jekyll – he showed no signs of being disturbed to be among so many of the un-dead. He leant on a black cane.

'Who is that?' she asked Lestrade.

'Charles Beauregard,' the new-born detective said, curling a lip. 'Have you heard of the Diogenes Club?'

She shook her head.

'When they say "high places", that's where they mean. Important people are taking an interest in this case. And Beauregard is their catspaw.'

'A striking man.'

'If you say so, mademoiselle.'

The coroner had restored order again. A clerk had nipped out of the room and returned with six more constables, all new-borns. They lined the walls like an honour guard. The anarchists were brooding again, their purpose obviously to cause enough trouble to be an irritant but not enough to get their names noted.

'If I might be permitted to address the implied question raised by the gentleman.' Dr Jekyll asked, eliciting a nod from Baxter, 'a knowledge of the position of the major organs does not necessarily betoken a medical education. If you are disinterested in preserving life, a butcher can have out a pair of kidneys as neatly as a surgeon. You need only a steady hand and a sharp knife, and there are plenty of both in Whitechapel.'

'Do you have an opinion as to the instrument used by the murderer?'

'A blade of some sort, obviously. Silvered.'

The word brought a collective gasp.

'Steel or iron would not have done such damage,' Dr Jekyll continued. 'Vampire physiology is such that wounds inflicted with ordinary weapons heal almost immediately. Tissue and bone regenerate, just as a lizard may grow a new tail. Silver has a counteractive effect on this process. Only silver could do such permanent, fatal harm to a vampire. In this instance, the popular imagination, which has tagged the murderer as "Silver Knife", has almost certainly got its facts straight.'

'You are familiar with the cases of Mary Ann Nichols and Eliza Anne Chapman?' asked Baxter.

Dr Jekyll nodded. 'Yes.'

'Have you drawn any conclusions from a comparison of these incidents?'

'Indeed. These three killings are indubitably the work of the same individual. A left-handed man of above average height, with more than normal physical strength . . .'

'Mr Holmes would've been able to tell his mother's maiden name from a fleck of cigar ash,' Lestrade muttered.

'. . . I would add that, considering the case from an alienist's point of view, it is my belief that the murderer is not himself a vampire.'

The anarchist was on his feet but the coroner's extra constables were around him before he could even shout. Smiling to himself at his subjugation of the court, Baxter made a note of the last point and thanked Dr Jekyll.

Geneviève noticed that the man she had asked Lestrade about was gone. She wondered if Beauregard noticed her as she had noticed him. From her side, a connection had been made. She was either having one of her 'insights' or had gone too long without feeding. No, she was certain. The man from the Diogenes Club – whatever that really was – was materially involved in the affairs of the Whitechapel Murderer, but she could not guess in what capacity.

The coroner began his elaborate summing-up, delivering the verdict of 'wilful murder by person or persons unknown', adding that the killer of Lulu Schön was judged to be the same man who had murdered, on 31st August, Mary Ann Nichols, and, on 8th September, Eliza Anne Chapman.

7

The Prime Minister

'WERE YOU AWARE,' began Lord Ruthven, 'that there are people in these isles whose sole objection to the marriage of our dear Queen – Victoria Regina, Empress of India, et cetera – to Vlad Dracula – known as Tepes, *quondam* Prince of Wallachia – is that the happy bridegroom happened once to be, in a fashion I shan't pretend to understand, a Roman Catholic?'

The Prime Minister waved a letter selected apparently at random from the piles of ignored correspondence littering the several desks in his Downing Street receiving room, Godalming knew better than to interrupt one of Ruthven's fits of loquacity. For a new-born eager to be initiated into the secrets of the elders, close attention to the centuries-old peer was a valuable, indeed indispensable, instrument of learning. When Ruthven talked a streak, volumes of ancient truth disclosed long-forgotten spells of power. It was hard not to be caught up in the force of his personality, to be transported on wings of rant.

'I have here,' Ruthven continued, 'a missive from a miserable society devoted to the thin memory of that constitutionalist bore Walter Bagehot. They tactfully complain that the Prince accepted the embrace of the Anglican Church an indecently short time before he accepted the embrace of the Queen. Our correspondent even goes so far as to suggest Vlad might conceivably not be sincere in his abjuration of the Pope of Rome, and that, with Cardinal Newman as his secret confessor, he has imported the perfidious taint of Leo the Thirteenth into the Royal Household. My curly-haired friend, some dunderheads find it easier to forgive a taste for virgin blood than the drinking of communion wine.'

Ruthven shredded the letter. Its confetti joined that of many other derided documents on the carpet. He grinned and breathed heavily, but there was no trace of his apparent excitement in his milk-white cheeks. It struck Godalming that the Prime Minister's rages were counterfeit, the impostures of a man more used to simulating than experiencing passion. He strode across the room, making and unmaking fists behind his back, grey eyes like fine-lashed marbles.

'Our Prince changed his faith before, you know,' Ruthven observed, 'and for the same reason. In 1473, he abandoned Orthodoxy and became Catholic so he could marry the sister of the King of Hungary. The manoeuvre won him freedom after twelve years as a hostage at Mathias's court, and a clear shot at regaining the Wallachian throne his bloody foolishness had lost him. That he stuck by Rome for four centuries afterwards tells you not a little about the man's innate dullness. If you wish to examine the true soul of conservatism, you should look no further than Buckingham Palace.'

By now the Prime Minister was addressing himself not to Godalming but to a portrait. Its beak-nosed profile was turned towards a balancing picture of the Queen that ornamented the same wall. Godalming had only met Dracula once; the Prince Consort and Lord Protector, then a mere Count going by the name of deVille, had not much resembled the proud creature captured in paint by Mr G. F. Watts.

'Imagine the brute, Godalming. Brooding for four hundred years in his stinking wreck of a castle. Plotting and scheming and swearing and gnashing his teeth. Festering in medieval superstition. Bleeding dry uncouth peasants. Running and rutting and raping and rending with the mountain beasts. Taking his coarse pleasure with those un-dead animals he calls wives. Shifting his shape like some were-wolf mountebank . . .'

Though the Prince Consort had personally sponsored the Prime Minister's appointment, relations between the vampire elders, formed over the course of centuries, were hardly congenial. In public, Ruthven displayed the expected fealty to the elder who had been King of the Vampires long before he was ruler of Great Britain. The un-dead had been an invisible kingdom for thousands of years; the Prince Consort had, at a stroke, wiped clean that slate and started anew, lording over warm and vampire alike. Ruthven, who had passed his centuries in travel and dalliance, was dragged out of the shadows with the other elders. Some might say that a chronically impoverished nobleman – who once remarked that his title and barren acres in Scotland could buy him a halfpenny bun if he had the ha'pence to go with them – had done well out of the changes. But His Lordship, a man whose title could hardly compare with Godalming's own, was a complainer.

'Now this Dracula has his *Bradshaw* by heart and calls himself a "modern". He can tell you all the times of trains from St Pancras to Norwich on bank holidays. But he can't believe the world has revolved since he got himself killed. Do you know how he died? He disguised himself as a Turk to spy on the enemy, then his own men broke his neck when he tried to come back to camp. The seed was already in him, put there by some fool of a *nosferatu*, and he crawled out of the earth. He is nobody's get. How he loves his native soil, to sleep in it at every opportunity. There's grave-mould in his bloodline, Godalming. That's the sickness he spreads. Think yourself lucky that you are of my bloodline. It's pure, We may not turn into bats and wolves, my son-in-darkness, but we don't rot on the bone either, or lose our minds in a homicidal frenzy.'

Godalming believed Ruthven had sought him out and made a vampire of him solely because of his involvement in what was now regarded as an underhanded conspiracy against the Royal Person. When warm, Godalming had personally destroyed the first of Dracula's British get. That made him a likely candidate for the pike between Van Helsing and that solicitor fellow Harker. He remembered with a shudder the Thor-like blows that drove the stake through his then-beloved Lucy, and felt a poisonous hate for the Dutchman who had persuaded him to such an extreme. He had been criminally foolish and was now eager to compensate. His turning, and Ruthven's adoption of him as protégé, had saved his heart for the moment, but he was too well aware of the Prince Consort's capriciousness and capacity for vengeance. And, of course, his father-in-darkness was not known for his own constancy or evenness of temperament. If he was to find a secure place in the changed world, he would have to be careful.

'His ideas were formed in his lifetime,' Ruthven continued, 'when you could rule a country with the sword and stake. He missed the Renaissance, the Reformation, the Age of Enlightenment, the French Revolution, the rise of the Americas, the fall of the Ottoman. He wishes to avenge the death of our gallant General Gordon by dispatching a force of ferocious vampire idiots to ravage the Sudan and impale all who owe allegiance to the Mahdi. I should let him do it. We could well live without his Carpathian cronies draining the public purse. Let a hundred or so of the clods get cut down by canny Mussulmen and be left to rot in the sun and we'd have all the barmaids in Piccadilly and Soho flying the Crescent in gratitude.'

Ruthven swept his hand through another pile of letters, and sent up a flurry which descended around him. The Prime Minister seemed barely out of his teens, with cold grey eyes and a dead white face. He betrayed no ruddy flush even when he had just fed. A connoisseur of delicate young girls, he nevertheless chose for his get able young men of position. He distributed his new-born children-in-darkness to government offices, even encouraging competition between them. Godalming, unsuited by his title to menial duties and yet hardly qualified for a cabinet post, was currently the most favoured of Ruthven's get, serving unofficially as a private messenger and secretary. He had always had a practical streak, a flair for working out the details of complicated plans. Even Van Helsing had trusted him to handle much of the spadework of his campaign.

'And have you heard of his latest edict?' Ruthven held up a scroll of official parchment, bound in scarlet tape. It unravelled, and Godalming saw the copperplate of a palace secretary. 'He wants to crack the whip on what he refers to as "unnatural vice", and has decreed that the punishment for sodomy shall henceforth by summary execution. The method will, of course, be his old reliable, the stake.'

Godalming glanced over the paper. 'Sodomy? Why should that so offend the Prince Consort?'

'You forget, Godalming. Dracula has not the Englishman's tolerance. He spent some years of his youth as a hostage to the Turks, and we must assume his captors made use of him from time to time. Indeed, his brother Radu, significantly known as "the Handsome", developed a taste for masculine attentions. Since Radu betrayed him in one of his family's innumerable internal intrigues, the Prince Consort has chosen to take an extreme position with regard to matters homosexual.'

'This seems a very minor business.'

Ruthven flared his nostrils. 'Your understanding is limited,

Godalming. Just consider: there is hardly an upstanding member of either house who has *not* at one time or another, buggered a telegraph boy. Come December, Dracula will have some very prominent fairies slowly sinking on to the Christmas trees they are surmounting.'

'A curious image, my lord.'

The Prime Minister waved away the remark, diamond-shaped nails catching the light.

'Tchah, Godalming, tchah! Of course, in that canny brain, our Wallachian Prince may have many purposes to one action.'

'Meaning?'

'Meaning that there is in this city a certain new-born poet, an Irishman, as known for his amatory preferences as for his unwise association with a countryman whose memory is much out of favour. And, dare I say it, better known for either attribute than for his verse.'

'You mean Oscar Wilde?'

'Of course I mean Wilde.'

'He is not much at Mrs Stoker's lately.'

'Neither should you be, if you value your heart. My protection can only cloak so much.'

Godalming nodded, gravely. He had his reasons for continuing to attend Florence Stoker's after-darks.

'I have a report on the doings of Mr Oscar Wilde somewhere,' Ruthven said, indicating another pyramid of papers. 'Commissioned in my private capacity as a gentleman of letters, with an interest in the continuing health of our finest creative minds. Wilde has embraced the vampire state with enthusiasm, you'll be pleased to know. Currently, sampling the blood of young men is his favoured pursuit, somewhat eclipsing his aesthetic fervour, and completely obliterating the flirtation with Fabian socialism that regrettably preoccupied him at the beginning of the year.'

'You've obviously taken an interest in the fellow. For myself, I always find him tiresome, tittering behind his hand to hide his bad teeth.'

Ruthven threw himself into a chair and ran a hand through his longish hair. The Prime Minister was something of a dandy, given to an extravagance of cuffs and cravats. *Punch* called him 'the compleat murgatroyd'.

'We contemplate the dread possibility that Alfred, Lord Tennyson, will hold the post of poet laureate for dreary centuries. Egads, imagine *Locksley Hall Six Hundred Years After*! I would rather drink vinegar than live in an England that would allow such a horror, and so I have been casting around for a merciful alternative. If things had been otherwise, Godalming, I should have chosen to be a poet, and yet tyrannous fate, with the invaluable assistance of the Prince Consort, has bound me to the rock of bureaucracy, the eagle of politics pecking at my liver.'

Now Ruthven stood up and wandered to his book-cases, where he remained, contemplating his beloved volumes. The Prime Minister had lengthy passages of Shelley, Byron, Keats and Coleridge by heart, and could disgorge chunks from Goethe and Schiller in the original. His current enthusiasms were French, and decadent. Beaudelaire, de Nerval, Rimbaud, Rachilde, Verlaine, Mallarmé; most, if not all, of whom the Prince Consort would have gleefully impaled. Godalming had heard Ruthven declare that a purportedly scandalous novel, *A Rebours* by J. K. Huysmans, should be placed before every schoolboy, and that he would, in a utopia, make vampires only of poets and painters. It was said, however, that one symptom of the un-dead state was a withering of the creative abilities. A proud philistine who would rather have hunt scenes on his walls than William Morris paper, Godalming never had anything that might be considered an artistic inclination, and so could not bear witness to the phenomenon.

'But,' the Prime Minister said, turning, 'of us elders, who else has the wit to mediate between Prince Dracula and his subjects, to hold together this new empire of living and dead? That lunatic Sir Francis Varney, whom we have packed off to India? I think not. None of our Carpathian worthies will serve, either: not Iorga, not Von Krolock, not Meinster, not Tesla, not Brastov, not Mitterhouse, not Vulkan. And what of the hand-kissing Saint-Germain, the meddling Villanueva, the upstart Collins, the impenetrable Weyland, the buffoon Barlow, the oily Duval? I "hai me doots", as the Scotchman says, I "hai me doots" indeed. Who then does that leave? The pale and uninteresting Karnstein, still mourning for his silly skewered girl? Come to that, what of the women? God, the vampire women! What a pack of foaming she-cats! Lady Ducayne and Countess Sarah Kenyon are at least English, even if they've not an ounce of brain between them. But Countess Zaleska of Romania, Ethelind Fionguala of Ireland, Countess Dolingen of Graz, Princess Asa Vajda of Moldavia, Elizabeth Bathory of Hungary? None of these titled tarts would be acceptable, I think, either to the Prince Consort or to the peoples of Britain. You might as well give the job to one of those mindless woman-things Dracula set aside to marry plump Vicky. No. Of the elders, there is only me. Here I am: Lord Ruthven, wanderer and wit. A land-poor Englishman, long absent from his homeland, recalled to be of service to his country. Who would have thought I would ever occupy the office of Pitt and Palmerston and Gladstone and Disraeli? And who could succeed me? *Après moi, le déluge*, Godalming. After me, the shower.'

8

The Mystery of the Hansom Cab

BEAUREGARD STROLLED IN the fog, endeavouring to digest all he had gleaned from the inquest. He would have to make a full report to the cabal; he must have the facts, such as they were, ordered.

His wandering was not random: from the Working Lads' Institute, he walked down Whitechapel Road, turned right into Great Garden Street, left into Chicksand Street. He allowed himself to be drawn to the site of the recent murder. Even with the churning fog and the Silver Knife panic, the streets were crowded. As midnight approached, the un-dead emerged. Public houses and music halls were illuminated, crammed with laughing and shouting people. Costermongers hawked sheet music, phials of 'human' blood, scissors, Royal souvenirs. Chestnuts roasted in a barrel-fire on Old Montague Street were sold to new-born and warm alike. Vampires had no need of solid food, but the habit of eating was hard to leave behind. Boys sold fancifully illustrated broadsheets with gruesome details piping hot from Lulu Schön's inquest. A good many more uniformed constables were about than was usual, mostly new-borns. Beauregard supposed any suspicious characters loitering around Whitechapel and Spitalfields must come in for close inspection, presenting the police with a thorny problem, since the district thronged with *nothing but* suspicious characters.

A street organ ground an air: 'Take a Pair of Crimson Eyes', from Gilbert and Sullivan's *The Vampyres of Venice: or: A Maid, a Shade and a Blade*. That seemed apt. The maid – so to speak – and the blade were obviously present in the case. The shade was the murderer, obscured by fog and blood.

Despite Dr Jekyll's testimony and Baxter's verdict, he considered the notion that the crimes to date were the work of different hands, ritual killings like thuggee stranglings or Camorra executions. The extent of the mutilation was superfluous to necessity if the murderer's purpose was simply to end life. The *Pall Mall Gazette* ventured that the savage excesses of the crimes were reminiscent of an Aztec rite. Even more, Beauregard was reminded of incidents in China, Egypt and Sicily, in connection with secret societies. The purpose of such atrocities was not merely to eliminate an enemy but also to deliver a message to the victim's confederates or any who might choose to stand with him. The metropolis was aswarm with secret societies and their agents; it was not improbable that there were already Freemasonries sworn to continue Abraham Van Helsing's crusade against the Prince Consort and his get. In a sense, as an agent of the Diogenes Club, Beauregard was actually a member of such a faction; the ruling cabal was divided in itself, torn between loyalty to the Queen and suspicion of the Lord Protector.

Sharp eyes took note of his good clothes but their owners mainly kept out of his way. Beauregard was conscious of the watch in his waistcoat and the wallet in his inside breast pocket. Nimble fingers were around, and long-nailed claws. Blood was not all the new-borns wanted. He swung his cane purposefully, warding off evil.

A thick-necked vampire with size twelve boots lounged opposite where Lulu had been killed, trying half-heartedly not to look like a detective constable posted on the off chance that the old saw about the murderer returning to the scene of the crime were true. The area around the Kosminskis' doorway had been picked clean by the police and souvenir hunters. He tried to imagine the last moments of the vampire girl. The detective, the monotony of his duty broken by the presence of a man in a cloak with morbid interests, lumbered from his spot. Beauregard had his card out ready. The new-born saw the words 'Diogenes Club' and did a curious little dance with his hands and face, half-salute and half-snarl. Then he stepped in front of the doorway, shielding Beauregard from sight, like the look-out for a cracksman.

He stood on the spot where the girl had died and felt nothing but the cold. Psychical mediums were reputedly able to track a man by invisible ectoplasmic residue, like a bloodhound following a trail. Any such who had offered assistance to the Metropolitan Police had not achieved notable results. The hollow where Silver Knife had worked was tiny. Lulu Schön, a small woman, had had to be twisted and trampled to be crammed down into it. Scrubbed-clean brickwork blotches, as shocking on the soot-blackened wall as an exposed patch of white bone, showed unmistakably where the blood-stains had been. There was nothing more, Beauregard thought, to be gained by this macabre visit.

He bade the detective a good-night and walked off to find a cab. A vampire whore in Flower & Dean Street offered to make him immortal for an ounce or two of his blood. He flipped her a copper coin and went on his way. How long would he have the strength to resist? At thirty-five, he was already aware that he was slowing. In the cold, he felt his wounds. At fifty, at sixty, would his resolve to stay warm to the grave seem ridiculous, perverse? Sinful, even? Was refusing vampirism the moral equivalent of suicide? His father had died at fifty-eight.

Vampires needed the warm to feed and succour them, to keep the city running through the days. There were already un-dead – here in the East End, if not in the salons of Mayfair – starving as the poor had always starved. How soon would it be before the 'desperate measures' Sir Danvers Carew advocated in parliament were seriously considered? Carew favoured the penning-up of still more warm, not only criminals but any simply healthy specimens, to serve as cattle for the vampires of breeding essential to the governance of the country. Stories crept back from Devil's Dyke that made ice of Beauregard's heart. Already the definition of criminality extended to include too many good men and women who were simply unable to come to an accommodation with the new regime.

At length, he found a hansom and offered the cabby two florins to take him back to Cheyne Walk. The driver touched his whip to the brim of his topper. Beauregard settled down behind the folding half-doors. With an interior upholstered in red like the plush coffins displayed in the shops along Oxford Street, the hansom was altogether too luxurious a conveyance for this quarter. He wondered whether it had carried a distinguished visitor in search of amorous adventures. Houses all over the district catered to every taste. Women and boys, warm and vampire, were freely available for a few shillings. Drabs like Polly Nichols and Lulu Schön could be had for coppers or a squirt of blood. It was possible the murderer was not from the area, that he was just another toff pursuing peculiar

pleasures. You could get anything in Whitechapel, either by paying
for it or stealing it

His duties had taken him to worse places. He had spent weeks
as a one-eyed beggar in Afghanistan, dogging the movements of
a Russian envoy suspected of stirring up the hill-tribes. During the
Boer Rebellion, he had negotiated a treaty with the Amahagger,
whose idea of an evening's entertainment was baking the heads of
captives in pots. However it had been something of a surprise to
return, after a spell abroad in the discreet service of Her Majesty, to
find London itself transformed into a city more strange, dangerous
and bizarre than any in his experience. No longer the heart of
Empire, it was a sponge absorbing the blood of the realm until
it burst.

The cab's wheels rattled on the road, lulling him like the soft crash
of waves under a ship. Beauregard thought again of his possible
secret society; the Hermetic Order of the Stake perhaps, or the
Friends of Van Helsing. In one feature, the crimes were unlike ritual
murders: in such cases it was important there be an unmistakable
signature, like the five orange pips sent by the Ku Klux Klan to a
traitor or the cold fish left beside a Sicilian who defied the mafia.
Here the only signature was a kind of directed frenzy. This was
the doing of a madman not an insurrectionist. That would not
prevent street-corner ranters like those who had interrupted the
inquest from claiming these pathetic eviscerations as victories for
the warm. It would not be beyond the capabilities of many a secret
society to take advantage of a hapless lunatic, systematically to drive
a man mad in a certain direction as if he were a weapon being aimed,
then discharging him into the streets to do his bloody business.

He might have drifted into sleep, to be awakened outside his
own front door by the cabby's rap, but something irritated him.
He had grown used to trusting his occasional feelings of irritation.
On several occasions, they had been the saving of his life.

The cab was in the Commercial Road, heading east, not west.
Towards Limehouse. Beauregard could smell the docks. He resolved
to see this out. It was an intriguing development. He had hopes that
the cabby did not merely intend to murder and rob him.

He eased aside the catch in the head of his cane and slid a few inches
of shining steel out of the body of the stick. The sword would draw
freely if he needed it. Still, it was only steel.

9

A Carpathian Quartet

B EFORE RETURNING TO the Hall, Geneviève slipped into the pub opposite Spitalfields Market. She was well known there, and in every other rowdy house within the so-called Terrible Quarter-Mile. As Angela Burdett-Coutts had shown, it was not sufficient to sit surrounded by improving tracts and soap in a comfortable church hall, waiting for the fallen to come and be improved. A reformer had to be familiar with the vilest sink-holes of drink and depravity. Of course, the Ten Bells on a week-night in 1888 was like one of the Aerated Bread Company's tea-rooms set beside a Marseilles brothel in 1786, a St Petersburg palace in the days of Great Catherine, or the château of Gilles de Rais in 1437. If her unfortunates could have seen their Miss Dee in earlier years, when the vicissitudes of a long life brought her to low circumstances, they might have been shocked. At times, she would have looked up to Polly Nichols or Lulu Schön as a scullery maid looks up to a duchess.

The atmosphere of the Ten Bells was steam-hot; thick with tobacco, beer and spilled blood. As she stepped through the doorway, her eye-teeth slid from their gumsheaths. She pinched shut her mouth, breathing through her nostrils. Animals trussed behind the bar squealed and fought their leather straps. Woodbridge, the barrel-bellied potman, took a sow by the ear and yanked her head around: the spigot-mouth of the tap driven into her neck was clotted. He gouged out the coagulated gore and turned the handle, disgorging a gushing dribble into a glass tankard. Pulling the pint, he joked in a rich Devon dialect with a new-born market porter. Geneviève knew too well the gamey taste of pig's blood. It could keep the red thirst at bay, but never slake it. She swallowed her spittle. These nights, she did not have the opportunity to form attachments. Her work occupied so much time that she fed only rarely and then not well. Although strong with the strength of centuries, she could not push herself beyond certain limits. She needed a willing partner and the tang of blood in her mouth.

She knew most of the regulars, at least by sight. Rose Mylett, a warm prostitute Geneviève thought was Lily's mother, was cutting her finger with a penknife and bleeding into tiny glasses of gin which she sold for a penny. Woodbridge's slightly hare-lipped son, Georgie, a soft-faced youth in an apron, darted between the tables, collecting the empties and wiping away glass-rings. Johnny Thain, a constable who had been putting in a deal of extra hours since he got a look at what Silver Knife left of Polly Nichols, was at a corner table with a couple of detectives, a tweed coat over his uniform. The casual trade fell into obvious groups: itinerant workmen hoping for a shift at the market, soldiers and sailors looking for a girl or two, new-borns thirsty for more than liquid pork.

By the bar, Cathy Eddowes was simpering up at a big man, stroking the tangle of his hair, pressing her cheek to a blocky shoulder. She turned from her potential client and waved at Geneviève. Her hand was wrapped in cloth, fingers sticking stiffly out of the bundle. If there were more time, she'd have been concerned. Mick Ripper, a knife-sharpener reputed to be the best three-fingered pickpocket in London, closed on Cathy's beau. He got near enough to see the man's face and backed off, plunging his hands deep into his pockets.

'Evenin', Miss Dee,' said Georgie. 'Rushed off 'em tonight, we are.'

'So I see,' she said. 'I hope we shall see you at the Hall for the new course of lectures.'

Georgie looked doubtful but smiled. 'If'n Dad lets me off of an evenin'. An' if'n it's safe to go out by night.'

'Mr Druitt will be taking a class in the mornings in the new year, Georgie,' she said. 'Mathematics. You're one of our promising young men. Never forget your potential.'

The lad had a gift for figures; he could keep in his head at once the details and totals of three separate rounds of varied drinks. That talent, nurtured in Druitt's classes, might lead him to a position. Georgie might exceed the high-water mark of his father, and become a landlord rather than a potman.

Cathy took a small table to herself and did not order a drink. She was stopping here just to put off her return to the Hall. She'd have to give a report on the inquest to Jack Seward, and did not just now want to think too much about the last moments of Lulu Schön's life. As an accordionist murdered 'The Little Yellow Bird', a few maudlin drunks tried, with only marginal success, to remember all the words in the right order.

> '*Goodbye, little yellow bird*,' Geneviève hummed to herself,
> '*I'd rather brave the cold, on a leafless tree,*
> *Than a prisoner be, in a cage of gold.*'

A group of noisy newcomers barged through the doors, bringing a gust of night's chill with them. The noise of the pub momentarily abated, and was then redoubled.

Cathy's prospective beau turned away from the bar, roughly pushing the new-born away. She rearranged a shawl around scab-dotted shoulders, and walked off with broken-heeled dignity. The man was Kostaki, the Carpathian who had been at the inquest. The three who had come in were his fellows, grim examples of the barbarian type Vlad Tepes had imported from his mountain homeland and set loose in London. She recognized Ezzelin von Klatka, a grey-faced Austrian with a close-cropped scalp and a moss-thick black beard. He had a reputation as an animal tamer.

Kostaki and von Klatka embraced, breastplates grinding as they grunted greetings in German, the language of preference for the mongrel *Mittel Europaër* who constituted the Carpathian Guard. Kostaki made introductions, and Geneviève gathered the others were Martin Cuda, a relative new-born who had not yet seen out his first century, and Count Vardalek, an effeminate and snake-like Hungarian who had the rank in the group.

Woodbridge offered the Guardsmen a pull of the pig, and von Klatka stared him into silence. The Prince Consort's Own did not favour animal blood. The group had the collective saunter Geneviève associated with Prussians or Mongols, the universal attitude of officers in an army of occupation. Carpathians marched around in a cloud of their own arrogance, condescending as much to the new-born as the warm.

Von Klatka picked a table in the centre of the room and stared down a couple of sailors until they chose to remove themselves to the bar, leaving their whores behind. The knight dismissed two of the girls, a new-born and a warm tart with no teeth, but let stay the last, a self-possessed gypsy who bore with pride the scars on her neck.

The Carpathians took chairs and leaned back in them, evidently at ease. They were illegitimate children of Bismarck and Geronimo: all wore highly polished boots and carried heavy swords, but their uniforms were augmented with oddments scavenged through the years. Von Klatka had around his neck a golden lanyard upon which were strung withered lumps of flesh she understood to be human ears. Cuda's helmet was adorned with a wolf's skin: head surmounting the crown and ringing the visor with teeth, eye-sockets sewn shut with red thread; thick-furred hide hanging down to the centre of his back, tail dangling almost to the floor.

Vardalek was the most extraordinary figure, his jacket a puffy affair of pleats and flounces, covered with kaleidoscope designs of spangle and sparkle. His face was powdered to conceal suppurating skin. Pantomime circles of rouge covered his cheeks and a scarlet cupid's-bow was painted over lips constantly distended by the two-inch fangs. His hair was stiff and golden, elaborately done up in bows and curls, twin braids dangling from the nape of his neck like rat's tails. This was the Count's party, and he was being escorted by the others on his tour of the fleshpots. Vardalek was one of those vampires who fussed about how close he was to the Prince Consort, claiming a dynastic connection as well as the obvious tie of bloodline. In a minute's chatter and on the flimsiest of pretexts, he mentioned the Royal Person no less than three times, always with mock-casual prefixes like 'as I was saying to Dracula . . .' or 'as our dear Prince mentioned the other night . . .'

The Hungarian surveyed the room and burst into high-pitched giggles, hiding his mouth behind a thin, green-nailed hand that protruded from an explosion of lace at his cuffs. He whispered to von Klatka, who grinned ferally and signalled to Woodbridge.

'That boy,' von Klatka said in approximate English, pointing a talon at Georgie. 'How much for that boy?'

The potman mumbled that Georgie was not for sale.

'Silly man, you understand not,' insisted von Klatka. 'How much?'

'He's my son,' Woodbridge protested.

'Then you should be honoured indeed,' shrilled Vardalek. 'That

your plumptious whelp should excite the interest of fine gentlemen.'

'This is the Count Vardalek,' explained Cuda, whom Geneviève
had marked as the snivelling toady of the group. 'He is very close
to the Prince Consort.'

Kostaki alone sat quietly, eyes forever watchful.

By now, everyone had ceased talking and was watching.
Geneviève was sorry that Thain and the detectives had left,
but these bullies were hardly likely to feel outranked by mere
policemen.

'Such a pretty lad,' said Vardalek, trying to wrestle the youth into
his lap. Georgie was stiff with terror, and the elder was strong in the
wrist. A long red tongue darted out of his cupid's-bow mouth and
scraped Georgie's cheek.

Von Klatka had out a wallet as fat as a meat pie. He threw a cloud
of banknotes in Woodbridge's face. The ruddy-cheeked potman
went grey, eyes heavy with tears.

'You don't want to be botherin' with the boy,' said Cathy
Eddowes, squeezing between von Klatka and Cuda, slipping her
arms around their waists. 'You gents wants yourselves a real
woman, a woman as 'as the *equipment*.'

Von Klatka pushed Cathy away, shoving her on to the flagstone
floor. Cuda clapped his comrade on the shoulder. Von Klatka glared
at Cuda and the junior vampire backed away, his face a stricken
white triangle.

Vardalek still cosseted Georgie, purring Magyar endearments
which the Devonshire boy could hardly be expected to appreciate.
Cathy crawled to the bar and pulled herself up. Pustules on her face
had burst and clear gum was oozing into one eye.

'Excellencies,' Woodbridge began, 'please . . .'

Cuda stood up and laid hands on the potman. The Carpathian
was a foot shorter than the beefy warm man, but the red fire in his
eyes made it plain he could rend Woodbridge apart and lap up the
leavings.

'What is your name, darling one?' Vardalek asked.

'G-G-Georgie . . .'

'Ah-hah, how is your rhyme? "Georgie-Porgie, pudding and
pie"?'

She had to intervene. Sighing, Geneviève stood up.

'Pudding and pie you shall be,' purred Vardalek, his teeth scraping Georgie's plump neck.

'Gentlemen,' she began, 'please allow these people to continue unmolested with their business.'

The Carpathians were shocked silent. Vardalek's mouth gaped open, and she saw that all but his fang-teeth were green ruins.

'Back off, new-born,' Cuda sneered. 'If you know what's best for you.'

'She's no new-born,' muttered Kostaki.

'Who is this impertinent little person?' asked Vardalek. He was licking tears from Georgie's cheeks. 'And why is she still un-dead seconds after insulting me?'

Cuda left Woodbridge and flew at her. Swift as an overcranked zoetrope, she leaned sharply to one side and jabbed an elbow into his ribs as he passed, shooting him across the room. His wolf-helmet came off as he fell, and someone semi-accidentally dumped a pot of slops into it.

'I am Geneviève Sandrine de l'Isle Dieudonné,' she declared, 'of the pure bloodline of Chandagnac.'

Kostaki, at least, was impressed. He sat up straight, as if to attention, bloody eyes wide. Von Klatka noted his comrade's changed attitude and, without moving from his spot, also withdrew from the confrontation. Geneviève had seen a similar attitude a few years ago in an Arizona poker parlour, when a dentist accused of cheating happened to mention to the three hefty cattlemen fumbling with their holster straps that his name was Holiday. Two of the drovers had then shown exactly the expressions worn now by von Klatka and Kostaki. She had not been in Tombstone for the funeral of the third.

Only Count Vardalek was left in the fight.

'Let the boy go,' she said, '*new-born!*'

Fury sparked in the Hungarian's eyes as he pushed Georgie away and stood up. He was taller than she, and almost as old. There was a terrible strength in his arms. His swelling nails turned to dagger-points, the lacquer on them shrivelling like butter on a griddle. He covered the distance between them in a snake's eye-blink. He was fast but he was of the diseased bloodline of Vlad Tepes. Geneviève's hands sprang out and she took a grip on his wrists, halting his finger-knives an inch from her eyes.

Vardalek snarled, foam blotting the powder on his chin, dripping on to the bulbous frills around his neck. His breath was proverbially foul, heavy with the grave. His stone-hard muscles writhed like pythons in her grasp, but she maintained her hold. Slowly, she forced his hands away from her face, raising his arms as if she were setting the hands of a huge clock at ten minutes to two.

In gutter Magyar, Vardalek alleged that Geneviève had regular carnal knowledge of sheep. That the milk from her breasts would poison the she-cats that were accustomed to suckle there. That seven generations of dung-beetles congregated in the hair of her worthless maidenhood. She kissed the air and squeezed, hearing his bones grind together, allowing the sharp points of her thumbs to cut into the thin veins of his wrists. Panic grew in his watery eyes.

Softly, so he alone could hear, she spoke in his own tongue, informing him that she was of the opinion that his ancestors knew only the love of mountain goats and asserting strongly the probability that his organ of generation was as flaccid as a newly lanced plague bubo. She asked what the Devil was employing for an arse while Vardalak was using that tender part of the diabolic anatomy for a face.

'Let go of him,' von Klatka said, without authority.

'Rip out 'is rotten 'eart,' said someone suffering from an attack of courage now that someone else was standing up to the Hungarian.

Vardalek's knees gave way as Geneviève pushed him back and down. He crumpled and sagged, but she still held him up. She made him kneel and he whimpered, looking up almost pitifully at her face. She felt dry air on her canine teeth and knew the muscles of her face were stretched into a beast-like mask.

Vardalek's head bent back, and his eyes rimmed with blood. His golden helmet of hair slipped, disclosing the angry red scalp his wig concealed. Geneviève let the elder go and he collapsed. Kostaki and von Klatka helped him up, Kostaki almost tenderly setting straight the Count's wig. Cuda was standing too, and had his sword drawn. Its blade caught the light, silver mixed in with the iron. Disgusted, Kostaki bade him put his weapon away.

Woodbridge had the door open, ready to usher them out. Georgie scurried off to wash Vardalek's spit off his face. Geneviève felt her face resuming its normal placid-pretty aspect, and stood by mildly. The background chatter resumed and the accordion player, proficient only within a narrow thematic range, started up 'She Was Only a Bird in a Gilded Cage'.

Von Klatka got Vardalek out into the street and Cuda followed them, filthy tail dragging. Kostaki remained, surveying the wreckage. He looked to where von Klatka had thrown his banknotes and gave a half-grin and a snort. The money had been whisked away as quickly as a sponge soaks up spilt beer. The gypsy girl was ostentatiously not where the notes had been. The Guardsman's white face cracked along lines when he changed expression, but the splits healed over instantly.

'Lady Elder,' said Kostaki, saluting her before turning to leave, 'my respects.'

10

Spiders in Their Webs

H E WAS IN Limehouse, somewhere near the Basin. In Beauregard's experience, the district's evil reputation was well deserved. More nameless corpses were washed up on the mudflats in a typical night than Silver Knife could account for in three months. With much creaking, rattling and shuffling, the hansom manoeuvred through an archway then came to a dead halt. The cabby must have had to bend double to scrape under the arch.

He gripped the hilt of his sword-cane. The doors were opened for him, and red eyes glittered in the dark.

'Sorry for the inconvenience, Beauregard,' purred a silky voice, male but not entirely masculine, 'but I trust you'll understand. It's a sticky wicket . . .'

He stepped down from the cab and found himself in a yard off one of the warren of streets near the docks. The fog here was wispy, hanging like undersea fronds of yellow gauze. There were people all about. The one who spoke was an Englishman, a vampire with a good coat and soft hat, his face in darkness. His posture, studied in its langour, suggested an athlete in repose; Beauregard would not care to go four rounds with him. The others were Chinese, pigtailed and bowed, hands in their sleeves. Most were warm but a massive fellow by the cab door was new-born, naked to the waist to show off his dragon tattoos and an un-dead indifference to autumn's chill.

As the Englishman stepped forward, moonlight caught his youthful face. He had pretty eyelashes like a woman's, and Beauregard recognized him.

'I saw you get six sixes from six balls in '85,' he said. 'In Madras. Gentlemen and Players.'

The sportsman shrugged modestly. 'You play what's chucked at you, I always say.'

He had heard the new-born's name in the Star Chamber,

tentatively linked with daring but somehow amusing jewel rob-
beries. He supposed the sportsman's involvement in this evident kidnapping confirmed that he was indeed the author of
those criminal feats. Beauregard believed even a gentleman should
have a profession, and always backed the Players against the
Gentlemen.

'This way,' said the amateur cracksman, indicating a wet stretch
of stone wall. The new-born Chinese pressed a brick and a section
of the wall tilted upwards, forming a hatch-like door. 'Duck down
or you'll bash your bean. Deuced small, these chinks.'

Beauregard followed the new-born, who could see in the dark
better than he, and was in turn followed by the rest of the party.
As the vampire-stooped, dragons on his shoulder-blades silently
roared and flapped. They proceeded down a sloping passageway,
and he realized they were below street level. The surfaces were
damp and glistening, the air cold and bad: these chambers must
be close to the river. As they passed a chute from which could
be dimly heard rippling water, Beauregard was reminded of the
nameless cadavers, supposing this place the source of quite a few
of their number. The passage widened and he deduced that this
part of the labyrinth dated back centuries. *Objets d'art*, mostly of
undoubted antiquity and oriental appearance, stood at significant
junctures. After many turns and descents and doors, his kidnappers
were sure he could never find his way unescorted to the surface. He
was pleased to be underestimated.

Something chattered behind a wall and he flinched. He could not
identify the animal din. The new-born turned to the noise and
yanked the head of a jade caterpillar. A door opened and Beauregard
was ushered into a dimly lit, richly furnished drawing room. There
were no windows, just chinoiserie screens. The centrepiece was a
large desk, behind which sat an ancient Chinaman. Long, hard
fingernails tapped like knife-points on his blotter. There were
others, in comfortable armchairs arranged in a half-circle about
the desk. The unseen chattering thing quieted.

One man turned his head, red cigar-end making a Devil's mask
of his face. He was a vampire, but the Chinaman was not.

'Mr Charles Beauregard,' began the Celestial, 'you are so kind to
join our wretched and unworthy selves.'

'You are so kind to invite me.'

The Chinaman clapped his hands, and nodded to a cold-faced servant, a Burmese.

'Take our visitor's hat, cloak and *cane*.'

Beauregard was relieved of his burdens. When the Burmese was close enough, Beauregard observed the singular earring, and the ritual tattooing about his neck.

'A dacoit?' he enquired.

'You are so very observant,' affirmed the Chinaman.

'I have some little experience of the world of secret societies.'

'Indeed you have, Mr Beauregard. Our paths have crossed three times: in Egypt, in the Kashmir, and in Shanghai. You caused me some little inconvenience.'

Beauregard realized to whom he was talking, and tried to smile. He assumed he was a dead man.

'My apologies, Doctor.'

The Chinaman leaned forward, face emerging into the light, fingernails clacking. He had the brow of a Shakespeare and a smile that put Beauregard in mind of a smug Satan.

'Think nothing of it.' He brushed away apologies. 'Those were trivial matters, of no import beyond the ordinary. I shall not prosecute any personal business in this instance.'

Beauregard tried not to show his relief. Whatever else he was, the criminal mandarin was known to be a man of his word. This was the person they called the 'Devil Doctor' or 'the Lord of Strange Deaths'. He was one of the Council of Seven, the ruling body of the Si-Fan, a *tong* whose influence extended to all the quarters of the Earth. Mycroft reckoned the Celestial among the three most dangerous men in the world.

'Although,' the Chinaman added, 'were this meeting to take place very far to the East, I fancy its agenda would not be so pleasant for you and, I confess, for myself. You understand me?'

Beauregard did, all too well. They met under a flag of truce, but it would be lowered as soon as the Diogenes Club again required him to work against the Si-Fan.

'Those affairs are not of interest to us at this moment.'

The amateur cracksman turned up the gaslight and faces became clear. The chattering thing burst into its screech and was quelled only by a mild glance from the Devil Doctor. In one corner was a large golden cage, built as if for a parrot with a six-foot wingspan, containing a long-tailed ape. It bared yellow teeth in bright pink gums that took up two-thirds of its face. The Chinaman was renowned for a strange taste in pets, as Beauregard had cause to recall whenever he used his snakeskin-handled boot scraper.

'Business,' snorted a military-looking vampire. 'Time is money, remember . . .'

'A thousand pardons, Colonel Moran. In the East, things are different. Here, we must bow to your Western ways, hurry and bustle, haste and industry.'

The cigar-smoker stood up, unbending a lanky figure from which hung a frock coat marked around the pockets with chalk. The Colonel deferred to him and sat back, eyes falling. The smoker's head oscillated from side to side like a lizard's, eye-teeth protruding over his lower lip.

'My associate is a businessman,' he explained between puffs, 'our cricketing friend is a dilettante, Griffin over there is a scientist, Captain Macheath – who, by the way, sends his apologies – is a soldier, Sikes is continuing his family business, I am a mathematician, but you, my dear doctor, are an artist.'

'The Professor flatters me.'

Beauregard had heard of the Professor too, Mycroft's brother, the consulting detective, had a craze of sorts for him. He might well be the worst Englishman unhanged.

'With two of the three most dangerous men in the world in one room,' he observed, 'I have to ask myself where the third might be.'

'I see our names and positions are not unknown to you, Mr Beauregard,' said the Chinaman. 'Dr Nikola is unavailable for our little gathering. I believe he may be found investigating some sunken ships off the coast of Tasmania. He no longer concerns us. He has his own interests.'

Beauregard looked at the others in the meeting, those still unaccounted for, Griffin, whom the Professor had mentioned, was an albino who seemed to fade into the background. Sikes was a pig-faced man, warm, short, burly and brutal. With a loud striped jacket and cheap oil on his hair, he looked out of place in such a distinguished gathering. Alone in the company, he was the image of a criminal.

'Professor, if you would care to explain to our honoured guest . . .'

'Thank you, Doctor,' replied the man sometimes called 'The Napoleon of Crime'. 'Mr Beauregard, as you are aware none of us – and I include you among our number – has what we might call common cause. We pursue our own furrows. If they happen to intersect . . . well, that is often unfortunate. Lately there have been the changes, but, whatever personal metamorphoses we might welcome, our calling has remained essentially the same. We are, as we always have been, a shadow community. To an extent, we have reached an accommodation. We pit our wits against each other, but when the sun comes up we draw a line. We let well enough alone. It grieves me greatly to have to say this, but that line seems not to be holding . . .'

'There was police raids all over the East End,' Sikes said, interrupting. 'Barmy Charlie Warren's sent in another bleedin' cavalry charge. Years of bloody work overturned in a single night. 'Ouses smashed. Gamblin', opium, girls: nuffin' sacred. Our business 'as been bought and paid for, an' the filthy peelers done us dirty when they went back on the deal.'

'I have no connection with the police,' Beauregard said.

'Do not think us naïve,' said the Professor. 'Like all agents of the Diogenes Club, you have no official position at all. But what is official and what is effective are separate things.'

'This persecution of our interests will continue,' the Doctor said, 'so long as the gentleman known as Silver Knife is at liberty.'

Beauregard nodded. 'I suppose so. There's always a chance the murderer will be turned up by the raids.'

'He's not one of us,' snorted Colonel Moran.

''E's a ravin' nutter, that's what 'e is. Listen, none of us is 'zactly squeamish – know what I mean? – but this bloke is takin' it too far. If an 'ore gets too rorty, you takes a razor to 'er fyce not 'er bleedin' froat.'

'There's never been any suggestion, so far as I know, that any of you are involved in the murders.'

'That is not the point, Mr Beauregard,' the Professor continued. 'Our shadow empire is like a spider-web. It extends throughout the world but it concentrates here, in this city. Thick and complicated and surprisingly delicate. If enough threads are severed, it will fall. And threads are being severed left and right. We have all suffered since Mary Ann Nichols was killed, and the inconvenience will redouble with each fresh atrocity. Every time this murderer strikes at the public, he stabs at us also.'

'My 'ores don't wanna go on the streets wiv 'im out there. It's 'urtin' me pockets. I'm seriously out of the uxter.'

'I'm sure the police will catch the man. There's a reward of fifty pounds for information.'

'And we have posted a reward of a thousand guineas but nothing has come of it.'

'Forget what they say about us on the screw stickin' together like Ikeys. If we tumbled old Silver Knife, 'e'd be narked to the esclop quicker'n an Irish dipper can flimp a drunkard's pogue.'

'I beg your pardon?'

'Mr Beauregard,' said the Doctor, 'what our associate is venturing to suggest is that we should like to add our humble efforts to those of your most estimable police. We pledge that any intimate knowledge which comes into our possession – as knowledge on so many matters so often does – shall be passed directly to you. In return we ask that the personal interest in this matter, which we know the Diogenes Club has required you take, be pursued with the utmost vigour.'

He tried not to show it, but was deeply shocked that the innermost workings of the ruling cabal were somehow known to the Lord of Strange Deaths. And yet the Chinaman evidently knew in detail of the briefing he had been given barely two days earlier. The briefing at which it had been assumed no more would be heard from the Si-Fan for some years.

'This bounder is letting the side down,' the amateur cracksman said, 'and it'd be best if he stripped his whites and slunk back to the bally pavilion.'

'We've put up a thousand guineas for information,' the Colonel said, 'and two thousand for his rotten head.'

'Unlike the police, we have no trouble with mendacious individuals coming forward offering false information in the hope of swindling us out of a reward. Such individuals do not long survive in our spider-web world. Do we have an understanding, Mr Beauregard?'

'Yes, Professor.'

The new-born smiled a thin smile. One murderer meant very little to these men, but a loose cannon of crime was an inconvenience they would not brook.

'And when the Whitechapel Murderer is caught?'

'Then it's business as usual,' said Moran.

The Doctor nodded sagely, and Sikes spat out: 'Too bloody right, pal.'

'Once our agreement is at an end,' the Chinaman announced, 'we shall revert to our former positions. And I would advise you to settle down with your Miss Churchward and leave the affairs of my countrymen to other hands. You have been unlucky with wives and you deserve your few years of contentment.'

Beauregard contained his anger. The threat to Penelope was beyond the limit.

'For myself,' said the Professor, eyes gleaming, 'I hope to disengage myself, and hand over the everyday running of my organization to Colonel Moran. I now have the opportunity to live for centuries, which will give me the time I need to refine my model of the universe. I intend to undertake a voyage into pure mathematics, a voyage which will take me beyond the dull geometries of space.'

The Doctor smiled, crinkling his eyes and lifting his thin moustache. Only he seemed to appreciate the Professor's grandiose schemes. Everyone else in the ring looked as if they had eaten bad eggs while the Professor's eyes glowed with the thought of an infinity of multiplying theorems, expanding to fill all space.

'Conceive of it,' the Professor said, 'one theorem encompassing *everything*.'

'A cab will take you to Cheyne Walk,' the Celestial explained. 'This meeting is at an end. Serve our purpose, and you will be rewarded. Fail us, and the consequences will be . . . not so pleasant.'

With a wave, Beauregard was dismissed.

'Our regards to your Miss Churchward,' said Moran, leering nastily, Beauregard fancied he detected a moue of distaste on the Chinaman's proverbially inscrutable face.

As the sportsman took him back up through the passages, Beauregard wondered how many Devils he would have to ally himself with to discharge his duty. He resisted the urge to demonstrate bravado by forging ahead and leading his guide to the entrance. He could have pulled off the stunt, but it might be as well to remain in the underestimation of the ring.

When they reached the surface, it was near dawn. The first streaks of blue-grey crept upwards from the East, and the seagulls drawn inland by the Thames squawked for breakfast.

The cab still stood in the yard, the driver perched on the box, swaddled in black blankets. Beauregard's hat, cloak and cane were waiting for him inside.

'Toodle-oo,' said the cricketer, red eyes shining. 'See you at Lord's.'

11

Matters of No Importance

'WHY SO QUIET, Penny?'
'What?' she blurted, shocked out of her angry reverie. The
noise of the reception was momentarily overwhelming, seeming to
resolve itself to a stage buzz of background chatter.

With sham outrage, Art rebuked her. 'Penelope, I believe you
were dreaming, I have been expending my meagre wit upon you
for minutes, yet you've not taken in a word. When I try to be
amusing you murmur "oh, how true" with a palpable sigh, and
when I endeavour to add a sombre note, to secure your sympathies,
you politely laugh behind your fan.'

The outing was wasted. It was to have been her first public
appearance with Charles, her first showing as an engaged woman.
She had planned for weeks, selecting exactly the right dress, the
correct corsage, the proper event, the suitable company. Thanks
to Charles's mysterious masters, it was a ruin. She had been out of
sorts all evening, trying not to revert to her old habit of wrinkling
her forehead. Her governess, Madame de la Rougierre, had often
warned her that if the wind changed her face would set that way;
now, if she examined herself in the glass for even the trace of a line,
she knew the old biddy had not been wrong.

'You are right, Art,' she admitted, quelling the interior fury that
always came to her when things were not *just so* 'I was gone.'

'That hardly says much for my powers of vampire fascination.'

When he tried to look comically offended, the tips of his teeth
protruded like grains of rice stuck to his lower lip.

Across the hotel restaurant, Florence was engaged in conversation
with a tiddly gentleman whom Penelope understood to be the critic
from the *Telegraph*. Florence was supposed to be the leader of
this tiny expedition into hostile territory – their sympathies were
naturally with the Lyceum, and this was the Criterion – but she

had abandoned her supporters to each other's company. That was typical of Florence. She was flighty, and, even at the advanced age of thirty, a flirt. No wonder her husband disappeared. As Charles had disappeared this evening.

'You were thinking of Charles?'

She nodded, wondering if there were anything in the stories about vampire mind-reading abilities. Her thoughts, she admitted, must just now be written in large print. She would concentrate on keeping her forehead smooth or she would end up like poor silly Kate, only twenty-two and her face already pulled out of shape by laughing and crying.

'Even when I have you all to myself for an evening, Charles is between us. Curse the fellow.'

Charles, due to accompany the first-night party, had sent his man with a message, excusing himself and entrusting Penelope to Florence's care for the evening. He was off on some government business she could not be expected to bother with. It was most vexing. After the wedding, unless she underestimated her own powers of persuasion, the situation in the Beauregard household would be much changed.

Her stays were so tight she could hardly breathe, and her *décolletage* so low the whole stretch of skin between her chin and bosom was insensate with the cold. And there was nothing to do with her fan but wave it about, for she could not risk setting it down on a chair and having some tipsy clod sit on it.

The original scheme had been for Art to chaperone Florence but he was as abandoned by her as Penelope had been by her fiancé and evidently felt obliged to loiter about like an ardent swain. They had been twice accosted by acquaintances who congratulated her, then indicated Art with an embarrassing 'and is this the lucky gentleman?' Lord Godalming was taking it with remarkable good humour.

'I did not mean to speak ill of Charles, Penny. I apologize.'

Since the announcement, Art had been most solicitous. He had once been engaged himself, to a girl Penelope remembered quite well, but something horrid had come of it. Art was easy to understand, especially set beside Charles. Her fiancé always paused before addressing her by name. He had never called her Pamela but they were both waiting in dread for that awful, inevitable moment. All through life, she had been plodding in her cousin's brilliant wake, chilling inside whenever anyone silently compared her with Pam, knowing she must eternally be judged the lesser of the Misses Churchward. But she was alive and Pam was not. She was older now than Pamela had been when she was taken from them.

'You can be sure that any matters which detain Charles are of the utmost importance. His name may never appear in the lists, but he is well known in Whitehall, if only to the best of the best, and rated highly.'

'Surely, Art, you are important too?'

Art shrugged, his curls shaking. 'I'm simply a messenger boy with a title and good manners.'

'But the *Prime Minister* . . .'

'I'm Ruthven's pet this month, but that means little.'

Florence returned, bearing an official verdict on the piece. It had been something called *Clarimonde's Coming-Out* by the famous author of *The Silver King* and *Saints and Sinners*, Henry A. Jones.

'Mr Sala says "there is a rift in the clouds, a break of blue in the dramatic heavens, and it seems as if we are fairly at the end of the unlovely".'

The play had been a specimen of the 'rattling farce' for which the Criterion was known. The new-born leading lady had a past and her supposed father but actual husband, a cynical Queen's Counsel, was given to addressing sarcasms directly to the dress circle, affording the actor-manager Charles Wyndham opportunities to demonstrate his aptitude for aphorism. Frequent changes of costume and backdrop took the characters from London to the country to Italy to a haunted castle and back again. By the final curtain, lovers were reconciled, cads were ruined, fortunes inherited justly and secrets exposed without harm. Barely an hour after the last act, Penelope could accurately describe to the smallest detail each of the heroine's gowns but could not recall the name of the actress who took her part.

'Penny, darling,' came a tiny, grating voice. 'Florence, and Lord Godalming. Hail and well met.'

It was Kate Reed, in a drab little dress, trailing a jowly new-born Penelope knew to be her Uncle Diarmid. A senior staffer at the Central News Agency, he was sponsor to the poor girl's so-called career in cheap journalism. He had a reputation as one of the grubbiest of the Grub Street grubs. Everyone except Penelope found him amusing, and so he was mostly tolerated.

Art wasted his time kissing Kate's knuckly hand and she turned
red as a beetroot. Diarmid Reed greeted Florence with a beery
burp and enquired after her health, never a sound tactic in
the case of Mrs Stoker, who was quite capable of describing
extensive infirmities. Mercifully, she took another tack and asked
why Mr Reed had lately not been attending the after-darks.

'We quite miss you in Cheyne Walk, Mr Reed. You always have
such stories of the highs and lows of life.'

'I regret that I've been trawling the lows of late, Mrs Stoker.
These Silver Knife murders in Whitechapel.'

'Dreadful business,' spluttered Art.

'Indeed. But deuced good for the circulation. The *Star* and the
Gazette and all the other dogs are in it to the death. The Agency
can't keep them fed. They'll take almost anything.'

Penelope did not care for talk of murder and vileness. She did
not take the newspapers, and indeed read nothing but improving books.

'Miss Churchward,' Mr Reed addressed himself to her, 'I understand congratulations are the order of the day.'

She smiled at him in such a way as not to line her face.

'Where's Charles?' asked Kate, blundering as usual. Some girls
should be beaten regularly, Penelope thought, like carpets.

'Charles has let us down,' Art said. 'Most unwisely, in my
opinion.'

Penelope burned inside, but hoped it did not show on her face.

'Charles Beauregard, eh?' said Mr Reed. 'Good man in a pinch,
I understand. You know, I could swear I saw the fellow in
Whitechapel only the other night. With some of the detectives
on the Silver Knife case.'

'That is highly unlikely,' Penelope said. She had never been to
Whitechapel, a district where people were often murdered. 'I cannot
imagine what would take Charles to such a quarter.'

'I don't know,' said Art. 'The Diogenes Club has queer interests,
in all manner of queer quarters.'

Penelope wished Art had not mentioned that institution. Mr
Reed's ears pricked up and he was about to quiz Art further when
they were all saved from embarrassment by another arrival.

'Look,' squealed Florence with delight, 'at who has come again
to plague us with his incorrigibility. It's Oscar.'

A large new-born with plenty of wavy hair and a well-fed look was swanning over to them, green carnation in his lapel, hands in his pockets to bulge out the front of his striped trousers.

'Evening, Wilde,' said Art.

The poet sneered a curt 'Godalming' of acknowledgement at Art, and then extravagantly paid court to Florence, pouring so much charm over her that a quantity of it naturally splashed over on to Penelope and even Kate. Mr Oscar Wilde had apparently once proposed to Florence, when she was Miss Balcombe of Dublin, but been beaten out by the now-never-mentioned Bram. Penelope found it easy to believe Wilde might have made proposals to a number of persons, simply so the rebuffs would give him something else about which to be wittily unconventional.

Florence asked him his opinion of *Clarimonde's Coming-Out*, whereupon Wilde remarked that he was thankful for its existence, for it might spur a canny critic, such as he obviously adjudged himself, to erect a true work of genius on its ruins.

'Why, Mr Wilde,' Kate said, 'it sounds as if you place the critic higher than the creator.'

'Indeed. Criticism is itself an art. And just as artistic creation implies the working of the critical faculty, and, indeed, without it cannot be said to exist at all, so criticism is really creative in the highest sense of the word. Criticism is, in fact, both creative and independent.'

'Independent?' Kate queried, surely aware she invited a lecture.

'Yes, independent. Just as out of the sordid and sentimental *amours* of the silly wife of a small country doctor in the squalid village of Ynville-l'Abbaye, near Rouen, Flaubert was able to create a classic, and make a masterpiece of style, so, from subjects of little or no importance, such as the pictures in this year's Royal Academy, or in any year's Royal Academy for that matter, Mr Lewis Morris's poems, or the plays of Mr Henry Arthur Jones, the true critic can, if it be his pleasure so to direct or waste his faculty of contemplation, produce work that will be flawless in beauty and instinct. Dullness is always an irresistible temptation for brilliancy, and stupidity is the permanent *Bestia Trionfans* that calls wisdom from its cave.'

'But what did you think of the play, Wilde?' asked Mr Reed.

Wilde waved his hand and made a face, the combination of gesture and expression communicating considerably more than his little

speech, which even Penelope found off the point, albeit elegantly
so. Relevance, Wilde once explained, was a careless habit that should
not be over-indulged.

'My Lord Ruthven sends his regards,' Art said.

The poet was almost flattered to be so noticed. As he began to
say something marvellously amusing but unnecessary, Art leaned
close to him and, in a voice so small only Penelope and Wilde could
make it out, said, 'and he would wish that you took great caution
in visiting a certain house in Cleveland Street.'

Wilde looked at Art with eyes suddenly shrewd and refused to
be drawn further. He escorted Florence off, to talk with Frank
Harris of the *Fortnightly Review*. Since turning, Mr Harris sported
goat-horns which Penelope found daunting. Kate tripped off in the
poet's wake, hoping to suck up enough to the editor to place with
him an article on women's suffrage or some such silliness. Even a
devoted libertine of Mr Harris's reputation would presumably think
Kate too undernourished a fish to count as worth netting, and cast
her back into the seas.

'What on earth did you say to so upset Wilde?' Mr Reed asked,
scenting a story. His nostrils actually did twitch whenever he
thought he was on the track of some scrap that might possibly
qualify as news.

'Just some craze of Ruthven's,' Art explained.

The news-gatherer looked at Art, his eyes like gimlets. Many
vampires had piercing gazes. At social gatherings, they could often
be found trying to outstare each other like a pair of horn-locked
moose. Mr Reed lost the contest and wandered off himself, searching
out his wayward niece.

'Sharp girl, that,' Art said, nodding after Kate.

'Pfui,' said Penelope, shaking her head. 'Careers are for girls who
can't get themselves husbands.'

'Meow.'

'Sometimes I think everything is going completely above me,'
she complained.

'Nothing to worry your pretty little head about,' he said, turning
back to her.

Art tickled her under the chin, and tipped her head up so
he could look into her eyes. She thought he might plan to
kiss her – here, in public, with all of theatre London about

– but he did not. He laughed and let go of her chin after a moment.

'Charles had better realize soon it is not safe to leave you lying around. Or else someone will steal you away and make of you a maiden tribute of modern Babylon.'

She giggled as she had been taught to do when anyone said anything she did not entirely understand. In the darks of Lord Godalming's eyes, something glinted. Penelope felt a tiny warmth growing in her breast, and wondered where such might lead.

12

Dawn of the Dead

DAWN SHOT THE fog full of blood. As the sun rose, new-borns scurried to coffins and corners. Geneviève trailed alone back to Toynbee Hall, never thinking to be afraid of the shrinking shadows. Like Vlad Tepes, she was old enough not to shrivel in the sun as did the more sensitive new-borns, but the vigour that had come with the blood of the warm girl ebbed as the light filtered through. She passed a warm policeman on the Commercial Road, and nodded a greeting to him. He turned away and kept on his beat. The feeling she'd had earlier, that someone was just out of sight dogging her footsteps, returned; she supposed it more or less a permanent delusion in the district.

In the last fortnight, she'd spent more time on Silver Knife than her work. Druitt and Morrison undertook double shifts, juggling the limited number of places at the Hall to deal first with the most needy. Primarily an educational institute, the hall was coming to resemble a field hospital. Seconded to a Vigilance Committee, she had been to so many noisy meetings that even now words persisted in her ears as music rings in the ears of those who sit too near the orchestra.

She stopped walking and stood, listening. Again, she felt followed. Her vampire sensitivities tingled and she had an impression of something in yellow silk, progressing with strange silent hops, long arms out like a somnambulist. She looked into the fog, but nothing emerged. Perhaps she'd absorbed one of the warm girl's memories or fancies and would be stuck with it until her blood was out of her system. That had happened before.

George Bernard Shaw and Beatrice Potter were making speeches all over the city, using the murders to call attention to conditions in the East End. Neither socialist was *nosferatu*; and Shaw at least had been linked, Geneviève understood, with a Republican faction.

In the *Pall Mall Gazette*, W. T. Stead was running a Silver Knife campaign, comparable to his earlier crusades against white slavery and child vampirism. In the absence of an actual culprit, the conclusion seemed to be that society at large was to blame. Toynbee Hall was momentarily the recipient of enough charitable donations to make Druitt propose that it would be a good idea to sponsor the murderer's activities as a means of raising funds. The suggestion did not amuse the serious-minded Jack Seward.

A poster on the wall of an ostler's yard promised the latest reward for information leading to the capture of Silver Knife. Rival groups of warm and new-born vigilantes roamed with billy-clubs and razors, scrapping with each other and setting upon dubiously innocent passers-by. The street girls were now complaining less about the danger of the murderer and more about the lack of custom noticeable since the vigilantes started harassing anyone who came to Whitechapel looking for a woman. The whores of Soho and Covent Garden were doing boom business. And boom gloating.

She heard a moan from an alleyway. Her canines shot out like flick-knives, startling her. She stepped into the shadowed recess, and saw a man pressing a red-headed woman against a wall. Geneviève was half-way to them, prepared to apprehend the murderer, when she saw that the man was a soldier in a long coat. His trousers around his ankles, he thrust hard against the woman with his pelvis, not a knife. He moved with desperate speed but wasn't getting anywhere. The woman, skirts bunched around her waist like a lifebelt, was braced in a corner, holding him up by his head, pressing his face to her feathered shoulder.

The whore was a good-looking new-born they called 'Carroty Nell'. During her turning, she'd called at the Hall, and Geneviève had helped her through, holding her down as she ran cold then hot and new teeth budded in her jaws. Her real name, Geneviève thought, was Frances Coles or Coleman. Her hair had grown much thicker, an arrow-shaped peak almost to the bridge of her nose. Stiff red vixen-bristles grew on her bare arms and the backs of her hands.

Carroty Nell licked shallow scratches on her customer's neck. She saw Geneviève but showed no sign of recognition, baring a row of fence-post fangs at the interloper, red-rimmed eyes weeping blood. Quietly, Geneviève backed out of the alley. The new-born was coaxing the soldier with abuse, trying to get him to spend his fourpence. 'Come on, you bastard,' she said, 'finish it, finish it . . .' Her client's hand came up and grabbed her hair, and he thrust harder and harder, gasping.

Back on the street, Geneviève stood still as her eye-teeth receded. She had been too ready to fight. The murderer was making her as jumpy as the vigilantes.

Geneviève had heard Silver Knife was a leather-aproned shoe-maker, a Polish Jew carrying out ritual killings, a Malay sailor, a degenerate from the West End, a Portuguese cattleman, the ghost of Van Helsing or Charley Peace. He was a doctor, a black magician, a midwife, a priest. With each rumour, more innocents were thrown to the mob. Sergeant Thick locked up a warm bootmaker named Pizer for his own protection when someone took it into his head to write 'Silver Nyfe' on his shopfront. After Jago, the Christian Crusader, argued that the killer could walk unhindered about the area killing at will because he was a policeman, a vampire constable called Jonas Mizen was dragged into a yard off Coke Street and impaled on a length of kindling. Jago was in jail himself but Lestrade said they'd have to let him out soon, since he had a convenient alibi for the time of Mizen's death. The Reverend John Jago, it seemed, had alibis to spare.

She passed the doorway where Lily slept. The new-born child was curled up for the day with some scraps of blanket given her at the Hall. She had wound herself up against the sun, making an Egyptian mummy of her tiny form. The girl's half-changed arm was worse, the useless wing sprouting from hip to armpit. Lily had a cat nestled against her face, its neck in her mouth. The animal was still barely alive.

Abberline and Lestrade had questioned dozens but made no useful arrests. There were always rival protesters outside the police stations. Mediums like Lees and Carnacki had been called for. A number of consulting detectives – Martin Hewitt, Max Carados, August Van Dusen – had prowled Whitechapel, hoping to turn up something. Even the venerable Hawkshaw had emerged from retirement. But with their acknowledged master in Devil's Dyke, the enthusiasm of the detective community ebbed considerably, and no solutions were forthcoming. A lunatic named Cotford was apprehended creeping about in minstrel's blackface, claiming to be

a detective 'in disguise'. He had been removed to Colney Hatch
for examination. Insanity, Jack Seward said, could be an epidemic
disease.

Geneviève found a shilling in her purse and slipped it into Lily's
blanket. The new-born murmured in her drowsiness but didn't
wake. As a hansom rumbled past, she glimpsed the profile of a
dozing man inside, his hat swaying with the movements of the
cab. Someone going home after a night in the fleshpots, she
guessed. Then she recognized the passenger. It was Beauregard,
the man she'd noticed at Lulu Schön's inquest, the man from the
Diogenes Club. According to Lestrade, his presence evidenced an
interest from very high places. The Queen, young again, had shown
public concern about 'these ghastly murders', but nothing had been
heard from Prince Dracula, to whom Geneviève assumed the lives
of a few streetwalkers, vampire or not, were of as much importance
as those of beetles.

The cab trundled into the fog. Again she felt there was something
out there, standing in the thick of it, watching her, waiting for a
chance to move. The feeling passed.

Gradually, as she came to realize how powerless she was to affect
the behaviour of this unknown maniac, she also sensed just how
important the case had become. Everyone began their arguments by
declaring that it was about more than just three butchered harlots. It
was about Disraeli's 'two nations'; it was about the regrettable spread
of vampirism among the lower classes; it was about the decline of
public order; it was about the fragile equilibrium of the transformed
kingdom. The murders were mere sparks, but Great Britain was a
tinderbox.

She was spending a lot of time with whores – she'd been an
outcast long enough to feel a certain kinship with them – and
shared their fears. Tonight, nearing dawn, she'd found a girl
in Mrs Warren's house off Raven Row and bled her, out of
need not pleasure. Warm Annie held her tenderly and let her
suckle from the flesh of her throat as if she were a wet-nurse.
Afterwards, Geneviève gave her a half-crown. It was too much,
but she had to make the gesture. The only decoration in Warm
Annie's room was a cheap print of Vlad Tepes riding into battle.
The only items of furniture were a wash-stand and a large bed, its
sheets cleaned so many times they were as thin as paper, the mattress

dyed with irregular brown patches. Brothels no longer had ornate mirrors.

After so many years, Geneviève should have become used to her predator's life, but the Prince Consort had turned everything topsy-turvy and she was ashamed again, not of what she must do to prolong her existence but of the things vampirekind, those of the bloodline of Vlad Tepes, did around her. Warm Annie had been bitten several times. Eventually she would turn. Nobody's get, she would have to find her own way, and doubtless end up as raddled as Cathy Eddowes, as truly dead as Polly Nichols, as beast-like as Carroty Nell. Her head was fuzzy from the gin her warm girl had drunk. That was why she had hallucinations. The whole city seemed sick.

13

Strange Fits of Passion

26 SEPTEMBER
In the Hall, the mornings are quiet. Whitechapel slumbers between
sunrise and what we used to call lunch-time. The new-borns scurry
for their earth-boxes. The warm of the area have never been day
people. I leave instructions with Morrison that I am not to be
disturbed and seclude myself in this office with my supposed work.
Records, I tell him. I am not lying. Keeping records is a habit. It used
to be so with us all. Jonathan Harker, Mina Harker, Van Helsing.
Even Lucy, with her beautiful hand and horrid spelling, wrote long
letters. The Professor was strict about the documents. History is
written by the victors; Van Helsing, through his friend Stoker,
always intended to publish. Like his foe, he was an empire-builder;
an account of his successful treatment of a scientifically corroborated
nineteenth-century case of vampirism would have added lustre to
his reputation. As it is, the Prince Consort took care to blot out
our history: my diary was destroyed in the fire at Purfleet, and Van
Helsing is remembered as second Judas.

He was not then Prince Consort, just Count Dracula. He deigned
to notice our little family; to strike at us again and again until we were
smashed and scattered. I have rough notes, cuttings and mementos,
kept here under lock and key. I believe it necessary, for my eventual
justification, to recreate the original records. This is the task I have
set myself for the quiet hours.

Who can say where it began? Dracula's death? His resurrection?
The laying of his colossal schemes against Great Britain? Harker's
dreadful experiences in Castle Dracula? The wreck of the *Demeter*,
washed ashore at Whitby with a dead man lashed to the helm?
Or, perhaps, the Count's first sight of Lucy? Miss Lucy Westenra.
Westenra. A singular name: it means Light of the West. Yes, Lucy.
For me, that was where it began. With Lucy Westenra. Lucy. On

24th May 1885. I can scarcely believe that the Jack Seward of that morning, twenty-nine and newly appointed to the supervision of Purfleet Asylum, ever really existed. The times before are a golden haze, half-remembered scraps from boys' adventures and medical directories. I had, I am assured, a most brilliant career: I studied and observed; I travelled; I had eminent friends. Then, things changed utterly.

I do not believe I truly loved Lucy until *after* her rebuff. I had reached the point in life when a man must consider the making of a match; she was simply the most suitable of my acquaintances. We were introduced by Art. Arthur Holmwood then, not yet Lord Godalming. At first, I thought her frivolous. Silly, even. After days among the screaming insane, sheer silliness was appealing. The convolutions of complex minds – I still believe it a gross error to assert that the mad are *simple*-minded – led me to consider as ideal the prospect of a girl as open and obvious as Lucy. On that day, I laid out my proposal. I had a lancet in my pocket for some reason and I fancy I fiddled with it throughout the preliminaries. Before my prepared speech – about how dear she was to me, though I knew her so little – was delivered, I knew I'd no hopes. She commenced a giggle, then covered her embarrassed amusement with forced tears. I extracted from her the confession that her heart was not her own. I knew at once I'd been cut out by Art. She didn't name him, but there was no doubt. Later, with Quincey Morris – incredibly, another of the guileless Lucy's conquests – I endured an evening of Art's prattling of future happiness. The Texan was all open-hearted decency, clapping Art's back for being the better man and all that. Fool smile plastered on my face, I downed tumbler after tumbler of Quincey's whisky, remaining sober as the good fellows joked towards inebriation. Lucy, meanwhile, packed herself off to Whitby, intent on subjecting Mina to an extended gloat. She had netted the future Lord Godalming, while the best her school-teaching friend could manage was a barely qualified Exeter solicitor.

I threw myself into work, the standard cure for a broken heart. I hoped poor Renfield would make my name. To be the discoverer of zoophagous mania would mark me as a coming man. Of course, in considering the merits of prospective fiancés ladies of breeding still unaccountably prefer an inherited title and unearned wealth to the isolation of unheard-of strains of mental disorder. That summer I followed the queer logic of Renfield's mania as he collected tiny lives. At first he aped the nursery rhyme: feeding flies to spiders, spiders to birds, birds to a cat. He intended to consume the accumulated life energy by eating the cat. When that proved impractical, he ate anything alive that happened by. He nearly choked to death disgorging feathers. My monograph was taking shape when I observed another obsession intermingled with zoophagia, a fixation upon the dilapidated estate neighbouring the grounds of the asylum. As the tourists now queuing for penny tours know, Carfax was the Count's first home in England. Several times, Renfield made an escape and rushed for the Abbey, babbling of the Coming of His Master and Salvation and the Distribution of Good Things. I assumed, with some disappointment, that he was developing an entirely commonplace religious mania, reinvesting the long-abandoned house with its sacred purpose. I was, for the first fatal time in the case, completely in error. The Count had established dominance over the madman, who was to be his catspaw. If it were not for Renfield, for the cursed clamp of his teeth about my hand, things might have been different. As Franklin has it, 'for the want of a nail . . .'

In Whitby, Lucy was taken sick. We did not know it, but Art had in his turn been cut out. In this world of titles, a Wallachian prince trumps an English lord. The Count, having come ashore from the *Demeter*, fixed his sights on Lucy and began to make a vampire of her. No doubt the fickle girl welcomed his advances. In the course of an examination, when she was brought to London and Art called me in, I ascertained that her hymen had been ruptured. I deemed Art a swine of the first water to so pre-empt his marriage vows. Having kicked about the world with the future Lord Godalming, I'd no illusions as to his respect for the sanctity of maidenhood. Now I can find it in myself to feel sorry for the Art of those days, worried sick over his worthless girl, made as big a fool as I by the Light of the West, who would submit by night to the Beast of the East.

It is possible that Lucy truly believed that she loved Art. However, it must have been a very surface love even before the arrival of the Count. Among the letters Van Helsing compiled was Lucy's account, gushed to Mina – who obligingly corrected the spelling in green ink – of the day upon which she supposedly received three proposals. The third was from Quincey, whom I suspect of sloshing a chew of tobacco from side to side in his mouth in the Westenra drawing room, embarrassed by the absence of a spittoon, giving the impression of a longhorn idiot. Lucy expends much wordage crowing to Mina and, compressing the events of a week into a single day, considerably exaggerates the eventfulness of her work-free life. In fact, she is so intent upon celebrating the feat of the three proposals that she barely has space to mention, in a hurried postscript, which of her suitors she bothered to accept.

Lucy's symptoms, now so familiar, were a complete puzzlement. The pernicious anaemia and the physical changes attendant upon her turning suggested a dozen different diseases. Her throat wounds were put down to everything from a brooch-pin to a bee-sting. I sent for my old teacher, Van Helsing of Amsterdam; he hastened over to England and made a diagnosis which he proceeded to withhold. In that, he did much harm, although I concede that, a scant three years ago, we'd hardly have credited nonsense about vampires. His grave error, I now recognize, was an out moded, almost alchemical, faith in folklore; scattering about him garlic flowers, communion wafers, crucifixes and holy water. If I had known then that vampirism was primarily a physical rather than a spiritual condition, Lucy might be un-dead still. The Count himself shared, and probably still does share, many of the Professor's misconceptions.

Despite Van Helsing, despite blood transfusions, despite religious impedimenta, Lucy died. Everyone was dying. Art's reprobate father finally succumbed, making his son a lord, leaving unsquandered a surprising portion of his fortune. Lucy's mother, shocked by a wolf in her bedroom, was carried off violet-faced by a coronary. She also, having beaten the gun in altering her will, left her property to Art; which might have proved severely embarrasing if, offended by Lucy's intercourse with the Count, he had called off the engagement.

Quite clearly, Lucy was – for a short time, at least – truly dead. Van Helsing and I both confirmed the condition. Now, much as it pains me, more I have to allow it possible her death, which seems to have addled her mind more than her turning, was due not to the Count but to Van Helsing's transfusions. The procedure is notoriously dangerous. *The Lancet* ran a series of articles last year about blood, a subject now of overpowering interest to the medical profession. A young specialist suggests there might be sub-categories of blood, conventional transfusion being possible only between those with similar types. It is possible that my own blood was the poison that killed her. Of course, there are among us many who can transfuse blood into themselves without thought of sub-category.

For whatever reason – and the repeated attentions of the Count can hardly have contributed to her well-being – Lucy died, and was interred in the Westenra vault in Kingstead Cemetery, near Hampstead Heath. There, she awoke in her coffin and rose as a new-born, emerging by night like a Drury Lane ghost, to seek out children to slake her newfound appetites. I understand from Geneviève that it is possible to pass from warmth to the un-dead state without an intervening period of true death. In her case, apparently, the turning was gradual. Vlad Tepes was killed, buried and – they say – *beheaded*, but transformed after death. Those of his bloodline tend to die before the change, although this is not true in every case. Art, for instance, has never died that I know of. It is possible that the fact of death is vital in shaping the *type* of vampire one becomes. Everyone changes, but some change more than others. The Lucy who came back was much different from the Lucy who went away.

A week after Lucy's death, we visited the tomb by day and examined her. She seemed asleep; I confess to thinking her more beautiful than ever. The triviality was gone; replaced by a certain cruelty of aspect, the effect was disturbingly sensual. Later, we spied, on the day she was to have been married, the new-born returning to her vault. She made advances to Art and may have bitten him slightly. I recall the red of her lips and the white of her teeth, and the strength of her slim body in its frail shroud. I remember the vampire Lucy, rather than the warm girl. She was the first such creature I had seen. Traits that are now commonplace – the juxtaposition of apparent langour with bursts of snake-speed, the sudden elongation of teeth and nails, the characteristic hiss of the red thirst – were, taken all at once, overwhelming. Sometimes I see Lucy in Geneviève, with her quick smile and sharp eye-teeth.

On the morning of the 29th, we trapped and destroyed her. We found her in the deathlike trance that comes upon new-borns in the hours of daylight, her mouth and chin still stained. Art did the deed, driving home the stake. I surgically removed her head.

Van Helsing filled the mouth with garlic. After sawing off the top of the stake, we soldered shut her lead inner-coffin and screwed fast the wooden lid. The Prince Consort had her remains exhumed and reburied in Westminster Abbey. A plaque above her grave damns Van Helsing for a murderer and, presumably thanks to Art, naming only Quincey and Harker, both safely dead, as accomplices. Van Helsing told us, 'Now, my friends, one step of our work is done, the one most harrowing to ourselves. But there remains a greater task: to find out the author of all this, our sorrow, and to stamp him out.'

14

Penny Stamps

H E AWOKE EARLY in the afternoon, and went down to breakfast – kedgeree and coffee – and the day's post, which Bairstow, his man, had laid-out on the parlour table. The only item of interest was an unsigned two-word telegram, 'IGNORE PIZER'. He assumed this to mean the Limehouse Ring had good cause to believe the recently arrested shoemaker unconnected with Silver Knife. Copied police reports and personal depositions had also been delivered, by hand from the Diogenes Club. Beauregard glanced through it all, and found nothing much new.

The *Gazette* reported 'the murder and mutilation of a vampire woman near Gateshead yesterday', predicting this fresh atrocity would 'revive in the provinces the horror which was beginning to die out in London'. The rest was puff – reading between the lines, Beauregard suspected the new-born had been destroyed by her husband, who resisted her attempt to make vampires of their children – although the paper made the sound point that rather than believing 'the murderous maniac of Whitechapel' to have made his way to the North, it was more likely that 'the Bitley murder is not a repetition, but a reflex, of the Whitechapel ones. It is one of the inevitable results of publicity to spread an epidemic. Just as the news of one suicide often leads to another, so the publication of the details of one murder often leads to their repetition in another murder. Reading of means to do ill makes ill deeds done.' One effect of the Silver Knife scare was a definitive refutation of the popular belief that vampires could not be killed. Silver might be hard to come by, but anyone could sharpen a table-leg or walking stick and shove it through a new-born's heart. The woman in Bitley was destroyed with a broken broom-handle.

Elsewhere in the papers there were editorials in support of the Prince Consort's newly published edict against 'unnatural vice'.

While the rest of the world advanced towards the twentieth century, Britain reverted to a medieval legal system. When warm, Vlad Tepes had so vigorously persecuted common thieves that it was reputedly possible for townships to leave gold drinking cups at public wells. His other current passion was that railways should run in accordance with their timetables; there was a notice in *The Times* of the appointment of an American new-born named Jones to oversee a commission for the extensive improvement of the service. The Prince Consort had his own private engine, the Flying Carpathian, and was often depicted at the throttle in *Punch*, an oversize cap on his head, toot-tooting the whistle and choo-chooing the boiler.

There were rumblings of anti-vampire riots in India, and the harsh methods Sir Francis Varney was employing against the insurrectionists. While the Prince Consort still favoured the stake, Varney's preferred method of execution was to cast offenders, warm and un-dead alike, into pits of fire. Native vampires among the mutineers were bound over the mouths of artillery pieces and had silver-seamed rockshards blown through their chests.

Thought of India prompted him to look up from the paper, to the black-rimmed photograph of Pamela on the mantel. She was smiling in the Indian sun in her white muslin dress, belly full of baby, a moment snatched from passing time.

'Miss Penelope,' Bairstow announced.

Beauregard stood up and greeted his fiancée. Penelope swept into the parlour, detaching her hat from her curls, carefully flicking some invisible speck from the stuffed bird perched on the brim. She wore something with ballooning sleeves and a tight shirtwaist.

'Charles, you're still in your dressing-gown, and it is practically three o'clock in the afternoon.'

She kissed his cheek, tutting that his face couldn't have felt a razor in recent hours. He called for more coffee. Penelope sat beside him at the table, and set her hat like an offering on the papers, absent-mindedly trimming them into an orderly pile. The stuffed bird looked startled to find itself wired in such a position.

'I'm not even sure it's proper for you to receive me in such a state,' she said. 'We're not married yet.'

'My dear, you gave me little time to consider propriety.'

She humphed in the back of her mouth, but did not endeavour to move her face. Sometimes, she affected expressionlessness.

'How was the Criterion?'

'Delightful,' she said, obviously not meaning it. The Churchward mouth turned down at the corners, a smile becoming a threat in an instant.

'You are angry with me?'

'I think I have a right to be, dear-heart,' she said, with a moue of reasonableness. 'Last night was fixed some weeks ahead. You knew it was to be important.'

'My duties . . .'

'I wished to show you off before our friends, before society. Instead, I was humiliated.'

'I hardly think Florence or Art would allow that.'

Bairstow returned and left the coffee things – a ceramic pot rather than silver – on the table. Penelope poured herself a cupful, then tipped in milk and sugar, not pausing in her critique of his behaviour.

'Lord Godalming was charming, as usual. No, the humiliation to which I refer was inflicted by Kate's dreadful uncle.'

'Diarmid Reed? The newspaperman?'

Penelope nodded sharply. 'The villain exactly. He had the nerve – in public, mind you – to suggest that you'd been seen in the company of policemen in some horrid, sordid nether region of the city.'

'Whitechapel?'

She gulped hot coffee. 'That's the very place. How absurd, how cruel, how –'

'True, I'm afraid. I thought I saw Reed. I must ask him if he has any thoughts.'

'Charles!' A tiny muscle in Penelope's throat pulsed. She set down her cup, but left her little finger crooked.

'There is no accusation, Penelope. I have been in Whitechapel on the business of the Diogenes Club.'

'Oh, *them.*'

'Indeed, and their business is also, as you know, that of the Queen and her ministers.'

'I doubt that the safety of the realm or the well-being of the Queen is one whit advanced by having you trail around with the lower orders, sniffing out the sites of sensational atrocities.'

'I can't discuss my work, even with you. You know that.'

'Indeed.' She sighed. 'Charles, I'm sorry. It's just that . . . well, that I'm proud of you, and I thought I deserved the opportunity to display you a little, to let the envious look at my ring, to draw their own conclusions.'

Her anger melted away, and she became again the fond girl he had courted. Pamela had been possessed of a temper, as well. He remembered Pam horse-whipping a blackguard of a corporal who was found to have interfered with the *bhisti*'s sister. The quality of her anger had been different, though; spurred by actual wrongs done to another, rather than imagined sleights against herself.

'I have been talking to Art.'

Penelope was working up to something, Beauregard realized. He knew the symptoms. One of them was a sick feeling in the pit of his stomach.

'It's about Florence,' she said. 'Mrs Stoker. We must drop her.'

Beauregard was astounded. 'I beg your pardon? She's a bit of a bore at times, but she means well. We've known her for years.'

He had thought Florence to be Penelope's closest ally. Indeed, Mrs Stoker had been highly instrumental in contriving occasions on which the couple were left alone together so that a proposal might be elicited. When Penelope's mother had been sick with a fever, Florence had insisted on taking charge.

'It is all the more important that we should openly distance ourselves from her. Art says –'

'Is this Godalming's idea?'

'No, it's mine,' she said, deliberately. 'I can have ideas of my own, you know. Art has told me something of Mr Stoker's affairs . . .'

'Poor Bram.'

'Poor Bram! The man is a traitor to the Queen you profess to serve. He has been hauled off to a work camp for his own good and may be executed at any moment.'

Beauregard had supposed as much. 'Does Art know where Bram is being held? What is his situation?'

Penelope waved the enquiry aside as irrelevant. 'Sooner or later, Florence must fall too. If only by association.'

'I hardly see Florence Stoker as an insurrectionist. What could she do, organize tea-parties for bands of ferocious vampire-killers? Distract politicians by simpering at them while assassins creep out of the bushes?'

Penelope tried to look patient. 'We must not be seen to be with the wrong people, Charles. If we are to have a future. I am only a woman, but even I can understand that.'

'Penelope, what has brought all this on?'

'You think me incapable of serious thought?'

'No . . .'

'You never considered Pamela to be such an empty-head.'

'Ah . . .'

She held his hand, and squeezed. 'I'm sorry. I did not mean to say that. Pam is out of this.'

He looked at his fiancée and wondered if he truly knew her. She was a long way from the pinafore and the sailor's cap.

'Charles, there is another prospect we must consider. After our marriage, we must turn.'

'Turn?'

'Art will do it, if we ask. Bloodline is important, and his is of the best. He's Ruthven's get, not the Prince Consort's. That could be to our advantage. Art says the Prince Consort's bloodline is dreadfully polluted, while Ruthven's is simon-pure.'

In her face, Beauregard could see the vampire Penelope might become. Her features seemed to push forwards as she leaned to him. She kissed him on the lips, warmly.

'You are no longer entirely young. And I shall be twenty soon. We have the chance to stop the clock.'

'Penelope, this is not a decision to be taken lightly.'

'Only vampires get anywhere, Charles. And among vampires, new-borns are less favoured. If we do not turn now, there will be a glut ahead of us, experienced un-dead looking down on us as those Carpathians look down on them, as the new-borns look down upon the warm.'

'It is not so simple.'

'Nonsense. Art has told me how it is accomplished. It seems a remarkably straightforward process. An exchange of fluids. There need be no actual contact. Blood can be decanted into tumblers. Think of it as a wedding toast.'

'No, there are other considerations.'

'Such as . . .?'

'Nobody knows enough about turning, Penelope. Have you not noticed how many new-borns are twisted out of true? Something beastly takes over, and shapes them.'

Penelope laughed scornfully. 'Those are very common vampires. We shan't be common.'

'Penelope, we may not have the choice.'

She withdrew and stood up. Incipient tears rimmed her eyes. 'Charles, this means a lot to me.'

He had nothing to say.

She smiled, and looked at him at an angle, pouting slightly. 'Charles?'

'Yes.'

She hugged him, pressing his head to her chest. 'Charles, please. Please, please, please . . .'

15

The House in Cleveland Street

'IT IS LIKE the warm days, is it not?' von Klatka said, his wolves straining at their leashes, 'When we fought the Turk?'

Kostaki remembered his wars, When Prince Dracula, genius of strategy, withdrew across the Danube to redouble an assault, he left a good many – Kostaki included – to be cut to tatters by the Sultan's curved scimitars. During that last mêlée something un-dead tore out his throat and drank his blood, bleeding from its own wounds into his mouth. He awoke new-born under a pile of Wallachian dead. Having learned little in several lifetimes, Kostaki again followed the standard of the Impaler.

'That was good fighting, my friend,' von Klatka continued, eyes alive.

They had come to Osnaburgh Street with a wagonload of ten-foot stakes. There was enough lumber to build an ark, Mackenzie of the Yard awaited them with his uniformed constables, The warm policeman stamped his feet against a cold Kostaki hadn't felt in centuries. Impatient steam leaked from his nose and mouth.

'Englishman, hail,' Kostaki said, clapping a salute against his fez.

'Scotsman, if you please,' said the Inspector.

'I seek your pardon.' A Moldavian survivor of the Imperial Ottoman chaos that was now Austria-Hungary, Kostaki understood the importance of distinctions between tiny countries.

A Captain in the Carpathian Guard, Kostaki was something between liaison officer and overseer. When directed so to do by the Palace, he took an interest in police matters. The Queen and her Prince Consort were much concerned with law and order. Only last week, Kostaki had trudged around Whitechapel, looking for the spoor of the crude villain they called Silver Knife. Now he was assisting with a raid on an infamous address.

They lined up either side of the wagon; Mackenzie's men, mostly new-borns, and a detachment of the Carpathian Guard. Tonight they would demonstrate that the posted edicts of Prince Dracula were not just time-wasting whims on parchment.

As Mackenzie shook hands with him, Kostaki refrained from exerting the iron *nosferatu* grip.

'We have plainclothes men blocking the escape routes,' the Inspector explained, 'so the house is completely bottled up. We go in through the front door and search from top to bottom, assembling the prisoners in the street. I have the warrants with me.'

Kostaki nodded agreement. 'It is a good plan, Scotsman.'

Mackenzie, like so many in this dreary land, was without humour. Unsmiling, he continued, 'I doubt if we'll meet much resistance. These invert fellows don't have the stomach for a scrap. Your English nancy-boy isn't best known for his backbone.'

Von Klatka spat blood into the gutter and snorted, 'Degenerate filth!' His wolves, Berserker and Albert, were eager to get their jaws around meat.

'Indeed,' agreed the policeman. 'Let's get it over with, shall we?'

They advanced on foot, the wagon following. What other traffic there was made way for them. As they passed, people tried to clear the street. Kostaki was proud of such a reaction. The reputation of the Carpathian Guard went before them.

Only a few years ago, he was no more than an un-dead gypsy, wandering Europe in hundred-year cycles, battening on to prey where he could find it, returning every generation to his castle to find it more neglected, forever posing as an increasingly remote descendant. Now he could walk unmolested down a London thoroughfare and not have to conceal what he was. Thanks to Prince Dracula, his red thirst was regularly slaked.

They marched into Cleveland Street and Mackenzie checked the house numbers. They were looking for Number 19. It was not much distinguished from its neighbours, respectable town-houses and the offices of ancient firms of solicitors. This was a well-lit, clean district, not like the East End. Kostaki mused briefly about the twisted wire contraptions fitted to chimneys in the fringes of his field of vision, but promptly dismissed the matter.

With a rasp, von Klatka slid his sword from its scabbard. Kostaki's comrade was a tireless warrior, ever eager for battle. It was a wonder he had lasted through the centuries since his warmth. Mackenzie stood aside and let Kostaki march up to the front door. He raised a gauntleted hand and took hold of the Knocker, which came off in his grip. That fool corporal, Gorcha, sniggered under his moustaches and Kostaki tossed the fragile bauble into the gutter. Mackenzie held his breath, the steam around him dissipating. Kostaki looked to him for approval: the policeman knew these people, this city, and deserved thus to be treated with respect. On the inspector's nod, Kostaki made a mighty fist, the blood-strength growing. His hand strained the seams of his reinforced glove.

He delivered a blow to the unpainted spot where the knocker had been, smashing in the door. He pushed through the splintered fragments that remained and shouldered his way into the foyer. Glancing about, he instantly took in everything. The dwarfish young man in footman's livery was no threat, but the shave-pated new-born in shirt-sleeves would fight. Constables and Guardsmen charged in after him and he was swept forwards towards the staircase.

The new-born put up his fists, but von Klatka set Berserker and Albert on him. The wolves latched on to his shins, and, as he yelled, von Klatka swiped with his sword. The vampire's head came free, blinking furiously, and landed upside-down at the feet of the footman. Mackenzie opened his mouth to rebuke von Klatka, who had grasped the stumbling headless body and shoved his face into the geyser of blood as if at a public fountain. Kostaki gestured at the policeman. This was no time for divisions.

'Good Lord,' said a warm constable, with disgust.

Von Klatka howled triumph and tossed the draining corpse away. He wiped blood out of his eyes. His wolves joined the noise.

'Rancid is blood of new-borns,' he said.

Kostaki laid a heavy hand on the shoulder of the footman. His spine was twisted and he had a small boy's face.

'You,' Kostaki said, 'your name is what?'

'Or-Or-Orlando,' said the creature, who, now Kostaki was close, turned out to be wearing powder and rouge.

'Orlando, guide us well,'

He spluttered, 'Yes, masterful sir.'

'Clever boy.'

Mackenzie had out a document. 'I have a warrant entitling us to search these premises, on the suspicion that indecent and unnatural

acts are being condoned for profit by the proprietor, one . . . um,'
he consulted the paper, 'Charles Hammond.'

'Mr Hammond is in France, your worship,' Orlando said. He
was dry-washing his hands, and experimenting with smiles of
insinuation. Kostaki could taste the fear boiling off him.

Gorcha, roaring like a bear, charged into the kitchens, laying about
him with a sword. There was a sound of breaking crockery and some
feeble whimpering.

'What is all this rot?' said someone from the landing above.

Kostaki looked up, and saw a thin, elegant new-born with
plastered-down hair and immaculate evening dress. He had with
him a boy in a stained nightshirt.

'Milord,' said Orlando, 'These gentlemen . . .'

The new-born ignored the footman and made an announcement.
'I am Bachelor Equerry to His Highness, Prince Albert Victor
Christian Edward, Heir Presumptive to the Throne. If this unwarranted intrusion is not withdrawn, the consequences for you will be
vastly unpleasant.'

'Tell him warrant we have,' von Klatka said.

'My lord, I am Kostaki of the Carpathian Guard, the private
regiment of His Highness, Vlad Dracula, known as Tepes the
Impaler, Prince Consort to Queen Victoria of these isles.'

The Lord goggled at Kostaki, patently appalled. These English
were always so shocked to be found out. They thought position
was protection. Kostaki called Gorcha away from the kitchen-maids,
and sent him up the stairs to haul down the Bachelor Equerry and his
rent-boy.

'Search the place,' Mackenzie ordered. His constables snapped
to, running up the stairs, barging into all the rooms. By now the
house was an uproar of screams and protests. The wolves were off
somewhere, doing mischief.

Two naked boys, faces painted gold, ran out from a back room,
laurels flying from their brows. Von Klatka opened his arms wide,
and swept them up, catching both at once. They struggled like fish
and von Klatka laughed at the absurdity.

'Pretty twins,' he said. 'Twins I have.'

Kostaki left the foyer to assess the work in the street. Cobblestones
had been torn up and stake-holes were being rapidly dug. Several of
the poles were already erect, ready to receive the offenders. A small

crowd had gathered on the other side of the street, gossiping use-
lessly among themselves. He growled, and they dispersed quickly.

'Thirsty work,' said one of the new-born labourers, settling a
stake into a hole.

The catch were already being collected outside the house. Von
Klatka was in charge, slapping exposed rumps with the flat of his
blade, jeering at the inverts. An upstairs window opened and a fat
man tried to throw himself out, naked rolls of flesh bouncing. He
was pulled back inside.

'You!' shouted the Bachelor Equerry, pointing at him. 'You shall
suffer for this outrage.'

Von Klatka slashed from behind at the Bachelor Equerry's legs,
catching him just above the knees. The silvered blade bit deep,
cracking bones. The new-born folded up into an attitude of prayer;
as the pain hit, he tried to shape-shift. His face pushed out into a
hairless snout; his ears slipped back, flaring wolfishly. His shirt-front
expanded, studs popping, as his ribs reconfigured. His arms became
clawed forelegs, but his wounded knees prevented the shift from
carrying much below his waist. On his dog-shaped head, slick hair
stretched so the pink scalp showed. The Bachelor Equerry opened
his throat and howled, widely spaced teeth loose.

'Von Klatka, impale him.'

Von Klatka and Gorcha took a foreleg each and hoisted the
Bachelor Equerry up on to their shoulders, his legs dangling,
trousers soaked with blood. He was reverting to his original shape.
The Carpathians settled His Lordship on the first point and he sank
belly-first on to it. His clothes ripped as he was penetrated, and a
gush of hot blood and shit squirted down the wooden pole as his
weight speared him. The stake, insufficiently banked, tilted and
nearly fell. Gorcha and von Klatka held the stake steady, a workman
piling cobbles into the hole, until it could stand by itself.

They were showing mercy. If the stake-end were rounded rather
than sharpened, death could take up to a week, the victim's organs
displaced rather than punctured. The Bachelor Equerry would die
as soon as the point breached his heart.

Kostaki looked about. Mackenzie was leaning against a wall,
regurgitating his last meal. He had done the same long ago, when
he first saw Prince Dracula deal with his enemies in the fashion that
earned him his nickname.

The assembled inverts saw what was happening to the Bachelor Equerry, and panicked. They had to be penned with swords. Several boys escaped, darting under Carpathian arms. Kostaki did not mind if a few scattered to the winds. The purpose of this raid was to catch the patrons of Number 19, Cleveland Street, not the unfortunates impressed into service there. One man, wearing the vestiges of canonical vestments, was on his knees praying loudly, a Christian martyr. A face-painted youth stood haughty with folded arms, gilded nakedness like imperial robes, outstaring his persecutors.

'Good grief,' said a well-dressed passer-by to his new-born wife, 'that man's a member of my club.'

Mackenzie was hysterical now, slapping the inverts, excoriating them in Scots. A bewhiskered man in the red tunic of some high-ranking officer pressed a pistol into Mackenzie's hand and begged to be decently shot as was his right. The policeman emptied the gun into the air and threw it away, spitting after it.

A knot of three new-born youths huddled together, shivering in ladies' night-dresses, hissing through dainty fangs. Their faces were smooth, their bodies womanish, Kostaki was reminded of Prince Dracula's concubines.

Mackenzie got himself under control and started properly to supervise his men. He presented the captives with death warrants; already filled out, but with blanks for their names. This business had to be done legally.

'Masterful sir,' wheedled a voice. It was Orlando. 'Sir, if I might make so bold as to mention, there is one who has escaped your justice. An important personage is to be found in a secret inner chamber, taking his gross pleasure with two poor lads stolen off the streets.'

Kostaki looked down on the hunched footman. Under his powder, his skin was pock-marked with disease.

'If accommodation were to be made, sir, I might see a way to assisting you, sir, in the execution of your, if I might say, sacred duty to his worshipful highness the Prince Consort, God bless him and keep him in his palace, sir.'

The warm young man's throat swelled with blood. Kostaki had not dealt with his own needs tonight. He grabbed Orlando by the neck and exerted pressure with his thumb.

'Out with it, worm!'

He had to relax his grip to allow the little man to speak.

'Behind the stairs, masterful sir, there's a secret door. And I'm the only one as knows the secret.'

Kostaki let him go and pushed him across the road.

'Sir, the one I speak of is a powerful individual, masterful sir, and I doubt if even you could subdue him by yourself.'

Kostaki detached Gorcha and a burly new-born police sergeant from the impaling party. The next of the inverts were being lifted up to their stakes. The dying yells were audible throughout the city. In Buckingham Palace, Prince Dracula would be raising a goblet of virgin wine to the enforcement of his edict.

Orlando scurried ratlike in front of them and sought out his secret door. Kostaki recognized his type: there were always those among the warm eager to serve the un-dead, just as there had been Wallachs who served the Turk.

'Remember, sir, I offered up voluntary-like the secret.'

Orlando tripped a catch and a section of wall-panel sprang out. The copper-smell of blood wafted from within, along with perfume and incense. Kostaki was first through the door. The room he entered was decorated as a bower; trees were painted on the walls, crêpe foliage hung from the ceiling, dry leaves were scattered all around. The remains of a basket of fruit were squashed into the japanned-wood floor. Curled up by the door was a dead youth, ragged gashes all over his nude body, face a perfect blue. He might turn, but Kostaki thought him too broken to be much use as a vampire.

'Here, masterful sir, behold the rutting beast, indulging his disgusting pleasures!'

In the middle of the room, surrounded by oriental cushions, churned a reptile form composed of two bodies. Underneath a writhing vampire was a squealing youth, blood slicking his back. The important personage was using the boy as a man uses a woman, simultaneously swallowing great gushing draughts from open veins. It was Count Vardalek, his back twice its normal length. Snake-teeth sprouted from the lower half of his face. His chin and lips were studded, fangs erupting through the flesh. His green-yellow eyes floated, pupils shrunk to pinpoints.

The Count looked up and spat venom.

'You see, sir,' Orlando said, grinning, 'a very important personage indeed, masterful sir.'

'Kostaki,' Vardalek said, 'what does this damned interruption mean?'

He was still moving sinuously, his body bearing upon the boy's like a serpent's coils. His sides were lightly scaled, and the scales caught the light, rainbow patterns reflecting.

'Captain Kostaki,' said Gorcha, standing by with his heavy musket, 'what should be done?'

'Get out, you fools,' Vardalek shouted.

Kostaki made a decision. 'There can be no exceptions.'

Vardalek gasped and gaped. He rose from his exhausted boy, and pulled a quilted robe about himself, spine settling as he dwindled to his usual height. His face rapidly resumed its human look. With a delicate touch, he reset his golden peruke on his sweat-slick skull.

'Kostaki, we are both . . .'

Kostaki turned away from his comrade, ordering, 'Bring him outside with the others.'

Out on the street, von Klatka's eyes bulged to see the Count being led to the stake.

Kostaki looked up at the sky. In his mountain homelands, he was used to the bright points of the stars. Here, gaslight, fog and thick rainclouds robbed him of the night's thousand eyes.

Gorcha and the Sergeant had to hold Vardalek steady. Kostaki and von Klatka stood close to the prisoner. He was smiling, but his eyes were afraid. He was not stupid. His long life was over. There would be no more gazelle-like lads for Count Vardalek.

'We have to do this thing,' Kostaki explained. 'Vardalek, you know Prince Dracula. If you were spared, we'd be impaled.'

'Comrades, this is absurd.'

Von Klatka was shifting from foot to foot like a warm fool. He wanted to intervene but he knew Kostaki was right. The Prince was proud to be known as harsh but just. His own regiment must be more rigid in its obedience to his rule than anyone else.

'What are a few boys, more or less?' Vardalek said.

'Sir, masterful sir . . .'

Kostaki raised a hand. A Guardsman took hold of Orlando and quieted him.

'I regret this deeply,' he explained.

Vardalek shrugged, endeavouring to retain his dignity. Kostaki had known the vampire since the 1600s. He had never exactly liked the arrogant Hungarian, but respected him as brave and wilful. Vardalek's preference for boys did not strike him as anything to fuss about, but Prince Dracula had strange prejudices.

'One thing you must know,' the Count said. 'That elder bitch the other night, the Dieudonné creature: my business with her is not finished. I have taken steps to even things.'

'That is to be expected.'

'I have commissioned her destruction.'

Kostaki nodded. Honour required as much.

'Masterful sir,' whined Orlando, 'now I have assisted the Prince Consort's justice, might I . . .'

'Your stake will be sharp, Vardalek,' he promised. 'And your heart will be set over its point. The end will be quick.'

'I thank you, Captain Kostaki.'

'On a stake set low so you can look down upon him, I shall have impaled the warm worm who betrayed you.'

'Masterful sir,' Orlando screeched, mouth breaking free of the Guardsman's hand, 'please, I, sir, I . . .'

Kostaki turned to the human and looked loathingly at him. Orlando's face was a wet twist of fear.

'And the stake which spits his guts shall be blunted.'

16

A Turning Point

27 SEPTEMBER

After my Lucy, Mina. His first get disposed of, the Count turned his attention to the wife of his solicitor. I believe he fixed on Mrs Harker even as he was paying his attentions to Lucy. The two women were together in Whitby when he came ashore. He saw them as a glutton sees a pair of fat pastries. I have tried to recreate the record lost in the fire at Purfleet, now I must at last turn to the journal entry I was prevented from making. On the night of the 2nd October 1885, a great stone was cast into the pond; we live now with the ripples, turned to tidal waves, of that splash.

While Van Helsing was lecturing our little circle on the habits of the common vampire, the Count was seducing Mina Harker. As with Lucy, she was to serve a double purpose, to slake his thirst and to become his get. From the first, his mission in Britain was evangelical; he was bent upon turning as many as possible, recruiting soldiers for his army. We made the asylum our fortress, and gathered behind its thick walls and iron bars as if they could keep out the vampire. In addition to the destroyers of Lucy, we took in Mina and her husband. Van Helsing must have known the Count would pursue the woman, and dug out all the holy impedimenta that had served so little use in the earlier case.

I was first alerted to the Count's invasion when an attendant intruded to tell me that Renfield had met with some accident. I came to his room and found the lunatic lying on his left side in a glittering pool of blood. When I went to move him, it became at once apparent that he had suffered terrible injuries; there was none of that unity of purpose between the parts of the body which marks even lethargic sanity. Van Helsing, in dressing-gown and slippers, tried to save the patient's life, but it was hopeless. Betrayed by his master, he raved and frothed. Quincey and Art arrived to get in the way. While the Professor was readying for a trephination, I attempted to administer an injection of morphia. Renfield bit my hand, deep. Months' practice biting off the heads of birds had given him strong jaws. If I had treated myself then, my hand mightn't have become worse than useless. But it was a crowded night, and when the sun came up, I had fled from Purfleet, no saner I fear than the poor dead man.

Renfield, babbling, told us of his attempt to defy his master. He had developed something of a crush on Mrs Harker, and anger at the Count's treatment of her broke his loyalty to the vampire. There was a touch of jealousy in his stand, I feel, as if he envied Dracula the slow taking of Mina's life. He alternated between maniacal rages and surprising courtesy. When I showed him to Quincey and Art, he recalled nominating Godalming's father for the Windham and took time to lecture Quincey on the greatness of the state of Texas, but he was always dismissive of Harker, jealous of the solicitor too. Before any of us, including the presumed expert Van Helsing, Renfield diagnosed Mina's condition. 'She wasn't the same,' he said; 'it was like tea after the teapot had been watered. I don't care for the pale people; I like them with lots of blood in them, and hers had all seemed to have run out . . . He had been taking the life out of her.'

Earlier that night, the Count had come to Renfield, apparently in a discarnate form resembling mist. The slave tried to throttle the master, only to be casually smashed against the wall. 'We know the worst now,' Van Helsing said. 'He is here and we know his purpose. It may not be too late.' With a more important life to save than Renfield's – that opinion being reinforced by the patient himself – Van Helsing abandoned plans to operate. He bid us gather up the weapons we had used against Lucy. Our group crept down the corridor towards the Harkers' bedroom, for all the world like the partisans of an outraged husband in a French farce. 'Alas, alas, that that dear Madam Mina should suffer,' Van Helsing lamented, shifting his crucifix from hand to hand like a pagan fetish. He knew confronting an elder by night, when his powers were at the height, would be a very different matter from trapping a feeble-minded new-born by day.

We paused outside the Harkers' door. Quincey said, 'Should we disturb her?' The Quincey Morris I remember from our Korea expedition would have shown no qualm about bursting at dead of night into a young lady's room, although he might have given pause if, as now, he knew the lady's husband were with her. The door was properly locked but we all put our shoulders to it. With a crash it burst open, and we almost fell headlong into the room. The Professor did actually fall, and I saw across him as he gathered himself up from hands and knees. What I saw appalled me. I felt my hair rise like bristles on the back of my neck.

The moonlight was so bright that through the thick yellow blind the room was light enough to see. On the bed beside the window lay Jonathan Harker, his face flushed and his breath coming heavily. Kneeling on the near edge of the bed facing outwards was his wife. By her side stood a tall, thin man, clad in black. His face was turned from us, but the instant we saw, we all recognized the Count. With his left hand he held both Mrs Harker's hands, keeping them away with her arms at full tension; his right hand gripped her by the back of the neck, forcing her face down on his bosom. Her white night-dress was smeared with blood, and a thin stream trickled down the man's bare breast which was shown by his torn-open shirt. The attitude of the two had a terrible resemblance to a child forcing a kitten's nose into a saucer of milk to compel it to drink.

As we burst into the room, the Count turned his face and a hellish look seemed to leap into it, With a wrench which threw his victim back upon the bed as though hurled from a height, he turned and sprang at us. By this time the Professor had gained his feet and was fumbling with one of his wafers. The Count suddenly stopped, just as Lucy had done outside the tomb. Further and further back he cowered, as we, lifting our crosses, advanced. A righteous Christian army, we would have done John Jago proud. We had the vampire in a corner and might have finished him or put him to flight but for a failure on our collective part. Before me was evidence that Dracula shared Van Helsing's belief in the power of sacred symbols to harm him, but my own faith faltered. I would rather have had a pistol in my hand, or Quincey's bowie knife, or one of my now-silvered scalpels. To face the Count with a penny ornament and a broken biscuit struck me then, and strikes me now, as sheer folly. As my doubt flared, I dropped my cross. And as a great black cloud passed over the moon, I heard terrible laughter in the dark. Quincey put a match to the gas and the light sprang up. All shadows banished,

the Count stood before us, blood dribbling from the shallow cut
in his chest. I had expected to find Dracula drinking the blood of
Mrs Harker, not vice versa.

'Well, well, well,' the Count said, casually buttoning his shirt, and
arranging his cravat. 'Dr Seward, I believe. And Lord Godalming.
Mr Morris of Texas. And Van Helsing. Of course, Van Helsing.
Professor is it, or Doctor? No one seems quite sure.'

I was surprised that he knew us, but, of course, he had information
from many: Harker, Renfield, Lucy, Mina. I had expected his voice
to be the thick-accented croak of an Attila unschooled in English.
But he spoke in a cultivated, almost proper manner. Indeed, his
command of our language was certainly far in excess of that of
Abraham Van Helsing or Quincey P. Morris, to name but two.

'You think to baffle me, you with your pale faces all in a row, like
sheep in a butcher's. You shall be sorry, each one of you. Your girls
whom you love are mine already; and through them you and others
shall yet be mine. My creatures, to do my bidding and to be my
jackals when I want to feed.'

Van Helsing, with a roar of rage, shoved his wafer at the Count,
but Dracula moved with incredible speed, stepping aside to let the
Professor fall a second time. He laughed again, a cruel chuckle from
the throat. I stood paralysed, my hand throbbing as if covered with
scorpions. Art, too, made no move. That shared lack of action
accounts for our both being, in a manner of speaking, alive three
years later.

Quincey, ever putting deed before thought, rushed at Dracula,
and stuck him through the heart. I heard the bowie sink in as if
penetrating cork. As the Count staggered back against the wall,
Quincey yee-hahed a victory yell. But the blade was plain steel,
not the wood that would have transfixed his heart nor the silver
that would have poisoned him. The vampire took the knife out of
his breast as if drawing it from a scabbard. The gash remained in
his shirt, but closed up in his flesh. Quincey said, 'Well, kiss my
sister's black cat's ass,' as Dracula closed on him. The Count gave
Quincey back his knife, plunging it into the hollow of his throat,
sucking briefly at the wound that erupted.

Our gallant friend was dead.

Next the Count picked up the unconscious Harker as easily as
he would a baby. Mina was by his side, eyes glazed as if drugged,

blood on her chin and bosom. Dracula kissed the solicitor's forehead, leaving a bloody mark.

'He was my guest,' he explained, 'but he abused hospitality.'

He looked at Mina, as if communicating with her mind. She hissed at him, startlingly like the new-born Lucy, setting her unholy blessing upon his intent. She was turning fast. With a quick snap, he broke Harker's neck in his great hands. He jabbed his thumb-nail into the pulsing vein of Harker's neck, and offered him to his wife. Mina, her hair swept aside with both hands, leaned over, and began to lap up the blood.

I helped the Professor to his feet. He shook with rage, his face purple with blood, foam about his mouth. He looked like one of the madmen in the other wing of the house.

'Now,' the Count said, 'leave me and mine be.'

Art had already backed out of the door. I followed, hauling Van Helsing with me. He was grumbling under his breath. Mrs Harker dropped her husband's lifeless body on the carpet and he rolled against the bed, open eyes staring. From the corridor, we saw Dracula pull Mina to him and press his face to her throat, his thick-nailed hands tearing at her chemise and the long tangle of her hair.

'No,' said Van Helsing, 'no.'

It took all my strength, and Art's too, to hold the savant back. We looked away from Dracula's feeding, but Van Helsing was transfixed. What he saw in the Harkers' bedroom was a personal affront.

A man in muddy striped pyjamas burst into the corridor from a stairwell, dragging a thin woman by her hair, waving an open razor. It was Louis Bauer, the Pimlico Square Strangler. A crowd of others, shambling in the darkness, followed. Someone sang a hymn with a ragged but pure voice, joined by animal-like whining. A hunched figure pushed to the front of the crowd. It was Renfield, twisted over where he was broken, his face and front a mess of blood.

'Master,' he shrieked, 'I atone . . .'

The swell of bodies pushed him forward. He should have been dead, but insanity can keep people with the most terrible injuries on their feet, if only for the length of a fit. He had let out the inmates. Renfield fell to his knees and was trampled under by his mad fellows. Bauer kicked his already snapped spine, finishing him at last. There was a fire in the building somewhere. And dreadful screams, either from rampaging patients or the staff who bore the brunt of their fury.

I turned to look for Art but he was gone. I've not seen him since. With my good arm around Van Helsing, I backed away from the mob. The Count, his business with Mina finished, emerged from the Harkers' room, and quieted the inmates with a glance, just as he was supposed to be able to quell wolves and other wild things.

I tugged on Van Helsing, leading him towards the back staircase Art must have taken. He resisted, still mumbling of holy hosts and un-dead leeches. Another man might have left him, but I was driven by a strength come too late. Because of me, Lucy was twice destroyed, Quincey and Harker were dead, Mina was the Count's slave. Even Renfield was on my conscience: he had been entrusted to my care, and I had used him for an experiment as he had used his spiders and bugs. I fixed upon Van Helsing as if he could be my salvation, as if rescuing him would make amends for the others.

Mina was by the Count now, already in the full throes of her turning. The process, I understand, is variable in its length of incubation. With Mrs Harker, it was rapid. It was hard to recognize in this new-born wanton, her night-clothes shredded away from the voluptuous white of her body, the prim and practical school-mistress of the lower middle classes whom I had met only a day or so before.

With a sudden shock of strength, I subdued the Professor. He went slack and I got him on to the stairs. I hurried as if we were pursued but no one followed us. Art must have taken one of the horses from the stable and proverbially failed to bolt the door after him, for there were several animals wandering loose on the lawns. Fire already burst from the lower windows of Purfleet Asylum. I could taste the smoke in the air. Like escaping madmen, we ran for the woods, avoiding the battered black bulk of Carfax Abbey. We were defeated utterly. The whole country lay before Count Dracula, ripe for the bleeding.

We stayed in the woods for days and nights. Van Helsing's mind and heart were gone, and my hand was a swollen mace of pain. We found a hollow protected somewhat from the elements and stayed there, starting at every sound. Even by day, we were too afraid to stir. Hunger became a problem. At one point, Van

Helsing tried to eat earth. If I slept, I was persecuted by dreams of Lucy.

They found us before the week was out. Mina Harker led them, wearing trousers and an old tweed jacket of mine, hair done up under a cap. The small band of new-borns were turned patients and one orderly. They had organized into a search party, discharging the Count's orders while he was removing his headquarters from Purfleet to Piccadilly. They seized upon Van Helsing and trussed him, slinging him over a horse's back for transport back to the Abbey. What became of him is too well known to recount, and too painful to think of.

I was left with Mina. The turn had affected her differently than it had her friend. While Lucy had become more sensual, more wilful, Mina was more severe, more purposeful. She accepted her place as one of Dracula's cast-offs and found her new state a liberation. In life, she had been stronger than her husband, stronger than most men. As an un-dead, she was stronger still.

'Lord Godalming is with us,' she told me.

I thought she intended to kill me on the spot, as she had done her foolish husband. Or else make me as she was. I stood up, my swollen and dirty hand in my pocket, hoping to meet whatever came with dignity. I cast about my mind for some suitable last words. She came close to me, a smile cutting into her cheeks, her sharp teeth white and hard in the moonlight. Almost lulled, I tugged at my collar, letting the night air against my throat.

'No, doctor,' she said, and walked away into the dark, leaving me alone in the woods. I tore at my clothes and wept.

17

Silver

OUTSIDE A PUBLIC house on the corner of Wardour Street,
two new-born street flowers discreetly offered themselves.
Beauregard recognized their silent protector as the dacoit from
Limehouse, tattoos covered by a long velvet coat. Wherever he
went in the city, in the world, he could never escape the webs of
the shadow people. The dacoit gave no sign of noticing him as he
passed, but somehow the girls knew not to bother him.

The address was in D'Arblay Street, an unobtrusive shop-front
between a cabinet-maker's and a jeweller's. The cabinet-maker's
had a selection of caskets, from plain plank boxes to gorgeously
finished items suitable for a Pharaoh's sarcophagus. A new-born
couple cooed over an especially fine coffin, large enough for a
family and ostentatious enough to cow a provincial alderman's
wife into a fit of silent envy. The other premises displayed an array
of jewel clusters and rings in the shapes or insignia of bats, skulls,
eyes, scarabs, daggers, wolfsheads, or spiders; trinkets favoured by
that type of new-born who styled themselves Gothick. Others called
them murgatroyds, after the family in *Ruddigore*, the Savoy Opera
of last year that so successfully lampooned the breed.

The denizens of Soho were more eccentric than their desperate
cousins in Whitechapel. Murgatroyds concerned themselves mainly
with ornament. Many of the women emerging as the sun set were
foreign; French or Spanish, even Chinese. They favoured shroud-
like dresses, thick cobweb veils, scarlet lips and nails, waist-length
coils of glossy black hair. Their beaux followed the fashions set
by Lord Ruthven; high-waisted, immodestly tight trews; floppy
Georgian cuffs; ruffle-fronted shirts in scarlet or black: ribboned
pompadours with artificial white lightning-streaks. Quite a few
vampires, especially the elders, regarded those who creep through
graveyard shadows in batwing capes and fingerless black gloves

as an Edinburgh gentleman might look upon a Yankee with a single Scots grandparent who swathes himself in kilts and tartan sashes, prefaces every remark with quotes from Burns or Scott and affects a fondness for bagpipes and haggis. 'Basingstoke,' muttered Beauregard, invoking the Gilbertian magic word supposed to render the most gloom-besotted murgatroyd into meek suburban mediocrity.

He walked to Fox Malleson's establishment and entered. The shop was empty, all the counters and shelves taken down. The window was painted over green. A vampire tough sat, eternally vigilant, by the door leading to the works. He presented the new-born with his card; he stood, considered for a moment, and pushed open the door, nodding for Beauregard to enter. The room beyond was full of opened tea-chests, in which were packed, amid quantities of straw, an assortment of silverware: tea and coffee pots, dinner services, cricket cups, cream jugs. Heaped on trays were the remains of rings and necklaces, gems prised out and gone. A heavy ring-base caught his attention, the gouged-out hollow at its centre like an empty eye-socket. He wondered if Fox Malleson were in partnership with the jeweller next door.

'Mr B, welcome,' said the short, old man who emerged from behind a curtain. Gregory Fox Malleson had so many chins that there seemed to be nothing between his mouth and collar but rolls of jelly. He had a good-humoured, kindly look, and wore a dirty apron, black silk sheaths over his sleeves and green-tinted protective goggles shifted up on to his forehead.

'It is always a pleasure to see one of the gentlemen from the Diogenes Club.'

He was warm. As a silversmith, he could hardly be anything else. The new-born outside would not dare to venture into the interior of Fox Malleson's works. The silver particles in the air might get into his lungs and condemn him to lingering death.

'I think you'll be pleased with what we've done for you. Come, come, this way, this way . . .'

He drew aside the curtain and admitted Beauregard into the work-rooms. A bed of hot coals burned forever in a smithy, pots of dull liquid silver standing over it. A gawky apprentice was melting down a mayoral chain, feeding it link by link into a pot.

'So hard to get raw materials these days. With all the new rules and regulations. But we muddle through, Mr B, oh yes we do. In our own way.'

Silver bullets cooled on a bench, like scones on a baker's tray.

'A commission from the Palace,' Fox Malleson said, with pride. He picked up a bullet between thumb and forefinger. The pads of his fingers all had hard burn-calluses. 'For the Prince Consort's Carpathian Guard.'

Beauregard wondered how *nosferatu* soldiers loaded their pistols. Either they had warm orderlies or thick leather gloves.

'Actually, silver's not much good for bullets. Too soft. You get the best effect with a core of lead. Silver-jackets, they're called. Burst in the wound. That'd polish off anyone, un-dead or not. Very nasty.'

'A costly weapon, surely?' asked Beauregard.

'Indeed so, Mr B. This is the Reid design. An American gentleman, Reid said bullets should be costly. A reminder that life is a currency not to be spent freely.'

'An admirable thought. Surprising from an American.'

Fox Malleson was reputedly the finest silversmith in London. For a time, his profession completely outlawed, he had been confined in Pentonville. But expedience prevailed. Power is based, at bottom, on the ability to kill; thus the means of killing have to be available, even if only to a select few.

'Look at the workmanship,' Fox Malleson said, holding up a crucifix. Even without its jewels, the craft was evident in the sculpting of the figure of Christ. 'You can see the suffering in the lines of the limbs.'

Beauregard examined it. A few truly feared the cross – the Prince Consort included, apparently – but most vampires were indifferent to religious artefacts. Some murgatroyds made a point of flaunting their immunity by wearing ivory crucifixes as earrings.

'Popish silliness, of course,' Fox Malleson said, a touch sadly. He passed the crucifix to his apprentice for the pot. 'Still, I miss artistry sometimes. Bullets and blades are all very well but they're just function. No form to speak of.'

Beauregard was unsure. The rows of bullets, like ranks of soldiers in pointed helmets, were shining and pleasing objects.

'That's why a commission such as yours is such a pleasure, Mr B. Such a pleasure.'

Fox Malleson took a long, thin bundle from a rack. It was wrapped in coarse cloth and tied up with string. The silversmith handled it as if it were Excalibur, and he the knight charged with it until the time Arthur should return.

'Would you care to examine?'

Beauregard loosed the strings and slipped away the cloth. His sword-cane had been polished and refinished. The wood shone, black with a red undertone.

'Lovely to see such work, Mr B. The original manufacturer was an artist.'

Beauregard pressed the catch and drew the sword. He laid down the sheathing wood and held up the blade, turning his wrist so it caught the red light from the embers. It sparkled and flashed and danced.

The weight was unchanged, the balance perfect. It felt as light as a willow switch, but a flick of the wrist was translated into a powerful slice. Beauregard cut at the air, smiling at the whistle.

'Beautiful,' he commented.

'Oh yes, Mr B, beautiful. Like a fine lady, beautiful and sharp.'

Beauregard laid his thumb against the cold flat of the blade, and felt the smoothness.

'I ask a favour of you,' the silversmith said. 'Don't use it for chopping sausage.'

Beauregard laughed. 'You have my word, Fox Malleson.'

He took the cane, and with a click sheathed the silver-coated sword. He would feel safer in Whitechapel, knowing he could defend himself against anyone.

'Now, Mr B, you must sign the Poisons Book.'

18

Mr Vampire

'YOU'RE TO COME quick, Miss Dee,' Rebecca Kosminski said, 'It's Lily, She's took poorly.'

The self-possessed little girl vampire led Geneviève through the streets away from the Hall. She was discharging her errand with meticulous attention. As they walked, Geneviève asked Rebecca about herself and her family. She was reluctant to give answers that suggested she was in a position to be pitied. The new-born already had an independent spirit. She dressed like a miniature adult and gave no answer when asked about favourite dolls. She had evolved away from the childhood of her body. The cruellest question anyone could ever ask Rebecca was: 'What would you want to be if you could grow up?'

In the Minories, Geneviève became aware again that she was being followed at a distance. Over the last few nights, she had almost always been half-conscious of something just out of mind's reach. Something in yellow that hopped.

'Are you very old, Miss Dee?' Rebecca asked.

'Yes. Sixteen years warm, and four hundred and fifty-six dark.'

'Are you an elder?'

'I suppose so. My first ball was in 1429.'

'Will I be an elder?'

It was unlikely. Few vampires lived as long as they would have unturned. If Rebecca lasted her first century, then she would most likely live several more. Most likely.

'If I become an elder, I hope to be just like you.'

'Be careful what you hope for, Rebecca.'

They came to the railway bridge, and Geneviève saw a huddle of women and men under the arches. The thing out of range stopped too, she thought. She had an impression of something truly old, but not truly dead.

'Here, Miss Dee.'

Rebecca took her hand and led her to the group. At the centre of attention was Cathy Eddowes, sitting on the cobbles with Lily's head in her lap. Neither new-born looked well. Cathy was thinner than she had been a few nights ago. Her rash had crept to cover her cheeks and forehead. The scarf wrapped about her head did not conceal the extent of her blemishes. The onlookers let Geneviève through and Cathy smiled up at her. Lily was in a kind of fit, with only the whites of her eyes showing.

'She nearly swallowed 'er tongue, poor mite.' Cathy said. 'I 'ad to stick me thumb in there.'

'What's wrong with Lily?' Rebecca asked.

Geneviève laid a hand on the child, and felt her shaking. Bones moved under her skin, as if her skeleton were trying to assume new form, misshaping her flesh.

'I don't really know.' Geneviève admitted. 'She's trying to shape-shift and she's not very good at it.'

'I'd like to shift my shape, Miss Dee. I could be a bird or a big cat . . .'

Geneviève looked at Rebecca and let the new-born look at Lily. Rebecca understood.

'I suppose I should wait until I'm older.'

'Keep that thought, Rebecca.'

A murgatroyd from the West End had turned Lily, for a lark, Geneviève resolved to find that new-born and inculcate in him an awareness of his responsibility to his abandoned child-in-darkness. If he would not listen, she might hurt him enough to convince him never again to be profligate with his Dark Kiss. Then she thought to herself, 'Careful.' She sounded too much like the Old Testament.

Lily's arm was still most sorely affected. It was a complete batwing now, withered and dead, the membrane stretched between bony spines. A tiny useless hand sprouted from a node of the ribs.

'She'll never fly,' Geneviève said.

'What's to be done?' Cathy asked.

'I'll take her to the Hall. Maybe Dr Seward has some treatment.'

'There's no 'ope, is there?'

'There's always hope, Cathy. No matter how much you suffer. You must see the doctor too. I've told you before.'

Cathy cringed. She was afraid of doctors and hospitals, more afraid than of policemen and jails.

'Strewth,' someone swore. 'What in God's blood is that?'

Geneviève turned to look. Most of the crowd faded away into the fog. She was left with Cathy, Lily and Rebecca. Something was coming near, emerging from the murk.

She would at last face the thing that had been dogging her. Standing, she looked about her. The railway arch was about twenty feet tall; a heavily loaded wagon could get through. The thing was coming the way she had come, down from Aldgate. She heard it first, like a slow beat of a drum. The thing bounced like a rubber ball, but with an unnatural slowness as if fog were as thick as water. Its silhouette became apparent. It was tall and wore a tasselled cap. Its yellow garment was a long robe, huge sleeves dangling from extended arms. It had been a Chinaman a long time ago. It still wore slippers on its small feet.

Rebecca stared at the vampire thing.

'That.' Geneviève said, 'is an elder.'

It kept leaping forwards like Spring-Heel'd Jack. Geneviève made out a face like an Egyptian mummy, with the addition of tusklike fangs and long moustaches. It set down a few yards away and let its arms fall, knife-taloned hands snickersnacking. The oldest vampire Geneviève had ever seen, the Chinese must have earned its wrinkles through countless centuries.

'What do you want with me?' she asked, first in Mandarin Chinese, then repeating herself in Cantonese. She had spent a dozen years travelling in China, but that had been a hundred and fifty years ago. She had lost most of her languages.

'Cathy,' she said, 'take Rebecca and Lily to the Hall. Do you understand me?'

'Yes'm,' the new-born said. She was terrified.

'Do it now, if you please.'

Cathy stood, cradling Lily against her shoulder, and took Rebecca by the hand. The three of them vanished at a trot through the arch, making to double around Fenchurch Street Station and back up towards Aldgate and Spitalfields.

Geneviève looked at the old vampire. She fell back on English, Elders went beyond the need for speech at some point, reading what they needed directly from others' minds.

'Well . . . we're alone now.'

It hopped and landed immediately in front of her, face to hers, arms on her shoulders. Muscles wriggled like worms under the thin leather of its face. Its eyes were closed but it could see.

She made a fist and punched at its heart. Her blow should have staved through the ribs; instead, she felt she had taken a swing at a granite gargoyle. There were strange bloodlines in China. Ignoring the pain, she half-turned in the vampire's near-embrace and brought up her leg, jamming her heel into its stomach and *pushing*, using its solidity to launch herself away. Her hands were out like springs when she landed on the cobbles on the other side of the bridge. She cowered in a street-lamp's circle of light as if it offered protection. Her ankle hurt too, now. She jumped to her feet and looked back. The Chinese vampire was gone. Either no real harm was meant her or it played with its prey. She knew which she felt the more likely.

19

The Poseur

LORD RUTHVEN STOOD at a podium, one hand fisted sternly on his extravagantly ruffled breast, the other resting upon an imposing stack of books. The Prime Minister's Carlyle, Godalming noticed, still had uncut pages. Ruthven wore a midnight black frock coat, frogged at the collar and on the pockets. A curly-brimmed top hat perched on his head; his face was a thoughtful blank. The portrait would be called The Great Man, or some such imposing title. My Lord Ruthven, the Vampire Statesman.

Several times Godalming had sat for painters; he had been possessed of a series of sudden, urgent needs to scratch or blink or twitch. Ruthven was uniquely able to stand motionless all afternoon, as patient as a lizard waiting on a rock for a morsel to crawl within range of a darting tongue.

'It is a shame we are denied the miracle of photography,' he declared, lips apparently unmoving. Godalming had seen attempted photographs of vampires. They developed in a blurred manner, the subjects appearing, if at all, as fuzzy silhouettes with corpse-like features. The laws that affected mirrors somehow thwarted the photographic process.

'But only a painter can capture the inner man,' Ruthven said. 'Human genius will always be superior to mechanical-chemical trickery.'

The artist at hand was Basil Hallward, the society portraitist. He deftly sketched a series of studies, a preliminary to the full-length picture. Although more fashionable than inspired, Hallward had his moments. Even Whistler doled out a few kind words for his early work.

'Godalming, what do you know about the Silver Knife business?' Ruthven asked, suddenly.

'The murders in Whitechapel? Three so far, I believe.'

'Good, you're up on it. Excellent man.'

'I just glance at the newspapers.'

Hallward released the Prime Minister and Ruthven sprang from his spot, eager to see the sketches, which the painter clutched to his heart.

'Come now, just a peep,' coaxed Ruthven, exerting considerable charm. At times, he was quite the larkish lad.

Hallward showed his pad and Ruthven flicked through, uttering approval.

'Very fine, Hallward,' he commented. 'I do believe you've caught me. Godalming, look here, look at this expression. Is this not me?'

Godalming agreed with Ruthven. The Prime Minister was delighted.

'You're too much the new-born to have forgotten your own face, Godalming,' Ruthven said, fingers at his own cheek. 'When I was as barely-cool as you, I swore it would never happen. Ah, the resolutions of youth. Gone, gone, gone!'

From philosophy, Ruthven switched to natural science. 'Actually, it is untrue that vampires lack a reflection. It is just that the reflection invariably does not *reflect* as it were, what is out here in the world.'

Godalming, like every new-born, had stared at a shaving glass for a few hours, wondering. Some disappeared completely, while others saw an apparently empty suit of clothes. Godalming's image was a black fudge like the photographs Ruthven had mentioned. The matter of mirrors was uniformly considered the most impenetrable of the mysteries of the un-dead.

'Anyway, Godalming . . . Silver Knife? This beastly murderer. He preys only on our kind, does he not? Slits throats and stabs hearts?'

'That is what they say.'

'A fearless vampire killer, like your old associate Van Helsing?'

Godalming's face burned; if still capable of blushing, he was doing so.

'I'm sorry,' the Prime Minister said with patent sincerity. 'I did not intend to raise that matter. It must be painful for you.'

'Things have changed, my lord.'

Ruthven fluttered his hand. 'You lost your fiancée to this Van

Helsing. Having suffered more at his hand than even Prince Dracula, you have been pardoned and forgiven your ignorance.'

Godalming remembered hammering at the stake, and Lucy's hissing, blood-spitting death. A death that need never have been. Lucy would have been one of the first ladies of the court; like Wilhelmina Harker or the Prince Consort's Carpathian mistresses. He would have lost her anyway.

'You've cause to curse the Dutchman's memory. For that reason, I wish you to represent my interests in the matter of Silver Knife.'

'I don't see what you mean.'

Ruthven was back at his podium, exactly in his former pose. Hallward's quick fingers filled in detail on a large sketch.

'The Palace has taken an interest. Our dear Queen is most upset. I have a personal note from Vicky. "This murderer is certainly not an Englishman," she deduces, "and if he is, he is certainly not a gentleman." Very astute.'

'Whitechapel is a notorious nest of foreigners, my lord. The Queen may be right.'

Ruthven smiled ironically. 'Rot, Godalming. We should all like to believe the English incapable of atrocious conduct, but such is not the case. Sir Francis Varney, after all, is an Englishman. The point is that our murderer is very choosy about his midnight surgical experiments.'

'You think he's a doctor?'

'That's hardly a fresh theory. It's of no importance. No, the thing is that he is a vampire killer. A homicidal lunatic, almost certainly, but also a vampire killer. Given the delicacy of the situation, he is treading a knife-edge with the public. No matter how they may disapprove and cry "monster", there is another view, a view which upholds the Silver Knife as an outlaw hero, a Robin Hood of the gutters.'

'Surely no Englishman could believe so?'

'Have you forgotten what it was like to be warm, Godalming? How did you feel when you were following Van Helsing about Kingstead Cemetery with hammer and stake?'

Godalming understood.

'The best thing would be, and I am not commissioning such an act by any means, if our madman were to take his silver knife to some warm tart, and thus display an all-inclusive mania. If there is any sympathy for him, such a step would cause it to evaporate.'

'Indeed so.'

'But even this exalted office does not give me power over the minds of mad murderers. A pity.'

'What would you have me do?'

'Poke around, Godalming. We are late off the mark. Many interested parties have been tracking our man. Carpathians have been seen attending inquests and loitering in vile places. And a connection of yours, one Charles Beauregard, has been acting on behalf of our more secret services.'

'Beauregard? He's a quill-pusher . . .'

'He is a member of the Diogenes Club, and the Diogenes Club is well placed.'

Finding a tiny fold of lip caught between his teeth, Godalming bit down, swallowing the brief tang of his own blood. It was becoming a habit.

'Beauregard has been haring around mysteriously. I have seen something of his fiancée. She is put out by his neglect.'

Ruthven laughed. 'Ever the curly-haired roué Godalming?'

'Not at all.' Godalming said, lying.

'At any rate, watch Beauregard. I've no reports of him beyond the most basic; which suggests to me that he is a shiny little tool Admiral Messervy and his crew wish to keep all to themselves.'

He could not imagine Beauregard even knowing where Whitechapel was. But he had been in India. Godalming had heard odd hints from Penelope, hints that now formed a wavering picture of a man very different from the dull companion of Florence Stoker's after-darks.

'At any rate, we are expecting Sir Charles Warren within the half-hour. I shall breathe fire in his face and impress upon him the importance of bringing this affair to a speedy and happy conclusion. Then I intend to saddle the Commissioner with you.'

Godalming was quietly proud. A clever new-born might advance himself by doing such a service to his Prime Minister.

'Godalming, this is an opportunity for you to erase for ever that question mark by your name. Bring us Silver Knife and it'll be as if you had never met Abraham Van Helsing. Few have a chance to change their past.'

'Thank you, Prime Minister.'

'And remember, our interests are singular. If the murderer is brought to book, then that will be good and just. But the most important aspect of the case is far removed from the fates of a few eviscerated *demi-mondaines*. When this is finished, the murderer must be reviled not revered.'

'I don't believe I fully understand.'

'Let me illustrate. In New Mexico, ten years ago, a new-born ran riot, killing without thought. A warm man, Patrick Garrett, loaded a shotgun with sixteen silver dollars and peppered his heart with razor-shards. The new-born was Henry Antrim or William Bonney, a cretin leech who deserved his fate. Soon after, stories began to circulate. Dime novels elaborated upon his youth and romantic appeal. Billy the Kid, they call him now, Billy Blood. Squalid murder and pathetic crime are forgotten and the American West has a a range-riding vampire demigod. You can read in the penny press how he rescued fair maidens and was rewarded with their freely bestowed favours, how he stood up for poor farmers against cattle kings, how he only became a killer to avenge the death of his father-in-darkness. It's all bunkum, Godalming, all a pretty lie for the newspapers. Billy Bonney was so low he'd bleed his own horse, but now he is a true hero. That will not happen in this case. When Silver Knife is hoisted to the stake, I want a dead madman not an unkillable legend.'

Godalming understood.

'Warren and the others merely wish to finish Silver Knife for 1888. I want you to make sure he is destroyed for all time.'

20

New Grub Street

S EPTEMBER WAS NEARLY done. It was the morning of the 28th. Silver Knife had not murdered since Lulu Schön, on the 17th. Of course, Whitechapel was now so crowded with policemen and reporters that the killer might be overcome with shyness. Unless, as some had theorized, he was a policeman or a reporter.

With the sun up, the streets were sparsely populated. The fog had blown away for the moment, giving him a cold, clear look at the place that had become his second home. Beauregard had to admit he did not much care for it, by day or night. After another fruitless shift with resentful detectives, he was tired to the point of exhaustion. Professional feeling was that the trail was cooling fast. The murderer might have succumbed to his own mania and turned his knife against himself. Or simply hopped on a steamer for America or Australia. Soon, everywhere in the world you could go, there would be vampires.

'Maybe he's just *stopped*,' Sergeant Thick had suggested. 'They do sometimes. He could spend the rest of his life sniggering every time he passes a copper. Maybe he doesn't get his jollies with the knife, maybe the thing is that he wants to have a secret all to himself.'

That had not sounded right to Beauregard. From the autopsies, he believed Silver Knife got his jollies cutting up vampire women. Although the victims were not conventionally violated, it was obvious the crimes were sexual in nature. Privately, Dr Phillips, the H Division Police Surgeon, theorized that the murderer might practise the sin of Onan at the site of his crimes. Little connected with this case was not utterly repulsive to decent sensibilities.

'Mr Beauregard.' A female voice interrupted his thoughts. 'Charles?'

A young person with a black bonnet and smoked glasses crossed the street to talk to him. Although it was not raining, she held aloft a black umbrella, shading her face. The wind caught and it tilted, swinging back the shadow.

'Why, it's Miss Reed!' Beauregard exclaimed, surprised. 'Kate?'

The girl smiled to be remembered.

'What brings you to these unsavoury parts?'

'Journalism, Charles. Remember, I scribble.'

'Of course. Your essay on the consequences of the match-girl strike in *Our Corner* was exemplary. Radical, of course, but exceedingly fair.'

'That is probably the first and only time the expression "exceedingly fair" will be used in connection with me, but I thank you for the compliment.'

'You underrate yourself, Miss Reed.'

'Perhaps,' she mused, before proceeding to her current business. 'I'm looking for Uncle Diarmid. Have you seen him?'

Beauregard knew Kate's uncle was one of the head men at the Central News Agency. The police thought highly of him, rating him one of the few scrupulous pressmen on the crime circuit.

'Not recently. Is he here? On a story?'

'*The* story. Silver Knife.'

Kate was fidgety, holding close a mannish document folder which seemed to have some totemic value. Her umbrella was larger than she could easily manage.

'There's something different about you, Miss Reed. Have you perhaps changed the style of your hair?'

'No, Mr Beauregard.'

'Odd. I could have sworn . . .'

'Maybe you haven't seen me since I turned.'

It hit him at once that she was *nosferatu*. 'I beg your pardon.'

She shrugged. 'That's all right. A lot of the girls are turning, you know. My – what do they call them? – father-in-darkness has many get. He is Mr Frank Harris, the editor.'

'I have heard of him. He is a friend of Florence Stoker's, isn't he?'

'He used to be, I think.'

Her patron, famous for championing people then breaking with them, was notoriously profligate with his affections. Kate was a direct young woman; Beauregard could see why she might appeal to Mr Frank Harris, the editor.

She must have some important mission to venture out by day, even heavily shrouded from the sun, so soon after turning.

'There is a café nearby where the reporters gather. It's not quite the place for an unaccompanied young lady, but . . .'

'Then, Mr Beauregard, you must accompany me, for I have something Uncle Diarmid must see immediately. I hope you do not think me forward or presumptuous. I would not ask if it were not important.'

Kate Reed had always been pale and thin. The turn actually made her complexion seem healthier. Beauregard felt the force of her will, and was not inclined to resist.

'Very well, Miss Reed. This way . . .'

'Call me Kate. Charles.'

'Of course. Kate.'

'How is Penny? I have not seen her since . . .'

'I'm rather afraid that neither have I. My guess is that she is in something of a pet.'

'Not the first time.'

Beauregard frowned.

'Oh, I am sorry, Charles. I didn't mean to say that. I can be a fearful twit at times.'

She made him smile.

'Here,' he said.

The Café de Paris was on Commercial Street, near the police station. A pie-and-eels-and-pitchers-of-tea establishment, formerly catering to market porters and police constables, it was now full of men with curly moustaches and check suits, arguing about bylines and headlines. The reason the place was such a hit with the press was that the proprietor had installed one of the new telephone devices. He allowed reporters, for a penny a time, to place calls to their head offices, even to the extent of dictating stories over the wire.

'Welcome to futurity,' he said, holding open the door for Kate.

She saw what he meant. 'Oh, how wonderful.'

An angry little American in a rumpled white suit and a straw hat from the last decade was holding the mouth- and ear-pieces of the apparatus, and yelling at an unseen editor.

'I'm telling you,' he shouted, loud enough to render the miracle of modern science superfluous, 'I've a dozen witnesses who swear the Silver Knife is a were-wolf.'

The man at the other end shouted, giving the exasperated reporter a chance to draw breath. 'Anthony,' he said, 'this *news*. We work for a *news*paper, we are supposed to print *news!*'

The reporter wrestled with the device, shutting off the call, and passed it on to the next man, a startled new-born, in the queue for the device.

'Over to you, LeQueux,' the American said. 'Better luck with your runaway steam-driven automaton theory.'

LeQueux, whom Beauregard had read in the *Globe* rattled the telephone, and began whispering to the operator.

A small group of urchins played marbles in a corner, while Diarmid Reed held court by an open fire. He sucked on a pipe as he lectured a circle of Grub Street toilers.

'A story is like a woman, lads,' he said. 'You can chase her and catch her, but you can't make her stay longer than she wants to. Sometimes, you come down to a kipper breakfast and she's upped stakes.'

Beauregard coughed to attract Reed's attention lest he embarrass himself before his niece. Reed looked up, and grinned.

'Katie,' he said, without a speck of regret for his indecent metaphor. 'Come in and have some tea. And Beauregard, isn't it? Where did you find my benighted niece? Not in some house hereabouts, I hope. Her poor mother always said she'd be the ruin of the family.'

'Uncle, this is important.'

He looked benignly sceptical. 'Just as your women's suffrage story was important?'

'Uncle, whether or not you agree with my views on that question, you must concede that a mass expression of them, involving many of the greatest and wisest in the land, is news. Especially when the Prime Minister responds by sending in the Carpathians.'

'Tell 'em, girl,' said the man in the straw hat.

Kate gave Beauregard her umbrella and unbuckled her document case. She laid a paper on the table, between teacups and ashtrays.

'This came in yesterday. Remember, you had me opening letters as a punishment.'

Reed was examining the paper closely. It was covered in a spidery red hand.

'You have brought this straight to me?'

'I've been looking for you all night.'

'There's a good little vampire,' said a stripe-shirted new-born newsman with waxed moustache points.

'Shut up, D'Onston,' Reed said. 'My niece drinks printers' ink, not blood. She's got news in her veins just where you've got warm water.'

'What is it?' LeQueux asked, breaking his telephone connection to catch up with the development.

Reed ignored the question. He found a penny in his waistcoat pocket and summoned one of the urchins.

'Ned, go to the police station and find someone above the rank of sergeant. You know what that means.'

The sharp-eyed child made a face that suggested he knew all about the varieties and habits of policemen.

'Tell them the Central News Agency has received a letter, *purporting* to be from Silver Knife. Just those words, exactly.'

'Pr'porten?'

'*Purporting.*'

The barefoot Mercury snatched the tossed penny out of the air and dashed off.

'I tell you,' he began, 'kids like Ned will inherit the earth. The twentieth century will be beyond our imagining.'

No one wanted to listen to social theories. Everyone wanted a look at the letter.

'Careful,' Beauregard said. 'That is evidence, I believe.'

'Well said. Now, back off boys, and give me some room.'

Reed held the letter carefully, rereading it.

'One thing,' he said when he had finished. 'This is an end for Silver Knife.'

'What?' said LeQueux.

'"*Don't mind me giving the trade name*", it says in the postscript.'

'Trade name?' D'Onstan asked.

'"*Jack the Ripper*". He signs himself "*Yours truly, Jack the Ripper*".'

D'Onstan whispered the name, rolling it around his mouth. Others joined in the chorus. The Ripper, Jack the Ripper. Jack. The Ripper. Beauregard felt a chill.

Kate was pleased, and looked modestly at her boot-toes.

'Beauregard, would you care?'

Reed gave him the letter, exciting grumbles of envy from the rival newspapermen.

'Read it out,' the American suggested. Feeling a touch self-conscious, Beauregard tried to recite.

'"*Dear Boss,*"' the letter began. 'The hand is hurried and spiky, but suggests an education, a man used to writing.'

'Cut the editorial,' LeQueux said, 'give it us straight.'

'"*I keep on hearing the police have caught me but they wont*" – no apostrophe – "*they wont fix me just yet. I have laughed when they look so clever and talk about being on the right track . . .*"'

'Bright boy,' D'Onstan said. 'He's got Lestrade and Abberline bang to rights there.'

Everyone shushed the interrupter.

'"*That joke about Silver Knife gave me real fits. I am down on leeches and shant quit ripping them till I do get buckled. Grand work the last job was. I gave the lady no time to squeal. How can they catch me now. I love my work and want to start again. You will soon hear of me with my funny little games.*"'

'Degenerate filth,' spluttered D'Onstan. Beauregard had to agree.

'"*I saved some of the proper red stuff in a ginger beer bottle over the last job to write with but it went thick like glue and I cant use it. Red ink is fit enough I hope. Ha ha. The next job I do I shall clip the ladys ears off and send to the police officers just for jolly wouldnt you . . .*"'

'Jolly wouldn't you? What is that, a joke?'

'Our man's a comedian,' said LeQueux. 'Grimaldi reborn.'

'"*Keep this letter back till I do a bit more work, then give it out straight.*"'

'Sounds like my editor,' said the American.

'"*My knife's so nice and silver and sharp I want to get to work right away if I get a chance. Good luck.*" And, as Reed said, "*Yours truly, Jack the Ripper. Dont mind me giving the trade name.*" There's another postscript. "*Wasnt good enough to post this before I got all the red ink off my hands, curse it. No luck yet. They say I'm a doctor now, ha ha.*"'

'Ha ha,' said an angry elderly man from the *Star*. 'Ha bloody ha. I'd give him a ha-ha if he were here.'

'How do we know he isn't?' said D'Onstan, rolling his eyes, wiping his moustache like a melodrama villain.

Ned was back, with Lestrade and a couple of constables, puffing as if they had been told the murderer himself, not merely a communication from him, were in the Café de Paris.

Beauregard handed the letter to the Inspector. As he read, his lips forming the words, the journalists discussed.

'It's a ruddy hoax,' someone said. 'Some joker making trouble for us all.'

'I think it's genuine,' opined Kate. 'There's a creepiness about it that sounds authentic to me. All that fake funny. The perverse relish drips off the page. When I first opened it, even before reading, I had a profound sense of evil, of loneliness, of purpose.'

'Whatever it is,' the American said, 'it's news. They can't stop us printing this.'

Lestrade put up his hand as if he might have some objection, but let it fall before he said anything.

'Jack the Ripper, eh,' said Reed. 'We couldn't have done better ourselves. The old Silver Knife moniker was wearing thin. Now, we've a proper name for the blighter.'

21

In Memoriam

29 SEPTEMBER

Today I went to Kingstead Cemetery to lay my annual wreath. Lilies, of course. It is three years to the day since Lucy's destruction. The tomb bears the date of her first death, and only I – or so I thought – remember the date of Van Helsing's expedition. The Prince Consort, after all, is hardly likely to make it a national holiday.

When I came out of the woods a little less than three years ago, I found the country turning. For months, as the Count climbed to his current position, I expected always to be struck down. Surely the invader who took such delight in the public ruination of Van Helsing would eventually reach out his claw and smash me. Eventually, as the fear subsided to a dull throb, I supposed I had become lost in the teeming crowds that so attracted our new master. Or maybe, with that diabolical cruelty for which he is famous, he had decided that allowing me my life would be a more fitting revenge. After all, I pose little threat to the Prince Consort. Since then, life has seemed à dream, a night-shadow of what should have been . . .

I still dream of Lucy, too much. Her lips, her pale skin, her hair, her eyes. Many times have dreams of Lucy been responsible for my nocturnal emissions. Wet kisses and wet dreams . . .

I have chosen to work in Whitechapel because it is the ugliest region of the city. The superficialities which some say make Dracula's rule tolerable are at their thinnest. With vampire sluts baying for blood on every corner and befuddled or dead men littering cramped streets, one can see the true, worm-eaten face of what has been wrought. It is hard to keep my control among so many of the leeches but my vocation is strong. Once, I was a doctor, a specialist in mental disorders. Now, I am a vampire killer. My duty is to cut out the corrupt heart of the city.

The morphine is making itself felt. My pain recedes and my vision becomes sharper. Tonight I shall see through the murk. I shall slice the curtain and face the truth.

The fog that shrouds London in autumn has got thicker. I understand all manner of vermin – rats, wild dogs, cats – have thrived. Some quarters of the city have even seen a resurgence of medieval diseases. It is as if the Prince Consort were a bubbling sink-hole, disgorging filth from where he sits, grinning his wolf's grin as sickness seeps throughout his realm. The fog means there is less distinction between day and night. In Whitechapel, many days, the sun truly does not shine. We've seen more and more new-borns go half-mad in the daytime, muddy light burning out their brains.

Today was unexpectedly clear. I spent a morning tending severe sunburns with liberal applications of linament. Geneviève lectures the worst cases, explaining that it'll take years for them to build a resistance to direct sunlight. It is hard to remember what Geneviève is; but at moments, when anger sparks in her eyes or her lips draw back unconsciously from sharp teeth, the illusion of humanity is stripped.

The rest of the city is more sedate, but no better. I stopped off at the Spaniards for a pork pie and a pint of beer. Above the city, looking down on the foggy bowl of London, its surface punctured by the occasional tall building, it would be possible, I hoped, to imagine things were as they had been. I sat outside, scarfed and gloved against the cold, and sipped my ale, thinking of this and that. In the gloom of the afternoon, new-born gentlefolk paraded themselves on Hampstead Heath, skins pale, eyes shining red. It is quite the thing to follow fashions set by the Queen, and vampirism – although resisted for several years – has now become acceptable. Prim, pretty girls in bonnets, ivory-dagger teeth artfully concealed by Japanese fans, flock to the Heath on sunless afternoons, thick black parasols held high. Lucy would have become one of them had we not finished her. I saw them chattering like gussied-up rats, kissing children and barely holding back their thirst. There is no difference, really, between them and the blood-sucking harlots of Whitechapel.

I left my pint unfinished and walked the rest of the way to Kingstead, head down, hands deep in my coat pockets. The gates hung open, unattended. Since dying became unfashionable, churchyards have fallen into disuse. The churches are neglected too, although the court has tame archbishops, desperately reconciling Anglicanism with vampirism. When alive, the Prince Consort slaughtered in defence of the faith. He still fancies himself a Christian. Last year's Royal Wedding was a display of High Church finery that would have delighted Pusey or Keble.

Entering the graveyard, I could not help but remember everything again, as sharp and hurtful as if it had been last week. I told myself we destroyed a *thing*, not the girl I had loved. Cutting through her neck, I found my calling. My hand hurt damnably. I have been trying to curb my use of morphine. I know I should seek proper treatment, but I think I need my pain. It gives me resolve.

During the changes, new-borns took to opening the tombs of dead relatives, hoping by some osmosis to return them to vampire life. I had to watch my step to avoid the chasm-like holes left in the ground by these fruitless endeavours. The fog was thin up here, a muslin veil.

It was something of a shock to see a figure outside the Westenra tomb. A slim young woman in a monkeyfur-collared coat, a straw hat with a red band on it perched on her tightly bound hair. Hearing my approach, she turned. I caught the glint of red eyes. With the light behind her, she could have been Lucy returned. My heart thumped.

'Sir?' she said, startled by my interruption. 'Who might that be?'

The voice was Irish, uneducated, light. It was not Lucy. I left my hat on, but nodded. There was something familiar about the new-born.

'Why,' she said, ''tis Dr Seward, from the Toynbee.'

A shaft of late sun speared through and the vampire flinched. I saw her face.

'Kelly, isn't it?'

'Marie Jeanette, sir,' she said, recovering her composure, remembering to simper, to smile, to ingratiate. 'Come to pay your respects?'

I nodded and laid my wreath. She had put her own at the door of the tomb, a penny posy now dwarfed by my shilling tribute.

'Did you know the young miss?'

'I did.'

'She was a beauty,' Kelly said. 'Beautiful.'

I could not conceive of any connection in life between my Lucy and this broad-boned drab. She's fresher than most, but just another whore. Like Nichols, Chapman and Schön . . .

'She turned me,' Kelly explained. 'Found me on the Heath one night when I was walking home from the house of a gentleman, and delivered me into my new life.'

I looked more closely at Kelly. If she was Lucy's get, she bore out the theory I have heard that vampire's progeny come to resemble their parent-in-darkness. There was definitely something of Lucy's delicacy about her red little mouth and her white little teeth.

'I'm her get, as she was the Prince Consort's. That makes me almost royalty. The Queen is my aunt-in-darkness.'

She giggled. My pocketed hand was dipped in fire, a tight fist at the centre of a ball of pain. Kelly came so close I could whiff the rot on her breath under her perfume, and stroked the collar of my coat.

'That's good material, sir.'

She kissed my neck, quick as a snake, and my heart went into spasm. Even now, I cannot explain or excuse the feelings that came over me.

'I could turn you, warm sir, make royalty of you . . .'

My body was rigid as she moved against me, pressing forward with her hips, her hands slipping around my shoulders, my back.

I shook my head.

''Tis your loss, sir.'

She stood away. Blood pounded in my temples, my heart raced like a Wessex Cup winner. I was nauseated by the thing's presence. Had my scalpel been in my pocket, I'd have ripped her heart out. But there were other emotions. She looked so like the Lucy who bothers my dreams. I tried to speak, but just croaked. Kelly understood. She must be experienced. The leech turned and smiled, slipping near me again.

'Somethin' else, sir.'

I nodded, and, slowly, she began to loosen my clothes. She took my hand out of my pocket and cooed over the wound. She delicately scraped away the scabs, licking with shudders of pleasure. Shaking, I looked about.

'We won't be disturbed here, doctor, sir . . .'

'Jack,' I muttered.

'Jack,' she said, pleased with the sound. 'A good name.'

She tugged her skirts up over her stocking-tops, and tied them around her waist, settling down on the ground, positioning herself to receive me. Her face was exactly Lucy's. Exactly. I looked at her for a long moment, hearing Lucy's invitation. I became painfully engorged. Finally, it was too much for me and, greatly excited and aroused, I fell upon the harlot, opening my clothes, and spearing her cleanly. In the lea of Lucy's tomb, I rutted with the creature, tears on my face, a dreadful burning inside. Her flesh was cool and white. She coaxed me to spend, helping me almost as a nursing mother helps a child. Afterwards, she took me wetly into her mouth and – with exquisite, torturous care – bled me slightly. It was stranger than morphine, a taste of rainbow death. Over in seconds, the act of vampire communion seemed in mind to stretch on for hours. I could almost wish that my life would drain away with my seed.

As I buttoned myself up, she looked elsewhere, almost modestly. I sensed the power she now had over me, the power of fascination a vampire has over its victim. I offered her coin, but my blood was enough. She looked at me with tenderness, almost with pity, before she left. If only I had had my scalpel.

Before making this entry, I conferred with Geneviève and Druitt. They are to take the night shift. We have become an unofficial infirmary and I want Geneviève – who, though formally unqualified, is as fine a general practitioner of medicine as I could wish – to be here while I am out. She is particularly concerned with the Mylett child, Lily. I fear Lily cannot last out the weekend.

The journey back from Kingstead is a blur. I remember sitting in an omnibus, lolling with the movement of the vehicle, my vision focusing and unfocusing. In the Korea, Quincey got me, in the spirit of experiment, to smoke a pipe of opium. This sensation was similar, but much more sensual. Every female I chanced to see, from skipping golden-haired children to ancient nurses, I desired in a vague, unspecifiable manner. I would have been too spent to act upon my desires, I think, but they still tormented me, like tinily ravenous ants crawling on my skin.

Now, I am jittery, nervous. The morphine has helped, but not much. It has been too long since I last delivered. Whitechapel has become dangerous. There have been people snooping around all the time, seeing Silver Knife in every shadow. My scalpel is on my desk, shining silver. Sharp as a whisper. They say that I am mad. They do not understand my purpose.

Returning from Kingstead, in the midst of my haze, I admitted something to myself. When I dream of Lucy, it is not of her as she was when warm, when I loved her. I dream of Lucy as a vampire.

It is nearly midnight. I must go out.

22

Good-Bye, Little Yellow Bird

T HE DIRECTOR HAD left her in charge of the night shift, which put
Montague Druitt in a black mood. When Geneviève wanted to
stay by Lily's bedside, Druitt harrumphed about the inconvenience,
unsubtly indicating she should delegate the general authority if she
wished to devote herself to this specific case. In the small downstairs
room where the child's cot was, Geneviève dispensed instructions.
Druitt stood at his ease, and affected not to notice the sawing of
Lily's lungs. Long, agonizing down-cut rasps came with every
exhalation. Amworth, the newly engaged nurse, fussed around the
patient, rearranging the blankets.

'I want you or Morrison in the foyer at all times,' she told him.
'The last few nights, there has been a stream of people coming
through, I don't want anyone in who has no business here.'

Druitt's brow wrinkled. 'You perplex me. Surely, we are for
all . . .'

'Of course, Mr Druitt. However there are those who would
exploit us. We have medicines, other items of value. Thefts have
been heard of. Also, should a tall Chinese gentleman present himself,
I would be grateful if you would refuse him admission.'

He did not understand; she hoped he would not be made to. She
did not really think the man could keep the hopping creature out
when it resumed its persecution of her. The elder was yet another
of the problems pressing around her, jostling for solutions.

'Very well,' Druitt said, and left. She noticed his one good coat
was trailing strands along the hem, and was almost through at
the elbows. With these people, good clothes were armour. They
separated the genteel from the abyss. Montague John Druitt, she
thought, had more than a passing acquaintance with the depths. He
was polite to Geneviève but something behind his reserve worried
her. He had been a schoolmaster, then half-heartedly embarked on

a law career, before coming to Toynbee Hall. He had achieved no distinction in any of his chosen professions. His special project was the raising of public subscriptions to fund a Whitechapel Cricket Club. He would run the side, recruiting likely players from the street, instilling in them the values and skills of the game he, not alone of his countrymen, regarded as almost a religion.

Lily began coughing up a red-black substance. The new nurse – a vampire with some experience – wiped clean the child's mouth, and pressed on her chest, trying to get the blockage cleared.

'Mrs Amworth? What is it?'

The nurse shook her head. 'The bloodline, ma'm,' she said. 'Nothing much we can do about it.'

Lily was dying. One of the warm nurses had given a little blood but it was no use. The animal she had tried to become was taking over, and that animal was dead. Living tissue was transforming inch by inch into leathery dead flesh.

'It's a trick of the mind,' Amworth said. 'Shape-shifting. To become another thing you must be able to *imagine* that other thing down to the smallest detail. It's like making a drawing: you have to get every little working thing right. The raw ability is in the bloodline, but the knack doesn't come easy.'

Geneviève was glad that those of the bloodline of Chandagnac could not shape-shift. Amworth smoothed Lily's wing like a blanket. Geneviève saw the disproportionate growth as a child's crayon drawing, bending the wrong way, not fitting together, Lily yelled, a stabbing pain inside her. She had gone blind on the streets, the sun burning out her new-born's eyes. The dead wing was leeching substance out of the bones of her legs, which crumbled and cracked in their sheaths of muscle. Amworth had put on splints, but that was just a delaying action.

'It would be a mercy,' Amworth said, 'to ease her passing.'

Sighing, Geneviève agreed. 'We should have a Silver Knife of our own.'

'Silver Knife?'

'Like the murderer, Mrs Amworth.'

'I heard this evening from one of the reporters that he has sent a letter to the newspapers. He wants to be called Jack the Ripper, he says.'

'Jack the Ripper?'

'Yes.'

'Silly name. No one will ever remember it. Silver Knife he was, and Silver Knife he'll always be.'

Amworth stood up and brushed off the knees of her long apron. The floor in the room was unswept. It was a constant struggle to keep dirt out of the Hall. It had not been meant for a hospital.

'There's nothing more to be done, ma'm. I must see to the others, I think we can save the Chelvedale boy's eye.'

'You go, I'll stay with her. Someone has to.'

'Yes ma'm.'

The nurse left and Geneviève took her place, kneeling by the cot. She took Lily's human hand and gripped tight. There was still un-dead strength in the child's fingers, and she responded. Geneviève talked to the girl softly, reverting to languages Lily could not possibly understand. Nestling in the back of her skull was a Medieval French mind that broke through sometimes.

Trailing around with her true father, she had learned, even in her short lifetime, to attend the dying. Her father, the physician, tried to save men their commanders would as soon have buried half-alive to get out of the way. The battlefield stink was in this room now, flesh gone rotten. She remembered the Latin droning of the priests and wondered whether Lily had any religion. She had not thought to call a pastor to the deathbed.

The nearest clergyman must be John Jago and the Christian Crusader would not consent to attend a vampire of any stripe. There was Reverend Samuel Barnett, Rector of St Jude's and founder-patron of Toynbee Hall, a tireless committee-member and social reformer, agitating for the cleaning-out of the vice dens of the 'wicked quarter-mile'. She remembered him spluttering red-faced with fury when preaching against the practice of women stripping to the waist to fight each other. Barnett, even without the unreasoning prejudice of Jago, disapproved of Geneviève and was openly suspicious of her motives for joining the East End Settlement Movement. She did not blame the Warriors of God for their distrust of her. Centuries before Huxley coined the term, she had been an agnostic. When Dr Seward had interviewed her for this position, he had asked: 'You're not Temperance, you're not Church, what are you?' 'Guilty,' she had thought.

She sang the songs of her long-ago childhood. She did not know if Lily could hear. The waxy red discharge from her ears suggested she might be deaf as well as blind. Still, the sound – maybe the vibrations in the air, or the scent of her breath – soothed the patient.

'*Toujours gai*,' Geneviève sang, voice breaking, hot bloody tears welling, '*toujours gai* . . .'

Lily's throat swelled up like a toad's and brackish blood, brown streaks in the scarlet, oozed out of her mouth. Geneviève pressed the swelling down, holding breath still in her nostrils to fend off the taste and smell of death. She pressed urgently, song and memory and prayer babbled together in her mind, leaking out of her mouth. Knowing she would lose, she fought. She had defied death for centuries; now the great darkness took its revenge. How many of Lily had died before their time to compensate for the long life of Geneviève Dieudonné?

'Lily, my love,' she incanted, 'my child, Lily, my dearest darling, my Lily, my Lily . . .'

The child's boiled eyes burst open. One milky pupil shrank minutely, reacting to the light. Through the pain, there was something close to a smile.

'Ma-ma,' she said, first and last word. 'Mma . . .'

Rose Mylett, or whoever was the child's human mother, was not here. The sailor or market porter who spent his fourpence to become her father probably didn't even know she had lived. And the murgatroyd from the West End – whom Geneviève would track down and *hurt* – was passed on to other pleasures. Only Geneviève was here.

Lily shook in a fit. Drops of sweated blood stood out all over her face.

'Mma . . .'

'It's mother, child,' Geneviève said. She had no children and no get. A virgin when turned, she had never passed on the Dark Kiss. But she was more this child's mother than warm Rosie, more her parent-in-darkness than the murgatroyd . . .

'It's mama, Lily. Mama loves you. You're safe and warm . . .'

She took Lily from her cot, and hugged her close, hugged her tight. Bones moved inside the girl's thin chest. Geneviève held Lily's tiny, fragile head against her bosom.

'Here . . .'

Pulling her chemise apart, Geneviève thumbnail-sliced a thin cut on her breast, wincing as her blood seeped.

'Drink, my child, drink . . .'

Geneviève's blood, of the pure bloodline of Chandagnac, might heal Lily, might wash out the taint of Dracula's grave-mould, might make her whole again . . .

Might, might, might.

She held Lily's head to her breast, guiding the girl's mouth to the wound. It hurt as if her heart were pierced by a silver ice needle. To love was to hurt. Her blood, bright scarlet, was on Lily's lips.

'*I love you, little yellow bird . . .*' Geneviève sang.

In the back of her throat, Lily made a throttling sound.

'*Goodbye, little yellow bird. I'd rather brave the cold . . .*'

Lily's head fell away from Geneviève's breast. Her face was smeared with blood.

'*. . . on a leafless tree . . .*'

The child's wing flapped once, a convulsive jerking-out that unbalanced Geneviève.

'*. . . than a prisoner be . . .*'

She could see the gaslight glowing like a blue moon through the thin membrane of the wing, outlining a tracery of disconnected veins.

'*. . . in a cage . . . of . . . gold.*'

Lily was dead. With a spasm of heart-sickness, Geneviève dropped the bundled corpse on the cot and howled. Her front was soaked with her own useless blood. Her damp hair was stuck to her face, her eyes gummed with clotted blood-tears. She wished she did believe in God, so she could curse Him.

Suddenly cold, she stood away. She rubbed the obstruction from her eyes and pushed back her hair. There was a basin of water on a stand. She washed her face clean, looking at the clean grain of the wooden frame which had once held a looking-glass. Turning from the basin, she realized there were people in the room. She must have made enough commotion to excite considerable alarm.

Arthur Morrison stood by the open door with Amworth behind him. There were others outside in the hall. People from outside, from the streets, *nosferatu* and warm alike. Morrison's face was dumbstruck. She knew she must be hideous. In anger, her face changed.

'We thought you should know, Geneviève,' Morrison said. 'There's been another murder. Another new-born.'

'In Dutfield's Yard,' said someone with the hot news, 'off Berner Street.'

'Lizzie Stride, 'er as only turned last week. Teeth not yet through. Tall gel, rorty-like.'

'Cut 'er froat, didn't 'e?'

'Long Liz.'

'Stride. Gustafsdotter. Elizabeth.'

'Ear to ear. *Thwick!*'

'She put up a barney, though. Sloshed 'im one.'

'Ripper was disturbed 'fore 'e could finish 'is job.'

'Some bloke with an 'orse.'

'Ripper?'

'Louis Diemschütz, one o' them socialisticals . . .'

'Jack the Ripper.'

'Louis was passin' by. Must of been the moment Jack was a-rippin' Lizzie's throat. Must of seen 'is rotten face. Must of.'

'Calls 'isself Jack the Ripper now. Silver Knife is gone and done.'

'Where's Druitt?'

'Damn bleedin' busybodies, them socialisticals. Always pokin' into a bloke's business.'

'Haven't seen the blighter all evening, miss.'

'Speakin' agin the Queen. And them's all Jews, y'know. Can't trust an Ikey.'

'Bet *'e's* an 'ook-nose. Jus' bet 'e is.'

'Ripper's still on the streets, 'e is. The coppers is givin' chase. By sun-up, they'll have 'is carcass.'

'If 'e's 'uman.'

23

Headless Chickens

IT WAS AS if the city were on fire!
Beauregard was at the Café de Paris when the cry went up.
With Kate Reed and several other reporters, he ran to the police
station. The street was full of people running and shouting. A
masked lout, a dozen assorted crucifixes strung about his neck,
drunkenly smashed windows, yelling that the Judgment of God
was at hand, that vampires were Demons of the Pit.

Sergeant Thick was minding the shop. A come-down for the
detective, but a responsible position. Apparently, Lestrade was at
the murder site and Abberline off duty. Kate dashed out to find
Dutfield's Yard, but Beauregard decided to stay.

'Nothing we can do yet, sir,' the sergeant said. 'I've put a dozen
men out, but they're just blundering in the fog.'

'Surely the murderer will be covered in blood?'

Thick shrugged. 'Not if he's careful. Or if he wears a reversible.'

'I beg your pardon?'

Thick opened his grey tweed coat and showed a tartan interior.
'Turns inside out. You can wear it both ways.'

'Clever.'

'This is a bloody messy job, Mr Beauregard.'

A couple of uniformed constables dragged in the window-
smasher. Thick hauled off the struggling man's flour-sack hood
and recognized one of John Jago's fearless Knights of Christendom.
The sergeant cringed away from the Crusader's whisky breath.

'The unholy leeches shall be . . .'

Thick balled the hood and shoved it in the vandal's mouth.

'Lock him up and let him sleep it off.' he ordered the constables.
'We'll talk about charges when the shopkeepers get up tomorrow
and see what damage he's done.'

For the first time he was at hand when the murderer was about his business, but he might as well be safe in bed in Chelsea for all he could do.

'Headless chickens, we are, sir,' Thick said. 'Running around in bloody circles.'

Beauregard hefted his sword-cane, and wished the Ripper would come out and fight.

'Cup of tea, sir?' Thick asked.

Before Beauregard could thank the sergeant, a warm constable, out of breath, shoved through the doors. He took off his helmet, gasping.

'What is it now, Collins? Some fresh calamity?'

'He's gone and done it again, sarge,' Collins blurted. 'Two for a penny. Two in one night.'

'What!'

'Liz Stride by Berner Street, now a bint called Eddowes in Mitre Square.'

'Mitre Square. That's off our patch. One for the City boys.'

The boundary between the jurisdictions of the Metropolitan and City Police ran through the parish. The murderer, between crimes, had crossed the border.

'It's almost as though he's trying to make us look complete bollock-heads. He'll be ripping them outside Scotland Yard next, with a note for the Commissioner written in scarlet.'

Beauregard shook his head. Another life wasted. This was no longer just a commission from the Diogenes Club. Innocent people were being killed. He felt an urgent need to do something.

'I had the news from PC Holland, one of the City blokes. He said this Eddowes – '

'Name of Catharine, I reckon. A familiar face around these parts. Spent more time sleeping it off in our cells than wherever she was lodging.'

'Yeah, I reckoned it'd be Cathy,' said Collins, pausing to look upset. 'Any rate, Holland says the bastard finished his job this time. Not like with Liz Stride, just a slash at the throat and a scarper in the dark. He was back to his usual, and gutted her proper.'

Thick swore.

'Poor bloody Cathy,' Collins said. 'She was a dreadful old tart, but she never did anyone no harm. Not real harm.'

'Poor bloody us, more like,' Thick said. 'After this, unless we get him sharp-ish, it's not going to be the easy life being a copper in this parish.'

Beauregard knew Thick was right. Ruthven would have someone important's resignation, maybe Warren's; and the Prince Consort would probably have to be restrained from impaling a few lower-ranking policemen, *pour encourager les autres*.

Another messenger appeared. It was Ned, the fleet-foot from the Café de Paris. Beauregard had given him a shilling earlier, impressing him into the service of the Diogenes Club.

Thick glowered like an ogre and the child skidded to a halt well away from him. He had been so eager on bringing Beauregard a message that he had dared venture into a police station. Now, his nervousness was reasserting itself; he trod as gingerly as a mouse in a cattery.

'Miss Reed says you're to come to Toynbee 'All, sir. Urgent.'

24

A Premature Post-Mortem

H ER EYES DRY, she wrapped Lily in a sheet. The corpse was already rotting, the skin of the face withering like the peel of an orange left too long in the bowl. The girl would have to be removed to quicklime and a pauper's grave before the smell became too bad to bear. The job of winding done, Geneviève would have to fill out a certificate of death for Jack Seward to sign and draft an account for the Hall's files. Whenever anyone died about her, another bead of ice clung to her heart. It would be easy to become a monster of callousness. A few more centuries and she could be a match for Vlad Tepes: caring for nothing but power and hot blood in her throat.

An hour before dawn, the news came. One of the ponces, arm carved up by someone's razor, was brought in; the crowd with him had five different versions of the story. Jack the Ripper was caught, and being held at the police station, identity concealed because he was one of the Royal Family. Jack had gutted a dozen in full view and eluded pursuers by leaping over a twenty-foot wall, springs on his boots, Jack's face was a silver skull, his arms bloodied scythes, his breath purging fire. A constable told her the bare facts. Jack had killed. Again. First, Elizabeth Stride. And now Catharine Eddowes. *Cathy*! That shocked her. The other woman, she said she didn't think she knew.

'She was in here last month, though,' Morrison said. 'Liz Stride. She was turning and wanted blood to keep her going. You'd remember her if you'd met her. She was tall, and kind of foreign, Swedish. Handsome woman, once.'

'He's takin' them two at a time,' the constable said. 'You almost have to admire him, the Devil.'

Everybody left again, for the second or third time, the crowd melting away from the Hall. Geneviève was alone in the quiet of the dawn. After a while, each fresh atrocity just added to an awful monotony. Lily had bled her dry. She had nothing more to feel. No grief left for Liz Stride or Cathy Eddowes.

As the sun rose, she fell into a doze in her chair. She was tired of keeping things together. She knew what would happen later. It had been getting worse with each murder. A troupe of whores would call, mainly in hysterical tears, begging for money to escape from the death-trap of Whitechapel. In truth, the district had been a death-trap long before the Ripper silvered his knives.

In her half-dream, Geneviève was warm again, heart afire with anger and pain, eyes hot with righteous tears. A year before the Dark Kiss, she had cried herself empty at the news from Rouen. The English had burned Jeanne d'Arc, slandering her as a witch. At fourteen, Geneviève swore herself to the cause of the dauphin. It was a war of children, carried to bloody extremes by their guardians. Jeanne never saw her nineteenth birthday, Dauphin Charles was in his teens; even Henry of England was a child. Their quarrels should have been settled with spinning-tops, not armies and sieges. Not only were the boy-kings now dead, so were their houses. Today's France, a country as strange to her as Mongolia, did not even have a monarch. If some of the English blood of Henry IV still flowed in Victoria's German veins, then it was also liable to have filtered down to most of the world, to Lily Mylett and Cathy Eddowes and John Jago and Arthur Morrison.

There was a commotion – *another* commotion – in the receiving rooms, Geneviève was expecting more injuries during the day. After the murders, there would be street brawls, vigilante victims, maybe even a lynching in the American style . . .

Four uniformed policemen were in the hallway, something heavy slung in an oilcloth between them. Lestrade was chewing his whiskers. The coppers had had to fight their way through hostile crowds. 'It's as if he's laughin' at us,' one of them said, 'stirrin' them all up against us.'

With the police was a new-born girl in smoked glasses and practical clothes, tagging along, looking hungry. Geneviève thought she might be one of the reporters.

'Mademoiselle Dieudonné, clear a private room.'

'Inspector – '

'Don't argue, just do it. One of them's still alive.'

She understood at once and checked her charts. She realized immediately that there was an empty room.

They followed her, straining under their awkward burden, and she let them into Lily's room. She shifted the tiny bundle and the policemen manoeuvred their baggage into its place, pulling away the oilcloth. Skinny legs flopped over the end of the cot, skirt-edge trailing on odd stockings.

'Mademoiselle Dieudonné, meet Long Liz Stride.'

The new-born was tall and thin, rouge smeared on her cheeks, hair a tatty black. Under an open jacket, she wore a cotton shift, dyed red in a splash from neckline to waist. Her throat was opened to the bone, cut from ear to ear like a clown's smile. She was gurgling, her cut pipes trying to mesh.

'Jackie Boy didn't have enough time with her,' Lestrade explained. 'Saved it all up for Cathy Eddowes. Warm bastard.'

Liz Stride tried to yell, but couldn't call up air from her lungs into her throat. A draught whispered through her wound. Her teeth were gone but for sharp incisors. Her limbs convulsed like galvanized frogs' legs. Two of the coppers had to hold her down.

'Hold her, Watkins,' Lestrade said. 'Hold her head still.'

One of the constables tried to get a hold on Liz Stride's head, but she shook it violently, ripping apart her wound even as it tried to mend.

'She won't last,' Geneviève told him. 'She's too far gone.'

An older or stronger vampire might have survived – Geneviève had herself lived through worse – but Liz Stride was a new-born and had been turned too late in life. She'd been dying for years, poisoning herself with rough gin.

'She doesn't have to last, she just has to give a statement.'

'Inspector, I don't know that she *can* talk. I believe her vocal cords have been severed.'

Lestrade's rat-eyes glittered. Liz Stride was his first chance at the Ripper, and he did not want to let her go.

'I think her mind's lost too, poor thing,' Geneviève said. There was nothing in the red eyes to suggest intelligence. The human part of the new-born had been burned away.

The door was pushed in and people crowded through. Lestrade turned to shout 'Out!' at them but swallowed his command.

'Mr Beauregard, sir,' he said.

The well-dressed man Geneviève had seen at Lulu Schön's inquest came into the room, with Dr Seward in his wake. There were more people – nurses, attendants – in the corridor. Amworth slipped in and stood against the wall. Geneviève would want her to look at the new-born.

'Inspector,' Beauregard said. 'May I . . .'

'Always a pleasure to help the Diogenes Club,' said Lestrade, his tone suggesting it was rather more of a pleasure to pour caustic soda into one's own eyes.

The man nodded a greeting to the new-born girl, acknowledging her with her name, 'Kate'. She stood out of his way, eyes lowered. If she wasn't in love with Beauregard, Geneviève would be very surprised. He slid between the constables with an elegant movement, polite but forceful. He flicked his cloak over his shoulders, to give his arms freedom of movement.

'Good God,' he said. 'Can nothing be done for this poor wretch?'

Geneviève was strangely impressed. Beauregard was the first person who had said anything to suggest he thought Liz Stride was worth doing something for, rather than a person something ought to be done about.

'It's too late,' Geneviève explained. 'She's trying to renew herself, but her injuries are too great, her reserves of strength too meagre . . .'

The torn flesh around Liz Stride's open throat swarmed, but failed to knit. Her convulsions were more regular now.

'Dr Seward?' Beauregard said, asking for a second opinion.

The director approached the bucking, thrashing woman. She had not noticed his return, but assumed the news must have dragged him back to the Hall. Geneviève saw again that he had a distaste – almost always held tightly in check – for vampires.

'Geneviève is right, I'm afraid. Poor creature. I have silver salts upstairs. We could ease her passing. It would be the kindest course.'

'Not until she gives us answers,' Lestrade interrupted.

'Heaven's sake, man,' Beauregard countered. 'She's a human being, not a clue.'

'The next will be a human being too, sir. Maybe we can save the next. The next ones.'

Seward touched Liz Stride's forehead and looked into her eyes, which were red marbles. He shook his head. In an instant, the wounded new-born was possessed of a surge of strength. She threw off Constable Watkins and lunged for the director, jaws open wide. Geneviève pushed Seward out of the way and ducked to avoid Liz Stride's slashing talons.

'She's changing,' Kate shouted.

Liz Stride reared up, backbone curving, limbs drawing in. A wolfish snout grew out of her face, and swathes of hair ran over her exposed skin.

Seward crab-walked backwards to the wall. Lestrade called his men out of danger. Beauregard was reaching under his cloak for something. Kate had a knuckle in her mouth.

Liz Stride was trying to become a wolf or a dog. As Mrs Amworth said, it was a hard trick. It took immense concentration and a strong sense of one's own self. Not the resources available to a gin-soaked mind, or to a new-born in mortal pain.

'Hellfire,' Watkins said.

Liz Stride's lower jaw stuck out like an alligator's, too large to fix properly to her skull. Her right leg and arm shrivelled while her left side bloated, slabs of muscle forming around the bone. Her bloody clothes tore. The wound in her throat mended over and reformed, new yellow teeth shining at the edges of the cut. A taloned foot lashed out and tore into Watkins's uniformed chest. The half-creature yelped screeches out of its neck-hole. She leaped, pushing through policemen, and landed in a clump, then scrabbled across the floor, one powerfully razored hand reaching for Seward.

'Aside,' Beauregard ordered.

The man from the Diogenes Club held a revolver. He thumb-cocked and took careful aim. Liz Stride turned, and looked up at the barrel.

'That's useless,' Amworth protested.

Liz Stride sprung into the air. Beauregard pulled the trigger. His shot took her in the heart and slammed her back against the wall. She fell, lifeless, on to Seward, her body gradually reverting to what it had been.

Geneviève looked a question at Beauregard.

'Silver bullet,' he explained, without pride.

'Charles,' Kate breathed, awed. Geneviève thought the girl might faint, but she didn't.

Seward stood up, wiping the blood from his face. Lips pressed into a white line, he was shaking, barely repressing disgust.

'Well, you've finished the Ripper's business, and that's a fact,' Lestrade muttered.

'I'm not complainin',' said the gash-chested Watkins.

Geneviève bent over the corpse and confirmed Liz Stride's death. With a last convulsion, an arm – still part-wolfish – sprang out, and claws fastened in Seward's trouser-cuff.

25

A Walk in Whitechapel

'I THINK AT the last she was lucid,' he said. 'She was trying to tell us something.'

'What do you suggest?' Geneviève replied. 'The murderer's name is . . . Sydney Trousers?'

Beauregard laughed, Not many of the un-dead bothered with humour.

'Unlikely,' he replied, 'Mr Boot, perhaps.'

'Or a boot-maker.'

'I have impeccable cause to believe John Pizer out of consideration.'

The corpse had been carted off to the mortuary, where the medical and press vultures were hungrily awaiting. Kate Reed was at the Café de Paris, telephoning in her story, under strict instructions not to mention his name. Drawing attention to the Diogenes Club would be bad enough, but he was really concerned with Penelope. He could well imagine her comments if his part in the last minutes of Liz Stride were made public. This was a different part of the woods, a different part of the city, a different part of his life. Penelope did not live here; and would prefer not to know of its existence.

He walked the distance between Berner Street and Mitre Square. The vampire from Toynbee Hall tagged along, less bothered than Kate had been yesterday by the pale sun. In daylight, Geneviève Dieudonné was quite appealing. She dressed like a New Woman, in tight jacket and simple dress, with sensible flat-heeled boots, beret-like cap and waist-length cape. If Great Britain had an elected parliament in a year's time, she would want the vote; and, he suspected, she would not be voting for Lord Ruthven.

They arrived at the site of the Eddowes murder. Mitre Square was an enclosed area by the Great Synagogue, accessible through two narrow passages. The entrances were roped off, the bloody patch guarded by a warm policeman. A few onlookers loitered, intent on filling out a suspects file. An Orthodox Jew, ringlets dangling in front of his ears, beard down to his belly, was trying to get some of these undesirables to stop hanging about the doors of the Synagogue.

Beauregard lifted the rope and let Geneviève pass. He showed his card to the policeman, who saluted. Geneviève looked around the dreary square.

'The Ripper must be a sprinter,' she said.

Beauregard checked his half-hunter. 'We bested his time by five minutes, but we knew where we were going. He may not have taken the shortest route, especially if his intent was to avoid the main roads. He was presumably just looking for a girl.'

'And a private place.'

'It's not terribly private here.'

There were faces behind the windows in the court, looking down.

'In Whitechapel, people are practised at not seeing things.'

Geneviève was prowling the tiny walled-in court, as if trying to get the feel of the place.

'This is perfect, public but private. Ideal for the practice of alfresco harlotry.'

'You're unlike other vampires,' he observed.

'No,' she agreed. 'I should hope to be.'

'Are you what they call an elder?'

She tapped her heart. 'Sweet sixteen in here, but I was born in 1416.'

Beauregard was puzzled. 'Then you're not . . .'

'Not of the Prince Consort's bloodline? Quite right. My father-in-darkness was Chandagnac, and his mother-in-darkness was Lady Melissa d'Acques, and – '

'So all this – ' he waved his hand '– is nothing to do with you?'

'Everything is to do with everyone, Mr Beauregard. Vlad Tepes is a sick monster and his get spread his sickness. That poor woman this morning is what you can expect of his bloodline.'

'You work as a physician?'

She shrugged. 'I've picked up many professions over the years. I've been a whore, a soldier, a singer, a geographer, a criminal. Whatever has seemed best. Now, doctoring seems best. My father, my true father, was a doctor, and I his apprentice. Elizabeth Garrett Anderson and Sophia Jex-Blake aren't the first women ever to practise medicine, you know.'

'Things have changed greatly since the fifteenth century.'

'So I understand. I read something about it in *The Lancet*. I wouldn't consider leeches, except in special cases.'

Beauregard found himself liking this ancient girl. Geneviève was unlike any of the women, warm or un-dead, he knew. Whether by choice or from necessity, women seemed to stand to one side, watching, passing comment, never acting. He thought of Florence Stoker, pretending to understand the clever people she entertained, turning petulant whenever anything was not done for her. And Penelope elevated an attitude of non-involvement to a sanctified cause, insisting that messy details be kept from her poor head. Even Kate Reed, new and new-born, contented herself with jotting down notes on life as an alternative to living it. Geneviève Dieudonné was not a spectator. She reminded him a little of Pamela. Pamela had always wanted, *demanded* to be involved.

'Is this affair political?'

Beauregard thought carefully before answering. He did not know how much he should tell her.

'I've made enquiries about the Diogenes Club,' she explained. 'You're some species of government office, are you not?'

'I serve the Crown.'

'Why your interest in this matter?'

Geneviève stood over the splash where Catharine Eddowes had died. The policeman looked the other way. A vampire had been at him to judge from the red marks streaking up from his collar almost to his ear.

'The Queen herself has expressed concern. If she decrees we try to catch a murderer, then . . .'

'The Ripper might be an anarchist of some stripe,' she mused. 'Or a die-hard vampire hater.'

'The latter is certain.'

'Why is everyone so sure the Ripper is warm?' Geneviève asked.

'The victims were all vampires.'

'So are a lot of people. The victims were also all women, all prostitutes, all near-destitutes. There could be any number of connecting factors. The Ripper always goes for the throat; that's a *nosferatu* trick.'

The policeman was getting fidgety. Geneviève disturbed him. Beauregard suspected she had that effect on not a few.

He countered her theory. 'As far as we can tell from the autopsies, the dead women were not bitten, not bled. Besides, as vampires, their blood would not interest another vampire.'

'That's not entirely true, Mr Beauregard. We become what we are by drinking the blood of another vampire. It is uncommon but we do tap each other. Sometimes it is a way of establishing dominance within a group, a petty tyrant demanding a tithe from his followers. Sometimes vampire blood can be a curative for those with debased bloodlines. And sometimes, of course, mutual bleeding can be simply a sexual act, like any other . . .'

Beauregard blushed at her forthrightness. The policeman was scarlet-faced, rubbing his angry wounds.

'The bloodline of Vlad Tepes is polluted,' she continued. 'One would have to be addle-pated with disease to drink from such a well. But London is full of very sick vampires. The Ripper could as easily be of their number as be some warm grudge-holder.'

'He could also be after the women's blood because he himself wants to become un-dead. You've the fountain of youth flowing in your veins. If our Ripper is warm but sick, he might be desperate enough to seek such measures.'

'There are easier ways of becoming a vampire. Of course, a lot of people distrust easy ways. Your suggestion has some merit. But why so many victims? One mother-in-darkness would suffice. And why murder? Any one of the women would have turned him for a shilling.'

They left the square and began drifting back towards Commercial Street. The thoroughfare was at the centre of the case. Annie Chapman and Lulu Schön had been killed in streets off the road. The police station from which the investigation was being conducted was there, and the Café de Paris, and Toynbee Hall. Last night, at some point, the Ripper must have crossed Commercial Street, and perhaps even have strolled, bloody knife under his coat, along its extension south of Whitechapel High Street, the Commercial Road, following his own route to Limehouse and the docks. There was a persistent rumour that the murderer was a seaman.

'Maybe he's a simple madman,' he said. 'Possessed of no more purpose than an orang-utan with a straight razor.'

'Dr Seward claims madmen are not so simple. Their actions might appear random and senseless, but there is always some pattern. Come at it from a dozen different ways and you eventually begin to understand, to see the world as the madman does.'

'And then we can catch him?'

'Dr Seward would say "cure him".'

They passed a poster listing the names of the latest criminals to be publically impaled. Tyburn was a forest of dying thieves, exquisites and seditionists.

Beauregard considered. 'I'm afraid there'll only be one cure for this madman.'

At the corner of Wentworth Street, they saw a gathering of policemen and officials in Goulston Street. Lestrade and Abberline were among them, clustered around a thin man with a sad moustache and a silk hat. It was Sir Charles Warren, the Commissioner of the Metropolitan Police, dragged down to a despised quarter of his parish. The group were standing by the doorway of a block of recently built Model Dwellings.

Beauregard sauntered over, the vampire girl with him. Something important, he assumed, was under discussion. Lestrade moved aside to let them into the group. Beauregard was surprised to find Lord Godalming with the civilian dignitaries. The new-born wore a large hat to shade his face, and was puffing on a cigar.

'Who is this man?' Sir Charles asked grumpily, indicating Beauregard and ignoring Geneviève as beneath his notice. 'You, fellow, go away. This is official business. Chop-chop, scurry off!'

Having made his reputation in the Kaffir War, Sir Charles was used to treating everyone without official rank as if they were a native.

Godalming explained: 'Mr Beauregard represents the Diogenes Club.'

The Commissioner, watery-eyed in the early morning sun, swallowed his irritation. Beauregard understood why the police resented his presence, but was not above taking a little pleasure in Sir Charles's discomfort.

'Very well,' Sir Charles said. 'I am sure your discretion is to be trusted.'

Lestrade made a disgusted face behind the Commissioner. Sir Charles was losing the support of his own men.

'Halse,' Lestrade said, 'show us what you found.'

A square of packing-case rested against the fascia by the doorway. Halse, a detective constable, lifted the make shift guard. A bloated rat, its body as big as a rugby ball, shot out and darted between the Commissioner's polished shoes, squeaking like rusty nails on a slate. The constable disclosed a chalk scrawl, grey-white against black bricks.

THE VAMPYRES
ARE NOT THE MEN THAT WILL BE
BLAMED FOR NOTHING

'So, obviously the vampires are to be blamed for something,' deduced the Commissioner, astutely.

Halse held up a ragged piece of once-white cloth, spotted with blood. 'This was in the doorway, sir. It's part of an apron.'

'The Eddowes woman is wearing the rest of it,' Abberline said.

'You are certain?' Sir Charles asked.

'It's not been checked. But I've just come from Golden Lane Mortuary, and I saw the other piece. Same stains, same type of tear. They'll fit like puzzle pieces.'

Sir Charles rumbled worldessly.

'Could the Ripper be one of us?' asked Godalming, echoing Geneviève's earlier musings.

'One of you,' Beauregard muttered.

'The Ripper is obviously trying to throw us off,' put in Abberline. 'That's an educated man trying to make us think he's an illiterate. Only one misspelling, and a double negative not even the thickest costermonger would actually use.'

'Like the Jack the Ripper letter?' asked Geneviève.

Abberline thought. 'Personally, I reckon that was a smart circulation drummer at the *Whitechapel Star* playing silly buggers to drive up sales. This is a different hand, and this is the Ripper. It's too close to be a coincidence.'

'The graffito was not here yesterday?' Beauregard asked.

'The beat man swears not.'

Constable Halse agreed with the inspector.

'Wipe it off,' Sir Charles said.

Nobody did anything.

'There'll be mob rule, a mass uprising, disorder in the streets. We're still few and the warm are many.'

The Commissioner took his own handkerchief to the chalk, and rubbed it away. Nobody protested at the destruction of evidence, but Beauregard saw a look pass between the detectives.

'There, job done,' Sir Charles said. 'Sometimes I think I have to do everything myself.'

Beauregard saw a narrow-minded impulsiveness that might have passed for stout-hearted valour at Rorke's Drift or Lucknow, and understood just how Sir Charles could make a decision that ended in Bloody Sunday.

The dignitaries drifted away, back to their cabs and clubs and comfort.

'Shall I see you and Penny at the Stokers'?' Godalming asked.

'When this matter is at a conclusion.'

'Give my kindest regards to Penny.'

'I'll be sure to.'

Godalming followed Sir Charles. And the East End coppers stayed behind to clean up.

'It should have been photographed,' Halse said. 'It was a clue, dammit, a clue.'

'Easy, lad,' said Abberline.

'Right,' said Lestrade. 'I want the cells full by sundown. Haul in every tart, every ponce, every bruiser, every dipper. Threaten 'em with whatever you want. Someone knows something, and sooner or later, someone'll talk.'

That would please the Limehouse Ring not a bit. Furthermore, Lestrade was wrong. Beauregard had a high enough estimation of the criminal community to believe that if any felon in London had so much as a hint of the identity of the Ripper, it would have passed directly to him. He had received several telegrams, indicating which avenues of inquiry would prove fruitless. The shadow empire had ruled out several investigative threads the police still pursued. It was perhaps disquieting to consider that the group in Limehouse had a higher percentage of first-rate minds than that which had just gathered in Goulston Street.

With Geneviève, he walked back towards Commercial Street. It was late afternoon already, and he had not slept in over a day and a half. Paper-boys were hawking special editions. With a signed letter from the killer and two fresh murders, the hysteria for news was at a peak.

'What do you think of Warren?' Geneviève asked.

Beauregard considered it best not to confide his opinion, but she understood it exactly in an instant. She was one of *those* vampires, and he would have to be careful what he thought in her company.

'Me, too,' she said. 'Precisely the wrong man for the position. Ruthven should know that. Still, better him than a Carpathian maniac.'

Puzzled, he put a suggestion to her. 'To hear you, one would think you prejudiced against vampires.'

'Mr Beauregard, I find myself surrounded by the Prince Consort's get. It's too late to complain, but Vlad Tepes hardly represents the best of my kind. No one dislikes a Jewish or Italian degenerate more than a Jew or an Italian.'

Beauregard found himself alone with Geneviève as the sun set. She took off her cap.

'There,' she said, shaking out her honey-coloured hair, 'that's better.'

Geneviève seemed to stretch like a cat in the sun. He could sense her increasing strength. Her eyes sparkled a little, and her smile became almost sly.

'By the way, who is Penny?' she asked.

Beauregard wondered what Penelope was doing exactly now. He had not seen her since their argument of a few days ago.

'Miss Penelope Churchward, my fiancée.'

He could not read Geneviève's expression but fancied her eyes narrowed a shade. He tried to think of nothing.

'Fiancée? It won't last.'

He was shocked by her effrontery.

'I'm sorry, Mr Beauregard. But believe me, I know this. Nothing lasts.'

26

Musings and Mutilations

2 OCTOBER

I feel their hot breath on my neck. Had Beauregard not finished her, Stride would have identified me. Others must have seen me about my nightwork: between Stride and Eddowes, I ran through the streets in a panic, bloodied and with a scalpel in my fist. I came close to being caught. I'd just begun work on Stride, when a cart thundered by. The horse snorted Hell clearing its throat. I bolted, sure the Carpathian Guards were at my heels. By some miracle, the carter never saw me. According to *The Times*, my 'person from Porlock' was Louis Diemschütz, one of the Jewish-socialist crew who congregate around the International Workingmen's Educational Club. With Eddowes, I was more fortunate. I'd calmed down enough to conduct business with her. She knew and trusted me. That helped greatly. With her, the delivery was successful.

Indeed, I think the Eddowes delivery my greatest achievement to date. At its conclusion, I was calmed. To throw my pursuers off the scent, I left a message on a wall. I walked back to the Hall, changed my clothes in good time, and was ready to meet the police when they arrived. All things considered, I carried off the unpleasantness with Stride well. Beauregard's steady eye and silver bullet finished my work. I feel better in myself than in some months. The pain in my hand has abated. I wonder if this is not an effect of the bleeding. Since Kelly tapped me, the pain has been receding. I've looked Kelly up in our files, and have an address for her off Dorset Street. I must seek her out and again solicit her attentions.

There are so many fabulations about the Ripper, fuelled by silly notes to the press, that I can hide unnoticed among them, even if the occasional rumour strikes uncomfortably close. After all, my name *is* Jack.

Today, a patient, an uneducated immigrant named David Cohen, confessed to me that he was Jack the Ripper. I turned him over to the police and he has been removed in a strait-waistcoat to Colney Hatch. Lestrade showed me the file of similar confessions. A queue of cranks waits to claim credit for my deliveries. And somewhere out there is the letter-writer, chortling over his silly red ink and arch jokes.

'Yours truly, Jack the Ripper'? Is the letter-writer someone I know? Does he know anything about me? No, he does not understand my mission. I am not a lunatic practical joker. I am a surgeon, cutting away diseased tissue. There is no 'jolly wouldn't you' to it.

I worry about Geneviève. Other vampires have a kind of red fog in their brains, but she is different. I read a piece by Frederick Treves in *The Lancet*, speculating on the business of bloodline, as delicately as possible suggesting that there might be something impure about the royal strain the Prince Consort has imported. So many of Dracula's get are twisted, self-destructing creatures, torn apart by changing bodies and uncontrollable desires. Royal blood, of course, is notoriously thin. Geneviève is sharp as a scalpel. Sometimes she knows what people are thinking. With her, I try to keep my mind on my patients, on schedules and timetables. There are traps in any train of thought: thinking of the injuries I treated in a new-born who was run down by a carriage reminds me of the injuries I have inflicted on other new-borns. No, not injuries. Cuts. Surgical cuts. There is no malice, no hate, in what I do.

With Lucy, there was love. Here, there is only the cool of medical procedure. Van Helsing would have understood. I think of Kelly, of our bestial moments together. She is so like the Lucy that was. As I remember the feelings in my skin, my mouth dries. I become aroused. The bites Kelly made itch. The itch is pain and pleasure at once. With the itch comes a need, a complicated need. It is unlike the simple craving for morphine I have experienced when the hurt gets too much to bear. It is a need for Kelly's kisses. But there is so much wrapped up in the need, so many thirsts.

I know what I do is right. I was right to save Lucy by cutting off her head and I have been right to deliver the others. Nichols, Chapman, Schön, Stride, Eddowes. I am right. But I shall stop. I am an alienist, and Kelly has made me turn my gaze back upon myself.

Is my behaviour so different from Renfield's, amassing tiny deaths as a miser hoards pennies? The Count made a freak of him as he has made a monster of me. And I *am* a monster, Jack the Ripper, Saucy Jack, Red Jack, Bloody Jack. I shall be classed with Sweeney Todd, Sawney Beane, Mrs Manning, the Face at the Window, Jonathan Wild: endlessly served up in *Famous Crimes: Past and Present*. Already, there are penny dreadfuls; soon, there will be music hall turns, sensational melodramas, a wax likeness in Tussaud's Chamber of Horrors. I meant to destroy a monster, not become one.

27

Dr Jekyll and Dr Moreau

'MY DEAR MLLE Dieudonné,' read the note, delivered by the estimable Ned, 'I have a call to make in connection with our enquiries, and should like a vampire with me. Could you make yourself available this evening? A cab will be sent to Whitechapel for your use. More later. Beauregard.'

As it eventuated, the cab contained Charles Beauregard himself, freshly shaved and dressed, hat in his lap, cane at his side. He was becoming accustomed to vampire hours, she realized, sleeping by day and thriving by night. He gave the cabby an address in the city. The hansom shifted pleasantly on its springs as it made its way out of the East End.

'Nothing is so reassuring as the interior of a hansom cab,' Charles declared. 'It is a miniature fortress on wheels, a womb of comfort in the dark.'

Considering her companion's evident inclination towards poetic thought, Geneviève was thankful she had taken care with her attire. She would not pass at the Palace, but her costume was at least not designed to radiate hostility to the male sex. She had bothered with a velvet cape and matching choker. She had spent some extra time brushing her hair, and now wore it loose about her shoulders. Jack Seward told her the arrangement was pleasing, and, denied the vain pleasures of a looking-glass, she would have to take his word.

'You seem different this evening,' Charles commented.

She smiled, trying to keep her teeth from showing. 'It's this dress, I'm afraid. I can hardly breathe.'

'I thought you didn't need to breathe.'

'That's a common fallacy. Somehow, those who know nothing are able to maintain entirely irreconcilable beliefs. On the one hand, vampires can be detected because they do not breathe. On the other, vampires have the rankest breath imaginable.'

'You are right, of course. That had never occurred to me.'

'We are natural beings, like any others,' she explained. 'There's no magic.'

'What about the business with mirrors?'

That was the thing they always came down to, the business with mirrors. No one had an explanation for that.

'Maybe a little magic,' she said, holding her thumb and forefinger nearly together. 'Just a touch.'

Charles smiled, a thing he did rarely. It improved his looks. There was something closed in the back of Charles Beauregard's mind. She could not truly read thoughts, but she was sensitive. Charles was intent on keeping his mind private. Not a trick that came naturally; his life in the service of the Diogenes Club must have taught it him. Her impression was that this courteous gentleman was an old hand at keeping secrets.

'Have you seen the newspapers?' he asked. 'There has been another communiqué from Jack the Ripper. A postcard.'

'"*Double event this time*",' she quoted.

'Quite. "*Had not time to get ears for police*".'

'Didn't he try to sever Cathy's ear?'

Beauregard had obviously memorized Dr Gordon Brown's report. 'There was some such injury, but it was probably incidental. Her face was extensively mutilated. Even if our letter-writer is not the murderer, he may have an inside source of information.'

'Like whom? A journalist?'

'That is a possibility. The fact that the letters were sent to the Central News Agency, and therefore available to all the newspapers, is unusual. Few outside the press even know what a news agency is. If the letters had been sent to a specific periodical, then individual journalists would benefit from the "scoop".'

'And also fall under suspicion?'

'Precisely.'

They were in the city now. Wide, well-lit streets, houses far enough apart to allow for grassy spaces and trees. Everything was so much cleaner here. Although in one square Geneviève noticed three bodies spitted on stakes. Children played hide-and-seek in the bushes around the impaled, red-eyed little vampires seeking out their plump playfellows and giving them affectionate nips with sharpening teeth.

'Upon whom are we calling?' she asked.

'Someone of whom you will approve. Dr Henry Jekyll.'

'The research scientist? He was at Lulu Schön's inquest.'

'That's the fellow. He has no gods but Darwin and Huxley. No magic at all is admitted past his doorstep. And, speaking of Dr Jekyll's doorstep, I should hope that this is it.'

The cab stopped. Charles climbed out and helped her down. She remembered to gather her dress and steady herself as she was extricated from the hansom. He told the cabby to wait.

They were in a square of ancient, handsome houses, now for the most part decayed from high estate and let in flats and chambers to all sorts and conditions of men: map-engravers, architects, Carpathians, shady lawyers, and the agents of obscure enterprises. One house, however, second from the corner, was still occupied entire; and at the door of this, which wore a great air of wealth and comfort though it was now in darkness except for the fan-light, Charles knocked. An elderly servant opened the door. Charles presented his card, which Geneviève gathered was a free pass to every dwelling or institution in the country.

'And this is Miss Dieudonné,' Charles explained, 'the elder.'

The servant took note, and admitted the visitors into a large, low-roofed, comfortable hall, paved with flags, warmed after the fashion of a country house by a bright, open fire, and furnished with costly cabinets of oak.

'Dr Jekyll is in his laboratory with the other gentleman, sir,' the servant said. 'I shall announce you.'

He vanished into another part of the house, leaving Geneviève and Charles in the hall. In the dark, she could see more clearly. There were strange shapes in the flickering of the firelight on the polished cabinets and the uneasy starting of the shadow on the ceiling.

'Dr Jekyll obviously doesn't believe in the incandescent lamp,' she commented.

'It's an old house.'

'I expected a man of science to live among the shining apparatus of the future, not lurk in the dark of the past.'

Charles shrugged, and leaned on his cane. The servant returned, and led them to the back of the house. They passed through a covered courtyard, and came to a well-lit building which abutted

Jekyll's house back-to-back. A red–baize door hung open and voices came from within.

Charles stood aside, and let her enter. The laboratory was a high-ceilinged space like an operating theatre, its walls covered with bookshelves and charts; there were tables and benches set up all around with intricate arrangements of retorts, tubes and burners. The place smelled strongly of soap, but other scents were not quite obliterated by regular scrubbing.

'Poole, thank you,' said Jekyll, dismissing his servant, who retreated to the main house with what Geneviève fancied was relief. The master had been in conversation with a broad-shouldered, prematurely white-haired man.

'Mr Beauregard, welcome,' Jekyll said. 'And Miss Dieudonné.'

He bowed slightly and wiped his hands on his leather apron, leaving smears of some substance.

'This is my colleague, Dr Moreau.'

The white-haired man raised a hand in greeting. Geneviève's impression was that she would not care for Dr Moreau.

'We have been talking of blood.'

'A subject of much interest,' Charles ventured.

'Indeed. Of paramount interest. Moreau has radical notions on the classification of blood.'

The two scientists had been standing by a bench upon which was unrolled a length of oilcoth. Spread on the cloth was an arrangement of dust and bone fragments roughly in the shape of a man: a curved piece that might have been a forehead, some yellow teeth, a few staves that suggested ribs, and a great quantity of crumbly red-grey matter which she regretted that she had cause to recognize.

'This was a vampire,' Geneviève said. 'An elder?'

A new-born would not decay so completely. Chandagnac had turned to ashes like these. He had been over four hundred at the time of his destruction.

'We were lucky,' Jekyll explained. 'Count Vardalek committed an offence against the Prince Consort and was executed. As soon as I had word of the case, I made an application for his remains. The opportunity has proved invaluable.'

'Vardalek?'

Jekyll waved away the name. 'A Carpathian, I believe.'

'I knew him.'

Jekyll, for a moment, was jarred out of his scientific enthusiasm. 'I am profoundly sorry, you must forgive me my lack of tact . . .'

'It is perfectly all right,' she said, imagining the Hungarian's painted face stretched over the skull remnants. 'We were not intimates.'

'We must study vampire physiology,' Moreau said. 'There are numerous points of interest.'

Charles was looking around the laboratory, peering casually at experiments in process. Sludge dripped into a beaker in front of his face, and fizzed into purple foam.

'You see,' Jekyll said to Moreau. 'The precipitate reacts normally.'

The white-haired scientist made no reply. Evidently, a point had been scored against him.

'Our concerns,' Charles began, 'are not so much scientific as criminal. We have been following the Whitechapel murders. The Jack the Ripper affair.'

Jekyll gave nothing away.

'You have yourself taken an interest? Attended inquests, and so forth?'

Jekyll conceded that he had, but volunteered no more.

'Have you formed conclusions?'

'About the murderer? Very few. It is my contention that we are all of us, if freed from the restraints of civilized behaviour, capable of any extreme.'

'Man is inherently a brute,' Moreau said. 'It is his secret strength.'

Moreau made hairy fists. It occurred to Geneviève that the scientist was physically enormously strong. There was something almost of the ape about his physique. It would be nothing to him to cut a throat or perform a swift dissection, dragging a silver blade through resisting meat, sawing apart bones.

'My concern,' Jekyll continued, 'is with the victims. The new-borns. Most of them are dying, you know.'

Geneviève did.

'Vampires are potentially immortal. But they are fragile immortals. Something inside drives them to self-destruction.'

'It's the shape-shifters,' Moreau said. 'They are evolution run backwards, an atavism. Mankind stands atop of the parabola of

life on earth; the vampire represents the step over the prow, the
first footfall on the path of regression to savagery.'

'Dr Moreau,' she said, 'if I understand you, I might be offended.'

Jekyll cut in. 'Ah, but Miss Dieudonné, you should not be.
You are the most interesting case imaginable. By your continued
existence, you demonstrate that vampires need not be retrograde
steps on the evolutionary ladder. I should like to examine you
properly. It is conceivable that you could be humanity perfected.'

'I do not feel like anyone's ideal.'

'Nor will you until you have a perfect world about you. If
we could determine the factors that differentiate an elder from a
new-born, we might eliminate much wastage of life.'

'New-borns are like young turtles,' Moreau said. 'Hundreds
hatch, but only a few crawl from sand to sea without being picked
off by sea-birds.'

Charles was listening intently, allowing her to quiz the scientists.
She wished she knew what he wanted to learn from them.

'Without wanting to contradict the pleasing suggestion that I
might be the culmination of a divine scheme, surely general
scientific opinion is that vampires do not constitute a separate
species of humanity but rather are a parasitical outgrowth of our
family tree, existing only by virtue of sustenance stolen from our
warm cousins?'

Jekyll looked almost angry beneath his mildness. 'I find it
disappointing that you entertain such outdated notions.'

'I merely entertain them, doctor. I should not ask them to move
into my house.'

'She's just drawing an argument out of you, Harry,' Moreau
explained.

'Of course, forgive me. To answer simply: vampires are no more
parasites for feeding off the blood of human beings than human
beings are parasites for feeding off the flesh of beef cattle.'

Geneviève's red thirst tickled the back of her throat. She had slept
the last few days away, and must feed soon or grow weak.

'Some of us call you "cattle". This dusty gentleman here was
known to employ the term.'

'It is understandable.'

'Vardalek was an arrogant Carpathian swine, doctor. I assure you
I hold the warm in no such contempt.'

'I'm glad to hear it,' put in Charles.

'Neither of you have chosen to seek the Dark Kiss?' she said. 'Surely, in the name of research, that would be a logical step.'

Jekyll shook his head. 'We wish to study the phenomenon at greater length. The vampire condition may be a cure for death, but in nine out of ten cases it is also a deadly poison.'

'Considering the vital import of the field, it has been shockingly neglected,' Moreau said. 'Dom Augustin Calmet is still cited as the standard reference . . .'

Calmet was the author of *A Treatise on the Vampires of Hungary and the Surrounding Regions*, first published in 1746, a collection of half-confirmed incidents and roughly embroidered folk tales.

'Even the late and ill-remembered Professor Van Helsing was at bottom a follower of Calmet,' Jekyll said.

'You gentlemen wish to be the Gallileo and Newton of the study of vampirism?'

'Reputation is not important,' Moreau said. 'Any buffoon can buy one. Look at the Royal Society, and recognize them, warm or un-dead, for a pack of bald-pate baboons. In science, proof is vital. And soon we shall have proof.'

'Proof of what?'

'Of the human potential for perfection, Miss Dieudonné,' said Jekyll. 'You are well-named. You might indeed be God-given. If we could all be as you . . .'

'If we were all vampires, upon whom would vampires feed?'

'Why, we would import Africans or South Sea Islanders,' Moreau said, as if pointing out to a dunderhead that the sky was blue. 'Or raise lesser beasts to human form. If vampires can shift their shapes, so can other creatures.'

'There are African vampires, Dr Moreau. Prince Mamuwalde is much respected. Even in the South Seas, I have kin and kind . . .'

Geneviève saw an unhealthy light behind Jekyll's eyes. Its twin could be observed in the eager look of Moreau: the lust of Prometheus, the desire for a consuming flame of knowledge.

'What a cold, dark, silence perfection would be,' Geneviève said. 'I imagine an ultimate universal improvement would be something very like death.'

28

Pamela

'I SEEM SUDDENLY to have developed a warm, almost affectionate, feeling for Dom Augustin Calmet,' Geneviève said. Beauregard was amused.

In the cab on the way back to Whitechapel, she was close beside him, Clayton, engaged for the night, knew where they were going. After his unexpected trip to Limehouse, Beauregard was happy to be driven about London by someone he knew to be in the employ of the Diogenes Club.

'Many brilliant men struck their contemporaries as mad.'

'I don't have any contemporaries,' she said. 'Except Vlad Tepes, and I've never met him.'

'You follow my reasoning, though?'

Geneviève's eyes flashed. 'Of course, Charles . . .'

She had the habit of using his Christian name. In another that might be unseemly, but it was absurd to insist on arbitrary rules of address with a woman old enough to be his ten-times great grandmother.

'It is possible the murders are experiments,' she continued. 'Dr Knox needed dead bodies, and wasn't too scrupulous where he got them; Dr Jekyll and Dr Moreau need un-dead bodies, and could quite conceivably not be above harvesting them from the streets of Whitechapel.'

'Moreau was mixed up in a vivisection scandal a few years ago. Something particularly revolting involving a skinned dog.'

'I can believe it. Inside his white coat, he's a cave-dweller.'

'And he is a man of some strength. Expert with the bullwhip, they say. He's knocked about the world a great deal.'

'But you don't think he's our murderer?'

Beauregard was mildly surprised to be so anticipated. 'I do not. For one thing, he is reckoned a surgeon of genius.'

'And Jack the Ripper knows his way about the insides of a body, but trawls through entrails with the finesse of a drunken pork butcher.'

'Exactly.'

He was used to having to explain his reasoning. It was refreshing, if not a little alarming, to be with someone who could keep up with him.

'Could he deliberately botch the job to throw off suspicion?,' she asked, then answering herself. 'No, if Moreau were stark mad enough to murder for an experiment, he wouldn't jeopardize his findings with intentional carelessness. If he were our Ripper, he'd abduct the victims and remove them to a private place where he could operate at his leisure.'

'The girls were all killed where they were found'

Beauregard nodded. 'And swiftly, in a frenzy. No "scientific method".'

The vampire bit her lip, and was for an instant the image of a serious sixteen-year-old in a dress made for an older and more frivolous sister. Then the ancient mind was back.

'So Dr Jekyll is your suspect?'

'He is a biological chemist, not an anatomist. I'm not at all up on the field, but I've been wrestling with his articles. He has some odd ideas. "On the Composition of Vampire Tissue" was his last piece.'

Geneviève considered the possibilities. 'It's hard to imagine, though. Next to Moreau, he seems so . . . *harmless*. He reminds me of a clergyman. And he is old. I can't picture him dashing about the streets by night, much less possessing the sheer strength the Ripper must have.'

'But there's something there.'

She thought a moment. 'Yes, you're right. There is something there. I don't think Henry Jekyll is Jack the Ripper. But there is an indefinably peculiar quality about him.'

Beauregard was grimly pleased to have his suspicions confirmed. 'He'll bear watching.'

'Charles, are you employing me as a bloodhound?'

'I suppose I am. Do you mind?'

'Woof woof,' she said, giggling. When she laughed, her upper lip drew back ferociously from sharp teeth. 'Remember not to trust me. I used to say the war would be over by winter.'

'Which war?'

'The Hundred Years War.

'Good guess.' He laughed.

'One year, I was right. By then, I didn't care any more. I think I was in Spain.'

'You were French originally. Why don't you live there?' he asked.

'France was English then. That was what they said the war was about.'

'So you were on our side?'

'Most definitely not. But it was a long time ago, and in another country, and that girl is long gone.'

'Whitechapel is a strange place to find you.'

'I'm not the only French girl in Whitechapel. Half the *filles de joie* on the streets call themselves "Fifi LaTour".'

He laughed again.

'Your family must have been French too, *Monsieur Beauregard*, and you reside in Cheyne Walk.'

'It was good enough for Carlyle.'

'I met Carlyle once. And many others. The great and the good, the mad and the bad. I used to fear someone would track me down by correlating all the mentions of me in memoirs through the ages. Track me down and destroy me. That used to be the worst that could happen. My friend Carmilla was tracked down and destroyed. She was a soppy girl, fearfully dependent on her warm lovers, but she didn't deserve to be speared and beheaded, then left to float in a coffin full of her own blood. I suppose I don't have to worry about that dread dark fate any more.'

'What have you been doing all these years?'

She shrugged. 'I don't know. Running? Waiting? Trying to do the right thing? Am I a good person, do you think? Or a bad person?'

She did not expect an answer. Her mix of melancholy and bitter came out as amusing. He supposed being amusing was her way of coping. She must be as weighted with centuries as Jacob Marley was with chains.

'Cheer up, old girl,' he said. 'Henry Jekyll thinks you're perfect.'

'Old girl?'

'It's just an expression.'

Geneviève hummed sadly. 'It's me exactly, isn't it though? An old girl.'

What was it she made him feel? He was nervous near her, but excited. It was much like being in danger, and he had trained himself to be cool under fire. When he was with Geneviève, it was like sharing a secret. What would Pamela have thought of his vampire? She had been perceptive; even with agony knifing into her, she could not be lied to. To the end, he told her that she would be all right, that she would see home again. Pamela shook away his assurances and demanded he listen. For Pamela, dying was hard: she was angry, not with the fool doctor, but with herself, angry that her body had failed her, was failing their baby. Her fury burned like a fever. Gripping her hand, he could feel it. She died with something unsaid; ever since, he had been picking at the scab, wondering if there was anything to understand, wondering what the urgent thought was, the thought Pamela was not able at the last to force into words.

'"I love you."'

'What?'

Geneviève's cheeks were dewed with tears. For once, she seemed younger than her face.

'That's what she was saying, Charles. "I love you." That's all.'

Angered, he gripped the handle of his cane and thumbed the catch. An inch of silver shone. Geneviève gasped.

'I'm sorry, I'm so sorry,' she said, leaning against him. 'I'm not like that, really. I don't pry. It's . . .' She was weeping freely, tears spotting her velvet collar. 'It was so clear, Charles,' she insisted, shaking her head and smiling at the same time. 'It came spilling from your mind. Usually, impressions are vague. For once, I had a perfect picture. I *knew*. What you felt . . . oh Lord, Charles, I'm so sorry, I didn't know what I was doing, please forgive me . . . and what *she* felt. It was a voice, cutting like a knife. What was her name?'

'Pen . . .' He swallowed. 'Pamela. My wife, Pamela.'

'Pamela. Yes, Pamela. I could hear her voice.'

Her cold hands latched upon his, forcing his cane shut. Geneviève's face was close. Red specks swam in the corners of her eyes.

'You're a medium?'

'No, no, no. You've carried the moment around with you, nurturing the hurt. It's in you, there to be read.'

He knew she was right. He should have known what Pamela was saying. He had not let himself hear. Beauregard had taken Pamela to India. He knew the risk. He should have sent her home when they found she was with child. But a crisis arose and she insisted on staying. She insisted, but he let her insist; he did not force her back to England. He was weak to let her stay. He did not deserve to understand her at the last. He did not deserve to be loved.

Geneviève was smiling through tears. 'There was no blame, Charles.

She was angry. But not with you.'

'I never thought . . .'

'Charles . . .'

'Well, I never *consciously* thought . . .'

She raised a finger and laid it against his face. Taking it away, she held it up before him. A tear stood out. He took a handkerchief, and wiped his eyes.

'I know what she was angry with, Charles. Death. Of all people, I understand. I think I would have liked, would have loved, your wife.' Geneviève touched her finger to her tongue, and shuddered slightly. Vampires could drink tears.

What Pamela would have thought of Geneviève hardly mattered. What was important, he realized with a lurch in his stomach, was what Penelope would think . . .

'I really didn't mean all this to happen,' she said. 'You must think me fearfully wet.'

She took his handkerchief, and dabbed her own eyes dry. She looked at the damp-spotted cloth. 'Well, well,' she said. 'Salt water.'

He was puzzled.

'Usually, I cry blood. It's not very attractive. All teeth and rat-tails, like a proper *nosferatu*.'

Now, he took her hand. The pain of memory was passing; somehow, he was stronger.

'Geneviève, you consistently underestimate yourself. Remember, I know for a fact that you don't know what you look like.'

'I can remember a girl with feet like a duck's, and lips that don't match. Pretty eyes, though. I'm not sure, but I hope that was my sister. Her name was Cirielle; she married the brother of a Marshal of France and died a grandmother.'

She was sharp again, in control of herself. Only the slight flush on her neck betrayed any emotion, and that was fading like ice in sunlight.

'By now my family must have spread over the globe, like Christianity. I expect everybody alive is related to me somehow.'

He tried to laugh but she was serious again.

'I don't like myself when I gush, Charles. I apologize for having embarrassed you.'

Beauregard shook his head. Something had broken between them, but he was not sure whether it had been a bond or a barrier.

29

Mr Vampire II

C HARLES'S TEAR STILL tingled on her tongue. She'd not meant to taste his grief but had been unable to help herself. In her old age, she was getting cranky and hard to fathom. Most elders went mad. Like Vlad Tepes. From Charles, she had a bubble of memory. The grip of a thin hand, the smell of dying blood, the heat and dirt of a far country, the fierce struggle of a woman to live, to bring life to the world. Alien feelings, alien pain. Geneviève could not become pregnant, could not give birth. Did that mean she was not truly alive? Not truly a woman? It was said that vampires were genderless, the sex of their bodies as functional as the eyes on the wings of a peacock. She could take pleasure in love-making, after a fashion; but it did not compare with feeding.

All this from a tear. She swallowed and licked the roof of her mouth until the mind-taste was gone.

'We're nearly at Toynbee Hall,' Charles said.

They were by Spitalfields Market, in Lamb Street just around the corner from Commercial Street. The market, open until dawn, was well lit, and crowded. The noise and smell were familiar.

With a lurch, they came to a halt. Geneviève was thrown forwards, against the wooden shield that fastened over the front of the hansom. Charles caught her and helped her up, but she found herself on her knees in the tiny floorspace. She could not see out of the cab. The horse neighed in hysteria, the cabby trying to rein her in with 'whoa' and a hard pull.

Geneviève knew something was wrong.

With a horrid wrench, the neighing abruptly stopped. The cabby swore and bystanders yelped in terror. Charles's face drained of emotion. He was a soldier moments before the charge. She'd been seeing that expression on the face of soon-to-be dead men for centuries. Her eye-teeth extended, and she salivated, ready for attack or defence.

There was a heavy thump on the top of the cab. She looked up. Five yellow fingers, with nails like hooked knives, stuck through the wood. They flexed like bone-jointed worms and a fist ripped away a section of the roof around the trap. Through the splintered slit, she glimpsed a ripple of yellow silk. Her hopping persecutor had returned. A wrinkled face pressed close to the hole, mouth gaping to show rows of lamprey-teeth. It grew and grew, ripping into the cheeks, exposing glisteningly muscled gums. The elder chattered, lips shrivelling to nothing, sparse moustaches sprouting from raw, wet flesh.

Hands took hold of either side of the hole, and peeled away more wood. Layers of varnished carriage-wood shattered, singing like broken violin strings.

Charles had drawn his sword-cane and was looking for a point of thrust. She had to carry the fight to the enemy before Charles tried to be her protector and got himself butchered.

From the floor of the cab, she launched, pushing hard, gripping the edges of the tear and pulling herself up. She burst through the gap, jagged edges ripping her good dress and blunting on her skin. The cab was rocking under the weight of the Chinese, who was balancing on the cabby's box. She saw the driver sprawled on the pavement a dozen yards away, trying to sit up amid a crowd of gawkers. A cold wind blew her unbound hair about her face and whipped her dress around her knees. The cab wobbled under their shifting weight, anchored only by the dead horse.

'Master,' she addressed herself to the vampire, 'what is your quarrel with me?'

The Chinese changed. His neck elongated, dividing into prickle-haired insect segments. The arms extending from his bell-shaped sleeves were several-elbowed, human-shaped hands as big as paddles. His head swung from side to side on his snakeneck, a yard of coiled pigtail lashing his shoulders. The queue ended with a spiked ball woven into his rope of hair.

Something at once wispy and prickly brushed her face. It was a cobwebby rope grown from the vampire's face. While she watched his hands, he had reached for her with his joined eyebrows. Hairs like pampas grass scratched her skin. She felt a trickle on her forehead. The creature was trying for her eyes. She made a fist and swung her forearm against the brow-snake, wrapping it about her wrist several times. She pulled hard; thin strings cut through her sleeve and noosed her wrist, but the vampire was off-balanced.

She was yanked from her own perch as the Chinese tumbled from the box. He slipped through the air like a fish through water and landed perfectly on his sandals. The brow-snake let go of her arm. Feet-first, she slammed into a wall. Then she fell on to cobblestones. Her ankles jarred from the impact with the wall, she tried to stand. The heel of her hand sank into a rotted half-cabbage and she skidded, sprawling again. She tasted filth against her face. Deliberately, she lifted herself on to her elbows, then on to her feet. The elder had managed to hurt her, which was not supposed to be easy. His power made her a child.

She got the wall behind her and gathered strength. Her face burned as the skin tightened. Her teeth and nails grew, splitting the flesh of her fingers and gums. She tasted her own blood.

They were in the market, in a messy space between stalls. A row of dangling beef carcasses lined the concourse between them, shifting on their iron hooks. The stench of dead animal blood was all around. The crowds had gathered in a circle, giving the elders room to fight but also cutting off any retreats.

Pushing against the wall, she flew at the vampire. He stood steady, arms apart. Her hands brushed his robe as, a quarter-second before she reached him, he stepped aside. As she passed, he stabbed her in the side with his pointed fingers. Her dress was shredded, and her skin punctured. She slammed into a cold side of beef, and staggered away, colliding with spectators. They held her up and, with a cheer, pushed her back at the Chinese. It was like a bare-knuckles fight, the crowd continually throwing the pugilists at each other. Until one or other refused to get up again.

She would have given odds against herself. According to superstition, she could halt the Chinese vampire's assault by tracing a prayer to Buddha on a sheet of yellow paper and pasting the incantation to his forehead. Or scatter sticky rice in his path to fix him to the earth and, holding her breath to be invisible to the un-dead, cut him into pieces with lengths of blessed, blood-inked string. Neither method appeared to be a practical option.

Long arms stretched like the steadying wings of a crane, the elder kicked her under the chin. His sandal toe hooked on her jaw, lifting her into the air. She landed badly, coming down heavily on a trestle table. Laid out in flour on wax paper had been a row of kidneys. The trestles collapsed and she was on the floor again, surrounded by lumps of purple meat. An unbroken lamp rolled on the cobbles, sooty flame bursting from its side-vent, a glass bulb of purple paraffin-oil weighting it down.

She looked up and saw the Chinese vampire strolling towards her. He had green eyes in his withered leather mask of a face. His movements were as precise and purposeful as a dancer's. His silks rustled as he walked, like the wings of insects. To him, this was a show, a demonstration. Like a bullfighter, he wanted applause as he made his kill.

There was a blur of movement behind the creature, and he paused, delicately cocking a pointed ear. Charles was closing on him, his sword a silver flash. If he could get the point into the elder's body and transfix him through the heart . . .

The vampire's arm bent backwards in three places and his hand fastened on Charles's wrist, halting the sword-lunge. As he twisted his grip, the sword revolved like the hand of a clock, never quite scraping the Chinese's garments. It fell with a clatter on the cobbles. The vampire flipped Charles over, tossing him away with his weapon. The crowd groaned in sympathy.

Geneviève tried to sit up. The kidneys were like large dead slugs, bursting under her weight. She was smeared with their discharges. The elder returned his attention to her and stretched out a bony arm, the sleeve of which seemed to swell in an unfelt breeze. From the dark of his robe was disgorged a fluttering cloud that grew like the impossible billows of a magician's scarf. Darting and chittering, the cloud swarmed towards her. A million tiny butterflies, many-coloured beauties whose wings caught the light like a scattering of diamond fragments, closed around her. They clustered on the meat, devouring it instantly, and bothered her face, seething around the scraps stuck to her skin, worrying the corners of her eyes.

She kept her mouth shut tight and shook her head violently. She wiped at her face with her wrists. Every time she cleared a swath, the butterflies would gather again. She reached out for the fallen lamp, and pinched out the flame. After yanking free the still-hissing wick, she emptied the lamp over her head. The butterflies were washed away, and the smell of paraffin-oil stung her nostrils. One spark,

and her head would be a candleflame. She scraped dead butterflies
out of her hair, and threw them away by the mucky handful.

The elder stood over her. He bent down and picked her up by
her shoulders. She hung from his hold like a length of cloth. She let
herself relax. Her toes scraped cobbles. Maybe there was amusement
in the dusty emerald of his ancient eyes. His needle-rimmed maw
came close to her face, and she smelled his perfumed breath. From
the teeth-circled red cleft emerged a pointed, tubular tongue like the
proboscis of a mosquito. He could drain her dry, leave her a husk.
She might live, but that would be the worst outcome.

Her feet flat on the ground now, she was looking up at the
creature. She let her head flop back, and exposed her throat in
submission. The tongue snaked towards her, its worm-toothed
aperture pulsing. She gave him a few seconds to relish victory
and grabbed him just under his armpits, her nails stabbing through
his robe and scrabbling against his ribs. Mouth agape, she lunged
up at his face and bit. She caught his tongue and clamped her
jaw tight around the wriggling meat. A peppery taste flooded her
mouth, choking her. The tongue, stronger than a snake, fought her
jaw-grip. She felt the filthy thing throb. Around his tongue, the
vampire screeched in fury. She was hurting him. Her teeth sawed
through gristle and muscle and, with a click, met. The tongue-end
in her mouth writhed, and she spat it out.

The vampire spun away from her, a gush of oily black exploding
from his mouth-hole and splashing down the front of its robe. He
still cried, screams emerging in bubbles of blood. The creature
would not be feeding on her. She wiped her mouth on her ruined
sleeve, coughing and spitting, trying to purge the taste. Her whole
mouth was numbed, her throat burned. The elder, spinning, flailed
at her again. His blows buffeted her against a wall and he began to
work on her like a boxer, hammering her belly and neck. He was
angry now, and not so precise. All he had was force, no skill. Pain
spread through her body. He took her head as he must have taken
the horse's and wrenched it to one side. Her neckbones parted and
she howled in her hurt. The vampire threw her down and kicked
her in the side. Then he jumped on her ribs. She heard her own
bones breaking.

She opened her eyes. The vampire was sneering down, keening
like a wounded seal. His lower face was a steaming mass of flesh

and teeth, trying to mend itself. Saliva and blood dripped on her.
Then he was gone and other faces were crowding round.

'Let me through,' someone said. 'Move aside, for the Lord's
sake . . .'

She hurt. Her ribs were fixing as she breathed, stabbing pains
receding with each wave. But her neck was out. And she was
bone-weary, her vision clouded red. She was aware of the filth in
which she lay, the crusted blood on her face. She no longer had
even one good dress.

'Geneviève,' a voice said, 'look at me . . .'

A face was close. Charles.

'Geneviève . . .'

30

The Penny Drops

DEEMING IT BEST not to move her, he sent Clayton to Toynbee Hall for Dr Seward. In the mean time, he did what he could to make her comfortable. A pail of clean-ish water had been filled from a standpipe; he took a cloth to her face, wiping off her mask of blood and dirt.

Whatever it had been, it had left, bounding with a peculiar hopping gait. Beauregard wished his sword-cane had skewered the thing. He was revising his opinions on vampires in general, but that monster should not be alive.

He dabbed her face and she held his hand tight. She groaned as broken bones moved. He was reminded of Liz Stride at the last. And of Pamela. Both of those were lost, death coming as a mercy. He determined to fight for Geneviève Dieudonné. If he could not preserve one life, what use was he? She tried to speak, but he soothed her to silence. He picked a crushed butterfly out of her hair and flicked it away. Her head sat unnaturally, neck kinked at an angle, a bone jutting under the skin. A warm woman would be dead.

The crowds who had enjoyed the fight were still there, putting the market back together. A few loafers hung about, hoping to see more blood. Beauregard would have liked to floor one or two of them with kung-fu kicks, just to give the public a show.

Clayton returned with a dumpy woman. It was Mrs Amworth, the vampire nurse. Another man from the Hall, Morrison, was with them, carrying a doctor's bag.

'Dr Seward is off somewhere,' Mrs Amworth explained. 'You'll have to make do with me.'

The nurse gently pushed him aside, and knelt by Geneviève. He still held her hand, but she winced as her arm shifted.

'You'll have to let go,' said Mrs Amworth.

He put Geneviève's hand down, arranging her arm by her side.

'Good, good, good,' Mrs Amworth said to herself as she felt Geneviève's ribs. 'The bones are setting properly.'

Geneviève half-sat, coughing, and then slumped.

'Yes, that hurts,' Mrs Amworth cooed, 'but only to make you better.'

Morrison opened the bag and set it within Mrs Amworth's reach. She took out a scalpel.

'You're going to cut?' he asked.

'Only her dress.'

The nurse slipped the blade under Geneviève's neckline at the shoulder and slit down the arm, peeling away what was left of the sleeve. There were purplish patches on her upper arm, which Mrs Amworth squeezed with both hands. There was a pop and the shoulder socketed properly. The livid blotches began to fade.

'Now, the trick,' Mrs Amworth said. 'Her neck is broken. We must set it quickly, or her bones will repair themselves wrongly and we'd have to break the spine again to fix her.'

'Can I help?'

'You and Morrison take her by the shoulders, and hold on for your lives. You, cabby, sit on her legs.'

Clayton was appalled.

'Don't be bashful. She'll thank you for it. Probably give you a kiss.'

The cabby anchored himself over Geneviève's knees. Beauregard and Morrison pinioned her shoulders. Only her head was free. Beauregard fancied Geneviève was trying to smile. She bared her fearful teeth.

'This will hurt, dear,' Mrs Amworth cautioned.

The vampire nurse took Geneviève's head, slipping her hands under her ears and getting a solid hold. Experimenting, she moved the head slightly from side to side, pulling the neck. Geneviève's eyes screwed shut, and she hissed, teeth meshing like the halves of a portcullis.

'Try screaming, dear.'

The patient took the advice, and gave vent to an elongated screech as Mrs Amworth pulled hard and popped Geneviève's skull back on to her spinal column. Then, straddling the patient, she took a strangler's grip on the throat and wrested the vertebrae into place. Beauregard saw the nurse straining as she accomplished her cure.

Her placid face was reddened, fangs burst from her mouth. He was, even after all his experiences, shocked at the transformation.

The four of them stood, leaving Geneviève to wriggle on the floor. Her screech was a series of yelps now. She shook her head, hair whipping about her face. He thought she was swearing in medieval French. She rubbed her neck and sat up.

'Now, dear, you must feed,' Mrs Amworth said. She looked around, and nodded at him.

Beauregard loosened his cravat, and undid his collar. Then, he froze. He felt the pulse in his neck against his knuckles. A shirt-stud came loose and wriggled between his shirt and waistcoat. Geneviève was sitting up, her back against a wall. Her face calmed down, losing the demon rictus, but her teeth were still enlarged, jutting like sharp pebbles. He imagined her mouth on his neck.

'Charles?' someone said.

He turned round. Penelope stood by a stack of cabbage crates. In a fur-collared travelling coat and gauze-clouded hat, she was as out of place as a Red Indian in the House of Commons.

'What are you doing?'

His instant reaction was to redo his cravat, but he fumbled and his collar flew absurdly loose.

'Who are these people?'

'She must feed,' Mrs Amworth insisted. 'Or she might collapse. She's all used up, poor thing.'

Morrison had rolled up his sleeve and presented his wrist, which bore several tiny scabs, to Geneviève's mouth. She held her hair out of the way and suckled.

Penelope looked away, nose wrinkling up in disgust. 'Charles, this is *filthy!*'

She nudged a head of cabbage aside with a pointed boot-toe. The loafers clustered behind Penelope exchanged inaudible jokes. The occasional explosion of rude laughter washed by without touching her.

'Penelope,' he said, 'this is Mademoiselle Dieudonné . . .'

Geneviève's eyes rolled up to look at Penelope. A dribble of blood emerged from the corner of her mouth, ran down Morrison's wrist, and dripped to the cobbles.

'Geneviève, this is Miss Churchward, my fiancée . . .'

Penelope did everything possible not to say 'ugh' out loud.

Geneviève finished, and returned Morrison's arm to him. He wrapped a handkerchief around his wrist, and refastened his cuff. Red-mouthed, she stood up. Her torn sleeve flapped away from her bare shoulder. She held half her bodice to her chest, and curtseyed, wincing somewhat.

There were policemen in the crowd now, and the loafers dispersed. Everyone in the market found something to do, picking through stalls, hefting crates, bartering prices.

Mrs Amworth put an arm around Geneviève to steady her, but Geneviève gently eased her away. She smiled at her own ability to stay upright. Beauregard thought she was light-headed, her feeding following so close upon her injuries.

'Lord Godalming said you might be found in the vicinity of the Café de Paris in Whitechapel,' Penelope said. 'I had hoped his information misleading.'

To attempt an explanation would be to admit a defeat, Beauregard knew.

'I have a cab,' she said. 'Will you return with me to Chelsea?'

'I still have business here, Penelope.'

She smiled with half her face, but her eyes were blue steel specks. 'I shall not enquire as to your "business", Charles. It is not my place.'

Geneviève wiped her mouth on a scrap of her dress. Sensibly, she faded into the background with Mrs Amworth and Morrison. Clayton stood about bewildered, a cabby without a cab. He would have to wait for the knacker to come for his horse.

'Should you wish to call on me,' Penelope continued, laying out an ultimatum, 'I shall be at home tomorrow afternoon.'

She turned and left. A porter whistled and she turned, cutting him into dead silence with a stare. The cowed man slunk into the shadows behind a row of beef sides. Penelope walked off, taking tiny steps, her veil drawn low over her face.

When she was gone, Geneviève said: 'So that's Penelope.'

Beauregard nodded.

'She has a nice hat,' Geneviève commented. Several people, including Mrs Amworth and Clayton, laughed, not pleasantly.

'No, really,' Geneviève insisted, gesturing in front of her face. 'The veil is a pretty touch.'

Inside himself, he was exhausted. He tried to smile but his face felt a thousand years old.

'Her coat is good, too. All those little shiny buttons.'

31

The Raptures and Roses of Vice

'Don't s'pose we done 'im in, does yer?' Nell asked, squatting on the bed, prodding the naked man with a long finger. He was face-down in a pillow, wrists and ankles loosely tied with scarves to brass bedposts. The nice white cotton sheets were spotted and stained.

Mary Jane was preoccupied with dressing. It was hard to set a bonnet without a mirror.

'Mary Jane?'

'Marie Jeanette,' she corrected, loving the sound like music. She had tried to be rid of her brogue, until she realized men found it pleasing. 'I've been tellin' you for close on a year. 'Tis Marie Jeanette. Marie Jeanette Kelly.'

'Yer Kelly don't go with yer "Marie Jeanette", Duchess.'

'Tish-tush. And pish-posh too.'

'That bloke what took yer to Paree didn't do the rest of us no favours.'

'*Any* favours.'

'Pardon me fer suckin', Duchess.'

'And don't you be talkin' unkindly of my "Uncle Henry". He was very distinguished. Probably still is very distinguished.'

'Unless 'e's a-rottin' from the pox yer give 'im,' Nell said, without real meanness.

'Be away with the cheek of you, now.'

Mary Jane was finally happy with her hat. She was careful about her appearance. She might have turned vampire and she might be a cocotte but she wasn't going to let herself go and become a fox-face horror like Nell Coles.

The other woman sat on the bed, and felt around the poet's neck, still sticky with his own blood.

'We done 'im, Mary Jane. 'E's bleedin' dead, an' 'e'll turn for certain.'

'Marie Jeanette.'

'Yeah, an' I'm Contessa Eleanora Francesca Muckety-Muck. Come 'ave a butchers.'

Mary Jane looked Algernon up and down. There were tiny bites, old and new, all over his body. His back and bottom were striped with purple welts. He had provided his own rods and encouraged them to put their backs into the whipping.

'He's an old hand at this, Nell. It'd take more than a flogging and a few love-bites to finish off this old cocker.'

Nell dipped a finger into the blood pooling in the small of Algernon's back and touched her rough lips. She got hairier with every moonrise. She had to brush her cheeks and forehead now, sweeping her thick red hair back into a flaring mane. She stood out in a crowd, which had been good for business. Customers were peculiar. She wrinkled her wide nose as she tasted the blood. Nell was one of those who got 'feelings' with her food. Mary Jane was glad that didn't happen to her.

Nell made a face. 'That's bitter,' she said. 'Who is the cove, anyway?'

'His friend said he was a poet.'

A square-rigged gent had sought them out, and paid for a carriage from Whitechapel to Putney. The house was almost in the country. Mary Jane understood Algernon had been sick and was taking the air for his health.

'Got enough books, ain't 'e?'

Nell couldn't read or write, but Mary Jane had her letters. The small bedroom was lined with bookshelves.

'Did 'e write 'em all?'

Mary Jane took a beautifully bound book down from a shelf, and let it fall open.

'"*Thou hast conquered, O pale Galilean: the world has grown grey from thy breath*",' she read aloud. '"*We have drunken of things Lethean, and fed on the fullness of death.*"'

'Sounds lovely. Yer reckon it's about us?'

'Doubt it. I think 'tis about Our Lord Jesus.'

Nell made a face. She cringed if someone showed her a crucifix, and couldn't bear to hear the name of Christ. Mary Jane still went to church when she could. She had been told God was forgiving. After all, the Lord returned from the grave and encouraged folk to drink His blood. Just like Miss Lucy.

Mary Jane put the book back. Algernon started gulping and Mary Jane held his head up. There was something in his throat. She burped him like a baby and let his head drop. A reddish stain seeped into his pillow.

'Come down and relieve us from virtue, Our Lady of Pain,' he said, clearly. Then he slumped insensible again, and started snoring.

'Don't sound dead, does he?'

Nell laughed. 'Garn, yer Irish cow.'

'Silver and stake my heart will break, but names'll never hurt me.'

The other woman fastened her chemise over furry breasts.

'Doesn't all that hair tickle?'

'Never 'ad any complaints.'

The poet had just wanted a whipping. When his back was bloody, he had let them bite him. It had been enough to finish him off. After that he had been harmless as a baby.

Since she turned, Mary Jane had been opening her legs less. Some men wanted the old-fashioned mixed in, but a lot only liked to be bitten and bled. She remembered with a thrill of nasty pleasure what it had been like when Miss Lucy was at her throat, tiny teeth worrying at the wound. Then the taste of Lucy's blood, and the fire running through her, turning her.

'Ladies of Pain, are we?' Nell said, belting her dress around thick red flanks.

Mary Jane's warm life was hazy in her mind. She had been to Paris with Henry Wilcox; that she knew. But she remembered nothing of Ireland, of her brothers and sisters. She learned from what folk who knew her said that she had come to London from Wales, that she had buried a husband, that she had been kept in a house in the West End. Once in a while she would have a glimpse of memory, seeing a face she knew or coming across an old keepsake, but her old life was a chalk picture in the rain, running and blurring. She had been seeing clearly since her turning, as if a dirty window had been wiped clean. Occasionally, when she was full of someone else's ginny blood, her former self would flood back, and she'd find herself puking in a gutter.

Nell was bending over Algernon, mouth to a bite on his shoulder, sucking quietly. Mary Jane wondered if the poet's blood was richer than a normal man's. Perhaps Nell would start spouting verses and rhymes. That'd be something to hear.

'Leave him be now,' Mary Jane said. 'He's had his guinea's-worth.'

Nell straightened up, smiling. Her teeth were yellowing, and her gums were black. She'd have to go to Africa and live in the jungle soon.

'I can't believe 'e's payin' a guinea. There ain't that much tin in the world.'

'Not in our world, Nell. But he's bein' a gentleman.'

'I knows gentlemen, Mary Jane. They is, as a rule, cheap as week-old pigsblood. And tight as a rat's arse-hole.'

They left the room arm in arm and went downstairs. Theodore, Algernon's friend, was waiting. He must be a good friend, to bring Mary Jane and Nell all the way out to Putney and to stand by all this time. A lot of folk would be disgusted. Of course, Theodore was a new-born and must be broad in the mind.

'How is Swinburne?' he asked.

'He'll live,' replied Mary Jane. Most girls had a fierce sort of contempt for customers like Algernon. They liked to look at a perfectly dressed gent and think of him wriggling naked in pain, sneering at them for preferring a whipping to a good shag. Mary Jane felt different. Maybe her turn had changed the way she felt about what folk did with each other. Sometimes she dreamed of opening the throats of angels as they sang, then straddling them as they died.

'How he loves you women,' Theodore said. 'He talks about your "cold immortal hands". Strange.'

'He knows what he likes,' Mary Jane said. 'No shame in bein' partial to something out of the ordinary.'

'No,' Theodore agreed, unsure. 'No shame at all.'

They stood in the reception room. There were portraits of famous men on the walls and still more books. Mary Jane had a picture of the Champ-Elysées, cut out of an illustrated paper, pasted to the wall of her room in Miller's Court. She saved up for a frame once when she was warm, but Joe Barnett, her man at the time, found the pennies in a mug and drank them away. He'd blacked her eye for holding back on him. When she turned, she'd thrown Joe out, but not before she had repaid him with interest for the bruises.

Theodore gave them a guinea apiece and escorted them out to the carriage. Mary Jane tucked her guinea safe into her poke, but Nell had to hold her coin up to catch the moonlight.

Mary Jane remembered to bid Theodore a good night and to curtsey as Uncle Henry had taught her. Some gentlemen had inquisitive neighbours, and it was only polite to act like a proper lady caller. Theodore didn't notice and turned back into the house before she had straightened up.

'A guinea, blimey!' Nell exclaimed. 'I'd 'a bitten 'is balls fer a guinea.'

'Get in the coach with you, you embarrassin' tart,' Mary Jane said. 'I don't know of what you're thinkin'.'

'I do believe I will, Duchess,' she said, squeezing through the door, wiggling her rump from side to side.

Mary Jane followed and settled down.

'Oi, you,' Nell shouted to the driver, ''ome, an' don't spare the 'orses.'

The carriage lurched into motion. Nell was still playing with her gold coin. She had tried to bite it. Now she was shining it against her shawl.

'I'll be off the streets fer a month,' she said, licking her fangs. 'I'll go up West an' find myself a guardsman with a knob like a firehose, an' suck the bastard dry.'

'But you'll be back in the alleys when the money's gone, on your back in the muck while some drunkard wobbles all over you.'

Nell shrugged. 'I 'ardly think I'll be marryin' royalty. Yer neither, Marie Jeanette de Kelly.'

'I'm not on the streets any more.'

'Just 'cos there's a roof over the bed yer shag in don't make it a church, girl.'

'No strangers, that's my rule now. Just familiar gentlemen.'

'*Very* familiar.'

'You should be listenin' to me, you know. It's not healthy on the streets these nights. Not with the Ripper.'

Nell was unimpressed. 'In Whitechapel, 'e'd 'ave to kill an 'ore a night til kingdom come til 'e got to me. There's thousands of us, an' there will be long after 'e's rottin' in Hell.'

'He's killin' them two at a time.'

'Garn!'

'You know 'tis true, Nell. 'Tis over a week since he did for Cathy Eddowes and the Stride woman. He'll be out and about again.'

'I'd like to see 'im try anythin' with me,' Nell said. She snarled, a mouthful of wolf-teeth glistening. 'I'd rip 'is 'eart out, an' eat the blighter.'

Mary Jane had to laugh. But she was being serious. 'The only safe thing is familiar gentlemen, Nell. Customers you know, and are sure of. The best thing would be to find a gentleman to keep you. Especially if he wants to keep you outside Whitechapel.'

'Only place that'd keep me is the zoo.'

Mary Jane had been *kept* once. In Paris, by Henry Wilcox. He was a banker, a colossus of finance. He had gone abroad without his wife, and she had travelled with him. He told everyone she was his niece, but the French understood the arrangement all too well. When he travelled on to Switzerland, he left her behind with an old frog rakehell to whom she did not take. 'Uncle Henry', it turned out, had lost her on a hand of cards. Paris had been lovely but she still came back to London, were she knew what folk were saying and she was the only person gambling with her life.

It was almost dawn when they got to Whitechapel. She'd not known enough at first to stay out of the sun, and her skin had burned to painful crackling. She had ripped dogs open for their juice. It had taken her months to catch up with the other new-borns.

She gave directions to the warm driver, realizing with a nice hot surge that the man was petrified of his vampire passengers. She rented a room just off Dorset Street, from McCarthy the chandler, for four and six a week. Some of the guinea would have to pay the arrears and keep McCarthy off her back. But the rest would be for her. Perhaps she could find a picture-framer?

Once they were out of the coach, it trundled off quickly, leaving them on the pavement. Nell gestured after the departing driver and howled like a comical animal. She even had fur growing around her eyes and up behind her pointed ears.

'Marie Jeanette,' croaked a voice from the shadows. Someone was standing under the Miller's Court archway. A gentleman, by his clothes.

She smiled, recognizing the voice.

Dr Seward stepped out of the dark. 'I've been waiting most of the night for you,' he said. 'I'd like –

'She knows what yer'd like,' Nell said, 'an' yer oughta be shamed of yerself.'

'Shush, furface.' Mary Jane said. 'That's no way to be talkin' to a gentleman.'

Nell stuck her snout in the air, rearranged her shawl, and trotted off, sniffing like a music hall queen. Mary Jane apologized for her.

'Do you want to come in, Dr Seward?' she asked. 'It's nearly sun-up. I have to have my beauty sleep.'

'I'd like that very much,' he said. He was fidgeting with his neck. She had seen her customers do that before. Once bitten, they always came back for more.

'Well, follow me.'

She led him to her room and let him in. Early sun fell through the dusty window on to the unwrinkled bedspread. She drew the curtains against the light.

32

Grapes of Wrath

THE CABAL WAS further depleted. Mr Waverly was gone, though no one remarked on his passing. Mycroft again held the chair. Sir Mandeville Messervy sat quiet throughout the interview, face fallen. Whatever path Beauregard pursued in Whitechapel, he could never know of the secret campaigns his masters waged in other quarters. In Limehouse, the Professor had referred to the business of crime as a shadow community; Beauregard knew this was a world of shadow empires. He was privileged to see the veil lifted, if only at odd moments.

He recounted his activities since the inquest on Lulu Schön, omitting nothing of importance. He did not, however, feel obliged to report the matters that passed between him and Geneviève in Clayton's cab shortly before the attack by the vampire elder. He was still unsure in himself what precisely he had shared in that moment of intimacy. He concentrated on the facts of the case, elaborating on the details available in the press, adding his own observations and comments. He spoke of Dr Jekyll and Dr Moreau, of Inspector Lestrade and Inspector Abberline, of Toynbee Hall and the Ten Bells, of Commercial Street Police Station and the Café de Paris, of silver and silver knives, of Geneviève Dieudonné and Kate Reed. Throughout, Mycroft nodded intently, fleshy lips pursed, fingers steepled under his soft chins. When Beauregard's account was concluded, Mycroft thanked him and said he was satisfied with the progress of the affair.

'Since these letters, the murderer is generally known by the "Jack the Ripper" soubriquet?' the Chairman asked.

'Indeed. You never hear of "Silver Knife" any more. Whosoever devised the name must have some species of genius. The consensus is that he must be a journalist. The fellows have the knack for the memorable phrase. The good ones, at least.'

'Excellent.'

Beauregard was puzzled. So far as he could see, he had been of no use at all. The Ripper had murdered again. Twice, with impunity. His own presence had deterred the madman not one whit, and any involvement he might be contracting in Whitechapel hardly bore upon the investigation.

'You must catch this man,' Messervy said, his first words since Beauregard entered the Star Chamber.

'We have every confidence in Beauregard,' Mycroft said to the Admiral.

Messervy grunted and slumped into his armchair. He wrestled with a pill-box and popped something into his mouth. Beauregard suspected the former Chairman had suffered an indisposition.

'And now,' Beauregard said, consulting his half-hunter, 'if you will excuse me. I must return to Chelsea on a personal matter . . .'

In her mother's house in Caversham Street, Penelope would be waiting in her cold fury. Waiting for an explanation. Beauregard would rather have faced the Chinese elder again, or Jack the Ripper himself. But he had a duty to his fiancée as solemnly undertaken as his duty to the Crown. He had no idea what conclusion their conversation would reach.

Mycroft raised an eyebrow, as if surprised personal matters should enter into it. Not for the first time, Beauregard wondered what manner of men were set over him in the Diogenes Club.

'Very well. Good day, Beauregard.'

Sergeant Dravot was not at his post outside the Star Chamber. A warm rough with the weather-beaten face and knuckles of an old-fashioned pugilist stood in his place. Beauregard went down to the foyer and left the Diogenes Club. He emerged into Pall Mall to find the afternoon chilly and overcast. Fog was again gathering.

He should be able to get a cab to Chelsea. Looking about, he noticed the streets were thick with people. He recognized a thumping sound as a marching drum. Then he heard the brass. A band was coming down Regent Street. He was not aware of any formally announced parade. Lord Mayor's Day was nearly a month off. With irritation, he realized the band would make hailing a hansom difficult. Traffic would be disrupted. Penelope would most definitely not understand.

The band rounded the corner and marched down Pall Mall,

towards Marlborough Street. Beauregard assumed they were zig-zagging through the streets, picking up followers, aiming to congregate in St James's Park. The uniformed bandmaster marching at the head of the parade held up a giant flag of St George, the standard of the Christian Crusade. The thin red cross on a white background billowed as the band advanced.

After the band came a choir, mainly of middle-aged women. They all wore long white dresses with red crosses on their fronts. They were singing some version of the song that had been 'John Brown's Body' and evolved into 'The Battle Hymn of the Republic'.

> *'In the beauty of the lilies, Christ was born across the sea.*
> *With a glory in his bosom that transfigures you and me:*
> *As he died to make men holy, let us die to make men free.*
> *While God is marching on . . .'*

The crowds now pressed around on all sides. Most of the onlookers, and all of the marchers, were warm, but three were a few jeering murgatroyds on the pavement, brought out by the gloom of the late afternoon, flapping their batwing cloaks and hissing through red lips. They were outnumbered and ignored. Beauregard thought their mocking attitude unwise. Potential immortality was not actual invincibility.

After the choir came an open carriage drawn by six horses. Standing on a platform, surrounded by worshipful acolytes, was John Jago. Behind him came an orderly rabble with banners bearing holy pronouncements, 'Thou Shalt Not Suffer a Vampire to Live' and 'Holy Blood, Holy Crusade'. Amid these marchers struggled a couple of hefty crusaders who carried between them a twenty-foot pole, upon which was impaled a papier-mâché figure, a vampire Guy Fawkes. The pole pierced its breast, and there was red paint splashed around the wound. It had red eyes, exaggerated fang-teeth, and was dressed in tatty black.

The murgatroyds fell silent for a moment. Beauregard knew there would be trouble. There were two mounted policemen in the street, but no one else with any authority. Warm people had flooded from somewhere. He could not move of his own accord, but found himself swept along with the march. Jago preached his usual hate and hellfire and Beauregard was pushed along beside his carriage. They swept down Marlborough Street towards the park. Once in the open, he could escape the crusaders.

One of the murgatroyds, a pale Adonis with black ribbons in his golden hair, picked a handful of horse-dung from the gutter and flung it, with a degree of accuracy that betokened no little skill as a bowler, at the preacher. The ball exploded against Jago's face, browning him like a fakir. For an instant, between the notes of the marching hymn, the crowd was as frozen as a photograph. Beauregard saw burning fury in Jago's eyes, a mixture of triumph and dawning fear in the face of the murgatroyd.

With a cry as loud as the last trump, the marchers fell upon the murgatroyds. There were four or five of the new-borns. Dandified in their dress, effete in their gesture, spinelessly vicious, cold-hearted poseurs: they encapsulated every fault commonly considered to epitomize the vampire. Beauregard felt himself thumped in the back by people struggling towards the scrum. Jago still preached, inciting the wrath of the righteous.

There was blood in the street. Pushed down to his knees, he knew that if he fell underfoot he would be trampled. To have survived so much in so many quarters of the globe only to be killed by an anonymous London crowd . . .

A strong hand took his arm and hauled him upright. His saviour was Dravot, the vampire from the Diogenes Club. He said nothing.

'Here's one of them,' shouted a red-haired man. Dravot's hand shot out and smashed the man's teeth, whirling him away into the mass of people. As he punched, Dravot's jacket fell open. Beauregard saw a pistol slung in a holster underneath his arm.

He tried to thank the sergeant. But his voice was lost in the shouting. And Dravot was gone. He took a knock on the chin from someone's elbow. He resisted the temptation to strike out with his cane. It was important to keep his cool. He did not want more people hurt.

The crowds parted and a screaming figure, blood in his hair and on his face, burst through, tripping and falling to his knees. The murgatroyd's coat was ripped apart. His mouth split open, teeth coming through in irregular lumps. It was the murgatroyd who had pelted Jago. Crusaders held the vampire's shoulders and someone thrust a broken pole-end into his throat, jamming it down through his rib-cage. Everyone fell back as soon as the spear was through him. From the pole fluttered half a banner. 'Death to . . .' The wooden spar missed the murgatroyd's heart. Although hurt, he was not killed. He got a grip on the pole, and started to draw it out of himself, snarling and spitting blood.

Beauregard could see St James's Palace across the road. People clung to the railings, climbing high to get a view. Straddling the top was Dravot, looking purposeful. Someone grabbed at his leg, but he kicked them off the perch.

The wounded murgatroyd ran through the crowd, screeching like a banshee, tossing people about like dressmaker's dummies. Beauregard was thankful he was not in the former fop's way. Jago shouted now, howling for blood. He sounded more like a vampire than the creatures he condemned. The preacher's arm went up in the air, fist raised against the Palace and the white-faced creatures behind the railings. In the hubbub, Beauregard heard the unmistakable crack of a gun going off. A red carnation appeared high up in Jago's lapel. He fell from his carriage, caught by the crowds.

Someone had shot Jago. Looking again at the railings, Beauregard saw Dravot was gone. Jago had blood all down his front. His supporters pressed rags to the wounds in his front and back. The bullet must have passed clean through, without doing much damage.

'I am the voice that will not be silenced,' Jago yelled. 'I am the cause which will not die.'

Then the crowds burst into the park and scattered, spreading out like spilled liquid towards Horse Guards Parade and Birdcage Walk. Beauregard could breathe again. Shots were fired into the air. Scuffles went on all around. The sun was going down.

He did not understand what he had seen. He thought Dravot had shot Jago but he could not be sure. If the sergeant had meant to kill the crusader, Beauregard assumed John Jago would be dead, brains spilled rather than blood. The Diogenes Club did not employ butter-fingered dead-eye marksmen.

There were more vampires around. The murgatroyds had fled, replaced by hard-faced new-borns in police uniforms. A Carpathian officer charged through the rabble on a huge black horse, waving a blooded sabre. A warm woman, shoulder slashed open, ran past, holding her baby to her, head down. The crusaders were losing their momentary advantage, and would soon be routed.

He had lost sight of Jago, and of Dravot. A horse sweeping past knocked him down. When he regained his feet, he found his watch smashed. It hardly mattered. The afternoon was over, and Penelope would be waiting no longer.

'Death to the Dead,' someone cried.

33

The Dark Kiss

WHEN THE STREETS were cleared, there were surprisingly few bleeding bodies dotted about. Compared with Bloody Sunday, it had been a minor skirmish. Godalming, dragged along by Sir Charles, could scarcely tell there had been a riot in St James's Park. Inspector Mackenzie, a dour Scot, was with them, trying to keep out of the Commissioner's way. During the hour of excitement just after nightfall, Sir Charles had been a changed person. The ground-down, persecuted bureaucrat whose foolish subordinates could not catch Jack the Ripper disappeared; he was again the military commander with lightning judgement under fire. 'These are Englishmen and women,' Mackenzie had muttered, 'not bloody Hottentots.'

It appeared the Christian Crusade had held an unannounced rally, intending to present a petition to Parliament. They demanded that the taking of another's blood without consent be considered a capital crime. Sundry vampires mixed in with the crusaders, and violence was exchanged. An unknown person had taken a shot at John Jago, who was now recuperating in a prison hospital. Several well-connected new-borns alleged that they had been assaulted by warm mobs, and a murgatroyd named Lioncourt was put out because a broken flagpole had been shoved through his best suit.

General Iorga, a commander of the Carpathian Guard, had been caught in the fighting. Now he stood with Sir Charles and Godalming, surveying the aftermath. Iorga was an elder, swanning about in his cuirass and long black cloak as if he owned the earth on which he walked. He was attended by Rupert of Hentzau, a young-seeming Ruritanian blood who thought a good deal of his gold-braided uniform and seemed as skilled at toadying as he was reputed to be with his rapier.

Sir Charles smiled grimly to himself as he handed out compliments to the men he thought of as his troops.

'We have won a significant victory here,' he told Godalming and Iorga. 'With no loss of life, we have routed the enemy.'

It had all blown up and dissipated so suddenly there had been no opportunity for the incident to develop. Iorga had ridden around doing damage but Hentzau and his comrades had not arrived on the scene in time to turn a scuffle into a massacre.

'The ringleaders must be found and impaled,' Iorga said. 'And their families.'

'That isn't how we do things in England,' Sir Charles said, without thinking.

The Carpathian's eyes blazed with hypnotic fury. According to General Iorga, this was no longer England, this was some Balkan pocket kingdom.

'Jago will be charged with unlawful assembly and sedition,' Sir Charles said. 'And his thugs will find themselves breaking rocks on Dartmoor for some years.'

'Jago should get Devil's Dyke,' Godalming put in.

'Of course.'

Devil's Dyke was partially Sir Charles's invention, an adaption of a system devised for making use of native prisoners-of-war, for concentrating civilian populations to prevent them from giving succour to their soldiery. Godalming understood the conditions in the camps made what was usually understood by penal servitude seem a breeze on the Brighton promenade.

'What about the fellow who started it?' asked Mackenzie.

'Jago? I've just said.'

'No, sir. I mean the bloody fool with the pistol.'

'Give him a medal,' Hentzau said, 'then cut off his ears as punishment for bad marksmanship.'

'He must be found, of course,' Sir Charles said. 'We can't have Christian martyrs hanging around our necks.'

'Our honour has been challenged,' said Iorga. 'We must exact reprisals.'

Even Sir Charles was less of a hothead than the General. Godalming was surprised by the elder's dimwittedness. Long life did not mean a continual growth of intelligence. He understood why Ruthven spoke of the Prince Consort's entourage in such contemptuous terms. Iorga was tubby around the middle and his face was painted. Once, for a moment only, Godalming had seen the rage-filled face of the Prince himself. Ever since, he had held the Carpathians in undue reverence, imposing the ferocity and stature of their leader on to the image of each of them. That was ridiculous. No matter how brutes like Iorga or blades like Hentzau might try to imitate Dracula, they were never more than feeble copies of the great original, essentially as trifling as the floppiest murgatroyd in Soho.

He pardoned himself and left the Commissioner and the General to continue mopping up. Both intended to stand around giving Mackenzie contradictory orders. As he passed Buckingham Palace, he tipped his hat to the Carpathians at the gates. The flag flew, indicating that Her Majesty and His Royal Highness were in residence. Godalming wondered if the Prince Consort ever thought of Lucy Westenra.

At the Victoria Station boundary of the park were several horse-drawn wagons, penned full of sorry-looking crusaders. Godalming understood that as riots went, tonight's affair had been strictly third class.

He whistled, red thirst pricking the back of his throat. It was good to be young, rich and a vampire. All London was his, more than it was Dracula's or Ruthven's. They might be elders, but, as he was realizing, that actually put them at a disadvantage. No matter how they tried, they could not be of the age. They were historical characters and he was contemporary.

When he first turned, he had been in a continual funk. He thought the Prince Consort would come for him any night, and serve him as he had served Van Helsing or Jonathan Harker. But he now had to assume he was forgiven. He might have destroyed Lucy Westenra, but Dracula had more important warm wenches to pursue. It was not inconceivable that he was grateful to Godalming for disposing of the get of his first dalliance in England. He would presumably not have wanted an un-dead Lucy for a bridesmaid, looking red daggers at the radiant Victoria as she was led down the aisle of Westminster Abbey by her devoted Prime Minister. That wedding had been the culmination of last year's Jubilee celebrations. The union of the Widow of Windsor and the Prince of Wallachia bound together a nation which, shaking as it changed, could as easily have flown apart.

He was expected at Downing Street at two o'clock tomorrow morning. Business was conducted through the night now. Then, before dawn, he was to attend a reception at the Café Royal, as Lady Adeline Ducayne welcomed a distinguished visitor, the Countess Elizabeth Bathory. Lady Adeline was taking such care to cosy up to the Countess because the Bathorys were distant connections of the Draculas. Ruthven described the Countess Elizabeth as 'an elegantly revolting alley-cat' and Lady Adeline as 'a wizened skeleton one generation out of the swamp', but he insisted Godalming be present at the affair in case matters of importance were discussed.

For the next six hours, he was at liberty. His red thirst grew. It was good to let the need gather, for it gave an edge to feeding. After a brief return to his town house in Cadogan Square to change into evening clothes, Godalming would go out on the razzle. He understood the pleasures of the hunt. He had several possibles picked out and would make one of those ladies his prey this evening.

His fangs were sharp against his lower lip. The prospect of the chase excited familiar changes in his body. His tastes were sharper, his palate more varied. His swollen teeth malformed his whistling. 'Barbara Allen' became a queer new tune no one would recognize.

In Cadogan Square, a woman approached him. She had two little girls with her, on leads, like dogs. They smelled of warm blood.

'Kind sir,' the woman said, hand out, 'would you care . . .'

Godalming was disgusted that anyone would stoop to selling the blood of their own children. He had seen the woman before, cadging coins off inexperienced new-borns, offering up the scabby throats of her smelly ragamuffins. It was inconceivable that any vampire past his first week could be interested in their thin blood.

'Go away, or I shall summon a constable.'

The woman departed, cringing. She dragged her children with her. Both little girls looked back at him as they were pulled off, hollow eyes round and moist. When they were all used up, would the woman find more children? He thought one of the girls might be new, and considered the possibility that the woman was not their mother but some horrid new species of pimp. He would bring the matter up with Ruthven. The Prime Minister was very perturbed by the exploitation of children.

He was admitted to his house by the manservant he had brought with him from Ring, the Holmwood country seat. His hat and coat were taken.

'There's a lady for you in the drawing room, my lord,' the valet informed him. 'A Miss Churchward. She has been waiting.'

'Penny? What on earth could she want?'

'She didn't say, my lord.'

'Very well. Thank you. I shall attend to her.'

He left the man in the hall and entered the drawing room. Penelope Churchward was perched primly on a stiff-backed chair. She had taken a piece of fruit – a dusty old apple, since he only kept food for his infrequent warm guests – and was flaying it with a small paring knife.

'Penny,' he said, 'what a pleasant surprise.'

As he spoke, he nicked his lip with a razor-tooth. When the red thirst was upon him, he had to watch his words. She set aside her apple and knife, and arranged herself to address him.

'Arthur,' she said, standing up, and extending her arm.

He carefully kissed her hand. She was different tonight, he knew with an instant intuition. Something in her attitude to him had been budding; now it was in full bloom. The chase had come to him.

'Arthur, I wish . . .'

Her sentence trailed off, but she had made her wish clear. Her collar was open, her throat exposed. He saw the blue vein in her white skin, and imagined it throbbing. A loose strand of her hair hung on her neck.

Steadily and with considered resolve, she allowed him to embrace her. She moved her head out of his way and he kissed her throat. Usually, his prey moaned as he first bit, gently piercing the skin. Penelope was relaxed and compliant, but made no sound. He clutched her tight to him as blood swelled into his mouth. In the moment of communion, he tasted not only her blood but her head. He understood her measured anger and sensed the rearrangement of the ordered paths of her thinking.

He gulped, taking more than he should. It was hard to draw away from the fountain. No wonder many new-borns killed their first fancies. Penelope's blood was of the finest. With no impurities, it slipped down his throat like honeyed liqueur.

She laid her hand on his cheek and pushed him away. The flow ceased, and he found himself sucking cold air. He would not be

stopped. He swept her up in his arms and threw her on to the
settee. Growling, he held her down and pulled at her collar. Her
chemise tore. He mumbled an apology and fell upon her, his mouth
gathering a fold of the flesh of her upper bosom. Her blood thrilled
him. His teeth caught in bitemarks, blood seeping around them as
he worried at the wound. She did not resist. Blood bubbled into his
mouth, and there were violet sunbursts behind his eyes. There was
no warm sensation to compare. It was more than food, more than
a drug, more than love. Never did he feel more alive than in this
moment . . .

. . . he found himself kneeling by the settee, prostrate on her
chest, silently sobbing. Minutes had been burned from his memory.
His chin and shirtfront were soaked with blood. Electrical charges
coursed through his veins. His heart burned as it filled with
Penelope's blood. For a moment, he was almost insensible. She
eased herself into a sitting position and lifted his head. He stared at
her with dazed eyes. Angry purple-wounds stood out on her neck
and breast.

Penelope smiled a tight, quiet smile at him. 'So that is what all
the fuss was about,' she commented.

She helped him up on to the settee like a mother posing a child
for a photograph. He sat, still tasting her in his mouth and head.
His shudders subsided. She dabbed her bites clean with a kerchief,
wincing in minor irritation. Then she buttoned her jacket up over
her ripped chemise. Her hair had come undone, and she fussed with
it for a moment.

'There now, Arthur,' she said. 'You've had your satisfaction of
me . . .'

He could not speak. He was glutted, helpless as a snake digesting
a mongoose.

'. . . now, I shall complete the exchange and have my satisfaction
of you.'

The paring knife was in her hand, shining.

'I understand this is quite simple,' she said. 'Be a dear and don't
struggle.'

Her knife was at his throat, slicing. It was sharp enough to slit
his tough skin, but he felt no pain. The knife was not silvered. The
gash would heal over almost instantly.

'Ugh,' she said.

Penelope swallowed her distaste and put her tiny mouth over the cut she had made. Shocked, he realized immediately what she was about. Her tongue kept apart the lips of the wound as she sucked blood from him.

34

Confidences

'Y OU SHOULD BE upstairs, resting,' Amworth told her. 'You'll mend sooner.'

'Why should I get well?' Geneviève asked. 'The hopping toad will only return and finish me off.'

'You don't know that.'

'Yes, I do. I don't know why it's going to destroy me, but I know it will. I've been in China. Those creatures don't give up of their own accord. They can't be reasoned with and they can't be stopped. I might as well go out in the street and wait for it to come for me. Then at least no one else would be in the way.'

Amworth was impatient. 'You hurt it last time.'

'And it hurt me worse.'

She was not entirely better. She often found herself moving her head around, to test her broken and re-set neck. Her head had not fallen off yet, but sometimes it felt about to.

Geneviève looked around the lecture hall that had become a makeshift infirmary. 'No Chinese callers?'

The nurse shook her head. She was listening to the chest of a little new-born girl. For a moment, Geneviève thought it was Lily. Then, she remembered. The patient was Rebecca Kosminski.

'I wish I knew which of the enemies I've cultivated was responsible.'

The Chinese vampire was a hireling. All over the East, such creatures were employed as assassins.

'I expect I'll be told. It would seem a waste not to let me know why my head is being torn off.'

'Shush,' Amworth said. 'You're frightening the girl.'

With a squirt of guilt, she saw the nurse was right. Rebecca looked thoughtful but her eyes had shrunk to tiny points.

'I'm sorry,' she apologized. 'Rebecca, I was just being silly, making up stories.'

Rebecca smiled. In a few years, she would never believe a lie that transparent. But now she was still a child inside.

Feeling useless – all her duties had been reassigned for a specified period of convalescence – Geneviève loitered in the infirmary for a few minutes then drifted out to the corridor.

The director's office was locked; Montague Druitt lurked outside. Geneviève bade him a good evening.

'Where's Dr Seward?' she asked.

Druitt was reluctant to talk to her but got the words out. 'He's off somewhere, with no explanation. It's most inconvenient.'

'Can I be of assistance? As you know, I have the director's confidence.'

Druitt shook his head, lips pressed tight. It was business for warm men, he was thinking. Geneviève could not tell what the man wanted. He was another of the Hall's scorched souls; she had no hope of making common cause with him, much less of being any help.

She left him in the corridor and traipsed out to the foyer, where an unfriendly warm nurse directed a stream of malingerers back into the fog, occasionally deigning to admit someone obviously suffering mortal injury.

Dr Seward had been much absent recently. She supposed he had some private grief. Like everyone else. Through all the pain of her broken bones, she still could not get the death of Pamela Beauregard out of her mind. Everyone lost people. She had been losing people for hundreds of years. But in Charles, the loss still burned.

'Miss Dieudonné?'

It was a new-born woman. She had come in from outside. She was dressed well, but not expensively.

'Do you remember me? Kate Reed?'

'Miss Reed, the journalist?'

'That's right. The Central News Agency.' She stuck out her hand to be shaken; Geneviève responded weakly in kind.

'What can be done for you, Miss Reed?'

The new-born let go of Geneviève's hand. 'I was hoping I could talk to you. It's about the other night. That Chinese thing. The butterflies.'

Geneviève shrugged. 'I don't know if there's anything I can tell you that you don't know. It was an elder. Evidently the butterflies are a quirk of its bloodline. Some German *nosferatu* have a similar affinity for rats, and you must have heard of the Carpathians and their pet wolves.'

'Why were you singled out for persecution?'

'I wish I knew. I have passed blamelessly through life doing nought but good deeds, and am beloved by all whose path I have crossed. It is beyond conception that anyone could nurture in their heart hostile feelings for me.'

Miss Reed did not appear to notice the irony. 'Do you think the assault has anything to do with your interest in the Whitechapel murders?'

That had not occurred to Geneviève. She considered a moment. 'I doubt it. Whatever you might have heard, I am scarcely an important figure in the investigation. The police have talked to me about the effects of the murders on this community, but that is the extent of my involvement . . .'

'And you've been consulted by Charles . . . by Mr Beauregard? The other night . . .'

'Again, he has spoken with me but nothing more. I understand I owe him a debt of gratitude for distracting the elder.'

Miss Reed was rather intent on digging out something. Geneviève had the impression that the lady journalist was more interested in Charles than in the Ripper.

'And what is Mr Beauregard's actual involvement in the investigation?'

'That, you would have to ask him.'

'I shall,' Miss Reed said. 'When he can be found.'

'He can be found here, Kate,' Charles said.

He had come into the foyer a few minutes ago. Geneviève had not noticed him standing quietly in the corner. Miss Reed's eyes narrowed and she slipped on a pair of smoked glasses. She had the new-born's pallor, but Geneviève discerned the ghost of a blush on her cheeks.

'Um,' Miss Reed said. 'Charles, good evening.'

'I come to call upon an invalid, but I find her quite recovered.'

Charles bowed to Geneviève. Miss Reed's line of questioning had petered out.

'Thank you for your time, Miss Dieudonné,' she said. 'I shall leave you to entertain your caller. Charles, good night.'

The new-born flitted out into the night.

'What was all that about?'

She shrugged, and her neck hurt. 'I don't know, Charles. Are you familiar with Miss Reed?'

'Kate's a friend of my . . . a friend of Penelope's.' At his own mention of his fianceé – whose veiled face and guardedly hostile eyes Geneviève had cause to remember – Charles's face fell, and he shook his head. 'Maybe she has been talking with Penelope,' he suggested. 'It is more than I have been.'

Despite herself, Geneviève was interested. She should be beyond such things, but in her weakness she reverted to a silly gossip.

'I had the impression that you were required to call upon Miss Churchward this afternoon.'

Charles half-smiled. 'You were not alone in that impression but circumstances intervened. There was trouble in St James's Park.'

She found Charles holding her hands as if feeling the bones for damage.

'Forgive me for being overly inquisitive but there is something about your domestic arrangements that puzzles me.'

'Oh, really,' he said, cooling.

'Yes. Am I correct in assuming that Miss Churchward, Penelope, is a connection of Mrs Beauregard, Pamela, your former wife?'

Charles's face betrayed nothing.

'I would assume them sisters were it not for the fact, demonstrated by Mr Holman Hunt and Miss Waugh, that if such were so, your engagement would consitute incest under English law.'

'Penelope is Pamela's cousin. They were brought up in the same household. As sisters, if you will.'

'So you intend to marry the *echt*-sister of your late wife?'

He picked his words carefully. 'That was indeed my intent.'

'Does this not strike you as a peculiar arrangement?'

Charles let go of her hands and turned away with a suspiciously casual aspect. 'No stranger than any other, surely.'

'Charles, I do not wish to embarrass you, but you must remember . . . the other night in the cab . . . through no fault of mine, I have some, uh, some understanding of your feelings, for Pamela, for Penelope . . .'

Sighing, Charles said, 'Geneviève, I appreciate your concern but I assure you it is quite needless. Whatever the motives for my engagement might have been, they now mean nothing. It is my understanding that, through no action of my own, I am released from my promise to Penelope.'

'My condolences.' She put her hand on his shoulder and turned him so she could see his eyes.

'Condolences are unnecessary.'

'I was flippant about Penelope the other night. I was light-headed, you understand. Close to hysterical.'

'You'd nearly been killed,' Charles said, with feeling. 'You were not responsible.'

'Nevertheless, I regret what I said, what I implied . . .'

'No,' Charles said, looking at her straight-on. 'You were exactly right. I was being unfair to Penelope. I do not feel for her as a man should for his wife. I was merely using her to replace the irreplaceable. She is better off without me. Just recently, I've been feeling . . . I don't know, feeling as if I'd lost an arm. As if I were not complete without Pamela.'

'You mean Penelope?'

'I mean *Pamela*, that's the terrible thing.'

'What will you do now?'

'I'll have eventually to see Penelope and clear things between us. She'll find a far better catch than me. As for myself, I have more important affairs to consider.'

'Such as?'

'Such as the Whitechapel Murders. Also, I want to see what I can do about saving your life.'

35

A Dynamite Party

'LOOK AT THEM,' said von Klatka, nodding at the wagon. 'Terrified of us, are they not? It is good, no?'

Von Klatka was enjoying himself too much. The Carpathian Guard had been called into the park too late to do much more than gloat. It was the best kind of victory, Kostaki reflected, with spoils but no losses. The police had already rounded up and penned most of the trouble-makers.

A row of worried faces peered through the bar-like slats of the nearest wagon. It held the women. Most wore white vestments with red crosses on the front.

'Christian Crusaders!' von Klatka sneered, 'fools!'

'We were the Christians once,' Kostaki said. 'When we followed Prince Dracula against the Turk.'

'An old battle, my comrade. There are new enemies to be conquered.'

He approached the wagon. The prisoners whimpered, cringing away from the slats. Von Klatka grinned and snarled. Some woman stifled screams and von Klatka laughed. Was there honour in this?

Kostaki saw a familiar face among the milling policemen. 'Scotsman,' he shouted, 'hail and well met.'

Inspector Mackenzie turned from his conversation with a turnkey and saw Kostaki bearing down on him. 'Captain Kostaki,' he acknowledged, tapping the brim of his hat. 'You've missed the merriment.'

Von Klatka prodded between the bars of the wagon, a naughty child in the zoo. One of the prisoners fainted and her comrades called for God or John Jago to protect them.

'Merriment?'

Mackenzie snorted bitterly. 'You might think it so. Not enough blood spilled for your tastes, I imagine. No one killed.'

'I am sure the omission will be remedied. There must be ring leaders.'

'Examples will be made, Captain.'

Kostaki sensed the warm policeman's discomfort, his swallowed anger. Few alliances truly lasted. It must be difficult for this man to reconcile his duties with his loyalties. 'I respect you, Inspector.'

The Scotsman was surprised.

'Have a care,' Kostaki continued. 'These are awkward times. All positions are precarious.'

Von Klatka reached into the wagon and tickled a shrinking girl's ankle. He enjoyed his sport. He turned to Kostaki, grinning for approval.

A vampire emerged from the shadows of the park. Kostaki immediately saluted. General Iorga – a blusterer if ever there was – had been caught in the rioting; now, he strode about, with that arrogant devil Hentzau in tow, as if fresh from winning the Battle of Austerlitz. Iorga grunted to get von Klatka's attention and was rewarded with another salute. He was one of those officers, as common in the armies of the living as of the un-dead, who need constant reassurance of their importance. The rest of his time not spent snivelling to his superiors was taken up with being beastly to his subordinates. For four hundred years, Iorga had vowed eternal fealty to the cause of Dracula, and for as long he had secretly hoped someone would hoist the Impaler on one of his own stakes. The General saw himself as King of the Vampires. In this, he was alone: set beside the Prince, General Iorga was a featherweight.

'There will be a celebration in the barracks tonight,' Iorga told them. 'The Guard has triumphed.'

Mackenzie shifted his hat to shade his disgusted face, but did not contradict the General in his poaching of credit for the rout of the rioters.

'Von Klatka,' Iorga said, 'cut out half a dozen of those warm women and escort them to our barracks.'

'Yes, *sir*,' von Klatka replied.

The prisoners cried and prayed. Von Klatka made great show of leering at each of the prisoners, rejecting this one as too old and fat, that one as too thin and stringy. He called the Captain over for an added opinion but Kostaki pretended not to hear.

Iorga and Hentzau strode off, capes flapping behind them. The

General aped the Prince's dress, though he was too plump to carry it off properly.

'He reminds me of Sir Charles Warren,' Mackenzie said. 'Struts around spitting orders with no idea what it's like out here at the sharp end.'

'The General is a fool. Most above the rank of Captain are.'

The policeman chuckled. 'As are most above the rank of Inspector.'

'We can agree on that.'

Von Klatka made his choices and the turnkey helped him haul the girls – for they tended to be the youngest – out of the wagon. They clung together, shivering. Their vestments were unsuitable for a chilly night.

'Good fat martyrs they make,' said von Klatka, pinching the nearest cheek.

The turnkey produced handcuffs and chains from the wagon and began to bind the chosen together. Von Klatka slapped one on the rear and laughed like a gay devil. The girl fell to her knees and prayed for deliverance. Von Klatka bent over and poked his red tongue into her ear. She reacted with comic disgust and the Captain was seized by convulsions of laughter.

'You, sir,' one of the women said to Mackenzie, 'you're warm, help us, save us . . .'

Mackenzie was uncomfortable. He looked away, putting his face in the dark again.

'I apologize.' Kostaki said. 'This is an absurdity. Azzo, get those women to the barracks. I shall join you later.'

Von Klatka saluted and dragged the girls off. He sang a shepherd's song as he led his flock away. The Guard were quartered near the Palace.

'You should not be asked to stand by for such things,' Kostaki told the policeman.

'No one should.'

'Perhaps not.'

The wagons trundled off, the prisoners to be distributed throughout London's jails. Kostaki assumed most would end up on stakes at Tyburn or put to hard labour in Devil's Dyke.

He was alone with Mackenzie. 'You should become one of us, Scotsman.'

'An unnatural thing?'

'What is more unnatural? To live, or to die?'

'To live off others.'

'Who can say they do not live off others?'

Mackenzie shrugged. He took out a pipe and filled it with tobacco.

'We have much in common, you and I,' Kostaki said. 'Our countries have been devoured. You, a Scotsman, serve the Queen of England, and I, a Moldavian, follow a Prince of Wallachia. You are a policeman, I a soldier.'

Mackenzie lit his pipe and sucked in smoke. 'Are you a soldier before or after you're a vampire?'

Kostaki considered. 'I should like to think I am a soldier. Which are you first, policeman or warm?'

'Alive, of course.' His pipe-bowl glowed.

'So, you have more kinship with this Jack the Ripper than with, say, Inspector Lestrade?'

Mackenzie sighed. 'You have me there, Kostaki. I confess it. I'm a copper first and a living man second.'

'Then, I repeat myself: join us. Would you leave our gift to braggarts like Iorga and Hentzau?'

Mackenzie considered. 'No,' he said, at last. 'I'm sorry. Maybe when I'm near death, I'll see things differently. But the Lord God didn't make us vampires.'

'I believe the contrary.'

There was noise in the near distance. Shouts of men, screams of women. Steel on steel. Something breaking. Kostaki began to run. Mackenzie tried hard to keep pace. The din came from the direction von Klatka had taken. Mackenzie clutched his chest and gasped. Kostaki left him behind and covered the distance in moments.

After sprinting through bushes, he found the scuffle. The girls were loose and von Klatka was on the ground. Five or six men in black coats, scarves tied over their faces, held him down, and one white-hooded fellow sawed at his chest with a shining dagger. Von Klatka yelled his defiance. Stuck in the ground was a stick from which hung the flag of the Christian Crusade. One of the masked men pointed a pistol. Kostaki saw the puff of smoke and prepared to shrug off yet another bullet. Then he felt a burst of pain in his knee. He had been shot with a silver ball.

'Back, vampire,' said the gunman, his voice muffled.

Mackenzie was with them now, Kostaki was ready to lunge forwards but the policeman held him back. His leg was numb. The bullet was lodged in his bones, poisoning him.

One of the freed women kicked von Klatka in the head, doing no damage at all. The man straddling the vampire had wrenched free his cuirass. With slices from a silver knife, he exposed von Klatka's beating heart. He was handed something like a candle by one of his comrades, and thrust it into von Klatka's rib-cage.

'For Jago!' the crusader shouted, from behind his cloth mask.

A lucifer flared and the crusaders scattered away from their handiwork. There was a circle of blood around von Klatka. He held his chest together, wounds closing. The candle stuck out from his ribs, a hissing flame at its end.

'Dynamite,' Mackenzie shouted.

Ezzelin von Klatka grasped at the burning fuse. But too late. His fist closed around the flame just as it expanded. A flash of white light turned night to day. Then a strong wind and a roar lifted Kostaki and Mackenzie off their feet. Mixed in with the blast were gobbets of vampire-flesh and scraps of von Klatka's armour and clothes.

Kostaki scrambled to his feet. First he made sure Mackenzie, who was holding his abused ears, was not seriously hurt. Then he turned to his fallen comrade. The whole of von Klatka's torso was blown to fragments. His head was burning, his flesh putrefying fast. A gaseous stench burst from his remains and Kostaki choked on it.

The Christian Crusade flag was fallen, dotted with burning specks.

'A reprisal for the attempt on Jago,' Kostaki said.

Mackenzie, shaking his head to try and get the ringing out of his ears, paid attention. 'Most likely. Dynamite's an old Fenian trick and there are a lot of Irish in with Jago's crew. Still . . .' His thought trailed off. There were people running towards them. Carpathians, roused from the barracks, breastplates hastily misbuckled, swords drawn.

'Still what, Scotsman?'

Mackenzie shook his head. 'The fellow who spoke, the one with the dynamite . . .'

'What of him?'

'I could have sworn he was a vampire.'

36

The Old Jago

'THERE ARE PEOPLE in this world of whom even vampires are afraid,' he said as they walked up Brick Lane.

'That, I know,' she admitted.

The elder was out in the fog waiting for his tongue to grow back. When ready, he would come for her again.

'I'm familiar with all the devils in all the hells, Geneviève,' Charles said. 'This is just a matter of invoking the correct demonic personage.'

She did not know what he was talking about.

He led her into one of the narrow, unpleasant-smelling streets that constituted the worst slum in London. Walls leaned together, dropping the occasional brick to the cobbles. Evil-looking new-borns congregated at every corner.

'Charles,' she said. 'This is the Old Jago.'

He allowed that it was.

She wondered if he had gone mad. Dressed as they were – which was to say, not in rags – they were practically parading with a sandwich board marked 'ROB AND KILL ME'. Red eyes glittered behind broken windows. Rat-whiskered children sat on doorsteps, waiting to fight for the leavings of larger predators. The further they penetrated into the rookery, the thicker the gathering crowds were. She was reminded of vultures. This was not England, this was a jungle. Places, she told herself, were not evil: they were what people made of them. In the dark, something laughed and Geneviève jumped. Charles calmed her and looked about, leaning on his cane as if taking the air at Hampton Court.

Hunched, shambling creatures lurked in courtyards. Hate came off them in waves. The Jago was where the worst cases ended up, new-borns shape-shifted beyond any resemblance to humanity, criminals so vile other criminals would not tolerate their society. A

Christian Crusade flag, the cross dyed in what probably was not blood, hung from one window. John Jago's mission was hereabouts, where few policemen dared venture. No one knew the clergyman's real name.

'What do we seek?' Geneviève asked, under her breath.

'A Chinaman.'

Her heart sank again.

'No,' he reassured, 'not *that* Chinaman. In this district, I imagine any Chinaman will serve.'

A burly new-born, bare-chested under his braces, detached himself from the shadows of a wall and stood before them, looking down on Charles. He smiled, showing yellow fangs. His arms were tattooed with skulls and bats. Having seen Charles save the day with Liz Stride, Geneviève thought he could best the vampire with silver blade or bullet. But he would not last long if a dozen of the rough's friends joined in. At least a dozen were scattered about, picking their teeth with grimy thumbnails.

'I say,' Charles began, drawling like a Mayfair ass, 'direct me to the nearest opium den, there's a good fellow. The viler the better, if you catch my drift.'

Something shone in Charles's hand. A coin. It disappeared into the rough's fist, and then his mouth. He bit the shilling in two and spat the halves out. They hardly had time to clatter before a tangle of children were fighting over them. The rough looked into Charles's face, trying to exert his new-won vampire powers of fascination. After a minute or two, during which Geneviève was increasingly uncomfortable, he grunted and turned away. Charles had passed a test. The rough nodded towards an archway and slouched off.

The arch led to an enclosed square, and was covered with a greasy grey blanket on a string. The makeshift curtain was swept aside by a slender hand and a warm cloud of scented smoke drifted out. The glow-worms of opium pipes lit up wizened faces. A warm sailor, with scabs on his neck and nothing in his eyes, tottered out, his pay burned away in dream-smoke. He would be lucky to get out of the Jago with his sea-boots.

'Just the thing,' Charles said.

'What are we doing?' she asked him.

'Rattling a web to attract a spider's attention.'

'Wonderful.'

A young Chinese, new-born and delicate, emerged from the courtyard. The roughs all deferred to her, which said much. She wore blue pyjamas and trod upon filthy cobbles with silk slippers. Her skin shone like fine porcelain. A tight bound rope of glossy black hair hung to her knees. Charles bowed to her, and she responded, arms outspread in welcome.

'Charles Beauregard of the Diogenes Club sends his regards to your master, the Lord of Strange Deaths.'

The girl said nothing. Geneviève imagined some of the loiterers had slipped away and found something else to interest them.

'I wish it known that this woman, Geneviève Dieudonné, is under my protection. I request that no further action be taken against her lest the bond of friendship between your master and myself be broken.'

The girl considered a moment and gave one sharp nod. She bowed once more and retreated behind the curtain. Through the thin blanket, Geneviève still saw the wavering red dots of the pipes.

'That should do it, I think,' Charles said.

Geneviève shook her head. She did not quite understand what had passed between Charles and the oriental new-born.

'I have friends in strange places,' he admitted.

They were alone. Even the children had disappeared. By invoking this 'Lord of Strange Deaths', Charles had cleared the street.

'So, Charles, I am under your protection?'

He looked almost amused. 'Yes.'

She did not know what to think. Somehow she did feel safer, but also a touch irritated. 'I suppose I should thank you.'

'It might be an idea.'

She sighed. 'So that was it, then? No battle of titanic forces, no magic destruction of the enemy, no heroic last stand?'

'Just a little diplomacy. Always the best way.'

'And your "friend" can really call off the elder, as a huntsman calls a dog to heel?'

'Indubitably.'

They were walking out of the Jago, back towards the 'safer' waters of Whitechapel. The slum was lit only by braziers of infernal embers in the courtyards, which gave the dark a reddish underglow. Now there were at least the usual hissing streetlights. By comparison, the fog here was almost friendly.

'The Chinese believe that if you save a person from death, you're responsible for the rest of their lives. Charles, are you prepared to take that burden? I've lived a long time and intend to live a great while longer.'

'Geneviève, I think you unlikely to place too great a strain on my conscience.'

They stopped and she looked at him. He was barely able to conceal his smug amusement.

'You only know me as I am now,' she said. 'I'm not the person I was, or the one I will be. Over the years, we don't change on the outside but inside . . . that's another thing.'

'I'll undertake the risk.'

With morning only an hour or so away, she was tired. She was still weak and should not have ventured out. The ache in her neck was worse than it had been. Amworth said that meant she was healing properly.

'I have heard the expression before,' she said.

'The expression?'

'"Lord of Strange Deaths". One who goes by that title is mentioned, if very infrequently, in connection with a criminal *tong*. His reputation is not of the best.'

'As I said, he is a devil from hell. But he is a devil of his word; he takes obligations seriously.'

'He has an obligation to you?'

'Indeed.'

'Then you've an obligation to him?'

Charles said nothing. His mind was a blank, except for the image of a railway station sign.

'You're doing that deliberately, are you not?'

'What?'

'Thinking of Basingstoke.'

Charles laughed. And, after a moment, she did too.

37

Downing Street, Behind Closed Doors

G ODALMING WAS LATE for his appointment. His neatly bandaged cut throbbed, the pain unlike anything since his turning. His head was fogged by Penelope; the old, warm Penelope who was no more, not the new-born he had left in Cadogan Square. In the cab, he slumped into a daze, reliving the passing of his bloodline. At once bloated and drained, he remembered the Dark Kiss. As himself and as Penelope. This would pass.

In Downing Street, he was ushered quietly into the Cabinet. In an instant, he was shocked sober. The room was filled, his private audience with Lord Ruthven superseded by what was obviously an important gathering. General Iorga and Sir Charles Warren were there. Also, Henry Matthews, the Home Secretary, and several other, equally distinguished vampires. Sir Danvers Carew, wearing his customary scowl, chewed an unlit cigar.

'Godalming,' Ruthven said, 'sit down. Lady Ducayne will have to excuse you. We are discussing the evening's atrocities.'

Godalming, befuddled, found a chair. He had missed the second act, and would have to pick up the thread.

'The Carpathian Guard has been grossly insulted.' Iorga said, 'and must be avenged.'

'Quite, quite, quite,' mumbled Matthews. Not generally reckoned to be among the Government's ablest men, he was sometimes unkindly likened to 'a French dancing master'. 'But it would be unwise to fly off the handle, what with the current delicate situation.'

Iorga thumped with a mailed fist, cracking the table. 'Our blood must have blood!'

Ruthven looked with distaste at the damage the Carpathian had done. The fine finish was ruined.

'Malefactors will not be allowed to escape unpunished,' the Prime Minister told the General.

'Indeed,' put in Sir Charles. 'We confidently expect arrests within twenty-four hours.'

'Just as you have confidently expected at every opportunity for the last few months in this Ripper case,' snorted Matthews.

The Home Secretary had quarrelled with the Commissioner before, notably in a bitter jurisdictional dispute over who was finally responsible for the newly formed Criminal Investigation Department of the Metropolitan Police. At first, each had claimed the dynamic detectives as their own, but, of late, both had been less keen; especially with the Whitechapel murders still unsolved.

Sir Charles was angered by the needling. 'As you well know, Home Secretary, the police failures in this matter owe more to your refusal to allot adequate funds than to any – '

'Gentlemen,' said Ruthven, quietly. 'This is not under discussion.'

The Home Secretary and the Commissioner slumped, each glaring at the other.

'Warren,' Ruthven addressed himself to Sir Charles, 'you are best placed to give an account of the position of the police force. Do so.'

Godalming listened intently. He might find out what this was about.

Sir Charles consulted his note book like an ordinary constable in court, and cleared his throat. 'At about midnight, an incident took place in St James's Park . . .'

'Within a few hundred yards of the Palace!' Matthews put in.

'. . . Indeed, in the immediate environs of Buckingham Palace, although at no time were the Royal Family endangered. An officer of the Carpathian Guard was escorting a group of insurrectionists arrested earlier, during the riots'

'Dangerous criminals!' Iorga blustered.

'That is conjecture. Reports vary. Inspector Mackenzie, a witness, describes the prisoners as "a group of frightened young women".'

Iorga grunted.

'A band of men cornered the officer, Ezzelin von Klatka, and destroyed him. In a particularly revolting manner.'

'How, exactly?' Godalming put in, intrigued.

'They stuck a stick of dynamite into his heart and set it off,' Ruthven said. 'An innovation, at least.'

'It was a pretty fine mess,' Sir Charles said.

'As our American cousins might have it, that's the Carpathian Guard all over,' Ruthven remarked.

Ioga's head was on the point of exploding. There was an angry red swelling around his eyes. 'Captain von Klatka died bravely,' he snarled, 'a hero.'

'Come, come, Iorga,' Ruthven said. 'A little levity is always welcome.'

'What of the culprits?' Carew asked.

'Men in masks,' Matthews said. 'A cross of St George was left by the body. Obviously, Sir Charles's previous reports on the disorganization of the Christian Crusade have been sorely in error.'

'Some see this as retaliation for the attack on John Jago,' Ruthven explained. 'Someone has painted thin red crosses all over the city.'

'Mackenzie says the murderer of von Klatka was a vampire,' Sir Charles said.

'Absurd,' Matthews shouted. 'You all cling together, you policemen. You cover your mistakes with lies.'

'Hold fire, Matthews,' Sir Charles responded. 'I merely repeat the claim of an observant man at the scene. For myself, I agree with you. It is unlikely that any vampire should wish harm to the Carpathian Guard. That would be practically the same as lifting a hand against our beloved Prince Consort.'

'Yes,' Ruthven said. 'It would, wouldn't it?'

'What's been done?' Carew said, his habitual angry look turning to black-faced fury.

Sir Charles sighed. 'I have issued orders for the arrest of the Crusade ring leaders still at liberty after this afternoon's disturbances.'

'Their heads should be on poles by sunrise.'

'General Iorga, we operate under the rule of law. We must first establish the guilt of the felons.'

Iorga waved the irrelevance away. 'Punish them all and let God decide who is guilty.'

Sir Charles continued. 'We know the churches and chapels where Jago's followers gather. All are being raided. In one night, we shall put an end to the Christian Crusade.'

Ruthven thanked the Commissioner. 'Excellent, Warren. I am myself arranging for the Archbishop to condemn the crusaders as heretics. They will no longer have even the notional support of the Church.'

'There must be further reprisals,' Iorga insisted. 'To stop the rot of rebellion. For von Klatka, a hundred must die.'

Ruthven considered the matter, before he took charge again. 'We now come to our larger purpose. Even without this fresh outrage I should have convened this meeting within a few nights. This is not an isolated incident. It has not been released to the public, but a week ago an assassin tossed a bomb at Sir Francis Varney during an official visit to Lahore. It failed to explode, but the villain escaped into the crowds. Also, there was this morning an organized mutiny in Devil's Dyke. That has been suppressed but several dangerous insurrectionists are being tracked on the Sussex Downs.'

Sir Charles looked stricken. This reflected badly on Scotland Yard. On his administration.

Ruthven continued. '*Silent enim leges inter arma*, as Cicero has it. Laws are dumb in time of war. It may be necessary to suspend Habeas Corpus. The Prince Consort has already taken the title of Lord Protector, assuming the constitutional burden formerly shouldered by our dear Queen. He may yet find it useful to extend his personal powers. In that event, we in this room would most likely constitute the entire government of Great Britain and its Empire. We would be king's ministers.'

Matthews was about to protest but fell silent. Still a new-born, like Sir Charles, he was in this room only on sufferance. Their seats could easily be filled by vampire elders. Or un-dead of the new breed, who had completely abandoned their warm ways. Godalming realized how close he was to power. He might soon learn what Ruthven was grooming him for.

A dour and silent vampire beside the Prime Minister gave him a ribbon-tied folder of papers. Godalming thought he was connected with the Secret Service.

'Thank you, Mr Croft,' Ruthven said, ripping the ribbon. He extracted a paper with finger and thumb and casually whirled it across the table to Sir Charles. 'This is a list of prominent people suspected of conspiracy against the Crown. They are to be arrested before the sun sets tomorrow.'

Sir Charles's lips moved as he read the list. He put it down and Godalming was able to glance over it.

Most of the names were familiar: George Bernard Shaw, W. T. Stead, Cunningham–Grahame, Annie Besant, Lord Tennyson. Others meant little: Marie Spartali Stilman, Adam Adamant, Olive Schreiner, Alfred Waterhouse, Edward Carpenter, C. L. Dodgson. There were some surprises.

'Gilbert?' Sir Charles asked. 'Why? The man's as much a vampire as you or I.'

'As much as you, maybe. He has lampooned us constantly. Many cannot see a vampire elder without sniggering. Not, I think, an attitude we wish to foster.'

It was hardly a coincidence that the bad baronet in *Ruddigore* whose name was a byword for a certain kind of vampire, was named Sir *Ruthven* Murgatroyd.

Matthews was looking over the list now, shaking his head. 'And Gilbert is not the only vampire here,' he said. 'You have down Soames Forsyte, my own banker.'

For once, Ruthven did not seem silly and trifling. Godalming saw cold steel claws inside the murgatroyd's velvet glove.

'Vampires are as capable of treason as the warm,' Ruthven explained. 'Every man and woman on that list has won their place in Devil's Dyke fair and square.'

Sir Charles was concerned. 'Devil's Dyke was not constructed with vampires in mind.'

'Then let us be thankful that we maintain the Tower of London. It shall be converted into a prison for vampires. General Iorga, have you under your command some officer whom you have had cause to reprimand for the severity of his treatment of underlings?'

Iorga grinned, a row of jagged beast-teeth flashing. 'I can think of several. Graf Orlok is well known for excess.'

'Excellent. Orlok shall be made Governor of the Tower of London.'

'But the man's a maniacal brute,' Matthews protested. 'He is no longer welcome at half the houses in London. He looks barely human.'

'Just the vampire for the job,' Ruthven commented. 'This is statesmanship, Matthews. There are positions for all. It is simply a matter of matching personality to the task.'

Mr Croft took a note, either of the Graf's appointment or of the Home Secretary's protest. Godalming would not care to be listed in Mr Croft's note book.

'Now, to other business. Warren, here is a draft of your new promotion policy.'

Sir Charles gasped as the paper was given him.

'Only vampires are to be advanced.' Ruthven said. 'This is to be a general rule in all branches of civil and military service. The warm may turn or stay where they are. It is of no consequence. And remember, Warren, only the *right sort* of vampires are to be promoted. I shall expect you to clean your house.'

Ruthven turned his attention to the Home Secretary and gave him another document. 'Matthews, this is a draft of the Emergency Powers Act which will pass in the House tomorrow evening. I consider it vital that we order the affairs of the daytime world rather more stringently than under the haphazard system we have tolerated until the present. There will be restrictions on travel, assembly and commerce. Public houses will only open during the hours of darkness. It is time we rearranged the clock and calendar for our convenience, rather than bowed to the wishes of the warm.'

Matthews swallowed the medicine. Sir Danvers Carew growled with something approaching pleasure. He was in line to replace Matthews when Ruthven made him resign.

'We are being forced to act swiftly,' Ruthven declared to the room in general. 'But this is no bad thing. We must keep to our decided course, whatever resistance we might meet. These are exciting nights, and we have a chance to lead the world. We are the wind from the East. We are the fury of the storm. In our wake, we will leave this country changed and tempered. Those who hesitate or stay their hands will be whisked away in the torrent. Like the Prince Consort, I intend to stand fast. Many will be destroyed utterly as the moon rises on our Empire. Mr Darwin was quite correct: only the fit shall survive. We must ensure that we are among the fittest of the fit.'

38

New-Born

ART HAD LEFT Penelope to see herself out. She was in a species of a swoon as he told her why he was dashing off. Something to do with the Prime Minister. Affairs of great import and urgency. Masculine matters, she assumed, and none of her concern. It seemed as if Art talked to her from the end of a long tunnel, a great wind blowing against him and carrying off his voice. Then he was gone and she was alone with herself . . .

. . . she was turning. It was not what she expected. She had been told it was quick: a brief pain like a tooth being pulled, then a period of dozing, comparable to the pupal stage of an insect, followed by a reawakening into the vampire state.

The pain, raging red throughout her body, was terrible. Suddenly, in a hot gush, her monthly was upon her. Her underthings were clogged. Kate had warned her, but she had forgotten. At the moment, there was little consolation in the prospect that this was the last time such feminine inconvenience would bother her. Vampire females, she understood, do not menstruate. That curse was lifted forever. As a woman, she was dead . . .

. . . on the divan where Art had taken her, where she had bled him, she gripped a bolster to her stomach. She had expelled every scrap of food from her stomach on to Art's Persian carpet. Then, in a more convenient moment, she had voided her bowels and bladder. She understood why, even as he was making a hasty escape, Art took the trouble to tell her where his privy was. During the turn, her body expelled all its wastes.

She felt feverish and empty, as if her insides had been scooped out. Her jaws ached as the buds of her teeth opened, sharp enamels scraping together. She had the enlarged, pointed teeth of the typical vampire. This was not a permanent condition, she knew. Her teeth would change in the moment of passion or anger. Or, as now, pain. Adapting to her new mode of feeding, her incisors became fangs.

Why had she chosen this? She could hardly remember.

Her hand was close to her face. She saw veins and tendons under the skin, undulating like worms. Her trimmed nails were daggerish diamond-shapes. There were even a few coarse black hairs. Her fingers had thickened and her engagement ring cut into her skin.

She tried to concentrate.

Her hand stopped writhing and dwindled into its familiar shape. With her tongue, she tested her teeth. They were small again, and she no longer felt that her mouth was full of pointed palings.

She was on her back, head lolling off the edge of the divan. She saw the room upside-down. Art's father stood on his head in a full-length portrait. A blue standing vase hung from the carpeted ceiling, dangling sharp fronds of white pampas grass. A frieze of delicately upturned flowers ringed the room. Inverted gaslights stuck out of the skirting board, blue flames jetting down towards the painted floor.

The flames grew until they were all she could see. The fever was in her brain. In the flames, she saw a man and a woman embracing. He was fully clothed in evening dress but she was naked and bloody. The faces were Charles's and Pamela's. Then her cousin's face became her own and Charles turned to Art. They were clothed in flame. The image lasted a moment, then flowed again until the faces were unrecognizable. They meshed and burned together, forming one four-eyed, two-mouthed, hair-swathed face. The conglomerate face of fire grew and engulfed her completely.

'Penelope for ever after,' she had shouted as a child. 'Long live Penny.'

The flame burned all around . . .

. . . with a single shiver, she was instantly awake. She tingled all over, clothing scraping her sensitive skin.

She sat up and arranged herself on the divan. The memory of her turn was fading fast. She felt her neck and breast and could not find a trace of the wounds Art had made.

The room was brighter and she saw into the shadowed corners. She saw things differently. There were subtler gradations of colour.

And she could smell more scents. The odours of her own bodily discharges were distinguishable, and not offensive. She thought all her senses were sharpened. Her tongue longed for new tastes. She wished to experiment.

She stood up and padded in her stockinged feet to the bathroom. There was, of course, no mirror. She divested herself of her soiled clothes, and wiped herself off with a balled petticoat. She washed herself all over. In her former life, she had rarely been as completely naked. Her old self seemed a dream. She was new-born. When satisfied that she was clean as any cat, she left the bathroom. She needed clothes. The garments of her warmth were useless now, sodden with useless blood.

Someone moved in one of the rooms off the corridor and she was instantly alert. She ran her tongue over sharp teeth. A door opened, and a thin face poked out. Shocked by her nudity, Art's manservant gulped and withdrew, locking his door behind him. She laughed. Flexing her hands, she wondered if she could wrench open the door and get to the man. She could smell his warm blood. 'Fi fi fo fum,' she whispered, her voice loud in her head.

Opening one of the doors, she found Art's dressing room. A suit of his morning clothes was laid out ready for him. Formerly, being tall had been an embarrassment. Her mother had trained her to sit down as often as possible and, without stooping, to arrange herself so she would not tower over a man. Now her height suited her well.

She pulled on Art's shirt and buttoned it up. She mastered the intricacy of the collar and the cuffs. Her fingers were abler now and solved all the problems presented to them. She threw aside Art's underclothes and pulled on his trousers, fiddling with the unfamiliar braces until the contraptions hung over her shoulders. The garment settled on her hips, and she pulled it up tight, crotch snug, then shortened the braces to suit her. She found a cravat and tied it around the too-large collar. A waistcoat and a coat completed the ensemble. Barefoot, she returned to the room where she had turned. Her shoes were under the divan, and still fitted her. She imagined she cut quite a dash, and wondered what her fiancé would think.

Running her hands through her hair, she wondered if she should do anything to make herself look less a fright. But she did not really care any more how she looked. The dead Penelope would have been shocked senseless. But the dead Penelope had been so different.

She felt a twinge of thirst. The taste of Art's blood lingered in her mouth. She had found it bitter and salty last night. But now it was sweet and delicious. And necessary. What to do? What to do?

She did not know if she was managing this terribly well. But if Kate Reed, who could barely pour tea from a pot without consulting Mrs Beeton, could become a successful vampire, then Penelope the Conqueror would not be daunted by the complications.

In the hall, she found an opera cloak, lined with red silk. It did not feel heavy. She tried to set one of Art's top hats on her head, but it slipped down around her ears and visored her eyes. The only headgear on Art's rack that could be made to suit her was a soft check cap with ear-flaps. It hardly went with the rest of the get-up she had appropriated but it would have to do. She was at least able to bundle up her hair under the cap and get it out of the way. Some vampire girls cut their hair short, like a man's. She might consider that . . .

. . . outside, the sun was rising. She thought she should get home and stay indoors. Maybe she should rest during the hours of daylight. Kate told her the sun could harm new-borns. She supposed she would have to put herself in the invidious and humiliating position of seeking Kate out and soliciting her advice on any number of unforeseeable points.

She left the house and found the early morning fog thick. Yesterday, she would not have been able to see the other side of Cadogan Square. Now she could distinguish things a little better, although her vision was better with shadows than with fog. If she looked up at the foggy clouds that blocked the sun, her eyes stung. She pulled her cap down, so the peak would shade her face.

'Missy, missy,' a voice said. A woman was coming at her out of the fog, dragging two small children.

The thirst was upon her again – the red thirst, they called it – and her mouth was parched, her teeth pricking. It was not to be compared with the needs she had known as a warm woman. It was an overpowering desire, a natural instinct on a level with the need to breathe.

'Missy . . .'

An old woman, her hand out, was before her. She wore a tatty poke bonnet and a ragged shawl. 'Do you thirst, missy?' The woman grinned. Most of her teeth were missing and her breath stank. Penelope could smell twenty layers of differing dirts. If Fagin had a widow, this was she.

'For sixpence, you could drink your fill. From one of my pretties.'

The woman picked up a bundle. It was a girl child, one of a pair. The face and hair were dirty but the girl was pale, mummy-wrapped in a long scarf. The woman disentangled the scarf from a thin, many-times-scabbed neck. 'Just sixpence, missy.'

The woman clawed at the little girl's neck, scraping scabs. Tiny drops of blood welled. The child made no sound. The blood-smell caught in Penelope's nostrils. It was a hot, spiced, penetrating scent. She *thirsted*.

The girl was handed to her. For a moment, she hesitated at the intimacy. When warm, she had not cared to be touched, had especially not cared to be touched by children. She had vowed after Pamela's death never to submit to a man's lusts, never to bear children. That eventually came to seem childish, but she had not relished the thought of her wedding night. That side of things had very little to do with her engagement. What she had done with Art had been more than a feeding, more than an agent of the turn. There had been a carnal element, repellant and exciting. Now, it was acceptable, even desirable.

'Sixpence,' the woman reminded, her voice dwindling as Penelope concentrated on the child's neck.

With Art, the drinking of blood had been an unpleasant necessity. She had felt a strange thrill, not quite indistinguishable from pain, when he bit her. Taking his blood had been a repugnant chore; this desire was different. The turn had awakened something in Penelope. As she touched her tongue to the open wound, her old self truly died. As the blood trickled into her mouth, the new-born she had become awoke.

She had chosen to become a vampire because she thought it proper. She had been angry with Charles, for his dalliance with that elder creature, for his failure to appear and make sufficient apology. He treated the warm woman badly, but perhaps his attitude would be different if she turned. All of that was absurdly by the bye.

She gulped, feeling the blood seeping throughout her. It did not just slip down her throat, but pumped into her gums, spreading through her face. She felt it swelling in her cheeks, throbbing in the veins under her ears, filling out her eyes.

'There now, missy. You'll polish her off. Have a care.'

The woman tried to pull the child away and Penelope threw her off. She was not satisfied yet. The child's whimpering was in her ears, an encouragement in the feeble whine. The girl wanted to be drained dry, as much as Penelope needed to take her blood . . .

. . . finally, it was over. The child's heart still beat. Penelope set her down on the pavement. The other girl – her sister? – quickly wrapped her up.

'A shilling,' the woman said. 'You took a shilling's worth.'

Penelope hissed at the pandering bitch, spitting through her fangs. It would be easy to open her from stomach to neck. She had the talons for the task.

'A shilling.'

The woman was resolute. Penelope recognized a kinship. They were both living with a need that superseded all other considerations.

In her front pockot, she found a watch and chain. She detached them from the waistcoat and tossed them to the panderer. The woman made a fist and snatched the prize from the air. Her mouth formed into a disbelieving grin.

'Thank you, ever so, missy. Thank you. Any time, you're welcome to my girls. Any time.'

Penelope left the woman in Cadogan Square and walked off in the fog, a newfound vitality electrifying her. She was stronger inside than she had ever been . . .

. . . she knew her way in the fog. The Churchward house was only a short distance away, in Caversham Street. As she walked, it was as if in all the city she alone knew where she was going. She could have found home with her eyes closed.

With the child's blood in her, she was light-headed. She had not often had more than a single glass of wine with dinner, but she recognized her current state as akin to intoxication. Once, she and Kate and another girl had emptied four bottles from her late father's prized cellar. Only Kate had not been sick afterwards and she had been infuriatingly superior about it. This was like that, but without the roiling in her stomach.

Occasionally, people would sense her coming and get out of her way. Nobody even stared or passed comment on her unusual dress. Men had kept the convenience of their clothing to themselves. She felt somewhat piratical, like Anne Bonney. Even Pam, she was sure, had never known anything as exhilarating as this. At last, she outshone her cousin.

The fog thinned, and her cloak hung heavy on her shoulders. She stopped, and found herself dizzy. Had the girl carried any disease? She clung to a lamp-post like a drunken toff. The fog was just whispy strands. A breeze was blowing from the river. She could taste the Thames on the wind. The world seemed to spin as the early fog dissipated. In the sky, a merciless ball of fire expanded, reaching out light-tendrils. She drew a hand over her face and felt her skin burning. It was as if a great magnifying glass were suspended in the air, concentrating the sun's rays on her as a boy directs a killing beam at an ant.

Her hand hurt. It was an angry lobster-red. The skin itched fearfully and split in one place. A curl of steamy smoke emerged from the crack. Pushing away from the lamp-post, she ran over uncertain ground, her cloak streaming behind her. The air dragged at her ankles like swamp-water. She was coughing, spitting up blood. She had glutted herself overmuch, and was paying for her greed.

Sun lay heavy on the streets, bleaching everything around to a shining bone-white. Even if she shut her eyes fast, an agony of light burst into her brain. She thought she would never reach Caversham Street and safety. She would stumble and fall in the road, and resolve into a smoking woman-shape of dust under the crumpled fan of Art's cape.

Her face was taut, as if it had shrunken on to her skull. She should never have ventured out into the sun on her first day as a new-born. Kate had told her. Someone got in her way and she bowled him over. She was still strong and swift. She bent double as she ran, the blast of the sun on her back, heating her body through several layers of cloth. Her lips were drawn away from her teeth, stiff and shrivelled. Every step hurt, as if she were skipping through a forest of razors. This was not what she had expected . . .

. . . a homing instinct brought her to the street, to her own front door. She fumbled with the bell-pull and hooked one foot under the boot-scraper to prevent herself from falling backwards. Unless admitted into the cool shade at once, she would die. She leaned against her door and banged with the heel of her hand.

'Mother, mother,' she croaked. She sounded like an old crone.

The door was opened and she fell into the arms of Mrs Yeovil, their housekeeper. The servant did not recognize Penelope, and tried to push her back out into the cruel day.

'No,' her mother said. 'It's Penny. Look . . .'

Mrs Yeovil's eyes grew wide; in their horror, Penelope saw her reflection more surely than she ever had in any mirror.

'Lord bless us,' the servant said.

Mother and Mrs Yeovil helped her into the hallway and the door was slammed shut. Pain still streamed through the stained-glass fanlight, but the worst of the sun was kept out. She lolled in the embrace of the two women. There was another person in the hallway, standing at the door of the withdrawing room.

'Penelope? My Lord, Penelope!' It was Charles. 'She's turned, Mrs Churchward,' he said.

For a moment, she remembered what it was all about, what it had all been for. She tried to tell him, but only a hiss came out.

'Don't try to talk, dear,' her mother said. 'It'll be all right.'

'Get her somewhere dark,' Charles said.

'The cellar?'

'Yes, the cellar.'

He pulled open the door under the stairs and the women carried her down into her father's wine cellar. There was no light at all and she was suddenly cool all over. The burning stopped. She still hurt but she no longer felt on the point of exploding.

'Oh, Penny, my poor dear,' her mother said, laying a hand on her brow. 'You look so . . .'

The sentence trailed off and they laid her out on cold but clean flagstones. She tried to sit up, to spit a curse at Charles.

'Rest,' he said.

They forced her back and she shut her eyes. Inside her head, the dark was red and teeming.

39

From Hell

17 OCTOBER
I am keeping Mary Kelly. She is so like Lucy, so like what Lucy became. I have paid her rent up to the end of the month. I visit her when work permits and we indulge in our peculiar exchange of fluids. There are distractions but I do my best to set them aside.

George Lusk, chairman of the Vigilance Committee, came to see me at the Hall yesterday. He had been sent half a kidney with a note headed '*From Hell*', claiming the enclosure was from one of the dead women, presumably Eddowes. '*Tother piece I fried and ate, it was very nise.*' With a horrid irony, he thought first to bring the grisly trophy to me, believing the meat from a calf or a dog and himself the victim of a jape. 'Jack the Ripper' jokes are an epidemic, and since Lusk had a letter about the murders published in *The Times*, he has fallen victim to not a few. With Lestrade and Lusk looking over my shoulder, I prodded and poked the kidney. The organ was certainly human and had been preserved in alcohol. I told Lusk the prank most likely the work of a medical student. From my days at Bart's, I recall fools who became devoted to such infantile and macabre practices. I cannot walk down Harley Street without remembering which society doctor once decamped from his lodgings leaving a dismembered torso to be discovered in his bed by the landlady. One oddity I observed was that the kidney almost certainly did come from a vampire. It displayed an advanced state of that distinctive species of liquid decay that comes upon the vampire after true death. I was not called upon to explain my familiarity with the innards of the un-dead.

Lestrade concurred, and Lusk, who is I understand quite a nuisance, was placated. Lestrade tells me the investigation is constantly muddied by similar false leads, as if Jack the Ripper were supported by a society of merry fellows intent on providing

him with a protective fog of confusion. I have thought myself that
I was not without friends, that some unknown power watched over
my interests. Nevertheless I believe I have played out, for the time
being, my string. The 'double event' – hideous expression, courtesy
of that bothersome letter-writer – has unnerved me, and I shall
suspend my night-work. It is still necessary but it has become
too dangerous. The police are against me and there are vampires
everywhere. It is my hope that others will take up my task. The
day after John Jago was wounded, a vampire fop was killed in
Soho, a stake through his heart and crusader cross carved in his
forehead. The *Pall Mall Gazette* ran an editorial suggesting that the
Whitechapel Murderer had gone West.

I am learning from Kelly. Learning about myself. She tells me
sweetly, as we lie on her bed, that she has gone off the game, that
she is not seeing other men. I know she lies but do not make an issue
of it. I open her pink flesh up and vent myself inside her and she
gently taps my blood, her teeth sliding into me. I have scars on my
body, scars that itch like the wound Renfield gave me in Purfleet.
I am determined not to turn, not to grow weak.

Money is unimportant. Kelly can have whatever I have left from
my income. Since I came to Toynbee Hall, I've been drawing no
salary and heavily subsidising the purchase of medical supplies and
other necessaries. There has always been money in my family. No
title, but always money.

I have made Kelly tell me about Lucy. The story, I am no longer
ashamed to realize, excites me. I cannot care for Kelly as herself,
so I must care for her for Lucy's sake. Kelly's voice changes, the
Irish-Welsh lilt and oddly prissy grammar fade, and Lucy, far
more careless about what she said and how she said it than her
harlot get, seems to speak. The Lucy I remember is smug and prim
and properly flirtatious. Somewhere between that befuddling but
enchanting girl and the screaming leech whose head I sawed free
was the new-born who turned Kelly. Dracula's get. With each
retelling of the nocturnal encounter on the Heath, Kelly adds new
details. She either remembers more or invents them for my sake.
I am not sure I care which. Sometimes, Lucy's advances to Kelly
are tender, seductive, mysterious, heated caresses before the Dark
Kiss. At others, they are a brutal rape, with needle-teeth shredding
flesh and muscle. We illustrate with our bodies Kelly's stories.

I no longer remember the faces of the dead women. There is only Kelly's face, and that becomes more like Lucy with each passing night. I have bought Kelly clothes similar to those Lucy wore. The nightgown she wears before we couple is very like the shroud in which Lucy was buried. Kelly styles her hair like Lucy's now. Soon, I hesitate to hope, Kelly will *be* Lucy.

40

The Return of the Hansom Cab

'It's been nearly a month, Charles,' Geneviève ventured, 'since the "double event". Perhaps it's over?'

Beauregard shook his head. Her comment had jolted him from his thoughts. Penelope was much on his mind.

'No,' he said. 'Good things come to an end; bad things have to be stopped.'

'You're right, of course.'

It was after dark and they were in the Ten Bells. He was as familiar with Whitechapel as he had become with the other territories to which the Diogenes Club had dispatched him. He spent his days fitfully asleep in Chelsea; his nights in the East End, with Geneviève, hunting Jack the Ripper. And not catching him.

Everyone was starting to relax. The vigilante groups who roamed the streets two weeks ago, making mischief and abusing innocents, still wore their sashes and carried coshes, but they spent more time in pubs than the fog. After a month of double- and triple-shifts, policemen were gradually being redistributed back to regular duties. It was not as if the Ripper did anything to reduce crime elsewhere in the city. Indeed, there had practically been open revolt within sight of Buckingham Palace.

Last night someone had dashed a tankard of pig's blood at the portrait of the Royal Family which hung behind the bar. Woodbridge, the landlord, had tossed the unpatriotic drunk out, but stains remained on the wall and the picture. The Prince Consort's face was distorted crimson.

There had been more trouble from the Crusade. With Jago in prison and most of his followers either under arrest or driven underground, Scotland Yard had assumed the movement would wither and die, but it was proving as stubborn as the original Christian martyrs. Thin red crosses were painted all over the city, invoking not

simply Christ but also England. Beauregard heard whispers that the
ravens had left the Tower of London the evening Graf Orlok took
office, and the kingdom was considered fallen. If ever the country
had an hour of direst need, this might well be considered it. There
was a minor Arthurian revival, encouraged rather than suppressed
by the Government's disapproval. The insurrectionists, hitherto
exclusively of the socialist, anarchist or protestant persuasions, now
numbered sundry British mystics and pagans among their ranks.
Lord Ruthven had banned Tennyson, especially the *Idylls of the King*,
and such formerly innocuous items as Bulwer-Lytton's *King Arthur*
and William Morris's *The Defence of Guenevere* also adorned the index
of prohibited works. With each proclamation, the nineteen century
edged closer to the fifteenth. Ruthven promised new uniforms for
all servants of the Crown; Beauregard suspected the designs would
emerge close to livery, with policemen in scuttle-helmets and tights,
emblem-bearing tabards worn over leather jerkins.

Neither Geneviève – after all, a fifteenth-century girl – nor
Beauregard drank. They just watched the others. Beside the squiffy
vigilantes, the pub was full of women, either genuine prostitutes
or police agents in disguise. That was one of several daft schemes
that had gone from being laughed at to being implemented. If
questioned, Abberline or Lestrade would throw up their hands and
find something else to talk about. Just now Scotland Yard's chief
embarrassment was an Inspector Mackenzie, who had been present
at, and unable to prevent, the assassination by dynamite of one of
the Carpathian Guard and had subsequently, unsurprisingly, joined
the growing list of mysterious disappearances. Disapproval poured
from the fountainhead of the Palace and splashed upon the Prime
Minister and the Cabinet, and then, with increasing force, down on
to the lower levels of society, becoming an absolute torrent on the
streets of Whitechapel.

There had been no sign of Geneviève's Chinese elder, so at least
the rattling that Beauregard had given the Devil Doctor's web had
yielded a result. His assumption was that anything evil and oriental
worked for the Lord of Strange Deaths. That was one of his few
successes in this business, but he could scarcely be proud of it. He
did not care to owe a favour to the Limehouse Ring above and
beyond the connection already made with them.

In the ruling cabal of the Diogenes Club, there was talk of outright rebellion in India and the East. A reporter for the *Civil and Military Gazette* had tried to assassinate the Governor-General. Varney was as popular as Caligula with the indigenous population and his own troops and civil service. Many in her realm ceased to recognize the Queen as their rightful ruler, if only because they sensed that since her rebirth she had not truly worn the crown. Each week, more ambassadors withdrew from the Court of St James. The Turks, whose memories were longer than anyone had expected, clamoured for reparations from Vlad Tepes, with regard to crimes of war committed in the Prince Consort's warm life.

Beauregard tried to look at Geneviève without her noticing, without her penetrating his thoughts. In the light, she looked absurdly young. Would Penelope – whose skin was still baked, and who had to be fed like a baby with drips of goat blood – ever again be as fresh? Even if, as Dr Ravna assured him would be the case, she made a complete recovery, would she be her old self? Penelope was a vampire now and he did not recognize the mind that could be glimpsed in her occasional coherent moments. He had to be guarded with Geneviève too. It was hard to keep his thoughts in rein and impossible fully to trust any vampire.

'You're right,' she said. 'He's still out there. He hasn't given up.'

'Perhaps the Ripper's taken a holiday?'

'Or been distracted.'

'Some say he's a sea captain. He could be on a voyage.'

Geneviève thought hard, then shook her head. 'No. He's still here. I can sense it.'

'You sound like Lees, the psychical fellow.'

'It's part of what I am,' she explained. 'The Prince Consort shape-shifts but I can sense things. It's to do with our bloodlines. There's a fog around everything but I can feel the Ripper out there somewhere. He's not finished yet.'

'This place annoys me,' he said. 'Let's get out and see if we can do some good.'

As they stood, he helped arrange her cloak on her shoulders. Woodbridge's son whistled and Geneviève, as accomplished a flirt as Penelope when the mood took her, smiled at him over her shoulder. Her eyes sparkled strangely.

They had been patrolling like policemen, interviewing anyone with the remotest connection to the victims or their circles. Beauregard knew more about Catharine Eddowes and Lulu Schön than about members of his own family. Poring through the scraps of their lives made them more real to him. No longer names in police reports, they now seemed almost friends. The press referred to the victims as 'street-walkers of the lowest sort' and the *Police Gazette* always depicted them as bloodthirsty harridans who invited their fate. But, talking with Geneviève or Sergeant Thick or Georgie Woodbridge, they came alive as women, shiftless and pathetic perhaps, but still feeling individuals, undeserving of the harsh treatment they had suffered and were still suffering.

Occasionally, he would whisper the name of 'Liz Stride' to himself. No one else – most especially not Geneviève – raised the matter, but he knew he had finished the Ripper's work with her. He had put her out of her misery like a dog but perhaps a vampire would not wish to be so saved. The question of the age was: how much does a human being have to change before she is no longer human? Liz Stride? Penelope? Geneviève?

When not following one of the false leads that cropped up nightly in this case, they just wandered, hoping to come across a man with a big bag of knives and darkness in his heart. It was absurd, when he thought about it. But the routine had attractions. It kept him away from Caversham Street, where Penelope still struggled with unfamiliar ailments. He was still unsure of his obligations to her. Mrs Churchward had revealed unexpected backbone in nursing her new-born girl. Having lost a niece raised as a daughter, she was determined to do do her best for her authentic offspring. Beauregard could not but feel that his involvement with the Churchward girls had not been remotely to their benefit.

'Don't blame yourself,' Geneviève said. He was almost used to her intrusions. 'It's Lord Godalming who should be horse-whipped with silver chains.'

Beauregard understood Godalming had turned Penelope, then left her to her own devices, whereupon she had blundered badly, exposing herself to the murderous sun and drinking tainted blood.

'To me, your noble friend seems an utter swine.'

Beauregard had not seen Godalming, who was very close with the Prime Minister, since. When this matter was concluded, he would take up his grievance with Arthur Holmwood. Geneviève told him the responsible, decent course was for the father-in-darkness to stay with his get and help the new-born cope with her turning. This was an age-old etiquette but Godalming had not felt honour-bound by it.

They pushed through the ornately glassed doors. Beauregard shivered in the cold but Geneviève just breezed through the icy fog as if it were light spring sunshine. He had constantly to remind himself this sharp girl was not human. They were in Commercial Street, near Toynbee Hall.

'I'd like to call in,' Geneviève said. 'Jack Seward has a new ladylove and has been neglecting his duties.'

'Careless fellow,' he observed.

'Not at all. He's just driven, obsessive. I'm glad he's found a distraction. He's been courting nervous collapse for years. He had a bad time of it when Vlad Tepes first came, I believe. It's not something he cares to talk about much. Especially not to me. But I have heard stories about him.'

Beauregard had heard a few rumours, too. From Lord Godalming, oddly enough, and from the Diogenes Club. His name had been linked with Abraham Van Helsing.

Down the street stood a four-wheeler, the horse funnelling steam from its nostrils. Beauregard recognized the driver. Above his scarf and below his cap were almond eyes.

'What is it?' Geneviève asked, noticing his sudden tension. She was still expecting the Chinese elder to pounce and rend out her windpipe.

'Recent acquaintances,' he said.

The door drifted open, creating a swirl in the fog. Beauregard knew they were surrounded: the tramp huddled in the alleyway across the road; the idler hugging himself against the cold; another, the one he couldn't see, lurking in the shadows under the tobacconist's shop; perhaps even the haughty vampire, in clothes too good for her, parading past as if *en route* to an assignation. He thumbed the catch of his cane, but did not think he could take them all on. Geneviève could take care of herself, but it was unfair to involve her further.

He assumed he was about to be called on to give an explanation for the lack of progress. From the point of view of the Limehouse

Ring, the situation deteriorated with every police raid and listing of 'emergency regulations'.

Someone leaned out of the carriage and beckoned them. Beauregard, with casual care, walked over.

41

Lucy Pays a Call

S HE WALKED WITH tiny steps to keep her skirts off the ground, as meticulous in her habits as any lady. Her new clothes, bought with John's money, still had a little shop-scratch about them. Few, observing her evening promenade, would recognize the Mary Jane Kelly with whom they were familiar. She felt as she had in Paris, a new-made girl free of her sad history.

In Commercial Street a fine gentleman was helping a pretty vampire into a coach. Mary Jane paused to admire the couple. The gentleman was courtly without effort, his every gesture precise and perfect; and the girl was a beauty even in the mannish dress so many affected these nights, her skin a radiant white, her hair honeyed silk. The coachman lightly whipped his horse and the carriage moved off. Soon, she too would only travel in coaches. Drivers would touch their hats to her. Fine gentlemen would assist her through doors.

She walked up to the doors of Toynbee Hall. The last time she had been here, her face was burned black after an accidental touch of the sun. Dr Seward, not yet *her* John, had examined her closely but with no interest, as if looking over a likely racehorse. He had prescribed veils and a spell indoors. Now she came not as a supplicant, but to pay a call.

She tired of waiting for someone to open the doors for her and daintily pushed them inwards. She stepped into the foyer and looked about. A matron bustled through, a roll of bedding hugged to her chest. Mary Jane hemmed to attract attention. Her cough, intended as a ladylike little sound, emerged as a deep, somewhat vulgar, throat-clearing. She was embarrassed. The matron looked her in the face, lips pursed as if instantly aware of every filthy detail of Mary Jane Kelly's past.

'I have come to call on Dr Seward,' Mary Jane said, trying hard with every word, every syllable.

The matron smiled unpleasantly. 'And who shall I say is calling?'

Mary Jane paused, then said: 'Miss Lucy.'

'Just Lucy?'

Mary Jane shrugged as if her name did not matter one whit. She did not care for the matron's attitude and thought it meet she be put in her place. She was, all considered, only a kind of servant.

'Miss Lucy, if you would care to follow me . . .'

The matron shoved through an inner door, and held it open with her cushion-like rump. Mary Jane passed through into a soap-smelling corridor and was led up a none-too-clean stairway. On the first-floor landing, the matron nodded towards a door.

'Dr Seward will be in there, Miss Lucy.'

'Thank you so much.'

Constrained by her burden, the matron attempted a creaky and impertinent curtsey. Suppressing nasty laughter, she sloped off up another staircase, leaving the visitor alone. Mary Jane had hoped to be announced, but contented herself with taking one hand from her muff and rapping on the office door. A voice from within rumbled something indistinguishable, and Mary Jane admitted herself. John stood at a desk with another, both poring over a pile of documents. John didn't look up, but the other man – a young fellow, dressed well but not a gentleman – did, and was disappointed.

'No,' he said, 'it's not Druitt. Where can Monty have got to?'

John ran his finger down a column of figures, totalling them in his head. Mary Jane knew her numbers but could never put them together: it was the root of her problem with the rent. Finally, John finished his calculation, jotted something down and raised his glance. When he saw her, it was as if someone had struck his head from behind with the blunt end of a ball-peen hammer. Unaccountable tears pricked the backs of her eyes, but she kept them in.

'Lucy,' he said, without expression.

The young man straightened and brushed his lapels with his knuckles, presenting himself to be introduced. John shook his head as if trying to put together two mismatched halves of a broken ornament. Mary Jane wondered if she had done something terribly wrong.

'Lucy,' he said again.

'Dr Seward,' began the young man, 'you are being remiss.'

Something inside John snapped and he began pretending every-thing was ordinary. 'Do forgive me,' he said. 'Morrison, this is Lucy. My . . . oh, a family friend.'

Mr Morrison's smirk was complex, as if he understood. Mary Jane thought she had seen him before; it was possible the young man knew her for who she was. She let him take her hand and bobbed her head slightly. A mistake, she knew at once; she was a lady, not a tweeny maid. She should have let Mr Morrison raise her hand to his lips, then nodded grudgingly as if he were the lowest thing on earth and she Princess Alexandra. For such an error, Uncle Henry would have taken the rod to her.

'I'm afraid you find me frightfully preoccupied,' John said.

'One of our stalwarts has gone missing,' Mr Morrison explained. 'You wouldn't have happened across a Montague Druitt on your travels?'

The name meant nothing to her.

'I feared as much. I doubt that Druitt is much in your line, anyway.'

Mary Jane pretended not to know at all what Mr Morrison meant. John, still taken aback, was fiddling with some doctor's implement. She began to suspect this social call to be not entirely a well-conceived endeavour.

'If you'll excuse me,' Mr Morrison said, 'I'm sure you've much to discuss. Miss Lucy, good night. Dr Seward, we'll talk later.'

Mr Morrison withdrew, leaving her alone with John. When the door was firmly shut, she slipped close to him and put her hands on his chest, her face by his collar, her cheek against the soft stuff of his waistcoat.

'Lucy,' he said, again. It was a habit of his, just to say the name out loud. He looked at Mary Jane, and saw the twice-dead girl in Kingstead.

His hands touched her about the waist, then climbed her back, finally fixing at her neck. Taking a grip, he thrust her away from him. His thumbs pressed under her chin. If she were warm, this might hurt. Her teeth grew sharp. John Seward's face was dark, his expression one with which she was familiar. Sometimes, this look would pass over him when they were together. It was his brute self, the savage she found inside every man. Then, something mild sparked in his eyes and he let her go. He was shaking. He turned away and steadied himself against his desk. She smoothed the strands of her hair that had come loose, and rearranged her collar. In his rough grip, her red thirst had been aroused.

'Lucy, you mustn't . . .'

He waved her away but she took a hold on him from behind, easing his collar away from his neck, undoing his stock.

'. . . be here. This is . . .'

She wet his old scars with her tongue, then opened them with a gentle bite.

'. . . another part of . . .'

Intently, she sucked. Her throat burned. She shut her eyes and saw red in the darkness.

'. . . my life.'

Taking her mouth from his neck for a moment, she chewed her glove, biting away the tiny shell buttons at her wrist. She freed her right hand and spat out the cloth skin. Her fingers had extended, nails splitting the seams. She reached into his clothes, displacing buttons. She stroked his warm flesh, careful not to cut. John moaned to himself slightly, lost.

'Lucy.'

The name spurred her, put anger in her appetite. She tugged at his clothes, and bit again, deeper.

'Lucy.'

No, she thought, gripping, Mary Jane.

Her chin and front were wet with his blood. She heard a choke in the back of his throat and felt him swallowing his own scream. He tried to say Lucy's name again but she worried him harder, silencing him. For the moment, in this heat, he was her John. When it was over, she would dab her lips and be his dream Lucy again. And he would rearrange his clothes and be Dr Seward. But now they were their true selves; Mary Jane and John, joined by blood and flesh.

42

The Most Dangerous Game

'GENEVIÈVE DIEUDONNÉ,' BEAUREGARD introduced her, 'Colonel Sebastian Moran, formerly of the First Bangalore Pioneers, author of *Heavy Game of the Western Himalayas*, and one of the greatest scoundrels unchanged . . .'

The new-born in the coach was an angry-looking brute, uncomfortable in evening dress, moustache bristling fiercely. When warm, he must have had the ruddy tan of an 'Injah hand', but now he looked like a viper, poison sacs bulging under his chin.

Moran grunted something that might count as an acknowledgement, and ordered them to get into the coach. Beauregard hesistated, then stepped back to allow her to go first. He was being clever, she realized. If the Colonel meant harm, he would keep an eye on the man he considered a threat. The new-born would not believe her four-and-a-half centuries stronger than he. If it came to it, she could tear him apart.

Geneviève sat opposite Moran and Beauregard took the seat next to her. Moran tapped the roof and the cab moved off. With the motion, the black-hooded bundle next to the Colonel nodded forwards, and had to be straightened up and leaned back.

'A friend?' Beauregard asked.

Moran snorted. Inside the bundle was a man, either dead or insensible. 'What would you say if I told you this was the veritable Jack the Ripper?'

'I suppose I'd have to take you seriously. I understand you only hunt the most dangerous game.'

Moran grinned, revealing tiger-fangs under his whiskers. 'Huntin' hunters. It's the only sport worth talkin' about.'

'They say Quatermain and Roxton are better than you with a rifle, and the Russian who uses the Tartar warbow is the best of all.'

The Colonel brushed away the comparisons. 'They're all warm.'

Moran had a stiff arm out, holding back the clumsy bundle. 'We're on our own in this huntin' trip,' he said. 'The rest of the Ring aren't in it.'

Beauregard considered.

'It's been nearly a month since the last matter,' the Colonel said. 'Saucy Jack's finished. Probably cut his throat on one of his own knives. But that's not enough for us, is it? If business is to get back to the usual, Jack has to be seen to be finished.'

They were near the river. The Thames was a sharp, foul undertaste. All the filth of the city wound up in the river, and was disseminated into the seven seas. Garbage from Rotherhithe and Stepney drifted to Shanghai and Madagascar.

Moran got a grip on the black winding sheet and wrenched it away from a pale, bloodied face.

'Druitt,' Geneviève said.

'Montague John Druitt, I believe,' the Colonel said. 'A colleague of yours, with very singular nocturnal habits.'

This was not right. Druitt's left eye opened in a rind of blood, He had been badly beaten.

'The police considered him early in the investigation.' Beauregard said – a surprise to Geneviève – 'but he was ruled out.'

'He had easy access,' Moran said. 'Toynbee Hall is almost dead centre of the pattern made by the murder sites. He fits the popular picture, a crackpot toff with bizarre delusions. Nobody – beggin' your pardon, ma'am – really believes an educated man works among tarts and beggars out of Christian kindness. And nobody is goin' to object to Druitt takin' the blame for the slaughter of a handful of harlots. He's not exactly royalty, is he? He don't even have an alibi for any of the killings.'

'You evidently have close friends at the Yard?'

Moran flashed his feral grin again. 'So, do I extend my congratulations to you and your lady friend?' he asked. 'Have you caught Jack the Ripper?'

Beauregard took a long pause and thought. Geneviève was confused, realizing how much had been kept from her. Druitt was trying to talk, but his broken mouth couldn't frame words. The coach was thick with the smell of slick blood and her own mouth was dry. She had not fed in too long.

'No,' Beauregard said. 'Druitt will not fit. He plays cricket.'

'So does another blackguard I could name. That don't prevent him from bein' a filthy murderer.'

'In this case, it does. On the mornings after the second and fourth and fifth murders, Druitt was on the field. After the "double event", he made a half-century and took two wickets. I hardly think he could have managed that if he'd been up all night chasing and killing women.'

Moran was not impressed. 'You're beginnin' to sound like that rotten detective they sent to Devil's Dyke. All clues and evidence and deductions. Druitt here is committin' suicide tonight, fillin' his pockets with stones and taking' a swim in the Thames. I dare say the body'll have been bashed about a bit before he's found. But before he does the deed, he'll leave behind a confession. And his handwritin' is goin' to look deuced like those bloody crank letters.'

Moran made Druitt's head nod.

'It won't wash, Colonel. What if the real Ripper starts killing again?'

'Harlots die, Beauregard. It happens often. We found one Ripper, we can always find another.'

'Let me guess. Pedachenko, the Russian agent? The police considered him for a moment or two. Sir William Gull, the Queen's physician? Dr Barnardo? Prince Albert Victor? Walter Sickert? A Portuguese seaman? It's a simple matter to put a scalpel into someone's hand and make him up for the part. But that won't stop the killing . . .'

'I didn't take you for such a fastidious sort, Beauregard. You don't mind servin' vampires, or –' a sharp nod at Geneviève '– consortin' with them. You may be warm but you're chillin' by the hour. Your conscience lets you serve the Prince Consort.'

'I serve the Queen, Moran.'

The Colonel started to laugh, but – after a flash of razor lightning in the dark of the cab – found Beauregard's sword-cane at his throat.

'I know a silversmith, too,' Beauregard said. 'Just like Jack.'

Druitt tumbled off his seat and Geneviève caught him. His groan told her that he was broken inside.

Moran's eyes glowed red in the gloom. The silvered length of steel held fast, its point dimpling his Adam's apple.

'I'm going to turn Druitt,' Geneviève said. 'He's too badly hurt to be saved any other way.'

Beauregard nodded to her, his hand steady. With a nip, she bit into her wrist, and waited for the blood to well up. If Druitt could drink enough of her blood as she drained him, the turn would begin.

She never had any get. Her father-in-darkness had served her well, and she would not be a profligate fool like Lily's murgatroyd or Lord Godalming.

'Another new-born,' Moran snorted. 'We should've been more selective when it all started. Too many bloody vampires in this business.'

'Drink,' she cooed.

What did she really know about Montague John Druitt? Like her, he was a lay practitioner, not a doctor but with some medical knowledge. She did not even know why a man with an income and position should want to work in Toynbee Hall. He was not an obsessive philanthropist like Seward. He was not a religious man like Booth. Geneviève had taken him for granted as a useful pair of hands; now, she would have to take responsibility for him, possibly for ever. If he became a monster, like Vlad Tepes or even Colonel Sebastian Moran, then it would be her fault. She would be killing all the people Druitt killed. He had been a suspect: even if innocent, there was something about Druitt that had made him seem a likely Ripper.

'Drink.' she said, forcing the word from her mouth. Her wrist was dripping red.

She held her hand to Druitt's mouth. Her incisors slid from their gumsheaths and she dipped her head. The scent of Druitt's blood was stinging in her nostrils. He had a convulsion and she realized his need was urgent. If he did not drink her blood now, he would die. She touched her wrist to his mashed lips. He flinched away, trembling.

'No,' he gargled, refusing her gift, 'no . . .'

A shudder of disgust ran through him and he died.

'Not everybody wants to live for ever,' Moran observed. 'What a waste.'

Geneviève reached across the space between them and backhanded the Colonel across the face, knocking away Beauregard's cane. Moran's red eyes shrank and she could tell he was afraid of her. She was still hungry, having allowed the red thirst to rise in her. She could not drink Druitt's spoiled dead blood. She could not even drink Moran's second-or third-hand blood. But she could relieve her frustration by ripping meat off his face.

'Call her off.' Moran spluttered.

One of her hands was at his throat, the other was drawn back, the fingers gathered into a point, sharp talons bunched like an arrowhead. It would be easy to put a hole in Moran's face.

'It's not worth it,' Beauregard said. Somehow, his words cut through her crimson rage and she held back. 'He may be a worm, but he has friends, Geneviève. Friends you wouldn't want to make enemies of. Friends who have already troubled you.'

Her teeth slipped back into her gums and her sharpened fingernails settled. She was still itchy for blood, but she was in control again.

Beauregard put up his sword and Moran ordered the cabby to stop the coach. The Colonel, his new-born's confidence in shreds, was shaking as they stepped down. A trickle of blood leaked from one eye. Beauregard sheathed his cane and Moran wrapped a scarf around his pricked neck.

'Quatermain wouldn't have flinched, Colonel,' Beauregard said. 'Good night, and give my regards to the Professor.'

Moran turned his face away into the darkness and the cab wheeled away from the pavement, rushing into the fog. Geneviève's head was spinning. They were back where they had started. Near the Ten Bells. The pub was no quieter now than when they left. Women loitered by the doors, strutting for passers-by.

Geneviève's hurt and her heart hammered. She made fists and tried to shut her eyes.

Beauregard held his wrist to her mouth. 'Here, take what you must.'

A rush of gratitude made her ankles weak. She almost swooned but at once dispelled the fog in her mind, concentrating on her need.

'Thank you.'

'It's nothing.'

'Don't be so sure.'

She bit him gently and took as little as possible to slake the red thirst. His blood trickled down her throat, calming her, giving her strength. When it was over, she asked him if it were his first time and he nodded.

'It's not unpleasant,' he commented, neutrally.

'It can be less formal,' she said. 'Eventually.'

'Good night, Geneviève,' he said, turning away. He walked into the fog and left her, his blood still on her lips.

She knew as little about Charles Beauregard as she had about Druitt. He had never really told her why he was interested in the Ripper. Or why he continued to serve his vampire queen. For a moment, she was frightened. Everyone around her wore a mask and behind that mask might be . . .

Anything.

43

Foxhole

T HE SURGEON HAD found it impossible to pick out all the silver shards from his knee. With each step, he felt again the hot explosion of pain. Some vampires could regenerate lost limbs as lizards grow new tails. Kostaki was not of that breed. Already, he had to live behind a dead face; soon, he might also have to stump along on a piratical peg-leg.

A couple of young bloods, sharp-eyed new-born toughs, lurched away from an ill-made and damp wall to bar the egress from the tiny courtyard. He showed his face and teeth, facing them down. Without a word, they slipped back to their shadows and allowed him to pass.

He was out of uniform, concealed by a large hat and cloak, limping through the night fog. The message had given an address in the Old Jago, a district which was to Whitechapel what Whitechapel was to Mayfair.

'Moldavian,' came a quiet voice. 'Over here.'

In the dark of an alley-mouth, Kostaki saw Mackenzie. 'Scotsman, well met.'

'If you say so.'

The Inspector's coat was holed and patched, and he wore a week's whiskers. Kostaki understood he had not been seen for some time. His fellows were concerned for his safety. The general assumption was that he had been removed to Devil's Dyke following an undiplomatic utterance.

'A fine pair of beggars we make.' Mackenzie said, shifting his shoulders inside his loose and dirty coat.

Kostaki grinned. He was pleased this warm man was not in a concentration camp. 'Where have you been?'

'Here, in the main,' said Mackenzie. 'And Whitechapel. This is where the trail goes to ground.'

'The trail?'

'Our masked fox with the dynamite. I've been tracking him since that night in the park.'

Kostaki remembered the flash of a pistol and dark eyes inside a concealing hood. The stick of dynamite fizzling in von Klatka's chest an instant before the blast. Then, a lumpy red rainstorm. 'You have found the murderer?'

Mackenzie nodded.

'I see the reputation of Scotland Yard is well earned.'

Mackenzie looked bitter. 'This is nothing to do with Scotland Yard. Not with Warren or Anderson or Lestrade. They were in the way, so I set out on my own.'

'A lone hunter?'

'Exactly. Warren insisted we look for a Christian Crusader, but I knew better. You were there, Kostaki. You must remember. The man in the hood. He was a vampire.'

The dark eyes. Maybe rimmed with red. Kostaki had not forgotten.

'And that vampire is here in this rookery.' Mackenzie looked up. In the lodging house opposite the alleyway there was a light. A third-storey room. Shadows moved on the thin muslin curtain. 'I've been watching him for days and nights. They call him "Danny" or "Sergeant". A very interesting fellow, our fox. He has surprising associations.'

Mackenzie's eyes shone. Kostaki recognized the pride of a predator.

'Are you sure this is him?'

'Sure as I can be. You will be too. When you see him, when you hear his voice.'

'How did you track him?'

Mackenzie smiled again and laid a finger beside his nose. 'I followed the trail. Dynamite and silver are hard to come by. There are only a few sources worth mentioning. I played the Irish card, asking around the mick pubs. It's certain his bully-boys were recruited from the Fenians. When it comes to mopping up, I've most of their names. I had a description of the Sergeant within two days. Then I found a few hard facts, details scattered on the ground like crumbs.'

The light dimmed and Kostaki shrank back deeper into the alley, pulling Mackenzie with him.

'You'll see now,' the Scotsman said. 'You'll see him.'

An ill-fitting door was pulled inwards and a vampire emerged from the building. It was the man Kostaki had seen in the park. There was no mistaking the upright bearing. And the eyes. He wore old clothes and a battered peaked cap, but his posture and flaring moustache suggested the British army. The vampire looked around him, staring for a long second into the alley. Then he consulted a pocket watch. Briskly, the Sergeant marched off.

Mackenzie breathed again.

When they could no longer hear the vampire's bootfalls, Kostaki said, 'It was him.'

'I never had any doubt.'

'Then why did you summon me?'

'Because I can trust you as no other. We have an understanding, you and I.'

Kostaki knew what Mackenzie meant.

'We must follow this Sergeant, find his confederates, root out and destroy his whole conspiracy.'

'That is where our situation becomes complicated. Men like Sir Charles Warren or your General Iorga detest surprises. They prefer a culprit to be someone they suspected. Often, they'll refuse to credit evidence simply because it contradicts a half-formed notion they've made the mistake of espousing. Sir Charles wants the dynamiter to be one of Jago's crusaders, not a vampire.'

'There have been vampire traitors before.'

'But not, I think, like our Sergeant. I am only beginning to make out the extent of his activities. He is the tool of greater forces. Perhaps greater forces than a simple policeman and a soldier can hope to best.'

They emerged from the alley and stood by the Sergeant's building. Without discussion, they understood that they would now break in and search the murderer's rooms.

While Mackenzie looked both ways, Kostaki splintered the door-lock with a firm grip. In the Old Jago, this would not be unusual or suspicious behaviour. A sailor, pockets pulled out and empty, zigzagged past, eyes rolling from gin or opium.

They slipped into the lodging house, and climbed three flights of narrow, precipitous stairs. Eyes looked at them through holes in doors, but no one intervened. They came to the room where the light had been. Kostaki broke another lock – somewhat stouter than he would have expected in this pit – and they were inside.

Mackenzie lit a stub of candle. The room was tidy, almost military in its precision. There was a cot, with a sheet tighter than a wrestler's stomach muscles. On a desk, writing materials were laid out square as if for an inspection.

'I have cause to believe our fox not only the destroyer of Ezzelin von Klatka,' Mackenzie declared, 'but also the would-be assassin who put a bullet into John Jago.'

'That makes little sense.'

'To a soldier, maybe not. But to a copper, it's the oldest game in town. You stir up both sides, set them at each other like dogs. Then sit back and watch the fireworks.'

Mackenzie was going through papers on the desk. There was a fresh bottle of red ink and a neat pot of pens beside the blotter.

'Are we dealing with an anarchist faction?'

'Quite the opposite, I should think. Sergeants do not make good anarchists. They have no imagination. Sergeants always serve. You can carve an empire with Sergeants behind you.'

'He is following orders, then.'

'Of course. This whole business has the whiff of the *ancien régime*, don't you think?'

Kostaki had an intuition. 'You admire this man? Or at least, admire his cause?'

'These nights, that would be a very unwise opinion to harbour.'

'Nevertheless . . .'

Mackenzie smiled. 'It would be hypocritical of me to mourn for von Klatka, or even to express sympathy for John Jago.'

'What if it had not been von Klatka, what if it had been . . .'

'You? Then, things might have seemed different. But only seemed. The Sergeant would make no distinction between you and your comrade. That is where I part company from his masters' thinking.'

Kostaki thought for a moment. 'I may lose my leg,' he said.

'I am sorry for that.'

'What do you intend to do about the Sergeant? Will you let him continue to serve his unknown cause?'

'I told you I was a copper before I was warm. When I have a case Warren can't ignore, I'll lay it before him.'

'Thank you, Scotsman.'

'For what?'

'For your trust.'

There were a great many pages of loose paper, covered with a cypher or shorthand that resembled hieroglyphic script.

'Hello,' Mackenzie said, 'what have we here?' He held up a pencilled draft of a letter. It was in plain English. 'Lestrade will be sick with envy,' he said. 'And Fred Abberline. Kostaki, look . . .'

Kostaki glanced at the paper. '*Dear Boss,*' it began, and it was signed '*Yours truly, Jack the Ripper.*'

44

On the Waterfront

T HE BODY HAD washed up on Cuckold's Point, at the curve of
Limehouse Reach. It had taken three men to drag it out of the
sucking mud and deposit it on the nearest wharf. Before Geneviève
and Morrison arrived, someone took the trouble to lay the corpse
out into a semblance of dignity, untangling the limbs and arranging
the water-and dirt-clogged clothes. A length of sailcloth was draped
over the dead man to protect the sensibilities of dock-workers and
waterfront idlers who happened by.

He had already been identified by an inscription in his watch and,
surprisingly, a cheque made out to his name. Nevertheless, they
were formally to confirm the corpse's identity. As the constable
lifted the sailcloth, several onlookers made exaggerated sounds of
disgust. Morrison flinched and turned away. Druitt's face had been
eaten by the fish, exposing empty eye-sockets and a devil's-grin of
bare teeth, but she knew him by his hairline and chin.

'It's him,' she said.

The constable dropped the cloth and thanked them. Morrison
seconded her statement. A wagon was ready to receive the body.

'I think he had family in Bournemouth,' Morrison told the
policeman. The constable took a dutiful note.

The Colonel had kept his word. Druitt's pockets were stuffed with
stones; no suicide note had been manufactured, but the inference was
inescapable. Another unpunished murderer was at liberty: the police
would mount no campaign against him, there would be no special
investigators from the Diogenes Club. What was so special about
the Ripper? Within fifty yards of the river, there would be a dozen
as cruel, as profligate. The Whitechapel Murderer was presumably
a madman; Moran and his kind had not even that excuse. Their
murders were simply stock-in-trade.

With Druitt hoisted on to the wagon, the show was over. The

idlers drifted off to the next spectacle and the policeman returned
to his duties. Geneviève was left with Morrison, at the edge of
the wharf. They walked towards Rotherhithe Street, a row of
rope-merchants', public houses, sailors' lodgings, shipping offices
and bawdy houses. This was the Arabian Nights quarter of London,
a bazaar in the thin fog. A hundred different languages mingled. It
was a heavily Chinese district and the rustle of silks still touched her
with dread.

At once, a veiled figure was in her way. A vampire in black
pyjamas. She bowed an apology and her veil parted. Geneviève
recognized the Chinese girl from the Old Jago, who had spoken
for the Lord of Strange Deaths.

'There will be reparation for this wrong,' she said; 'you have the
word of my master.'

Then, the girl was gone.

'What was that about?' Morrison asked.

Geneviève shrugged. The girl had spoken in Mandarin. If Charles
was to be credited, she could guarantee that Colonel Moran would
not avoid the consequences of his actions. But if punished, it would
not be for brutal murder but for *unnecessary* brutal murder.

The girl had disappeared into the crowds.

Geneviève did not intend to return immediately to the Hall. She
wanted to seek out Charles, not so much for himself but to enquire
after the condition of his unfortunate fiancée. Penelope Churchward,
whom she had met once and hardly warmed to, was the latest of her
concerns. With multitudes shovelled into the furnace, how many
could she save? Not Druitt, certainly. Not Lily Mylett. Not Cathy
Eddowes.

Morrison was talking to her, confiding in her. Having heard
nothing, she begged his pardon.

'It's Dr Seward,' he repeated himself. 'I'm worried that he's
making a fool of himself with this Lucy of his.'

'Lucy?'

'That's what she calls herself.' Morrison was one of the rare
individuals who had met Jack Seward's mysterious lady-love, and
he had not been impressed. 'Personally, I think we've seen her
before. Under another name and in shabbier clothes.'

'Jack has always ridden himself too hard. Perhaps this *amour* is the
cure for his habitual exhaustion.'

Morrison shook his head. He was finding it hard to express his exact thoughts.

'Surely, you can have no social objection to this girl? I had thought those concerns well behind us,' said Geneviève.

Morrison looked sheepish. Himself of modest birth, his work should have given him an understanding of the situations of even the meanest and most degraded. 'There's something wrong with Dr Seward,' he insisted. 'He is calm and even-tempered on the surface, more so than of late. But underneath he is losing his grasp. He forgets our names sometimes. He misremembers which year it is. I believe he is retreating to some Arcadian time, before the coming of the Prince Consort.'

Geneviève pondered the notion. Recently, she found Jack hard to read. He had never been as open to her as others – as Charles, for instance, or even Arthur Morrison – but in the past few weeks he had given away almost nothing, as if his mind were behind lead shutters as stout as the cabinet in which he locked his precious wax cylinders.

They stopped walking and she took Morrison's hand. At the touch of his skin, tiny memories burst. She still had Charles's blood in her; with it came fly-blown specks of faraway lands. She kept seeing a face in pain, which she assumed to be his late wife.

'Arthur,' she said, 'madness is epidemic with us. It is everywhere, like evil. There is little we can do to ease the condition, so we must learn to live with it, to make it serve us. Love is always a species of insanity. If Jack can find some purpose in this spinning world, what harm can it do?'

'Her name isn't Lucy. I think it's something Irish . . . Mary Jean, Mary Jane?'

'Hardly proof of direst perfidy.'

'She is a vampire.' Morrison stopped, realizing what he had said. Embarrassed, he tried to smooth over his prejudice. 'I mean . . . you know . . .'

'I appreciate that you are concerned,' she told him, 'and to an extent I share your misgivings. But I don't see what we can honourably do.'

Morrison was plainly torn inside. 'Still,' he said, 'something is wrong with Dr Seward. Something should be done. Something.'

45

Drink, Pretty Creature, Drink

H ER TOUCH HAD changed him. For two days, Beauregard had been troubled by dreams. Dreams in which Geneviève, sometimes herself and sometimes a needle-fanged cat, lapped at his blood. It had always been in his stars. The way things were, he would sooner or later have been tapped by a vampire. He was luckier than most, to have given blood freely rather than be drained by force. He had certainly been more fortunate than Penelope.

'Charles,' Florence Stoker said, 'I've been running on for close to an hour, and I declare you've not heard a single word. It's plain from your face that your thoughts are in the sickroom. With Penelope.'

Oddly guilty, he let Florence continue in her belief. After all, he *should* be thinking of his fiancée. They were in the drawing room, awkwardly superfluous. Florence consumed cup after tiny cup of tea. Mrs Churchward occasionally darted in with a noncommittal report and Mrs Yeovil, the housekeeper, would regularly appear with more tea. But, absorbed in his own thoughts, he paid them no mind. Geneviève had taken blood from him, but given something of herself in return. She ran and turned about like quicksilver in his mind.

Penelope was attended by Dr Ravna, the specialist in nervous disorders. A vampire, he had a reputation in the field of diseases of the un-dead. Dr Ravna was with the invalid now, attempting some treatment.

Beauregard had been in his daze for two nights and had neglected his duties in Whitechapel. Penelope's infirmity provided an excuse but an excuse was all it was. He could not stop thinking of Geneviève. He was afraid he wanted her to drink from him again. Not the simple thirst-slaking of an opened wrist but the full embrace of the Dark Kiss. Geneviève was an extraordinary woman by the standards of any age. Together, they could live through the centuries. It was a temptation.

'I suppose the wedding will have to be cancelled,' Florence said. 'A great pity.'

There had been no possibility of a formal discussion, but Beauregard assumed his engagement to Penelope was now at an end. It would be best if lawyers could be kept out of it. There was no real fault on either part, he hoped, but neither he nor Penelope was the person they had been when they entered into their understanding. With all the other troubles, the last thing he needed was a suit for breach of promise. It was hardly likely, but Mrs Churchward was old-fashioned and might consider that her daughter had been insulted.

Geneviève's lips had been cool, her touch gentle, her tongue roughly pleasant as a cat's. The draining of his blood, so slow and so tender, had been an exquisite sensation, instantly addictive. He wondered what she was doing just now.

'I cannot understand what Lord Godalming was thinking of,' Florence continued. 'He has acted most peculiarly.'

'How unlike Art.'

A screech sounded through the ceiling, barely human, followed by a whimper. Florence cringed and Beauregard's heart contracted. Penelope was in pain.

The Jack the Ripper business was dragging on without fruit. The faith expressed in his abilities as an investigative agent by the Diogenes Club and the Limehouse Ring might well be misplaced. He had, after all, accomplished little.

A personal note of apology had arrived from the Professor, informing him that Colonel Moran had been severely reprimanded for his interference. Also there had been a peculiar missive in green ink on thin parchment, informing him that Mr Yam, whom he took to be the Chinese elder, would no longer be inconveniencing Mlle Dieudonné. Apparently, a commission had been undertaken, but the Lord of Strange Deaths no longer felt obliged to carry it out. Beauregard made a connection with a news item buried in the pages of *The Times*. A singular invasion, a burglary-in-reverse, had occurred at the home of Dr Jekyll. Apparently, an unknown person effected an entry into his laboratory and scattered fifty gold sovereigns over the ashes of the elder vampire that the scientist had been examining.

'Sometimes I wish I had never heard of vampires,' Florence said. 'I told Bram as much.'

Beauregard mumbled some assent. The doorbell rang and he heard Mrs Yeovil scuttling past the room to admit the caller.

'Another well-wisher, I should think.'

Yesterday, Kate Reed, Penelope's new-born journalist friend, had come by and loitered in embarrassed impotence for half an hour, mumbling sympathetically, then found an excuse to dash off somewhere. She had hardly set Penelope a good example.

The front door was pulled open, and a familiar voice explained: 'I don't have a card, I'm sorry.'

Geneviève. He was on his feet and in the hallway before he could think, Florence trailing after him. She stood on the doorstep.

'Charles,' she said. 'I assumed I would find you here.'

She stepped past Mrs Yeovil and slipped off her green cloak. The housekeeper hung it up.

'Charles,' Florence prompted. 'You are being remiss.'

He apologized and effected an introduction. Geneviève, on her best behaviour, touched Florence's hand and made a passable curtsey. Mrs Churchward was in the hallway now, come down to investigate the new arrival. Beauregard made a further introduction.

'I understand you are in need of a doctor familiar with infirmities of the un-dead,' Geneviève explained to Penelope's mother. 'I have not a little experience.'

'Dr Ravna of Harley Street is with us, Miss Dieudonné. I should think his services sufficient.'

'Ravna?' Her face betrayed her opinion.

'Geneviève?' he asked.

'There's no polite way of saying it, Charles. Ravna is a crank and a buffoon. He's been a vampire six months, and already he's self-declared himself the Calmet of the age. You'd be better off with Jekyll or Moreau, and I wouldn't trust them to lance a boil.'

'Dr Ravna comes most highly recommended,' Mrs Churchward insisted. 'He is welcome in all the best houses.'

Geneviève waved that aside. 'Society has been known to make mistakes.'

'I hardly think . . .'

'Mrs Churchward, you must let me see your daughter.'

She fixed her eyes on Penelope's mother. Beauregard felt the persuasive force of her glance. The wound on his wrist tickled. He was sure everyone noticed how often he fidgeted with his cuff.

'Very well,' Mrs Churchward said.

'Think of it as a second opinion,' Geneviève said.

Leaving Florence and Mrs Yeovil behind, Geneviève and Beauregard followed Mrs Churchward upstairs. When Mrs Churchward opened the sickroom door, a dreadful odour seeped out. It was the smell of things dead and forgotten. The room was heavily curtained, a single fishtail gaslight casting a pale half-circle on the bed.

Dr Ravna, sleeves rolled up, was bending over the patient, taking a set of tongs to a wriggling black thing fastened to her chest. The bedclothes were rolled back, and Penelope's chemise was open. A half-dozen black streaks were fixed to her breast and belly.

'Leeches!' Geneviève exclaimed.

Beauregard swallowed his nausea.

'You damned fool!' Geneviève pushed the specialist aside and laid her hand on Penelope's brow. The patient's skin was yellowish and shiny. She was red around the eyes and angry marks dotted her exposed body.

'The impure blood must be drawn out,' Dr Ravna explained. 'She has drunk from a poison well.'

Geneviève pulled off her gloves. She plucked a leech from Penelope's chest and dropped it into a basin. Working methodically and without distaste, she detached all the sluglike things. Bloodspots welled where their mouths had been. Dr Ravna began to protest, but Geneviève stared him silent. When the job was done, she rolled up the bedspread, and tucked it around Penelope's neck.

'Fools like you have much to answer for,' she told Dr Ravna.

'My credentials are of the finest, young lady.'

'I'm not young,' she said.

Penelope was conscious but apparently unable to speak. Her eyes darted and her hand took Geneviève's. Even ignoring the obvious symptoms of her illness, Penelope was different. Her face had changed subtly, her hairline shifted. She looked like Pamela.

'I just hope your leeches haven't destroyed her mind utterly,'

Geneviève told Dr Ravna. 'She was already sick and you've dangerously weakened her.'

'Is there anything that can be done?' Mrs Churchward asked.

'She needs blood,' Geneviève said. 'If she's drunk tainted blood, she needs good blood to counteract it. Draining her veins is worse than useless. Without blood, the brain is starved. Maybe irreparably injured.'

Charles unfastened his cuff.

'No,' Geneviève said, waving his unspoken offer away. 'Your blood won't do.'

She was firm on the point. Beauregard wondered whether her motives were entirely medical.

'She needs her own blood, or something close. What Moreau says is true. There are differing types of blood. Vampires have known that for centuries.'

'Her own blood?' Mrs Churchward said. 'I don't understand.'

'Or something close, the blood of a relative. Mrs Churchward, would you be willing . . .'

Mrs Churchward could not conceal her disgust.

'You nursed her once,' Geneviève explained. 'Now you must do it again.'

Penelope's mother was horror-struck. Her hands were held to her, wrists crossed over her throat.

'If Lord Godalming were truly a gentleman, this would not be necessary,' Geneviève told Beauregard.

Penelope hissed, eye-teeth bared. She sucked at the air, tongue out to catch whatever sustenance there was.

'Your daughter will live,' Geneviève told Mrs Churchward. 'But everything that makes her who she is could be washed away and you would be left with a blank, a creature of appetites but no mind.'

'She looks like Pamela,' Beauregard said.

Geneviève was concerned. 'Damn, that's bad. Penelope is shrinking inside, reshaping herself, losing herself.'

Penelope whimpered and Beauregard blinked away tears. The smell, the stifling heat of the room, the cowed doctor, the patient in pain. All were too familiar.

Mrs Churchward approached the bed. Geneviève beckoned her and took her hand. She brought mother and daughter together, and slipped away from them. Penelope reached up and embraced her mother. Mrs Churchward pulled her collar away from her throat, quivering with distaste. The patient sat up in bed and attached her mouth to her mother's neck.

A shock froze Mrs Churchward. A red trickle coursed down Penelope's chin on to her night-dress. Geneviève sat on the bed and stroked Penelope's hair, cooing encouragements.

'Careful,' she said. 'Not too much.'

Dr Ravna retreated, leaving behind his leeches. Beauregard felt like an intruder, but remained. Mrs Churchward's expression softened and a certain dreaminess crept into her eyes. Beauregard understood how she felt. He gripped his wrist tight, sliding the stiff linen of his cuff over the bitemarks. Geneviève eased Penelope away from her mother's neck and settled her back on to her pillows. Her lips were scarlet, her face ruddy. She seemed fuller, more like her old self.

'Charles,' Geneviève said sharply. 'Stop dreaming.'

Mrs Churchward was tottering on the verge of a faint. Beauregard caught her and helped her into a chair.

'I never . . . thought . . .' she said. 'Poor, poor Penny.'

She understood her daughter better now, Beauregard knew.

'Penelope,' Geneviève said, trying to get the invalid's attention. Penelope's eyes wandered and her mouth trembled. She licked away the last of the blood. 'Miss Churchward, can you hear me?'

Penelope purred an answer.

'You must rest,' Geneviève told her.

Penelope nodded, smiled and allowed her eyes to flutter shut.

Geneviève turned to Mrs Churchward and snapped her fingers in front of her face. Penelope's mother was jolted from her daydream. 'Two days from now, the same, you understand? With supervision. You must not let your daughter take too much blood from you. And that must be the last time. She must not become dependent on you. Another feeding will bring her up to strength. Then, she must fend for herself.'

'Will she live?' Mrs Churchward asked.

'I can't promise an eternity, but if she's careful she should survive the century. Perhaps the millennium.'

46

Kaffir War

E ACH NIGHT, SIR Charles sent out constables with paint pots to obliterate the day's Crusader Crosses from walls within sight of Scotland Yard. But after dawn the thin red signs would appear again, daubed on anything conveniently white or white-ish in the vicinity of Whitehall Place and Northumberland Avenue. Godalming watched as the Commissioner barked orders at his latest group of amateur redecorators.

Living loiterers in thick coats and scarves watched, hostile natives on the point of attacking the fort. One of Sir Charles's wiser measures was to prepare the Yard for siege, ensuring rifles were readily available and all doors and windows defensible. Whenever the situation skewed from a police to a military matter, the Commissioner had a spurt of competence that was almost heartening. Good soldier, terrible copper; that would be the verdict on Sir Charles Warren.

The fog was back, thicker than ever. Even vampires found it impenetrable. Seeing in the dark was not the same as seeing through the sulphur-soup. Godalming still watched over Sir Charles for the Prime Minister. The Commissioner was steadily losing his grip. When he next met with Ruthven, Godalming intended to recommend replacement. Matthews had been after Sir Charles's scalp for months, so the Home Secretary – himself hardly secure in his position – would be mollified.

Somehow Crusaders had managed to paint their cross on the main doors of the Yard. Godalming suspected Jago had warm sympathizers on the force. Whoever was appointed in Sir Charles's stead would have to purge the ranks before order could be re-established.

The Cross of St George was an obvious symbol for insurrection-ists, being simultaneously the crucifix vampires are proverbially unable to face and the standard of an England bridling under the Prince Consort.

'This is intolerable.' Sir Charles fumed. 'I am surrounded by blackguards and blunderers.'

Godalming kept quiet. The punishment for unauthorized wall-painting and slogan-scribbling was now five strokes of the lash, administered in public. At this rate it would soon be summary impalement, or at least the chopping off of the offending hand.

'That dolt Matthews and his penny-pinching,' Sir Charles continued. 'We need more men on the streets. Troops.'

Only Godalming paid attention to the Commissioner. His subordinates got on with the business of policing, trying to ignore the ravings of their commanding officer. Dr Anderson, Sir Charles's Assistant Commissioner, had extended his walking holiday in Switzerland, while Chief Inspector Swanson was doing his best to seem part of the wallpaper, hoping to keep his head down until the shooting was over.

A derelict-looking man approached Sir Charles and began talking to him. Instantly, Godalming was interested. He sauntered near enough to listen. The ragged man had come with a limping companion who stood back a dozen yards. This companion was an elder vampire, whose face was on the point of falling off his skull. Godalming assumed he was of the Carpathian Guard. He was certainly not an Englishman.

'Mackenzie!' Sir Charles shouted. 'What do you mean by this? Where have you been?'

'On a trail, sir.'

'You've been remiss in your duty. You are relieved of your rank, and subject to severe disciplinary action.'

'Sir, if you'll listen . . .'

'And look at yourself, you're a disgrace to the force! A ruddy disgrace!'

'Sir, consider this . . .' MacKenzie, whom Godalming understood to be an Inspector, gave the Commissioner a piece of paper.

'It's another of these blasted crank letters!' Sir Charles exclaimed.

'Indeed, but unfinished, unsent. I know who the author is.'

Godalming now knew this was important. An unholy light sparked in Sir Charles's eyes. 'You know the identity of Jack the Ripper?'

Mackenzie smiled, eyes mad. 'I didn't say that. But I know who is composing letters over the signature.'

'Then find Lestrade. It's his case. No doubt he'll thank you for weeding out another interfering lunatic.'

'This is of paramount importance. It's to do with the business in the park the other night. It's to do with everything. John Jago, the dynamiters, the Ripper . . .'

'Mackenzie, you're raving!'

To Godalming, both policeman seemed on the verge of madness. But the piece of paper was a nugget of something. He stepped in and looked at it.

'"*Yours truly, Jack the Ripper,*"' he read aloud. 'Is this in the same hand as the others?'

'I'll stake ten guineas on it,' Mackenzie said. 'And I'm a Scotsman.'

They were in a crowd now. Uniformed men clustered around, and not a few of the loiterers. Mackenzie's elder comrade also joined the group. A new-born constable stood to attention behind Mackenzie, ready for action.

'Sir Charles,' Mackenzie said, 'it's a vampire. Treason is involved. Dynamite treason. I've reason to believe we've been duped all along. Highly placed interests are intervening.'

'A vampire! Nonsense. Rattle the cages of the crusade and you'll get your man. And he'll be a warm johnny.'

Mackenzie raised his hands in frustration. It was as if he had battered his forehead against the Commissioner's obstinacy.

'Sir, does the name of the Diogenes Club mean anything to you?'

Sir Charles's face went grey. 'Don't be ridiculous, man.'

Godalming was intrigued. The Diogenes Club was Charles Beauregard's outfit and Beauregard had arisen throughout this whole affair. It was possible the Scotsman had picked up a genuine trail and run his quarry to ground.

'Sir Charles,' he said. 'I think we should have Inspector Mackenzie's report *in camera*. It is possible that we are near to solving several mysteries.'

He looked from the Commissioner's face to the Inspector's. Both were set, unwilling to bend to the other. Beside Mackenzie was the Carpathian, red eyes fixed on Sir Charles. Behind them was the massively moustached, dark-eyed constable.

At once, with a dizzying vampire insight, Godalming knew the constable was as fake as a seven-pound note.

Fire belched and noise rang out. People scattered, yelling. Bags of paint exploded against Portland stone dressings. Windows were smashed by well-aimed projectiles. Shots were discharged and a woman screamed. Everyone in their little group tried to throw themselves to the ground. The Carpathian collided with Godalming, and he staggered under the weight, trying to remain on his feet. The false policeman had his arm drawn back. Something flashed. Godalming collapsed and was forced to the grimy cobbles. The Carpathian rolled off him. Sir Charles swore mightily and waved a revolver.

Mackenzie drew in air for a breath, then held it. He was on his knees, mouth open, eyes rolled up. The Jack the Ripper letter, caught by a gust, whirled off a few yards, then stuck flat as a poster to a wet wall, written-side in. Mackenzie gasped and blood came from his mouth. The Carpathian was trying to help him stand. He took his hand away from the Scotsman's back and it was bloody.

Someone kicked Godalming in the head. Police whistles shrilled. Sir Charles, thinking himself in the thick of an African battle, was in charge again, dispensing orders, bringing constables to snap to attention, gesturing with his pistol.

Reinforcements poured out of the Yard, summoned by the disturbance. Many brandished guns: Sir Charles liked his men to go armed, no matter what regulations specified. The Commissioner directed them to put down the mob. With truncheons out, a platoon of policemen battered the few remaining loiterers, driving them towards the Embankment. Godalming saw that the new-born who had stabbed Mackenzie was with this group, applying his stick to the head of a clergyman. The constables drove the rabble into the fog. The assassin would not return.

Mackenzie was face-down on the cobbles, unmoving. The dark patch on the back of his coat showed he had been neatly skewered through the heart. The Carpathian stood over him, blood-dipped knife in his hand and no expression on his dead face.

'Arrest this murderer,' Sir Charles ordered.

The three new-born constables around them hesitated. Godalming wondered if they could subdue the elder. The Carpathian contemptuously cast away the knife and held out his hands. One of the coppers obliged, fastening purely formal handcuffs around the elder's wrists. He could have broken them with a flex but let himself be taken.

'We shall have an explanation of you,' Sir Charles said, holding up a finger as if daring the vampire to bite it off.

The constables hauled the Carpathian away.

'That's better,' the Commissioner said, surveying the calm. The streets had been cleared. Paint dripped on the walls. The cobbles were littered with still-rolling missiles and the odd constable's helmet, but peace had been enforced. 'That's much more like it. Order and discipline, Godalming. That's the stuff we need. Mustn't slacken.'

Sir Charles returned to the building, striding purposefully, followed by several of his men. The natives had been momentarily repulsed but Godalming heard the jungle drums summoning more cannibals. He remained in the fog for a moment, his mind racing. Of all who had been there, only he – and the assassin – really knew what had happened. He was coming into his full powers, acquiring the insights and sensitivities if not of an elder then of a vampire who could no longer be described as a new-born. He could survey calm and see the chaos beneath. Lord Ruthven had told him to look for an advantage, then to pursue it ruthlessly. This knowledge could be turned to his supreme advantage.

47

Love and Mr Beauregard

H E STOOD IN front of his open fireplace, hands behind him, feeling the heat. Even the short stroll from Caversham Street to Cheyne Walk had chilled him to the bone. Bairstow had set the fire earlier and the room was warm and welcoming.

Geneviève wandered around the room like a cat getting acquainted with a new home, alighting on this and that and examining, almost tasting, an object, before replacing it, sometimes making a slight adjustment to a position.

'This was Pamela?' she said, holding up the last photograph. 'She was beautiful.'

Beauregard agreed.

'Many women wouldn't care to be photographed when they were with child. It might seem indecent,' she said.

'Pamela was not like many women.'

'I don't doubt it, to judge by her influence on her survivors.'

Beauregard remembered.

'She didn't wish you to give up the rest of your life, though,' she said, setting the picture down. 'And she certainly did not want her cousin to reshape herself in her image.'

Beauregard had no answer. Geneviève made him see his late engagement in an unhealthy light. Neither Penelope nor he had been honest with themselves or each other. But he could not blame Penelope, or Mrs Churchward, or Florence Stoker. It had all been his own fault.

'What's gone is gone,' Geneviève continued. 'I should know. I've buried centuries.'

For a moment she bent over and did a comic impersonation of a shaking dowager. Then she straightened and brushed a wave of hair away from her forehead.

'What will happen to Penelope?' he asked.

She shrugged. 'There are no guarantees. I believe she will survive, and I think she will be herself again. Maybe she will be herself for the first time.'

'You don't like her, do you?'

She stopped her wandering and cocked her head in thought. 'Perhaps I'm jealous.' Her tongue passed over her bright teeth and he realized she was closer to him than modesty recommended. 'Then again, perhaps she isn't very nice. That night in Whitechapel, after I had been hurt, she didn't strike me as entirely sympathetic. Lips too thin, eyes too sharp.'

'Do you realize how great a thing it was for her to come to such a quarter? To seek me out. It ran against everything she had been taught, everything she believed about herself.'

He still found it hard to credit that the old Penelope had ventured out by herself, let alone travelled to a place she must have viewed as belonging to the neighbourhood of the pits of Abaddon.

'She doesn't want you any more,' she said, bluntly.

'I know.'

'She'll be incapable of being a good little wife now she's new-born. She'll have to find her own way in the night. She might have the makings of a very fine vampire, for what that's worth.' Her hand was on his lapel, sharp nails resting against the material. The heat from the fire made him almost uncomfortable. 'Come on and kiss me, Charles.'

He hesitated.

She smiled, her even teeth almost normal. 'Don't worry,' she said. 'I won't bite.'

'Liar.'

She giggled and he touched his mouth to hers. Her arms slipped tight around him. Her tongue ran over his lips. They moved away from the fire, and, not without some awkwardness, settled on a divan. His hand slid into her hair.

'Are you seducing me, or am I seducing you?' she said. 'I forget which.'

She was amusing at the strangest times, he noticed. His thumb felt the nape of her cheek. She kissed his wrist, touching her tongue to the healed-over bites. A jolt ran through him. He felt it most in the soles of his feet.

'Does it matter?' he replied.

She pressed his head down into a cushion, so he could see the ceiling, and kissed his neck.

'This may not be the love-making you are used to,' she said. Her teeth were sharper now, and longer.

Her chemise was free of her skirt and undone. She had a pretty, slim shape. His clothes were loose, too.

'I could say as much to you.'

She laughed, a full-throated man's laugh, and nipped his neck, hair falling in front of her face, whisping over his mouth and nose, tickling. His hands worked under her chemise, up and down her back and shoulders. He felt the vampire strength of the muscles sliding under her skin. She picked the studs out of his collar and shirtfront with her teeth and spat them away. He imagined Bairstow finding them one by one over the next month and laughed.

'What's funny?'

He shook his head and she kissed him again, on the mouth, eyes and neck. He was aware of the pulsing of his blood. Gradually, between caresses, they divested each other of the four or five layers of clothing deemed proper.

'If you think this a Herculean labour,' she said as he discovered yet another set of hooks on the thigh of her skirt, 'you should have tried to court a high-born lady in the late fifteenth century. It is a miracle my generation have any descendants at all.'

'Things are easier in hotter climates.'

'Easier does not always mean more pleasant.'

They lay together, warmed by their bodies.

'You have scars,' she said, following the slice-mark under his ribs with a fingernail.

'The service of the Queen.'

She found the two bullet-wounds in his right shoulder, entry and exit, and tongued the long-healed pockmark under his collarbone.

'What exactly is it that you do for Her Majesty?'

'Somewhere between diplomacy and war there is the Diogenes Club.'

He kissed her breasts, his own teeth pressing delicately into her skin.

'You have no scars at all. Not so much as a birthmark.'

'For me, everything heals on the outside.'

Her skin was pale and clear, almost but not quite hairless. She adjusted her position to make it easier for him. She bit her full underlip as he gently settled his weight on to her.

'There now,' she said. 'At last.'

He sighed slowly as they slipped together. She held him tight with her legs and arms and reached up with her head, attaching her mouth to his neck.

Icy needles shocked him and, for a moment, he was in her body in her mind. The extent of her was astonishing. Her memory receded into the dim distance like the course of a star in a far galaxy. He felt himself moving inside her, tasted his own blood on her tongue. Then he was himself again, shuddering.

'Stop me, Charles,' she said, red drops between her teeth. 'Stop me if it hurts.'

He shook his head.

48

The Tower of London

A LETTER UNDER the seal of Lord Ruthven was passport enough to gain him an audience. The new-born Yeoman Warder seemed to plod down the stone-walled stairwell while Godalming followed with a darting lightness of step. It was an effort to contain his energies. He was excited, almost exploding. The guard was so much slower than he, in thought and motion. He was only gradually becoming aware of the breadth of his new capabilities. He had not found his limits yet.

Just after nightfall, he had encountered while walking in Hyde Park a young lady of his acquaintance. Her name was Helena Such-and-So-Forth, and she had sometimes come to Florence's after-darks, usually with one of Mrs Stoker's fat-headed theatrical cronies. He had reached out with his gaze and held her fascinated. Guiding her into a convenient gazebo, he had made her shrug her way out of her garments. Afterwards, he opened her neck and sucked her almost dry. She had been alive when he left, barely.

Now he was full of the taste of Helena. Sometimes there were little explosions inside his skull and he knew more about the warm girl. Her tiny life was his. With each feeding, he became stronger.

Above was the White Tower, the oldest part of the fortress. Nearby was the Cell of Little Ease, a four-foot-square chamber constructed so a prisoner could not lie down. It had held such enemies of the Crown as Guy Fawkes. Even the less-unpleasant rooms were bubbles in stone, allowing no possibility of escape. Each stout wooden door was inset with a tiny grille. From some of the tenanted cells, Godalming heard the groans of the damned. The prisoners were near starvation. Many had taken to biting their own veins, seriously injuring themselves. Graf Orlok was notoriously harsh on his own kind, punishing them for their treasons with an imprisonment that amounted to slow death.

Kostaki was kept in one of these cells. Godalming had made enquiries about the Guardsman. An elder, he had been with the Prince Consort since Dracula's warm days. Since his arrest, he had apparently not uttered a single word.

'Here, sir.'

The Yeoman Warder, faintly silly in his comic-opera costume, took out his keyring and unfastened the triple locks. He set down his lantern to wrestle with the door and his enlarged shadow danced on the stone behind him.

'That will be all,' Godalming told the guard as he stepped into the cell. 'I'll call out when I'm finished.'

In the gloom, Godalming saw burning red eyes. Neither the prisoner nor he needed a lantern.

Kostaki looked up at his visitor. Godalming found it impossible to perceive an expression on his ragged face. It was not rotten, but hung on his skull like old linen, stiff and musty. Only his eyes betokened life. The Carpathian, who lay on a straw-stuffed cot, was chained. A silver band, padded with leather, circled his good ankle, and stout silver-and-iron links fixed him to a ring that was set into the stone. One of the elder's legs lay useless, a wadding of soiled bandage about the smashed knee. The stench of spoiled meat filled the cell. Kostaki had been shot with a silver ball. The elder coughed. The poison was in his veins, spreading. He would not last.

'I was there,' Godalming announced. 'I saw the supposed police-man murder Inspector Mackenzie.'

Kostaki's red eyes did not move.

'I know you are falsely accused. Your enemies have brought you to this filth.' He gestured around the low-ceilinged, windowless cell. It might as well be a tomb.

'I passed six decades in the Château d'If,' Kostaki announced. 'These are by comparison quite comfortable quarters.' His voice was still strong, surprisingly loud in the confined space.

'You'll talk to me?'

'I have done so.'

'Who was he? The policeman?'

Kostaki fell silent.

'You must understand, I can help you. I have the ear of the Prime Minister.'

'I am beyond help.'

Water seeped up between the cracks of the flagstones. Patches of green-white moss grew on the floor. There were spots of similar mould on Kostaki's bandages.

'No,' Godalming told the elder, 'the situation is very grave, but it can be reversed. If those who scheme against us can be thwarted, then there are many advantages to be won.'

'Advantages? With you English, there are always advantages.'

Godalming was stronger than this foreign brute, sharper in his head. He could turn the situation so he emerged as sole victor. 'If I find the policeman, I can uncover a conspiracy against the Prince Consort.'

'The Scotsman said the same thing.'

'Is the Diogenes Club mixed up in this?'

'I don't know what you're talking about.'

'Mackenzie mentioned them. Just before he was killed.'

'The Scotsman kept much to himself.'

Kostaki would tell what he knew. Godalming was certain of it. He could see the gears turning in the elder's head. He knew which levers to depress.

'Mackenzie would wish this cleared up.'

Kostaki's great head nodded. 'The Scotsman lead me to a house in Whitechapel. His quarry was a new-born, known as "the Sergeant" or "Danny". At the last, his fox turned on him.'

'This was the man who killed Mackenzie?'

Kostaki nodded, indicating his wound. 'Aye, and the man who did this to me.'

'Where in Whitechapel?'

'They call the place the Old Jago.'

He had heard of it. This business kept running back to Whitechapel: where Jack the Ripper murdered, where John Jago preached, where agents of the Diogenes Club were often seen. Tomorrow night, Godalming would venture out into Darkest London. He was confident this Sergeant was no match for the vampire Arthur Holmwood had become.

'Keep up your pluck, old man,' Godalming told the elder. 'We'll have you out of here directly.'

He withdrew from the cell and summoned the Yeoman Warder,

who refastened the thick door. Through the bars, Kostaki's red eyes winked out as he lay back on his cot.

At the end of the corridor, framed by an arch, stood a tall, hunched *nosferatu* in a long, shabby frock coat. His head was swollen and rodent-like with huge pointed ears and prominent front fangs. His eyes, set in black caverns that obscured his cheeks, were constantly liquid, darting here and there. Even his fellow elders found Graf Orlok, a distant family connection of the Prince Consort's, a disquieting presence. He was a crawling reminder of how remote they all were from the warm.

Orlok scuttled up the passageway. Only his feet seemed to move. The rest of him was stiff as a waxwork. When he was close, his flamboyant eyebrows bristled like rat's whiskers. His smell was not as strong as that in Kostaki's cell, but it was fouler.

Godalming greeted the Governor but did not shake Orlok's withered claw. Orlok peered into Kostaki's cell, pressing his face close to the grille, hands against the cold stone either side of the door. The Yeoman Warder tried to edge away from his commanding officer. Orlok rarely asked questions but had a reputation for gaining answers. He turned away from the cell and looked at Godalming with active eyes.

'He still won't talk,' Godalming told the *nosferatu*. 'Stubborn fellow. He'll rot here, I suppose.'

Orlok's rat-shark-rabbit teeth scraped his lower lip, the nearest he could manage to a smile. Godalming did not envy any prisoner entrusted to the care of this creature.

The Yeoman Warder escorted him up to the main gate. The skies above the Tower were lightening. Godalming still trembled with the sustenance he had taken from Helena. He had the urge to run home, or to dive under Traitor's Gate and swim.

'Where are the ravens?' he asked.

The Yeoman Warder shrugged. 'Gone, sir. So they say.'

49

Mating Habits of the
Common Vampire

H IS HOUSE WAS interesting, his books and pictures confirming
her intuitions. In his library, Geneviève found a reading desk
piled with volumes, many with places marked. Charles's interests
were eclectic; currently, he was absorbed by *The Modern Apostle,
and Other Poems* by Constance Naden, *After London* by Richard
Jefferies, *The True History of the World* by Lucian de Terre, *Essays
on the Endowment of Education* by Mark Pattison, *Science of Ethics*
by Leslie Stephen and *The Unseen Universe* by Peter Guthrie
Tait. Among his books, Geneviève found framed photographs
of Pamela, a strong-faced woman with a pre-Raphaelite cloud of
hair. In pictures, Charles's wife was always frozen in sunlight, at
ease in her stillness while others in her group posed stiffly.

She found pen and ink on a stand and considered leaving a note.
With the pen in her hand, she could not think of anything she needed
to say. Charles would wake up and find her gone but she had no
excuses to make. He knew about being bound by duty. Finally she
just wrote that she would be at the Hall this evening. She assumed
he'd return to Whitechapel and that he would look in on her. Then
they might have to talk. After a moment, she signed the note, 'love,
Geneviève', the accent a tiny flick above her flowing signature. Love
was all very well; it was the talking about it that enervated her.

On the third attempt, Geneviève found a cabman willing to
take an unescorted vampire girl from Chelsea to Whitechapel. Her
destination might not be outside the Four-Mile Radius, that arbitrary
circle beyond which hansom cabs were not obliged to venture, but
cabbies often had to be overpaid to discharge duties which lay in
that easterly direction.

En route, lulled by the gentle trundle of the wheels and her sense
of satisfied repletion, she tried not to think about Charles and the

future. By now she had suffered enough involvements to guess accurately what they could expect of life together. Charles was in his middle thirties. She would stay sixteen, unchanged. In five or ten years, she would seem his daughter. In thirty or forty, he would be dead; especially if she continued to feed off him. Like many vampires, she had, with the insistent complicity of her victims, destroyed those about whom she cared deeply. An alternative would be to turn him; as his mother-in-darkness, she would nurture him into a new life, finally losing him to the wider world as all parents must lose their children.

They crossed the river. And the city became noisier, more cramped, more populated.

There were vampire couples, even vampire families, but she thought them unhealthy. After centuries together, they tended to meld into one creature with two or more bodies, leeching off each other so much that they lost their original individualities. If anything, their reputation for extreme cruelty and ruthlessness was worse than that of the worst of the un-dead outlaws.

It was a cold, drab morning. They were well into November, past Hallowe'en and Guy Fawkes' Night, neither much celebrated this year. The fog was so thick that the sun did not penetrate down to the streets. The cab made slow progress.

This time, the world was truly different. Vampires were no longer secret things. She and Charles would not be unique, hardly even out of the ordinary. Their little love must be playing out in a thousand variations up and down the country. Vlad Tepes had not bothered to think through the implications of his rise to power. Alexander-like, he cut the knot; loose ends fell where they might, without any guidance or judgement.

Last night, with Charles, it had been more than feeding. Despite her worries, she remained elated by his blood. She could still taste him, still feel him inside.

The cabby opened his trap and told her they were in Commercial Street.

50

Vita Brevis

H E DID NOT intend to roll up in a hansom and saunter about the vilest hole in London as if taking a constitutional in Piccadilly. Not that any driver would dare venture into the Old Jago, for fear his brass would be tarnished, his fare stolen and his horse exsanguinated. The last time Godalming had been in Whitechapel, dogging Sir Charles's heels, he had gathered how teeming the quarter was. It might take weeks of patient work to find his Sergeant but find the man he would. With Mackenzie dead and Kostaki imprisoned, he had no rivals on this track. Only he knew the face of the quarry.

As he strolled up Commercial Street, Godalming whistled 'The Ghost's High Noon', from *Ruddigore*. Not politically a sound tune for an intimate of Lord Ruthven, it was hard to work out of the head. Besides, when he had unshakeable evidence that the Diogenes Club conspired against the Prince Consort, he would be forgiven anything. His long-ago warm association with Van Helsing would be wiped from the record. He could name his own position. Arthur Holmwood was on his way up.

His nocturnal vision had improved markedly. The entire quality of his perceptions shifted with each night. The fog that shrouded the people on the street was to him merely a faint fuzziness. He could distinguish an infinite variety of tiny sounds, scents and tastes.

Even if Ruthven lived for ever, it was unlikely he could keep eternally on the right side of the Prince Consort. He was too temperamental for his position. Eventually, he would fall from grace. When that happened, Godalming would be in a position to dissociate himself from his patron. Perhaps even to replace him.

Some time tonight, he must feed. His appetites grew with the increase of his sensitivities. What was once a fumbling business – wrestling some warm tart before ripping into her with swollen, painful teeth – became easier as he found himself more able to impose his will upon the warm. He merely had to issue mental orders to his chosen conquest and she would come to him, baring her neck for his satisfaction. It was smooth and peculiarly delightful. His approach became delicate and he was able more to relish the pleasures of feeding.

It was time he made more vampires, like Penelope Churchward. He would need concubines, catspaws, maidservants. Each powerful elder had his retinue, adoring get who served their master's interests. For the first time, he wondered what had happened to the new-born Penny. She had stolen a suit of his clothes. He must seek her out and bend her to his purpose.

'Art?' came an educated girl's voice. 'I say, it's Lord Godalming, isn't it?'

He looked at the girl and his thoughts crawled down. It was like being dragged from a mountain peak into a muddy trough; forced to consider petty pursuits after having had the prospect of things colossal.

'Miss Reed,' he purred, 'how pleasant to find you.'

Kate Reed looked at him strangely, almost shocked. He considered feeding off her, but was not ready. Vampire blood was heady. Only true elders could survive a diet of the stuff, exorting tribute from their vassals. He was not yet strong enough, but Kate might make a suitable vassal in the new century. Doubtless weak, she could be easily shaped into a pliable devotee.

The girl looked taken aback; disgust leaked out of her head. 'I'm sorry,' she said, 'I see I was mistaken.'

Since turning, she had changed. Godalming had badly underestimated Kate Reed. She had found him entirely transparent. His thoughts had been written on his face, or so boldly in his head that even a poor new-born could distinguish them. He would have to be more careful. The girl retreated swiftly, almost running. She would not welcome his attentions in the near future. Still, he had time. Eventually, he would claim her. He would make a project of it.

He resumed his whistling, but the tune was shrill and erratic to his own ears. With considerable irritation, he realized Kate Reed had rattled him. He was so taken with his new abilities and perceptions that he had neglected the mask that had been a part of him long before he left his warm days behind. He had let another see him as he truly was, which was unforgivable. His father, his human father, would have thrashed him soundly for showing his hand in such a blatant fashion.

He wanted to be among people, hidden in a crowd. There was a public house, the Ten Bells, on the other side of the road. He might find a woman there. He crossed the street, dodging out of the path of a cart, and pushed into the pub . . .

. . . there were a few warm folks scattered in the crowd, but mostly the Ten Bells was a vampire pub. Godalming resisted the meagre temptations of a pint of pig's blood, but found company with a pair of new-born whores. To everyone but his quarry, he would seem a slumming murgatroyd from the West End. He wore his frilliest shirt and his tightest jacket, and looked the part of a bloodthirsty, empty-headed poseur.

The whores were called Nell and Marie Jeanette; they were lightly sozzled on gin and pig's blood. Nell was remarkably hirsute with a striking faceload of stiff red bristles. Marie Jeanette was Irish with absurd pretensions and new clothes. This one, who was almost pretty, had an appointment later, presumably with a deep-pocketed admirer. She was just passing the time but Nell was seriously on the prowl and took elaborate care to seem intrigued, often commenting on his general good appearance and obvious sharpness. He did his best to seem a drunken, affected idiot.

Nell was outlining a supposedly tempting scheme, involving a warm third party. She was proposing that they get together in her nearby room, and he could have his pleasure of the two of them, satisfying all his interests in one bed. She kept rubbing her whiskered cheek against him, letting him sniff her animal musk.

'Yer has to rub me the right way, Artie,' she said, smoothing the fur on her arm, then ruffling it up. 'Depending on what yer likes.'

He looked across the pub and saw a man at the bar, back to the room. Godalming, with a rush of excitement, *knew*. He pressed close to Nell's neck, making sure his face was in shadow. A pint of pig in his hand, the man turned, one heel up on the bar-rail, and looked about him. It was the Sergeant. He took a deep draught of his drink, then wiped the gory residue out of his moustache with the back of his hand. He was in a check suit not a constable's uniform, but there was no mistaking him.

'That man at the bar,' Godalming said, 'with the extravagant moustache. Do you know him? Don't be obvious about looking.'

If Nell noticed he was suddenly twice as intelligent and half as interested in her, she accepted the change without complaint. She was used to the requirements of her gentleman friends. Like a good little spy, she took a neatly surreptitious look and whispered to him, 'He's a regular. Danny Dravot.'

The name meant nothing but hearing it gave him a ticklish thrill in his stomach. His quarry had a face and a name. Dravot was almost in Godalming's power.

'I thought I might have known him in the army,' he said.

'He was in India, I hears. Or maybe Afghanistan.'

'A sergeant, I'll wager.'

'Some does call him that.'

Marie Jeanette was listening to them. She must be feeling left out, awaiting her tardy suitor.

'Does yer want me to invite him over?' Nell asked.

Godalming looked at Dravot's glittering red eyes. Though sharp and clever, they did not seem to notice him. 'No,' he told the whore. 'He's not the fellow I thought he was.'

Dravot finished his pint and left the Ten Bells. Godalming waired a moment and stood up, leaving the two whores cold. They would be puzzled but go on to the next customer. Whores were no threat.

''Ere, where yer goin'?' Nell protested.

He lurched away from the table, pretending to be drunk.

''E's a rum 'un,' Nell told Marie Jeanette.

The doors were pulled open just as he reached them and he slipped out into the street, shoving aside a newcomer. Dravot was briskly marching away, towards the Old Jago. Godalming made as if to follow but a hand was laid on his shoulder.

'Art?'

. . . of all the people in the Empire, he had run into Jack Seward! The doctor was much changed. Still warm, he seemed ten years older, face weathered, hair streaked grey, colour bad. His clothes had been good once, but were missing a few buttons and none the better for dusty stains.

'Good God, Art, what . . .?'

Dravot stopped to talk with a knife-grinder. Godalming thanked Providence, and wondered how he might get rid of his unwanted old friend.

'You look . . .' Unable to complete a sentence, Seward shook his head and grinned. 'I don't know what to say.'

Godalming could tell Seward was sick in his head. When last he had seen him – in Purfleet when, as a warm fool, Godalming had dared defy Dracula and wound up fleeing for his life, leaving behind his companions to face the Count – Seward had been nervous but in command of himself. Now he was a broken man. Still ticking but completely broken, like a watch that skips hours and sometimes runs backwards for the odd minute.

Dravot was deep in conversation with the knife-grinder. The man must be one of his confederates.

'You're a vampire!' exclaimed Seward.

'Obviously.'

'Like *him*. Like Lucy.'

Godalming remembered Lucy, screeching as he pounded the stake into her. The dreadful grinding of the saw against her neckbone as Van Helsing and Seward removed her garlic-stuffed head. The old anger came back. 'No, not like Lucy.'

Dravot started walking off again. Godalming stepped around Seward and hesitated. If he broke into a run, the Sergeant would know he was pursued and take steps to evade the huntsman. Coldly ignoring Seward, he began to walk, pretending to amble, but actually moving at a measured pace, fixing Dravot in his eye. The doctor caught up and trotted at his side, giving out little yelps to get his attention like an overly-insistent mendicant. Behind them, someone else had come out of the Ten Bells. She shouted after Seward. It was Marie Jeanette. Seward had certainly changed his habits since Godalming last knew him.

'Art, why did you turn? After all he did to us, why . . .?'

Dravot slipped into a side-street. Godalming thought the Sergeant had been alerted by the commotion.

'Art, why . . .?'

Seward was near hysteria. Godalming shoved him away, and hissed. He must be rid of this nuisance. The doctor fell back against a lamp-post, appalled and shocked.

'Leave me be, Jack.'

The doctor shook, old fears returning. Godalming heard the rapid clip of Marie Jeanette's boots as she ran towards them. Good. The whore would distract Seward. He turned away and followed Dravot. The Sergeant had doubled back away from the Jago, walking round the market towards Aldgate. Damn. It was in the open now. Godalming would have to outpace the new-born and bring him down. He had a revolver loaded with silver. He needed Dravot alive but he was ready to cripple the Sergeant to bring him in. The more he was hurt, the keener he would be to expose his confederates. Dravot was the key. If he could be turned properly, the future was laid out to Godalming's advantage. He was sure of his own faculties, of his strength. His curved fangs were comfortable in the grooves they had worked inside his mouth. He no longer chewed himself.

Through the warren-like maze of streets round the market, Godalming hunted Sergeant Danny Dravot. Even when the quarry got out of his sight, he seemed to leave a glowing trail in the fog. Godalming could hear the distinctive quality of his boot-steps streets away. This could be dangerous. The Sergeant had shown consummate cool in his assassination of Inspector Mackenzie. Remembering Kate Reed, he checked his confidence. He would not be brought low by overestimating his own powers.

Cautiously, he followed Dravot. They were past the market now and straggling back towards Commercial Street. Godalming rounded a corner into Dorset Street and could not see the Sergeant. Off this road were a series of tiny residential courts. The fox must have slipped into one of them. The fog eddied by an arched opening. Godalming was sure he had his man cornered. The only other egress from the court would be through one of the dwellings.

Whistling again, light-headed with incipient victory, he strolled towards the court. His step was nimble and he was ready for a great test of his strength. First, he would batter the new-born with his fists, pulling out the revolver only to settle the matter at the end. It was important that he prove his dominance over the lesser vampire.

A couple appeared at the end of Dorset Street, moving towards him. It was Seward and his whore. They did not matter. It would be useful to have witnesses to this business. Jack Seward would serve the cause of Arthur Holmwood after all.

'Jack,' he said, 'I have a criminal trapped. Stay by this court and summon a constable if one happens to pass.'

'A criminal!' exclaimed Marie Jeanette. 'Faith, in Miller's Court?'

'A desperate man,' he told them. 'I am an agent of the Prime Minister, on urgent official business.'

Seward's face was dark. Marie Jeanette could not keep up with the developments.

'I live in Miller's Court,' the whore said.

'Who is the man?' Seward asked.

Godalming was peering into the fog. He thought he could see the Sergeant, standing in the courtyard, awaiting him.

'What has he done?'

Godalming knew what would most impress these fools. 'He's the Ripper.'

Marie Jeanette gasped and held her hand to her mouth. Seward looked as if he had been stomach-punched.

'Lucy,' the doctor said, a hand inside his coat, 'stand back.'

A chink appeared in Godalming's confidence. Dravot dared him to enter Miller's Court. Seward and Marie Jeanette were pestering fleas and should be brushed off. He had a destiny to fulfil. But something tiny was wrong.

'You called her Lucy,' he said. 'Her name isn't Lucy.'

He turned to Seward, who pressed close against him, arm moving fast. Godalming felt a silver shock in his chest. Something sharp was stuck into him, sliding swiftly and smoothly between his ribs.

'And that man in there,' Seward said, nodding into the courtyard . . .

Great pain spread through Godalming's chest. He was packed in ice, but a white-hot needle transfixed him. His vision blurred, his hearing was a fuzzy jangle, all senses were stripped from him.

'. . . his name isn't Jack.'

51

In the Heart of Darkness

MIDNIGHT WAS HOURS past. Geneviève sat in Jack's chair, contemplating the disarray of papers crawling over his desk. On her return, Morrison had recounted five separate crises that had arisen since her departure yesterday afternoon. As tactfully as possible, the young man accused her of neglecting her duties, as of late had the director. The shot had gone home. Something would have to be done soon. Jack was off with his vampire minx, and she herself had hardly been any better, with Charles.

The purpose of the Hall was changing. Lecture schedules had fallen into disrepair with Druitt's death. The institution's primary educational purpose was collapsing. In the meantime, with the Infirmary worked ragged, the Hall was taking more and more of the medical slack. Lecture halls were becoming wards. Jack, when he could be distracted from his own interests, authorized the engaging of more medical staff. The immediate problem was sparing enough qualified people for a board of interview. And, as ever, money was in short supply. Those who had been generous in the past seemed to be finding other interests. Or turning. Vampires were notoriously uncharitable.

She was torn between the fast-fading elation of her last feeding and the thousand gnat-bite problems of Toynbee Hall. Recently there had been too many strands to her life, too many demands on her time. Important matters were neglected.

She stood up and wandered about the room. One wall was lined with Jack's medical books and files. In its corner, under a glass case, was his prized phonograph. As Acting Director, this office should be her home. But she had been haring off to the Old Jago, to Chelsea. Now, she wondered whether she had been hunting Jack the Ripper or Charles Beauregard.

She found herself standing by the tiny window that looked out on to Commercial Street. The fog was thick tonight, a street-level sea of churning yellow that lapped at the buildings. For the warm, the November cold would be as sharp as a razor. Or a scalpel.

The Ripper had not murdered since the last weekend of September. She dared hope he had vanished for good. Perhaps Colonel Moran had been right, perhaps Montague Druitt had been the Silver Knife? No. That was impossible. And yet Moran had said something that night which ticked away in the back of her mind.

Opposite the Hall, wrapped in a black cloak, stood a man, fog swirling around and above him. He seemed to be wrestling with some inner question, just as she was. It was Charles.

Moran had said the Hall was in the centre of a pattern, a pattern dotted on to the map by the murders.

Charles crossed the road with a sudden resolve, the fog parting for him.

52

The Last of Lucy

S HE WAS WHO-the-bloody-ever she wanted to be. Whoever *men* wanted her to be. Mary Jane Kelly. Marie Jeanette. Uncle Henry's niece. Miss Lucy. She'd be Ellen Terry if it helped.

John sat by her bedside. She was telling him again how she'd been turned. Of the night on the heath when his precious Lucy had given the Dark Kiss. Now she told the story as if she were Lucy, and Mary Jane some other person, some worthless whore . . .

'I was so cold, John, so hungry, so *new* . . .'

It was easy to know how Lucy had felt. They had both been gripped by the same soul-deep panic upon awakening from death-sleep. The same desperate, bottomless thirst. Only Lucy awoke in a crypt, respectfully laid out and mourned for. Mary Jane was on a cart, minutes away from a lime pit, jumbled in among other unclaimed bodies.

'She was just an Irish whore. Of no importance, John. But she was warm, plump, alive. Blood pounding in her sweet neck.'

He was listening, head bobbing. She supposed he was mad. But he was a gentleman. And he was good to her, good for her. Earlier, with the strange toff, he had protected her. That madman, with his talk of Jack the Ripper, had threatened her, and John Seward fought him off. She'd not expected him to be so valiant in her defence.

'The children hadn't been enough, John. My thirst was terrible, eating me inside.'

Mary Jane had been confused by the new desires. It had taken her weeks to adjust. That time was like a dream now. She was losing Mary Jane's memories. She was Lucy.

With his doctor's hand, John smoothed her shift over her breast. He was the image of the considerate lover. She'd seen him from another side earlier. When he cut down the toff with a knife. His face had been different when he stabbed. John told her she was avenged, and she knew he meant Lucy. The toff had destroyed Lucy. But with his death, that part of the story was washed from John's mind. Perhaps it would come to her as she became more Lucy and less Mary Jane. As Lucy's memories seeped into her mind, Mary Jane slowly sank into a dark sea.

Mary Jane had not mattered at all and she should be glad to see her so drowned. In the cold, dark depths, it would be easy for Mary Jane to fall asleep and wake up entirely as Lucy.

But, her heart caught . . .

It was hard to keep pace as things changed but it was important to make the effort. John was her best hope for escape from this poor room, from these mean streets. Eventually, she'd persuade him to keep her in a house in the better part of the city. She'd have fine clothes and servants. And well-spoken children with pure, sweet blood.

She was sure the toff deserved to die. He'd been mad. There'd been no one hiding in Miller's Court, waiting for him. Danny Dravot was not the Ripper. He was just another old soldier, full of lies about heathens he'd slaughtered and brown wenches he'd bedded.

As Lucy, she remembered Mary Jane fearfully clutching her throat. Lucy slipped out from between the crypts.

'I needed her, John,' she continued. 'I needed her blood.'

He sat by her bed, reserved and doctorly. Later, she'd pleasure him. And she'd drink from him. Each time she drank, she became less Mary Jane and more Lucy. It must be something in John's blood.

'The need was an ache, an ache such as I'd never known, gnawing at my stomach, filling my poor brain with a red fever . . .'

Since her rebirth, the mirror in her room was useless to her. No one ever bothered to sketch her picture, so it was easy to forget her own face. John had shown her pictures of Lucy, looking like a little girl dressed up in her mother's clothes. Whenever she imagined her face, she saw only Lucy.

'I beckoned her from the path,' she said, leaning over from the pile of pillows on the bed, her face close to his. 'I sang under my breath, and I waved to her. I *wished* her to me, and she came . . .'

She stroked his cheek and laid her head against his chest. The tune came to her, and the words. 'It Was Only a Violet I Plucked from My Mother's Grave'. John held his breath, sweating a little.

His every fibre was held tense. Her thirst for him rose as she retold the story.

'There were red eyes before me, and a voice calling. I left the path, and she was waiting. It was a cold, cold night but she wore only a white shift. Her skin was white in the moonlight. Her –'

She caught herself. She was speaking as Mary Jane, not Lucy. Mary Jane, she said inside, be careful . . .

John stood up, gently pushing her away, and walked across the room. He took a grip on her washstand and looked in the mirror, trying to find something in his reflection.

Mary Jane was confused. All her life, she'd been giving men what they wanted. Now she was dead and things were the same. She went to John and hugged him from behind. He jumped at her touch, surprised. Of course, he hadn't seen her coming.

'John,' she cooed at him, 'come to bed, John. Make me warm.'

He pushed her away again, roughly this time. She was unused to her vampire's strength. Imagining herself still a feeble girl, she was one.

'Lucy,' he said, emptily, not to her . . .

Anger sparked in her mind. The last of Mary Jane, trying to keep mouth and nose above the surface of the dark sea, exploded. 'I'm not your bloody Lucy Westenra,' she shouted. 'I'm Mary Jane Kelly, and I don't care who knows it.'

'No,' he said, reaching into his jacket, gripping something hard, 'you're not Lucy . . .'

Even before the silver knife was out, she realized how foolish she'd been. Not to have seen earlier. Her throat stung lightly. Where it had been cut.

53

Jack in the Machine

A WARM MATRON sat at the desk in the foyer, devouring the latest
Marie Corelli, *Thelma*. Beauregard understood that since her
turning, the celebrated authoress's prose had further deteriorated.
Vampires were rarely creative, all energies diverted into the simple
prolonging of life.

'Where is Mademoiselle Dieudonné?'

'She is filling in for the director, sir. She should be in Dr Seward's
office. Shall you be wanting to be announced?'

'No need to bother, thank you.'

The matron frowned and mentally added another complaint to
a list she was keeping of Things Wrong With That Vampire
Girl. Beauregard was briefly surprised to be party to her clear
and vinegary thoughts, but swept the passing distraction aside as
he made his way to the director's first-floor office. The door was
open. Geneviève was not surprised to see him. His heart skipped as
he remembered her, close to him, body white, mouth red.

'Charles,' she said.

She stood by Seward's desk, papers strewn about her. He found
himself embarrassed. After what had passed between them, he did
not quite know how to act in her presence. Should he kiss her? She
was behind the desk, and the embrace would be awkward unless she
made room for it. Looking about for a distraction, his attention was
drawn to a device in a glass dust-case, an affair of brass boxes with
a large trumpet-like attachment.

'This is an Edison–Bell phonograph, is it not?'

'Jack uses it for medical notes. He has a passion for tricks
and toys.'

He turned. 'Geneviève . . .'

She was near now. He had not heard her come out from behind
the desk. She kissed him lightly on the lips and he felt her inside

him again, a presence in his mind. He was weak in the legs. Loss of blood, he supposed.

'It's all right, Charles,' she said, smiling. 'I didn't mean to bewitch you. The symptoms will recede in a week or two. Believe me, I have experience with your condition.'

'*Nunc scio quid sit Amor*,' he quoted from Virgil. At last I know what Love is like. He could not think along a straight line of reasoning. Butterfly insights fluttered in the back of his mind, never quite caught.

'Charles, this might be important,' she said. 'It's something Colonel Moran said, about the Ripper.'

By an effort of will, he concentrated on the pressing matter.

'Why Whitechapel?' she asked. 'Why not Soho or Hyde Park or anywhere? Vampirism is not limited to this district, nor prostitution. The Ripper hunts here because it is most convenient, because he *is* here. Somewhere near . . .'

He understood at once. His weakness washed away.

'I've just pulled out our records,' she said, tapping one of the piles on the desk. 'The victims were all brought in at one time or another.'

He remembered Moran's reasoning.

'It all comes back to Toynbee Hall by so many routes,' he said. 'Druitt and you work here. Stride was brought here, the killings are in a ring about the address. You say all the dead women were here . . .'

'Yes, and in the last year or so. Could Moran have been right? Could it have been Druitt? There have been no more murders.'

Beauregard shook his head. 'It's not over yet.'

'If only Jack were here.'

He made a fist. 'We'd have the murderer then.'

'No, I mean Jack Seward. He treated all the women. He might know if they had something in common.'

Geneviève's words sank into his brain and lightning swarmed behind his eyes. Suddenly, he *knew* . . .

'They had Seward in common.'

'But –'

'*Jack* Seward.'

She shook her head but he could tell she was seeing what he saw, coming quickly to a realization. Together, their minds raced.

He knew her thoughts and she knew his. They both remembered Elizabeth Stride grasping Seward's ankle. She *had* been trying to tell them something. She had been reaching out to identify her murderer.

'A doctor,' she said. 'They'd trust a doctor. That's how he got close enough to them, even when the scare was in full flood . . .'

She was thinking back, a thousand tiny details leaping at her. Many small mysteries were solved. Things Seward had said, had done. Absences, attitudes. All were explained.

'"Something is wrong with Dr Seward", I was told,' she said. 'Damn me for a fool, damn me for not listening, damn me, damn me . . .' She made fists against her forehead. 'I'm supposed to see into men's minds and hearts, and I even ignored Arthur Morrison. I'm the worst fool that ever lived.'

'Are there diaries here?' Beauregard asked, trying to draw her out of her fit of self-recrimination. 'Private records, notes, anything? These maniacs are often compelled to keep memorabilia.'

'I've been through his files. They contain only the usual material.'

'Locked drawers?'

'Only the phonograph cabinet. The wax cylinders are delicate and have to be protected from dust.'

Beauregard took a good hold and wrenched the cover off the contraption. He pulled open the drawer of the stand. Its fragile lock splintered. The cylinders were ranked in tubes, with neatly inked labels.

'Chapman,' he read aloud, '*Nichols, Schön, Stride/Eddowes, Kelly, Kelly, Kelly, Lucy* . . .'

Geneviève was by him, delving deeper into the drawer. 'And these . . . *Lucy, Van Helsing, Renfield, Lucy's Tomb.*'

Everyone remembered Van Helsing; Beauregard even knew Renfield was the Prince Consort's first disciple in London. But . . .

'Kelly and Lucy. Who are they? Unknown victims?'

Geneviève was going again through the papers on the desk. She talked as she sorted. 'Lucy, at a guess, was Lucy Westenra, Vlad Tepes' first English get. Dr Van Helsing destroyed her, and Jack Seward was in with Van Helsing. He was always expecting the Carpathian Guards to come for him. It is almost as if he has been in hiding.'

Beauregard snapped his fingers. 'Art was in that group, too. Lord

Godalming. He'll be able to fill in details. It comes to me now. Lucy Westenra. I met her once, when she was warm, at the Stokers'. She was part of that set.'

A pretty, silly-ish girl, not unlike a young Florence. All the men mooned around her. Pamela had not liked her, but Penelope, a child then, doted on the girl. He realized that his former fiancée styled her hair like Lucy's. It made her look less like her cousin.

'Jack loved her,' Geneviève said. 'That was what drew him in with the Van Helsing circle. What happened must have driven him out of his wits. I should have realized. He calls *her* Lucy.'

'Her?'

'His vampire mistress. It's not her real name, but it's what he calls her.'

Geneviève was sorting through the extended drawer of a stout filing cabinet, flicking past individual files with a nimble finger.

'As for Kelly,' she said, 'we have lots of Kellys on our books. But only one who fits Jack's requirements.'

She handed him a sheet of paper, the details of a patient's treatment. Kelly, Mary Jane. 13 Miller's Court.

Geneviève's face was ash-grey. 'That's the name,' she said. 'Mary Jane Kelly.'

54

Connective Tissue

O N THE 9TH of November, 1888, Geneviève Dieudonné and Charles Beauregard left Toynbee Hall at almost precisely four *ante meridiem*. Dawn was still hours off, the moon clouded over. The fog, although slightly thinned, was sufficient to impair even a vampire's night-sight. Nevertheless, their journey was accomplished swiftly.

Geneviève and Beauregard proceeded along Commercial Street, turned west into Dorset Street by the Britannia, a public house, and sought out the address they had for Mary Jane Kelly. Miller's Court was accessible through a narrow brick archway on the north side of Dorset Street, between Number 26 and a chandler's shop.

Neither took much note of a rag-wrapped personage huddled just inside the court, assuming him to be a tramp. Dorset Street was referred to locally as 'Dosset Street', because of the number of vagrants attracted to the temporary lodgings, or 'doss houses', offered there. It was common for those who lacked the fourpence for a bed to sleep rough. In actuality, the personage was Arthur Holmwood, Lord Godalming, and he was not sleeping.

Geneviève and Beauregard expended a few moments on determining which doorway gave entrance to Number 13, a single-room dwelling at the ground-floor back of 26 Dorset Street. They were drawn by a line of thin red firelight spilling on to the doorstep.

The quarter-hour had not yet sounded. By the time of their arrival, Dr John Seward had been at his work for more than two hours. The door of 13 Miller's Court was not locked.

55

Fucking Hell!

CHARLES SWORE, fighting to keep his breath, Geneviève, no shock to spare for his surprising vocabulary, had to agree with him.

The greasy smell of dead blood hit her like a bullet in the belly. She had to hold the doorframe to keep from fainting. She had seen the leavings of murderers before; and blood-muddied battlefields, and plague holes, and torture chambers, and execution sites. 13 Miller's Court was the worst of all.

Jack Seward knelt in the middle of a ruin barely recognizable as a human being. He was still working, apron and shirtsleeves dyed red. His silver scalpel flickered in the firelight.

Mary Kelly's room was cramped: a bed, a chair, a fireplace, and barely enough floor to walk round them. Jack's operation had spread the girl across the bed and the floor, and up the walls to the height of three feet. The cheap muslin curtains were speckled with halfpenny-sized dots. There was a mirror, its dusty glass marked with bloody splashes. In the grate, a bundle of clothes burned, casting a red light that seared into Geneviève's night-sensitive eyes.

Jack was not overly concerned with their intrusion.

'Nearly done,' he said, easing out something from a pie-shaped expanse that had been a face. 'I have to be sure Lucy is dead. Van Helsing says her soul will not rest until she is truly dead.'

He was calm, not ranting. He performed his butchery with a surgeon's precision. In his mind, there was purpose.

'There,' Jack said. 'She is delivered. God is merciful.'

Charles had his pistol out and aimed. His hand was trembling. 'Put down the knife and step away from her,' he said.

Jack placed the knife on the bedspread and stood up, wiping his hands on an already-bloody patch of apron.

'See, she is at peace,' Jack said. 'Sleep well, Lucy my love.'

Mary Jane Kelly was truly dead. Geneviève had no doubt about that.

'It's over,' Jack said. 'We've beaten him. We've defeated the Count. The contagion cannot spread.'

Geneviève had nothing to say. Her stomach was still a tight fist. Jack seemed to notice her for the first time.

'Lucy,' he said, alarmed. He was seeing someone else, somewhere else. 'Lucy, it was all for you . . .'

He bent to pick up his silver scalpel and Charles shot him in the shoulder. He spun round, fingers grasping air, and slammed against the mantel. He pressed his gloved hand to the wall and sank downwards, knees protruding as he tried to make his body shrink. Huddled against the fireplace, he held his wound. The shot had gone completely through and torn the murder out of him.

Geneviève snatched the scalpel away from the bed. Its silver blade made her itch, so she shifted to hold it by the enamelled grip. It was such a small thing to have done so much hurt.

'We have to get him out of here,' Charles said. 'A mob would tear him apart.'

Geneviève hauled Jack upright and between them they managed to heave him into the courtyard. His clothes were tacky from the drying gore.

It was nearing morning, and Geneviève was suddenly tired. The cold air did not dispel the throbbing in her head. The image of 13 Miller's Court was imprinted in her mind like a photograph upon paper. She would never, she thought, lose it.

Jack was easy to manipulate. He would walk with them to a police station, or to Hell.

56

Lord Jack

IT HAD BEEN dizzyingly hot inside Mary Jane Kelly's room; the chill of the court was sobering. Once out of the charnel house, Beauregard realized that though the mystery was solved, he was faced with a quandary. The women were dead, Seward hopelessly mad. What justice would be served by turning him over to Lestrade? In whose interests was he to act now? Sir Charles Warren's, by letting the police take credit for an arrest? The Prince Consort's, by turning over another vanquished foe to the spikes outside the Palace?

'He bit me,' the Ripper said, remembering some trivial incident, 'the madman bit me.' Seward held out his gloved, swollen hand. Blood was pooled in the palm.

'Vlad Tepes will make him immortal, just so he can torture him forever,' Geneviève said.

Someone came out of the chandler's shop and stood in the archway. Beauregard saw red eyes in the dark and made out the silhouette of a big man in a check ulster and a billycock hat. How much had this vampire witnessed? He stepped into the court.

'Well done, sir. You've put an end to Jack the Ripper.'

It was Sergeant Dravot from the Diogenes Club.

'All along, sir, there were two murderers, working together,' said Dravot. 'It should have been obvious.'

The world was spinning again, the cobbles beneath him falling away. Beauregard did not know where it would stop.

Dravot bent down and whipped a ragged blanket away from a human bundle that had been shoved into a corner. A dead white face stared up, lips drawn back in a last snarl.

'It's Godalming!' Beauregard exclaimed.

'Lord Godalming, sir,' Dravot said. 'He was in it with Dr Seward. They fell out last night.'

Beauregard could not make all the pieces fit. He knelt by the body. There was a large patch of black blood on Godalming's breast, soaking his shirt. In the patch was a ragged wound, over the heart.

'How long have you known all this, Dravot?'

'You caught the Rippers, sir. I've just been looking out for you. The cabal set me up as your guardian angel.'

Geneviève was standing apart from them, holding Jack Seward's arm. Her face was shadowed.

'And Jago? Was that you?' asked Beauregard.

Dravot shrugged. 'Another matter, sir.'

Beauregard stood, pushing the cobbles with his cane, and brushed off his knees. 'There'll be a fearful scandal. Godalming was well thought of. He had a reputation as a coming man.'

'His name will be entirely blackened, sir.'

'And he was a vampire. That will cause a stir. The assumption was that the Ripper was warm.'

Dravot nodded.

'I should think the cabal will be delighted,' Beauregard continued. 'This will embarrass a great many people. There will be repercussions. Careers will be smashed, reputations overturned. The Prime Minister will look foolish.'

Geneviève spoke bitterly. 'It's all very tidy, gentlemen. But what about Jack?'

Dravot and Beauregard looked at her. And at Seward. The Ripper was propped against the wall of the court. His face was wearily free of expression. Blood dribbled from his wound.

'His mind is gone completely,' Geneviève said. 'Whatever glue held him together is dissolved.'

'It would be best if Mr Beauregard did the honours.'

Geneviève looked at Dravot with something approaching loathing. Beauregard felt he had no choice. His actions had been directed by others. He was almost at the end of his duty. With a great weariness, he realized he had done little but leap hurdles on a course set out for him.

'Hold him up,' Beauregard said. 'Against the wall.'

Geneviève's hand was at Seward's throat, her nails extending. 'Charles,' she said. 'You don't have to. If it must be done, I can . . .'

He shook his head. She could not spare him this. It had been the same with Elizabeth Stride. He had simply been merciful. 'It's alright, Geneviève,' he said. 'Just hold him.'

She knew what he was about and gave her consent. She took her hand from Seward's throat. 'Goodbye, Jack,' she said. He gave no sign of understanding.

Beauregard drew his sword-cane. The rasp cut through the tiny night-sounds. Geneviève nodded and Beauregard slipped his blade through Seward's heart. The point scraped brickwork. Beauregard withdrew the sword, and sheathed it. Seward, cleanly dead, crumpled. He fell beside Godalming. Two monsters together.

'Good work, sir,' Dravot said. 'You cornered the murderers and Dr Seward became frenzied. He destroyed his confederate and you bested him in single combat.'

Beauregard was irritated to be treated as if he were a schoolboy being tutored by his fellows in an excuse.

'And what of me?'

Beauregard and Dravot both looked at Geneviève.

'Am I a "loose end"? Like Jack, like Godalming? Like that poor girl in there?' She nodded to Mary Jane Kelly's doorway. 'You let him butcher her, didn't you?'

Dravot said nothing.

'You or Jack killed Godalming. Then, knowing what he was, you stood back in the shadows and let him account for her. It was tidier that way. You didn't even dirty your hands.'

Dravot deferred. Beauregard was sure the Sergeant had a revolver about him, loaded with silver bullets.

'We came along at a convenient time,' she continued. 'To finish off the story.' Geneviève held out Seward's scalpel. 'Do you want to use this? That would be neater.'

'Geneviève,' Beauregard said, 'I don't understand . . .'

'No, you wouldn't. Poor Charles. Between bloodsuckers like Godalming and this creature, Dravot, you're a lost lamb. Just as Jack Seward was.'

Beauregard stared long at Geneviève before he turned to Dravot. If it came to it, he would protect her with his life. There were limits to his devotion to the plans of the Diogenes Club.

The Sergeant was gone. Beyond the archway, the fog was dispersing. It was nearly dawn. Geneviève came to him and he embraced her. The world stopped tilting and turning. Together, they were the fixed point.

'What happened here,' she asked, 'what truly happened?'

He did not yet know.

Together, bone-tired, they emerged from Miller's Court. On the other side of Dorset Street, a pair of constables strolled, chatting together on their beat. Geneviève whistled, to get their attention. Her trilling was not a human sound. It pierced his eardrums like a needle. The coppers, truncheons out, trotted towards them.

'You'll be the hero,' she whispered to him.

'Why?'

'You've no choice.'

The policemen were with them. They both looked terribly young. One was Collins, whom he remembered from his visit with Sergeant Thick. Collins recognized Beauregard and all but saluted.

'There's a dead woman in that court,' Beauregard told them. 'And a pair of murderers, also dead. Jack the Ripper is finished.'

Collins looked shocked. Then he grinned. 'Is it over?'

'It's over,' Beauregard said, uncertain but convincing.

The two constables dashed into Miller's Court. After a moment, they rushed out again and began blowing their whistles. Soon the area would be thick with policemen, journalists, sensation-seekers. Beauregard and Geneviève would have to explain at length, more times than either could really bear.

In his mind, Beauregard saw Jack Seward on his knees in the ground-floor back room with the bloody thing that had been Mary Jane Kelly. Geneviève shuddered along with him. The memory was something they would share for ever.

'He was mad,' she said, 'and not responsible.'

'Then who,' he asked, 'was responsible?'

'The thing who drove him mad.'

Beauregard looked up. The last moonlight shone down through thinning fog. He fancied he saw a bat, large and black, flit across the face of the moon.

The Home Life of Our Own
Dear Queen

N ETLEY APPLIED THE whip to the team. The imposing carriage had prowled through Whitechapel's cramped streets as irrit- ably as a panther in Hampton Court Maze, unable to move with its accustomed elegance and speed. In the wider thoroughfares of the city, it rolled at a rapid pace. The suspension was perfect, lulling her along without even the creak of wood and iron. Hostile eyes were drawn to the gilt coat of arms that stood out like a red-and-gold scar on the polished black door. Despite the luxurious interior, Geneviève found comfort impossible. With black leather upholstery and discreet brass lamps, the Royal Coach was too much like a hearse.

They proceeded down Fleet Street, past the boarded-up and burned-out offices of the nation's great periodicals. There was no fog tonight, just a razored wind. There were still newspapers, but Ruthven had installed tame vampire editors. Even fervent loyalists were bored by bland endorsements of the latest laws or endless encomia to the Royal Family. Very rarely an item would be printed which, combined with certain private knowledge, might actually qualify as a piece of news, such as the recent note in *The Times* of the explusion from the Bagatelle Club of Colonel Sebastian Moran, his hitherto uncanny abilities at the whist table, which extended to somewhat unorthodox manipulations of the cards, now being severely impaired by his unexplained loss of both little fingers.

As they passed the law courts, a scatter of broadsheets blew across the dark pavements of the Strand. Passers-by, even those marked by their dress as of the upper orders, hastily picked up these papers and stuffed them into their coats. A constable did his best to collect as many as possible, but they rained down from some garret heaven like autumn leaves. Hand-printed in basements, these were impossible to stamp out: no matter how many premises were raided, how many scribblers arrested, the hydra-headed spirit of dissent persisted. Kate Reed, Charles's admirer, had become a leading luminary of the underground press. In hiding, she had won a reputation as an Angel of the Insurrection.

In Pall Mall, Netley, whom Geneviève judged a fidgety sort, stopped at the Diogenes Club. After a moment, the door was held open and Charles joined her in the coach. After kissing her, lips cold on her cheek, he sat opposite, discouraging further intimacy. He wore immaculate evening dress, the scarlet lining of his cloak like spilled blood on the coach seat, a perfect white rose in his lapel. She glanced at the door as it was shut and saw the closed face of the moustached vampire from Miller's Court.

'Good night, Dravot,' Charles said to the servant of the Diogenes Club.

'Good night, sir.'

Dravot stood at the kerb, at attention but suppressing a salute. The coach had to take a circuitous route to the Palace. The Mall had been blocked by Crusaders for most of last week; the remains of barricades still stood, and great stretches of St James's Street had been torn up, cobbles converted to missiles.

Charles was subdued. She had seen him several times since the night of 9th November, and even been admitted into the hallowed Star Chamber of the Diogenes Club to give evidence at a private hearing of the ruling cabal. Charles had been called upon to account for the deaths of Dr Seward, Lord Godalming and, incidentally, Mary Jane Kelly. The tribunal had as much to do with deciding which truths should be concealed as which should be presented to the public at large. The chairman, a warm diplomat who had weathered the changes, took in everything, but gave no verdict, each grain of information shaping the policies of a club that was often more than a club. Geneviève supposed it a hiding place for pillars of the *ancien régime*, if not a nest of insurrectionists. Apart from Dravot, there were few vampires in the Diogenes Club. Her discretion, she knew, had been vouched for by Charles. Otherwise she assumed the Sergeant would call upon her with a garotte of silver wire.

As soon as they were underway, Charles leaned forwards and took her hands. He fixed her with his eyes, intently serious. He and she had been together two nights ago, in private. His collar hid the marks.

'Gené, I implore you,' he said, 'let me stop the coach outside the Palace and turn you loose.' His fingers pressed her palms.

'Darling, don't be absurd. I'm not afraid of Vlad Tepes.'

He let her go and sat back, obviously distressed. Eventually, he would confide in her. She had learned that, in many things, Charles's desires conflicted with his duty. Just now, she was Charles's desire. His duties lay in directions she could not immediately discern.

'It's not that. It's . . .'

. . . the disarray in which Beauregard found Mycroft had an air of the Final Act. At this meeting, he alone was the cabal.

The Chairman toyed with the scalpel. 'The famous Silver Knife,' he mused, testing the blade with his thumb. 'So keen.'

He laid down the instrument and let loose a sigh that set his cheeks wobbling. He had lost some of his prodigious weight and his skin was slackening, but his eyes were still sharp.

'You're to be invited to the Palace. Pay your regards to our friend in the Queen's service. You must not be startled by him. He is the gentlest of fellows. A touch *too* gentle, if truth be told.'

'I have heard him spoken of highly.'

'He was a great favourite of the late Princess Alexandra. Poor Alex.' Mycroft steepled his fat fingers and rested his chins on them. 'We demand much of our people. There's precious little public glory in this bloody business, but it must be done.'

Beauregard looked at the shining knife.

'Sacrifices must be made,' added Mycroft.

Beauregard remembered Mary Jane Kelly. And others, some only names in newspapers, some frozen faces: Seward, Jago, Godalming, Kostaki, Mackenzie, von Klatka.

'We would all do what we ask of you,' Mycroft insisted.

Beauregard knew that was true.

'Not that many of us remain.'

Sir Mandeville Messervy awaited execution on a charge of high treason, along with other worthies; the dramatist Gilbert, the financial colossus Wilcox, the arch-reformatrice Beatrice Potter, the radical editor Henry Labouchère.

'Chairman, one thing perplexes me still. Why me? What did I do

Dravot could not have? You let me run through the maze but he was there always. He could have accomplished this all on his own account.'

Mycroft shook his head. 'Dravot is a good man, Beauregard. We did not choose to burden you with knowledge of his part in our larger plans, lest it interfere . . .'

Beauregard swallowed the pill without choking.

'But Dravot is not you. He is not a *gentleman*. No matter what he did, he would never, *never*, be invited into the Royal Presences.'

At last, Beauregard understood . . .

. . . an engraved invitation had been delivered into Geneviève's hand by a pair of fully uniformed Carpathian Guardsmen; Martin Cuda, who pretended not to remember her and kept his head down, and Rupert of Hentzau, a Ruritanian blood whose studied sardonic smile constantly threatened to become a cruel laugh. As the more-or-less permanent Acting Director of Toynbee Hall, she was busier than ever but a summons from the Queen was not to be ignored. Presumably, she was to be commended for her part in ending the career of Jack the Ripper. A private honour, perhaps, but an honour nevertheless.

Their names had been kept out of it. Charles insisted public credit be taken by the police. It was generally believed that Constable Collins had come upon Godalming and Seward as they left the room where they had together mutilated Mary Jane Kelly. Hastily summoned reinforcements trapped them in Miller's Court and both were killed in the confusion. Either the murderers did for each other to escape the stake, or the police, enraged and appalled, destroyed them on the spot. Influenced by the recent habits of justice in London, most favoured the latter explanation, although Tussaud's Chamber of Horrors offered a vivid recreation, complete with actual clothes, of the two Rippers gutting each other.

At Scotland Yard, Sir Charles Warren had resigned in exchange for an overseas posting, and Caleb Croft, an elder with a reputation as a hatchet man, was his replacement. Lestrade and Abberline were on fresh cases. The city hunted a new maniac, a warm murderer of brutish disposition and appearance named Edward Hyde. He had trampled a small child, then raised his ambitions by shoving a broken walking-stick through the heart of a new-born

Member of Parliament, Sir Danvers Carew. Once Hyde was apprehended, another murderer would come along, and another, and another . . .

Red light rippled in the carriage as they passed Trafalgar Square. Although the police kept dousing the bonfires, insurrectionists always rekindled them. Scraps of wood were smuggled in, and even items of clothing used for fuel. New-borns, superstitiously afraid of fire, didn't care to get too near. Crowds scuffled with policemen by the fires, while an engine crew, perhaps half-heartedly, tried to train hoses. Captain Eyre Massey Shaw, the popular superintendent of the London Fire Brigade, had recently been removed from office, allegedly because of a refusal to deal with the Trafalgar Square conflagration; Dr Callistratus, a sullen Transylvanian with no appreciable experience of, or interest in, fire-fighting, was installed in Shaw's stead and was reportedly unable to occupy his office due to the pile of resignations heaped against the door. She looked out at the blazes heaped round the stone lions, flames leaping up a third of the height of Nelson's Column. Originally a memorial to the victims of Bloody Sunday, the fires now had fresh meaning. Word of a new mutiny had come from India. Sir Francis Varney had been dragged by sepoys from the Red Fort in Delhi and bound over the muzzle of one of his own guns to be blown away. A jumble of old scrap-iron and silver salts shot through his chest, Varney was cast into a fire and burned down to ash and bones. Many warm British troops and officials had thrown in with the native rebels. According to the broad sheets, who plainly had highly positioned sources. India was in open revolt, and there were further stirrings in Africa and points east.

Placards were waved and slogans shouted. JACK STILL RIPS, a graffito read. The letters still came, red-inked scrawls signed 'Jack the Ripper'. They had been received by the press, by the police, by prominent individuals. Now they called for the warm to rally against their vampire masters or for British new-borns to resist foreign elders. Whenever a vampire was killed, 'Jack the Ripper' took credit. Charles said nothing, but Geneviève suspected many of the letters were issued from the Diogenes Club. A dangerous game was played out in the halls of secret government. Even if a madman became a hero, a purpose was served. To those for whom Jack the Ripper was a martyr, there was Jack Seward taking his silver knife to the vampire oppressors. To those for whom Jack the Ripper was a monster, there was Lord Godalming, the arrogant un-dead disposing of common women he regarded as trash. The story had a different meaning for each retelling, the Ripper a different face. For Geneviève, that face would always be Danny Dravot, fingers bloody with ink, standing by while Mary Jane Kelly was ripped apart.

Public order in the city was at the point of breaking down. Not just in Whitechapel and Limehouse, but in Whitehall and Mayfair. The heavier the hand of the authorities became, the more people resisted. The latest fashion was for warm Londoners of all classes to black their faces like minstrels and call themselves 'natives'. Five army officers awaited court martial and summary impalement for refusing to order their men to fire upon a peaceful demonstration of mock blackamoors.

After some negotiations, and not a little shouted abuse from a black-faced matron, Netley was allowed to take the carriage through Admiralty Arch. The coachman must have wished he was able to paint out the crest on his conveyance.

A vampire but not of the bloodline of Vlad Tepes, Geneviève was left, as ever, on the sidelines. It had been refreshing at first, after centuries of dissembling, not to have to pretend to be warm; but eventually the Prince Consort had made things as uncomfortable for most of the un-dead as for the living he called cattle. For every noble murgatroyd in his town house with his harem of willing blood-slaves, there were twenty of Mary Jane Kelly, Lily Mylett, or Cathy Eddowes, as miserable as they had ever been, vampire attributes addictions and handicaps rather than powers and potentials . . .

. . . with Geneviève, he called upon the Churchwards. Penelope was out of bed now. They found her in a Bath chair in the heavily curtained parlour, a tartan rug over her legs. A new-purchased coffin, lined in a white satin, stood on trestles in place of the occasional table.

Penelope was getting stronger. Her eyes were clear. She had little to say.

On the mantel, Beauregard noticed a photograph of Godalming, posed stiffly by a potted plant with a studio background, ringed with black crepe.

'He was, in a manner of speaking, my father,' Penelope explained.

Geneviève understood in a way Beauregard could never hope to.

'Was he really such a monster?' Penelope asked.

Beauregard told the truth. 'Yes, I'm afraid he was.'

Penelope almost smiled. 'Good. I'm glad. I shall be a monster too.'

They sat together, untouched cups on the low table, darkness gathering . . .

. . . the carriage sped smoothly down Bird Cage Walk towards Buckingham Palace. Insurrectionists hung in chains from cruciform cages lining the road, some still alive. Within the last three nights, open battle had raged between the warm and the un-dead in St James's Park.

'Look,' Charles said, sadly, 'there's Van Helsing's head.'

Geneviève craned and saw the pathetic lump on the end of its pike. Some said Abraham Van Helsing was still alive, in the Prince Consort's thrall, raised high so that his eyes might see the reign of Dracula over London. That was a lie; what was left was a fly-blown skull.

The main gates loomed before them, newfangled barbed wire wrapped around the upright bars. Carpathians, midnight-black uniforms slashed with crimson, hauled the huge ironwork frames aside as if they were silk curtains, and the coach slid through. Geneviève imagined Netley sweating like a frightened pig at an Indian Officers' Ball. The Palace, illuminated by watch-fires and incandescent lamps, poured black smoke into the sky, its face an image of Moloch the Devourer.

Charles's face was a blank, but he was focused in his mind. 'You can stay in the carriage,' he said, urgent, persuasive. 'Safe. I shall be all right. This will not take long.'

Geneviève shook her head. She supposed she had been avoiding Vlad Tepes for centuries, but she would face whatever was inside the Palace.

'Gené, I beg you.' His voice almost broke.

Two nights ago, she had been with Charles, delicately lapping blood from cuts on his chest. She knew and understood his body now. Together, they made love. She knew and understood him.

'Charles, why are you so worried? We're heroes, we have nothing to fear from the Prince. I am his elder.'

The carriage halted by the maw-like porch, and a periwigged footman opened the door. Geneviève stepped down first, relishing the soft crunch of the clean gravel under her shoes. Charles followed, taut as a drawn bowstring, gathering his cloak about him. She took his arm and nuzzled against him, but he would not be comforted. He eagerly anticipated what he would find inside the Palace, but his anticipation was blackened by dread.

Beyond the Palace fences stood crowds, as usual. Sullen sightseers peered through the bars, awaiting the Changing of the Guard. Near the gates, Geneviève saw a familiar face, the Chinese girl from the Old Jago. She stood with a tall, old oriental man whose aspect was somehow sinister. Behind them, in shadow, was a taller, older oriental form, and Geneviève had a flash of a past terror, returning. When she looked again, the Chinese party were gone, but her heart remained beating too fast. Charles had still not told her the full story behind his bargain with the elder assassin.

The footman, a vampire youth with a gold-painted face, lead them up the broad stairs, and struck the doors with his tall stick. They opened as if by some unheard mechanism, disclosing the marbled length of a vaulted reception hall.

With her single decent dress ruined, she had been forced to commission a replacement. Now she wore it for the first time, a simple ball-gown free of bustles, frills and flounces. She doubted Vlad Tepes thought much of formality but supposed she should make an effort for the Queen. She could remember the family as electors of Hanover. Her only unusual ornament was a small gold crucifix on the latest of innumerable replacement chains. It was all she had from her warm life. Her real father had given it to her, claiming it blessed by Jeanne d'Arc. She doubted that but somehow had contrived to keep it through the ages. Many times, she had walked away from entire lives – houses, possessions, wardrobes, estates, fortunes – keeping only the cross the Maid of Orleans had probably never touched.

Thirty-foot diaphanous silk curtains parted in the draught, and she and Charles passed through. The effect was of a giant cobweb, billowing open to entice the unwary fly. Servants appeared, under the direction of a vampire lady-in-waiting, and Charles and Geneviève were relieved of their cloaks. A Carpathian, his face a mask of stiff hair, stood by to watch Charles hand over his cane. Silver was frowned on at the Court. She had no weapons to yield . . .

. . . he had tried everything to dissuade her from accompanying him, short of disclosing to her the duty he must perform. Beauregard knew he would die. His death would have purpose, and he was prepared for it. But his heart sickened at what might become of Geneviève. This was not her crusade. If it were possible, he would help her escape even at the cost of his own life. But his duty was more important than either of them.

When they were together, warmed by their communion, he told her what he had told no other woman since Pamela.

'Gené, I love you.'

'And I you, Charles. I you.'

'I you what?'

'Love, Charles. I love you.'

Her mouth was on him again and they rolled together, getting comfortable . . .

. . . an armadillo wriggled by her feet, its rear parts clogged with its own dirt. Vlad Tepes had raided Regent's Park Zoo and had exotic species roaming loose in the Palace. This poor edentate was merely one of his more harmless pets.

The lady-in-waiting who guided them through the cathedral-like space of the reception hall wore black velvet livery, the Royal Crest upon her bosom. With tight trews and gold-buckled knee-boots, she looked like the principal boy. Although handsome, her face had lost any feminine softness it might have possessed when its wearer was warm.

'Mr Beauregard, you have forgotten me,' she said.

Charles, involved in his own thoughts, was almost shocked. He looked closely at the lady-in-waiting.

'We met at the Stokers',' she explained. 'Some years ago. Before the changes.'

'Miss Murray?'

'The widow Harker now. Wilhelmina. Mina.'

Geneviève knew who the woman was: one of Vlad Tepes's get.

After Jack Seward's Lucy, the first of the Prince Consort's conquests in Britain. Like Jack and Godalming, she had been in with Van Helsing's group.

'So that fearful murderer was Dr Seward,' Mina Harker mused. 'He was spared only to suffer, and to make others suffer. And Lord Godalming too. How Lucy would have been disappointed in her suitors.'

Geneviève saw into Mina Harker, and realized the woman was condemned – had condemned herself – to exist with the consequences of failure. Her failure to resist Vlad Tepes, her circle's failure to trap and destroy the invader.

'I had not expected to find you here,' Charles blurted.

'Serving in Hell?'

They were at the end of the hall. More doors loomed above them. Mina Harker, eyes like burning ice, looked at them both as she struck a panel, the rapping of her knuckles as loud in the echoing space as shots from a revolver . . .

. . . Beauregard remembered the warm Mina Harker, unfussy and direct when set beside Florence, Penelope or Lucy, siding with Kate Reed in the belief that a woman should earn a living, should be more than a decoration. That woman was dead and this white-faced court servant was her pale ghost. Seward had been a ghost too, and Godalming. Between them, the Prince Consort and the skull on the pike had to account for a great deal of human wreckage.

The inner doors opened in noisy lurches and a startling servant admitted them to a well-lit antechamber. The extensive and grotesque malformations of his body were emphasized by a tailored parti-coloured suit. He was not the new-born victim of catastrophically failed shape-shifting, but a warm man suffering from enormous defects of birth. His spine was drastically kinked, loaf-shaped excrescences sprouting from his back: his limbs, with the exception of the left arm were bloated and twisted. His head was swollen by bulbs of bone, from which sprouted wisps of hair, and his features were almost completely obscured by warty growths. Mycroft had prepared Beauregard for this, but he still felt a heart-stab of pity.

'Good evening,' he said. 'Merrick, is it not?'

A smile formed somewhere in the doughy recesses of Merrick's face. He returned the greeting voice slurred by excess slews of flesh around his mouth.

'How is Her Majesty this evening?'

Merrick did not reply, but Beauregard imagined expression in the unreadable expanse of his features. There was a sadness in his single exposed eye and a grim set to his growth-twisted lips.

He gave Merrick a card and said, 'Compliments of the Diogenes Club.' The man understood and his huge head bobbed. He was another servant of the ruling cabal.

Merrick lead them down the hallway, hunched over like a gorilla, a long club-handed arm propelling his body. It apparently amused the Prince Consort to keep this poor creature on hand. Beauregard could not help but feel an additional disgust for the vampire. Merrick knocked on doors three times his height . . .

. . . she realized, ridiculously late, that Charles was not afraid of whatever he would face in the Palace. He was afraid for her, afraid of the consequences of something soon to happen. He took her hand and held it tight.

'Gené,' Charles said, voice just above a whisper, 'if what I do brings harm to you, I am sincerely sorry.'

She did not understand him. As her mind raced to catch up with him, he leaned over and kissed her, on the mouth, the warm way. She tasted him, and was reminded of everything . . .

. . . her voice was cool in the dark.

'This can be for ever, Charles. Truly for ever.'

He remembered his meeting with Mycroft.

'Nothing is for ever, my darling . . .'

. . . the kiss broke, and he stood back, leaving her baffled. Then the doors were opened and they were admitted into the Royal Presences.

Ill lit by broken chandeliers, the throne-room was an infernal sty of people and animals, its once-fine walls torn and stained. Dirtied and abused paintings hung at strange angles or were piled loose behind furniture. Laughing, whimpering, grunting, whining, screaming creatures congregated on divans and carpets. An almost naked Carpathian wrestled a giant ape, their feet scrabbling and slipping on a marble floor thick with discharges. The stench of dried blood and ordure was as strong as it had been in Number 13 Miller's Court.

Merrick announced them to the company, his palate suffering as he got out their names. Someone made a crude remark in German. Gales of cruel laughter cut through the din, then were cut off by a wave of a ham-sized hand. The gesture gave the congregation pause; the Carpathian jammed the ape's face against the floor and snapped the animal's spine, prematurely ending the contest of strength.

Upon the raised hand, an enormous gemstone ring held the burning reflections of seven fires. She recognized the Koh-i-Noor, or Lake of Light, the largest diamond in the world, and the centrepiece of the collection known as the Crown Jewels. Her eyes was drawn to the shining light, and to the vampire who wielded it. Prince Dracula sat upon his throne, massive as a commemorative statue, his enormously bloated face a rich red under withered grey. Moustaches stiff with recent blood hung to his chest, his thick hair was loose about his shoulders, and his black-stubbled chin was dotted with the gravy of his last feeding. His left hand loosely held the orb of office, which seemed in his grip the size of a tennis ball.

Charles shook in the presence of the enemy, the smell smiting him like blows. Geneviève held him up and looked around.

'I never dreamed . . .' he muttered, 'never . . .'

An ermine-collared black velvet cloak, ragged at the edges, clung to Dracula's shoulders like the wings of a giant bat. Otherwise he was naked, his body thickly coated with matted hair, blood clotting on his chest and limbs. His white manhood coiled in his lap, tipped scarlet as an adder's tongue. His body was swollen with blood, rope-thick veins visibly pulsing in his neck and arms. In life, Vlad Tepes had been a man of less than medium height; now he was a giant.

A warm girl ran across the room, pursued by one of the Carpathians. It was Rupert of Hentzau, his uniform in tatters, a ruddy flush on his face. The plates of his skull dislocated as he shambled, distorting and reassembling his face. He brought the girl down with a swipe of a paw, scraping silk and skin from her back. Then he began to tear at her back and sides with triple-jointed jaws, taking meat as well as drink. As Hentzau fed he became wolfish, wriggling out of his boots and breeches, his laugh turning to a howl. The girl was instantly dead.

Dracula smiled, yellow teeth the size and shape of pointed thumbs. Geneviève looked into the broad face of the King of Vampires.

The Queen knelt by the throne, a spiked collar round her neck, a massive chain leading from it to a loose bracelet upon Dracula's wrist. She was in her shift and stockings, brown hair loose, blood on her face. It was impossible to see the round old woman she had been in this abused, wretched figure. Geneviève hoped her mad, but feared her well aware of what was happening about her. Victoria turned away, not looking at the Carpathian's meal.

'Majesties,' Charles said, bowing his head.

An enormous fart of laughter exploded from Dracula's jaggedly fanged maw. The stench of his breath filled the room. It was everything dead and rotten.

'I am Dracula,' he said, in surprisingly unaccented and mild English. 'And who might these welcome guests be?'

. . . his head was in the eye of a nightmare maelstrom. In his heart was steel resolve. All he saw made him *justum et tenacem propositi virum*, a man upright and tenacious of purpose. Later, if he still lived, he might succumb to nausea. Now, in this vital moment, he must have complete control of himself.

Never entirely a soldier, Beauregard had learned strategy at school and in the field. He knew, without seeming to notice, the relative positions of all in the throne-room. Few of them mattered, but he was especially aware of Geneviève, Merrick and, without quite knowing why, Mina Harker. All, as it happened, were behind him.

The man and the woman on the dais were the focus of his attention; the Queen, whose visible distress gripped his heart, and the Prince, who sat at his ease on the throne, embodying the chaos about him. Dracula's face seemed painted on water; sometimes frozen into hard-planed ice, but for the most part in motion. Beauregard discerned other faces beneath. The red eyes and wolf teeth were fixed, but around them, under the rough cheeks, was a constantly shifting shape; sometimes a hairy, wet snout, sometimes a thin, polished skull.

A fastidious dressed vampire youth, an explosion of lace escaping at his collar, mounted the dais.

'These are the heroes of Whitechapel,' he explained, a fluttering handkerchief before his mouth and nose. Beauregard recognized the Prime Minister.

'To them we owe the ruination of the desperate murderers known as Jack the Ripper,' Lord Ruthven continued. 'Dr John Seward of infamous memory, and, ah, Arthur Holmwood, the terrible traitor . . .

The Prince grinned ferociously, moustaches creaking like leather straps. Ruthven, Godalming's father-in-darkness, was plainly put out at the reminder of the ghastly deeds in which his protégé was popularly believed to have collaborated.

'You have served us well and faithfully, my subjects,' Dracula said, his praise sounding like a threat . . .

. . . Ruthven stood by Prince Dracula's side, completing the triumvirate of rulers, the elder vampires and the new-born Queen. There was no-doubt that Vlad Tepes was the apex of this trinity of power.

Geneviève had met Ruthven nearly a century previously, while travelling in Greece. He struck her then as a dilettante, desperately amusing himself with romantic trifles but oppressed by the aridity of his long life. As Prime Minister, he had exchanged ennui for uncertainty, for he must know the higher he was raised the greater was the likehood that he would eventually be dashed down to the depths. She wondered if any other could see the fear that nestled like a rat in the bosom of Lord Ruthven.

Dracula looked Charles up and down, almost benevolently. Geneviève sensed her lover's blood boiling, and realized she had adopted an aggressive posture, teeth bared and fingers hooked into claws. She forced herself to stand demurely before the throne.

The Prince turned his attention to her and raised a thick eyebrow. His face was a mass of healed-over scars which swarmed about his smooth features.

'Geneviève Dieudonné,' he said, rolling her name around his tongue, trying to squeeze meaning from the syllables. 'I have had word of you before, in earlier times.'

She held out her empty hands.

'When I was new to this blessed state,' he continued, gesturing expressively, 'you were spoken of highly. It has been a wearisome task, keeping abreast of the peregrinations of our kind. The occasional report of you has come to me.'

As he spoke, the Prince seemed to swell. She suspected he chose to go naked not simply because he was able to, but because clothes could not contain his constant shifting of shape.

'You counted a distant kinswoman of mine as a friend, I believe.'

'Carmilla? That is so,' said Geneviève.

'A delicate flower, sadly missed.'

Geneviève nodded agreement. This monster's solicitousness was sickly-sweet, hard to swallow without choking. As fondly and without thought as a master pets an old hunting dog, Prince stretched out a hand and caressed the Queen's tangled hair. Panic bloomed in Victoria's eyes. At the base of the throne-dais clustered a knot of shrouded *nosferatu* women, the wives Dracula had set aside. Beauties all, they rent their garments immodestly, exposing limbs and breasts and loins. They hissed and lusted like cats. The Queen was plainly in terror of them. Dracula's enormous fingers encircled Victoria's fragile skull and squeezed slightly.

'My lady,' he continued, 'why have you not come before to my court? We should have welcomed you to our sadly missed Castle Dracula in Transylvania or to our more modern estate here. All elders are welcome.'

Dracula's smile was persuasive, but behind it were his teeth.

'Do I so offend you, my lady? You wandered from one place to the next for hundreds of years, always in fear of the jealous warm. Like all un-dead, you were outcast on the face of the earth. Was this not injustice? Harried by inferiors, we were denied the succour of church and the protection of law. You and I, we have both lost girls that we have loved, to peasants with sharpened spikes and silver sickles. I am named Tepes and yet it was not Dracula who pierced the heart of Carmilla Karnstein, nor that of Lucy Westenra. My dark kiss brings life, eternal and sweet; it is the silver knives that bring cold death, empty and endless. The dark nights are ended and we are raised to our rightful estate. This have I done for the good of all who are *nosferatu*. None need hide his nature among the warm, none need suffer the brain fever of the red thirst. Daughter-in-darkness of Chandagnac, you share in this; and yet you have no love for Dracula. Is this not sad? Is this not the attitude of a shallow and ungrateful woman?'

Dracula's hand was about Victoria's neck, thumb stroking her throat. The Queen's eyes were downcast.

Were you not alone, Geneviève Dieudonné? And are you not among friends now? Among equals?'

She had been un-dead a half-century longer than Vlad Tepes. When she turned, this prince was a babe in arms, shortly to be delivered into a life in captivity.

'Impaler,' she declared, 'I have no equal.'

. . . as the Prince glowered at Geneviève, Beauregard stepped forward.

'I have a gift,' he said, his hand inside the breast of his tailcoat, 'a souvenir of our exploit in the East End.'

Dracula's eyes showed the philistine avarice of a true barbarian. Despite lofty titles, he was barely a generation away from his mountain bully-boy ancestors. This prince liked nothing more than pretty things. Bright, shining toys. Beauregard took a cloth bundle from his inside pocket, and unwrapped it.

Silver light exploded.

Vampires had been feeding in the shadows, noisily suckling the flesh of youths and girls. Now everyone was quiet. It must be an illusion, but the tiny blade gleamed, a miniature excalibur illuminating the whole room. Fury twisted Dracula's brow, then contempt and mirth turned his face into a wide-mouthed mask. Beauregard held up Jack Seward's silver scalpel.

'You think to defy me with this little needle, Englishman?'

'It is a gift,' Beauregard replied. 'But not for you.'

Geneviève edged away, uncertain. Merrick and Mina Harker were too far off to affect this action. Carpathians detached themselves from their amusements and formed a half-circle to one side. Several of the harem stood, red mouths wet and eager. No one was between Beauregard and the dais, but if he made a move towards Dracula, a wall of solid bone and vampire-flesh would form.

'For my Queen,' Charles said, tossing the knife.

Tumbling silver reflected in Dracula's eyes, as anger exploded dark in the pupils. Victoria snatched the scalpel from the air . . .

*   *   *

. . . it had all been for this moment, to get Charles into the Royal Presence, to serve this one duty. Geneviève, the taste of him in her mouth, understood . . .

. . . the Queen slipped the blade under her breast, stapling her shift to her ribs, puncturing her heart. For her, it was over swiftly. With a moan of joy, she fell from the dais, blood gouting from her fatal wound, and rolled down the steps, chain rattling with her as it unravelled. *Sic transit Victoria Regina.*

The Prime Minister beat his way through the harem, pushing the harpies aside, and clutched the Queen's body. Her head flopped as he extracted the scalpel with a single pull. Ruthven pressed his hand over her wound as if willing her back to life. It was no use. He stood, still gripping the silver knife. His fingers began to smoke and he threw away the scalpel, admitting with a yelp to his own pain. Surrounded by Dracula's wives, their faces transforming with hunger and rage, the Prime Minister shook inside his murgatroyd's finery.

Beauregard waited for the deluge.

The Prince – Consort no more – was on his feet, cloak rippling around him like a thundercloud. Tusks exploded from his mouth, his hands became spear-tipped clusters. His power was dealt a blow from which it could never recover. Albert Edward, Prince of Wales, was King now; and the stepfather who had dispatched him to pleasurable but purposeless exile in Paris was scarcely likely to exert any great influence over him. The Empire Dracula had usurped would rise against him.

If Beauregard died now, he would have done enough.

Dracula raised a hand, the useless chain dangling from his wrist, and pointed at Beauregard. Beyond speech, he spat out rage and hate.

The late Queen had been the Grandmother of Europe. Seven of her children still lived, four of them warm. By marriage and accession they linked the remaining Royal houses of Europe. Even if Bertie were set aside, there were sufficient claimants to contest the throne. By a nice irony, the King Vampire could be brought low by a gaggle of crowned haemophiliacs.

Beauregard walked backwards. The vampires, suddenly sober, gathered. The women of the harem and the officers of the guard. The women pounced first and bore him onto the floor, ripping . . .

. . . Charles had tried to save her from harm by keeping her out of the designs of the Diogenes Club, but she'd stubbornly insisted on seeing Dracula in his lair. Now they would probably both die.

She was thrust aside by Dracula's women. They were on Charles, claws and mouths red. She felt the razor-kiss of their nails on his face and hands. She pulled one – that Styrian bitch Countess Barbara de Cilly of Graz, unless Geneviève was mistaken – from the fray and pitched her screeching across the room. Geneviève bared her teeth and hissed at the fallen woman.

Anger gave her strength.

She strode to the huddle that had formed over Charles and hauled him free, thumping and stabbing with her hands. In their lair, the courtiers were soft, replete. It was comparatively easy to cast aside Dracula's women. Geneviève found herself spitting and shrieking with the other she-creatures, pulling handfuls of hair and scratching at red eyes. Charles was bloodied, but still living. She fought for him as a mother wolf fights for her cubs.

The hell-cats scrabbled backwards, away from Geneviève, giving her room. Charles was at her side, still in a daze. Hentzau stood before them, Dracula's champion. His lower body was human, but he had an animal's teeth and claws. He made a fist and a point of bone slid from his knuckles. It grew long and straight and sharp.

She stepped back, out of range of the bone-rapier. The courtiers retreated, forming a circle like a prize-fight crowd. Still shackled to his dead Queen, Dracula watched. Hentzau whirled about, his sword moving faster than she could see. She heard the whisper of the blade and, moments later, realized her shoulder was opened, a red line trickling on her dress. She snatched up a footstool and raised it as a shield, parrying the next slice. Hentzau cut through cover and cushion, fixing his blade-edge in wood. As he pulled free, horsehair bled from the gash.

'Fighting with the furniture, eh?' Hentzau sneered.

Hentzau made passes near her face and locks of her hair floated free. From somewhere by the doors came a shout, and something was thrown to the floor before Charles . . .

*   *   *

. . . the strangled voice was John Merrick's. At his feet was his sword-cane. The poor creature had wrested it from the custody of a footman. Beauregard had not expected to survive his Queen. For him, these seconds were an afterlife.

The Guardsman who had extruded a sword from his skeleton closed on Geneviève. Hentzau did not reckon a warm man worth the worry. He was light on his feet, a fencer's muscles moving in his knees, his sword-arm keen enough to fetch off a head.

Beauregard picked up his cane and drew the silver-edged sword. He understood how the Ruritanian must feel, with a weapon as an extension of his arm.

With a tap, Hentzau whisked Geneviève's stool from her hands. He grinned and drew back for a thrust at her heart. Beauregard sliced down, knocking Hentzau's point out of true, and slashed back, the edge of his blade slipping under the Guardsman's jaw, sliding through coarse fur, opening skin and scraping bone.

The Ruritanian howled in silver pain and turned on Beauregard. He launched an assault, sword-point darting like a dragonfly. Even in agony, he was fast and accurate. Beauregard parried a rapid compass of attacks. Suddenly, a thrust came. He felt a fish-hook sting just under his ribs. Throwing himself backwards, half-seconds ahead of the piercing blade, his heels skidded on the marble. He fell badly, *knowing* Hentzau would close on him and puncture his arteries. The women of the harem would drink from his fountaining wounds.

Hentzau raised his sword-arm like a scythe; the blade began a swishing descent. Beauregard knew the arc would terminate in his neck. He thought of Geneviève. And Pamela. With a convulsion, he brought up his own arm to ward off the blow. The handle of his sword slipped slightly in his sweat-slick fist and he gripped it hard.

A shock of impact ran through his whole body. Hentzau's arm sliced against Beauregard's silver. The Guardsman staggered back. His sword-arm fell in a dead lump, cut clean through at the elbow. As blood geysered, Beauregard rolled out of the way.

He regained his footing. The Guardsman gripped his stump and stumbled. His face turned human, moulting hair. After Hentzau's howl had subsided to a succession of choking sobs, there came an exaggerated clanking sound. Beauregard and Geneviève turned to its source.

Prince Dracula stood on the dais. He had detached the Queen's chain from his arm, and dropped it . . .

. . . he came down from his throne, steam pouring from his nostrils. For centuries he had thought himself a higher being, apart from humanity; less blinded by selfish fantasies, she knew she was just a tick in the hide of the warm. In his bloated state, the Prince was almost lethargic.

Geneviève held Charles to her and turned to the doors. Before them stood the Prime Minister. He was civilized, almost effete, in this company.

'Aside, Ruthven,' she hissed.

Ruthven was uncertain. With the Queen truly dead, things would change. Willing to try anything, Geneviève held out her crucifix. Ruthven, surprised, almost laughed. He could have barred their path, but he hesitated – ever the politician – then stepped out of the way.

'Very clever, my lord,' she told him, quietly.

Ruthven shrugged. He knew an empire had foundered. She guessed he would immediately concentrate on his own survival. Elders were skilled in survival.

Merrick held the doors open. In the antechamber, a startled Mina Harker stood, unsure in her shock. Everyone was reeling, trying to keep up with the rapid changes. Some of the courtiers had given up and returned to their pleasures.

Dracula's shadow grew, his wrath reaching out like a fog.

Geneviève helped Charles out of the throne-room. She licked blood from his face, and felt the strength of his heart. Together, they would ride this whirlwind.

'I couldn't tell you,' he tried to explain.

She shushed him.

Merrick shut the doors and put his enormous back to them. He made a long howl that might have meant 'go!' Something smashed against the other side of the doors and a clawed hand punched through above Merrick's head, a dozen feet from floor-level, tearing at the wood. The hand made a fist, and enlarged its hole. The doors shook as if a rhinoceros were slamming against them. An upper hinge flew apart.

She saluted Merrick and limped away, Charles by her side . . .

           ★   ★   ★

. . . he told himself not to look back.

As they ran, Beauregard heard the doors behind them bursting outwards, and Merrick being crushed under falling wood and stamping feet. Another ill-used hero, lost too swiftly to be mourned.

Sweeping past Mina Harker, they emerged from the antechamber into the reception hall, which was full of vampires in livery. A dozen different rumours animated them.

Geneviève pulled him onwards.

He heard the thunder of pursuit. Among the clatter of boots, there was a single flap. He felt the draught of giant wings.

Bewildered guards let them through the Palace doors . . .

. . . her blood raced. There was no carriage, of course. They would have to make their way on foot and disappear in the crowds. In the most populated city in the world, it should be easy to hide.

As they stumbled down the wide steps, a cadre of Carpathians quick-marched up, swords rattling in their scabbards. At their head was the General everyone made fun of behind his back, Iorga.

'Quick,' Geneviève shouted, 'the Prince Consort, the Queen! All will be lost!'

Iorga tried to look resolute, not delighted at the prospect of some unknown harm to his commander-in-chief. The cadre redoubled their speed and jammed into the great doorway just as Dracula's retinue tried to come through. They would be through the main gates by the time the Carpathians had disentangled themselves.

Charles, the exhilaration of his duel fading, wiped his face with his sleeve. She took his arm and they strolled lopsidedly away from the clamour.

'Gené, Gené, Gené,' he murmured through blood.

'Shush,' she said, guiding him onwards. 'We must hurry.'

. . . people, warm and un-dead, streamed in from all sides. The Palace was being attacked and reinforced at once. In the park, a choir of demonstrators sang hymns, blocking the path of a fire engine. In the grounds, loose horses ran, kicking up scuds of gravel.

He needed to draw breath. Geneviève, her grip on his arm fierce, let him pause. The instant he stopped running, he was aware of the mauling he had sustained. He supported himself with his naked sword and gulped cold air into his lungs. His mind and body shook. It was as if he had died back in the throne-room and was now an ectoplasmic form liberated from earthly flesh.

Ahead, people swarmed over the Palace gates. The weight of numbers made them swing inwards, knocking over a couple of Guardsmen. This riot came at a most convenient time. The Diogenes Club took care of its own. Or his other friends, the Limehouse Ring, were intervening on his behalf. Or else he was lost in the tides of history, and this was simply a fortunate occurrence.

Holding aloft torches and wooden crucifixes, a crowd of roughs, faces streaked with burnt cork, shoved into the courtyard. Their leader was a nun, her wimple disclosing a Chinese cameo of a face. Tiny and lithe, she summoned her followers, and pointed up at the skies.

A deeper darkness than night fell. A great shadow was all around, thrown over the crowds. Twin red moons looked down. Slow-flapping winds knocked people off their feet. The bat-shape filled the sky over the Palace.

For a moment, the crowds fell silent. Then a voice was raised against the shape. More voices joined. Torches were tossed into the air, but fell short. Stones pulled from the drive were hurled. Shots were fired. The huge shadow soared higher.

Iorga's men, regathered after their undignified tumble, charged the crowds, laying about themselves with sabres. The mob was easily beaten back through the main gates. Beauregard and Geneviève were sucked out of the courtyard with the retreat. A lot of noise had been made, but little damage was done. The Chinese nun was the first to disappear into the night, her followers scattering after her.

Well away from the gates, he allowed himself to look back. The shadow had alighted on the roof of Buckingham Palace. A gargoyle-shape looked down, wings settling like a cloak. Beauregard wondered how long the Prince could cling to his perch.

In the night, fires burned high. The news would soon spread, a match touched to the powder-keg. In Chelsea and Whitechapel and Kingstead; in Exeter and Purfleet and Whitby; in Paris and Moscow and New York: there would be repercussions, rippling out to change the world. The park was full of shouting. Dark figures danced and fought . . .

*   *   *

. . . she felt a twinge of regret for her lost position. She would not return to Toynbee Hall and her work would pass to others. With or without Charles, in this country or abroad, in the open or in hiding, she would start anew, building another life. All she took with her was her father's crucifix. And a good dress, somewhat spotted.

She was sure the creature on the roof of the Palace, even with his night-eyes and lofty vantage point, could not see them. The further away they walked, the smaller he became. After they were past the piked skull of Abraham Van Helsing, Geneviève looked back and saw only darkness.

Author's Note and Acknowledgements

A T THE AGE of eleven, I was allowed up late to watch *Dracula*, the 1930 Tod Browning version with Bela Lugosi, on television. I can't overestimate the effect this simple act has had on the subsequent course of my life. So my first acknowledgement must be to my parents, Bryan and Julia Newman, who put up with my bizarre interests throughout my teenage years and beyond. Among my first attempts at writing was a one-page play, based on the film, which I wrote, starred in, and directed in Tony Collins's drama class at Dr Morgan's Grammar School in autumn 1970. Shortly afterwards, I read (and reread) Bram Stoker's novel, and went out of my way to catch as many Dracula movies as possible. I even had the Aurora glow-in-the-dark hobby kit ('Frightning Lightning Strikes!') of Lugosi as the Count. Among my friends of the time, and down to the present day, who endured this craze and saw movies with me, I must thank Alex Dunn (*Young Frankenstein*), Rodney Jones (*The Satanic Rites of Dracula*), Dean Skilton (*Blacula*) and Brian Smedley (*Dracula AD 1972*). Also, from the late '70s and early '80s – when I caught up with Murnau's *Nosferatu* and was able to compare new versions with Louis Jourdan, Klaus Kinski, Frank Langella and George Hamilton – I acknowledge David Cross (*Plan 9 From Outer Space*), Steve Roe (*The Games of the Countess Dolingen of Graz*), Stefan Jaworzyn (*Dracula vs Frankenstein*), Nigel Floyd (*The Monster Squad*) and Tom Tunney (Madeline Smith's Greatest Admirer). When I happened to return to the building that had been Dr Morgan's assembly hall in February 1989, the stage was set for that year's school play, *Dracula*, which I regarded as a personal vindication.

Here's how this book evolved: I first had the idea for an

alternative outcome to the Dracula story in the early '80s – I remember discussing it with Neil Gaiman and Faith Brooker around 1984 – but the outline lay about gathering dust, and the odd character, until Stephen Jones asked me to write something for an anthology project he was working on in 1991, *The Mammoth Book of Vampires*. Steve's request prompted me finally to set down the parameters for *Anno Dracula*, in that I felt a mammoth book of vampires should have some showing from the king of the un-dead. The result was 'Red Reign', which first appeared in Steve's book and which has been extensively cannibalized – and, to give value for money, sneakily altered – here. Meanwhile I had already been drawn to vampires in my work as Jack Yeovil for GW Books, developing not only a system of vampirism that, crossbred with Bram Stoker's, survives in this book, but also a Genevieve who is something of a trans-continual cousin to the Geneviève of this novel. I should like to thank Bryan Ansell, Phil Gallagher, Neil Jones, Tom Kirby, Martin McKenna, Lindsey Paton and David Pringle for their influence on, and encouragement of, this strand of my work, and admirers of Geneviève and her Kith and Kind should check out Jack Yeovil's novels *Drachenfels* and *Beasts in Velvet* and the stories 'No Gold in the Grey Mountains' and 'Red Thirst', plus the forthcoming *Genevieve Undead*, which contains the novellas 'Stage Blood', 'The Cold Stark House' and 'Unicorn Ivory'.

Of course, this novel would not exist without Stoker's 1897 *Dracula*. And in taking hold of the material Stoker laid down, I must also acknowledge a debt to many scholars. Most often consulted were Leonard Wolf's *The Annotated Dracula* and Christopher Frayling's *Vampyres: Lord Byron to Count Dracula*, which point out many of the byways I found myself exploring, but I should not care to underestimate Basil Copper's *The Vampire in Legend, Fact and Art*, Richard Dalby's *Dracula's Brood*, Daniel Farson's *The Man Who Wrote Dracula*, Donald F. Glut's *The Dracula Book*, Peter Haining's *The Dracula Centenary Book*, Raymond T. McNally and Radu R. Florescu's *In Search of Dracula*, Michel Parry's *The Rivals of Dracula*, Barry Pattison's *The Seal of Dracula*, David Pirie's *The Vampire Cinema*, Alan Ryan's *The Penguin Book of Vampire Stories*, Alain Silver and James Ursini's *The Vampire Film*, David J. Skal's *Hollywood Gothic: The Tangled Web of Dracula from Novel to Stage to Screen* and Gregory Waller's *The Living and the Undead*. In addition, for numerous historical, literary and frivolous details, I must credit W. S. Baring-Gould's *Sherlock Holmes: A Biography* and *The Annotated Sherlock Holmes*, Paul Begg, Martin Fido and Keith Skinner's invaluable *The Jack the Ripper A to Z*, Richard Ellman's *Oscar Wilde*, Philip José Farmer's *Tarzan Alive* and *Doc Savage: His Apocalyptic Life*, Andrew Goodman's *Gilbert and Sullivan's London*, Steve Gooch's translation of *The Lulu Plays* of Frank Wedekind, Melvin Harris's *The Ripper File*, Michael Harrison's *The World of Sherlock Holmes*, Beth Kalikoff's *Murder and Moral Decay in Victorian Popular Literature*, Laurence Lerner's *The Victorians*, Norman and Jeanne Mackenzie's *The Time Traveller: The Life of H. G. Wells*, Sally Mitchell's *Victorian Britain: An Encyclopedia*, Arthur Morrison's *A Child of the Jago* (with a biographical study by P. J. Keating) and David Pringle's *Imaginary People: A Who's Who of Modern Fictional Characters*. In particular, thanks are due to Norman Mackenzie and Laurence Lerner; this is the second novel (the first was *Jago*) to come out of my experience with their Late Victorian Revolt course at the University of Sussex in 1979. Among the friendly eyes who glanced over the manuscript in various forms, I should like to credit Eugene Byrne, for his detailed historical carping, Steve Jones, Antony Harwood, Lucy Parsons and Maureen Waller.

On the dating of *Dracula*: Stoker does not specify which year the events of his novel are supposed to take place. Frayling argues persuasively that he intended 1893, while Wolf and Haining pick 1887. The fact is that neither choice will entirely suffice. Published in 1897, the novel ends with a present-day chapter locating the bulk of the story seven years in the past, but numerous small details – like the use of the phrase 'new woman', coined in 1892, or even the comparative sophistication of Dr Seward's phonograph – jar with this. I have plumped – as did Jimmy Sangster, Terence Fisher and Hammer Films for their 1958 *Dracula* (*Horror of Dracula* to heathen Americans) – for 1885, and opted to shift on to an alternate timetrack half-way through Stoker's Chapter 21, on page 249 of Wolf's annotated edition. Stoker's *Dracula* is already an alternate world story, set in a timeline where social and mechanical progress has advanced slightly faster than in our own, where Chicksand Street and Piccadilly are considerably longer thoroughfares than those we make do with, and where London boasts a Kingstead Cemetery in the region of Hampstead Heath presumably corresponding to our own Highgate Cemetery. In reworking history, I have taken as a starting point Stoker's imagined world rather than our own, even to the extent of finally presenting to the public Kate Reed, a character conceived by Stoker for *Dracula* but omitted from the novel. The other major hands who contributed to the creation of this consensus world where Dr Jekyll and Dr Moreau can share research or Inspector Lestrade and Inspector Mackenzie maintain a friendly rivalry should be well known enough to need to no further acknowledgement, but, given the importance some minor figures took as the book grew, I should perhaps direct the interested reader to Alexander Dumas (in *The Pale-Faced Lady*), Eric, Count Stenbock (in 'The True Story of a Vampire', which I found in James Dickie's anthology *The Undead*), George A. Romero (in *Martin*) and the ever-dependable Anonymous (in 'The Mysterious Stranger') for our Carpathian worthies Kostaki, Vardalek, Cuda and von Klatka. The mothers- and fathers-in-darkness of the other vampires who flit through these pages will, I hope, accept the tip of the hat, and understand that I have done my best to take care of their bloodlines.

As usual, I have to mention various people who happened to be nice to me during the composition of this novel, subtly influencing the text through late-night phone calls, freely given answers to bizarre questions, increasingly deranged dinner conversations in peculiar locales, and general pleasant enthusiasm. In particular, Susan Byrne eased me through difficulties round about Chapter 14. Also, thanks to Julie Akhurst, Pete Atkins, Clive Barker (for the afternoon when I drunkenly complained about the length of *Imajica*), Saskia Baron, Clive Bennett, Anne Billson (coming soon: her vampire novel), Steve Bissette, Peter Bleach, Scott Bradfield, Monique Brocklesby (more blood, more blood), John Brosnan, Molly Brown (Chapter 45!), Allan Bryce, Mark Burman, Ramsey Campbell, Jonathan Carroll, Kent Carroll, Dave Carson (yer man), Tom Charity, Steve Coram, Jeremy Clarke, John and Judith Clute (more paronomasia, now!), Lynne Cramer, Stuart Crosskell, Colin Davis, Meg Davis, Phil Day, Elaine di Campo, Wayne Drew, Alex Dunn, Malcolm and Jax Edwards, Chris Evans, Richard Evans, Dennis and Kris Etchison, Tom FitzGerald, Jo Fletcher, Christopher Fowler, Barry Forshaw, Adrian and Ann Fraser, Kathy Gale (Nodding Dog, Nodding Dog), Steve Gallagher,

David Garnett, Lisa Gaye, John Gilbert (for the afternoon when I drunkenly complained about not being paid), Charlie Grant, Colin Greenland, Beth Gwinn, Rob Hackwill, Guy Hancock, Phil Hardy (Crouch End Luncheon Society), Louise Hartley-Davies, Elizabeth Hickling, Susannah Hickling, Rob Holdstock, David Howe, Simon Ings, Peter James, Trevor Johnstone, Alan Jones, Graham Joyce (Endless Evil in Leicester), Roz Kaveney, Joanna Kaye (one of the slim dark ones), Leroy Kettle, Mark Kermode (sorry, no Linda Blair), Roz Kidd (for an interesting afternoon in Islington), Alexander Korzhenevski, Karen Krizanovich (cute nose), Andy Lane (background on the Limehouse Ring), Joe Lansdale, Stephen Laws (who'd certainly drink at the Ten Bells), Christopher Lee (and Gitte, for two weeks in another town), Amanda Lipman, Paul J. McAuley (Partner in Many Crimes), Dave McKean, Tim Mander, Nigel Matheson, Mark Morris, Alan Morrison (and Gowan, for getting me on a train), Cindy Moul (kisses), Dermot Murnaghan (for George Formby), Sasha Newman, David Newton, Terry Pratchett, David Roper, Jonathan Ross, Nick Royle, Geoff Ryman, Clare Saxby, Trevor Showler, Skipp 'n' Spector, Adrian Sibley, Dave Simpson, Brian Stableford, Janet Storey (sort of), Dave and Danuta Tamlyn, Lisa Tuttle, Alexia Vernon, Karl Edward Wagner, Howard Waldrop (I'm not worthy!), Mike and Di Wathen, Sue Webster, Chris Wicking, F. Paul Wilson, Doug Winter, Miranda Wood, John Wrathall and all the murgatroyds.

By coincidence, I am signing this wrap-up on 3 May, precisely the day that *Dracula* begins, with Joathan Harker's arrival in Transvlania. So this is where we came in . . .

Kim Newman,
Crouch End, 1992